An unwanted gift

Emma read her mother's handwriting.

> *Within this box I have placed your inheritance. I awaken the gift of power that sleeps in your spirit. You stand revealed by the stars and moonlight. You have received your wyrd. It is time for you to claim your place among your near and distant kin.*
>
> *You were born with a gift. A power to walk through time and set things right. Perhaps you have suspected it for many years. Now that you have been challenged, you must be certain.*
>
> *Do not be afraid of the darkness. In this box you will find everything you need to defeat it. May your light shine bright, Merle Acalia.*
>
> *Have no fear. When the time is right, we shall meet as equals.*

The paper slipped through Em's fingers and fell to the floor...

Out of *Time*

Lynn Abbey

ACE BOOKS, NEW YORK

OUT OF TIME

An Ace Book / published by arrangement with
the author

PRINTING HISTORY
Ace mass-market edition / July 2000

The Penguin Putnam Inc. World Wide Web site address is
http://www.penguinputnam.com

Check out the ACE Science Fiction & Fantasy newsletter
and much more on the Internet at Club PPI!

ISBN: 0-441-00751-1

ACE®
Ace Books are published
by The Berkley Publishing Group,
a division of Penguin Putnam Inc.,
375 Hudson Street, New York, New York 10014.
ACE and the "A" design are trademarks
belonging to Penguin Putnam Inc.

PRINTED IN THE UNITED STATES OF AMERICA

10 9 8 7 6 5 4 3 2 1

Out of
Time

One

Morning had the crystal clarity that came to the Midwestern town of Bower only in autumn and only after a hard freeze had put an end to summery thoughts. The sky was a deep blue—strong, almost electric, and framed by the gold and orange leaves clinging defiantly to trees that no longer wanted them.

A breeze completed the perfect morning, stirring the leaves into music and bearing the odor of nothing at all. Locking the front door of her townhouse behind her, Emma Merrigan forgave such a morning for arriving on Thursday, not Saturday.

Beads of translucent moisture covered the windshield of Em's far from new but well-maintained car. She swiped the windshield with her bare fingers and was relieved to see that they left liquid tracks across the glass. In Michigan in the first full week of November, frost was more likely than dew. This year they'd had a long, beautiful Indian summer, but the longer it lasted, the harder it would end. There could be six inches of snow on the ground by sunset.

Emma had seen more than one winter arrive just that fast, just that unwelcome. Once the Canadian Arctic air broke free, there was nothing but a picket fence in western Ontario to stop its southward march.

Like winter, Em was running late this year. She hadn't

finished any of the chores prudent Midwesterners scheduled between Labor Day and Halloween—not the least of which was getting her *real* winter coat—the down-filled, calf-length epitome of frigid chic—back from the dry cleaner. As the wipers beat away the dew, she made a mental note to stop on her way home from work.

Emma's workdays began with a short drive from the townhouse to the parking structure beside the university library where a credit-card-sized piece of plastic velcroed inside the windshield exchanged greetings with a much larger box suspended from a concrete overhang. It was a new system, installed just before Labor Day, and lost in thoughts of coats, unchanged antifreeze, and a furnace that needed cleaning, Em had the car stopped and the window rolled halfway down before the gate popped up.

Feeling foolish even though the attendant's box was abandoned and she was the only witness to her creeping senility, Em gunned the car up the ramp.

"We'll see how great all this is come January."

For twenty-five years Emma had worked at the library and parked in this structure. She'd watched countless attendants come and go and gotten to know them well, even if they'd never known each other's names. She'd known what losing that job had meant to some of them.

"Just wait until there's a layer of ice and crud between us and that California camera!"

Not that there was an *us* in Emma's life this autumn. Her dad had died last February after a mercifully short illness. He was the last of the people who'd counted on her. Two husbands were gone, lost to the dark memories of divorce, the second far more painful than the first. Two children, a boy and a girl from that second husband and his first wife but attached to Emma, even after the second divorce, were gone too. Emma had stood by them until they'd gotten themselves launched. Lori, the youngest, had headed for the East Coast; Jay-Jay, who called himself Jeff now that he was grown up, had gone the other way. She stayed in touch with them, but it was a point of pride as bright as the sun that they didn't *need* her.

As for other family, Emma had been an only child, raised by her father. She'd grown up believing that her mother had died not long before her first birthday and that Dad had loved his wife too much to consider remarriage after her death, even for his daughter's sake.

And perhaps Arch Merrigan had loved Eleanor, but death hadn't separated Emma's parents. She'd learned the shocking truth about her motherless life while doing undergrad research in the same library where she now worked. Come to think of it, Emma had learned the truth on another November morning, thirty-one years ago.

Partway across the bridge between the parking structure and the library, Emma paused at the handrail. She stared through the wire mesh. Blue skies and breezes faded from perception, replaced by a front-page headline from the *Bower Tribune*, sharper in memory than it had been in the microfiche reader.

Professor's wife vanishes. Police puzzled.

The words weren't the banner headline; that had celebrated the sheathing of Main Street's dated brick-and-marble facades in "up-to-the-minute decorative aluminum," but the article had been set in type large enough to catch Em's eye as she'd scanned fiche after fiche, researching a Political Science assignment on local reaction to the Berlin Airlift.

Em didn't remember if she'd turned in the Poli-Sci paper. She did remember, and with chest-tightening shock that never diminished, the day-by-day sheets of microscopic print informing Bower of a postwar mystery. In those family-value days, no wife could leave her infant daughter without creating a mystery. The FBI invaded with a platoon of agents who had seemed both drab and exotic in the grainy photographs.

Her father was cleared of all suspicion in the second day's

article. In the third, police and FBI were questioning a garage mechanic who'd gassed up the Merrigan Oldsmobile, checked its oil, and was, apparently, the last person to see Eleanor before she vanished, along with the Olds. On the sixth, he too was declared an innocent man.

After that the articles grew shorter and more cautious: Eleanor Merrigan herself became the mystery. No one, not even Em's father, knew much about her before they'd met and quickly married. Eleanor had joined her husband's church, but didn't attend. She'd joined the university wives' club, the garden club, and all the other civic-minded clubs where professors' wives stayed out of sight, out of trouble, but no one remembered her. Apparently, Em's mother had done a better job of staying out of sight than out of trouble.

One interviewee—a woman whose name Emma hadn't recognized—suggested that Eleanor Merrigan might have "gone back to that foreign place where she came from."

Two weeks after the story broke, the FBI located the Merrigan car near a train station in Buffalo, New York. The doors were locked, the keys were under the front seat, the fingerprints were all the same and presumed to be Eleanor Merrigan's. The last article Emma read began with the cold verdict, *Foul play not suspected in wife's disappearance.* The FBI had recalled its aliens and the Bower police chief was quoted: "There's nothing more we can do except hope Mrs. Merrigan comes to her senses. She's left a fine husband all alone with that little girl."

Emma recalled turning off the fiche reader and staring at its blank screen. She recalled each step and thought of a dream-walk across campus to the engineering quad and her father's office. The department secretary—her hair was blond, her dress was green, and her name one of the few things Em had forgotten about that day—had reminded Emma that on Tuesdays Dr. Merrigan spent his afternoon at the lab; she'd have better luck finding him there, or—better—simply waiting for him at home.

But Emma hadn't wanted to find her father among colleagues, or—worse—in the house where Eleanor Merrigan's presence had never faded from carpets, drapes, and furniture that hadn't changed in Emma's lifetime. And she didn't have to. Dad had given her keys to the house and his office when she was in fifth grade and some of her properly parented friends had yet to unlock a door for themselves. Over the secretary's protests, Em had let herself into his office.

Sitting in Dad's chair, in his most personal room, she'd studied Eleanor's portrait, hung where Dad could see it, but obscured from other angles. Eleanor had been considerably younger than her husband, beautiful, smiling, and never more a stranger to her daughter than she'd been on that day.

Dad had arrived not more than a half-hour later—as Emma had known he would. In the university's tight-knit community word traveled fast that Dr. Archibald Merrigan's sanctuary had been violated.

The day had been as sour as Em's mood: soot gray and sleety. Dad was breathing hard and dripping cold water onto the bare floor when he opened the door. He'd known from the start why she was sitting in his chair, staring into a shadowed corner. Truth had shown on his face when their eyes met, though perhaps, in hindsight, he'd merely reacted to what he saw on hers.

"Your mother warned me our marriage wouldn't be forever, Em. Five years, she said. When you came along, I thought she'd changed her mind. She hadn't."

"You looked for her. You and the police and the *FBI!* After they found the car, you knew she wasn't hurt or dead or kidnapped. You must have known where she went," Em had countered with angry statements of hope rather than questions.

"I didn't know, but I'd promised her I wouldn't pursue her. Once I knew it wasn't an accident—we traced her as far as New York City—I accepted it. She was gone. I had you to think about."

They'd argued. The bitterness and hurt of two silent decades was briefly given voice. Neither of them had ever *had* Eleanor, except to think about. They had each other—politely, properly, and proudly—and having that, but nothing more, their argument had ended with a tearful hug. By unspoken agreement, truth never again threatened the fiction they had both accepted: Dr. Merrigan, professor and widower, and Emma, his motherless daughter.

Truth or fiction, growing up hadn't been easy. In the beginning Dad hired a housekeeper, an elderly Italian woman, very exotic for Bower in the Fifties. "If the father is dead," Mrs. Carbone had said at least once a day, "the family suffers. If the mother dies, the family cannot exist."

Mrs. Carbone herself died when Em was seven. After that, Em remembered learning how to cook and clean. She took care of herself most of the time, though there was always someone—a colleague's wife or friend's mother—to take her shopping in August before school opened and a nurse, no less, from the university hospital to watch over her when she got sick.

Money hadn't been a problem. Dad was a tenured professor and the university took care of its own. When the time came, Emma had had the grades and the connections to attend whichever school she'd desired. It was the Sixties; father and daughter had disagreed about everything from music to politics, but Em had never seriously considered leaving Bower, never moved out to a dorm or off-campus apartment.

She didn't date until her senior year when she caught the eye of a young man about to get one of the university's first computer science degrees. They married a week after graduation and went to live in New York City where Em's new husband had a promising career until he drew a dangerously low number in the Vietnam draft lottery. Rob wanted to go to Canada; she didn't. They parted company easily, though not without regrets. Emma lingered in New York, writing computer programs for a large insurance company (her ex had shown her the basics, also COBOL, Fortran, and several flavors of assembler) until the following December when she came home for the holidays and never went back.

Emma had lived at home for another three years; it was familiar and cheap, though she could have afforded to move out. Soon after she'd returned to Bower, Dad had pulled a few strings—tugged them gently—and she'd started working at the university library.

The second time she married, Emma was in love. Jeff was an old high-school classmate, recently divorced. He had two children living with him and no interest in the university, unless its football team was doing particularly well. They were friends before they became lovers and she'd expected their marriage to last forever.

Time had proven Emma wrong in ways that still hurt but, determined not to repeat her mother's crime, she'd overstayed her welcome to complete the raising of children who were never hers. In the end, after a second prolonged, messy divorce, Em had reclaimed her maiden name and made a down payment on a two-bedroom townhouse.

"Beautiful day, Emma!"

A woman's voice broke Em's reverie. She saw the sky and the wire mesh of the pedestrian bridge again and nodded behind a smile.

"Definitely one to remember come January."

Emma fell in step beside the taller, younger woman. Sunshine and blue skies were the order of the morning's conversation as they waited for the elevator. Em rode down two floors to the third and, amid weather-heavy greetings, threaded her way through corridors and cubicles to the coffee maker.

Her office was on the border between the library's original brick walls and the largely glass addition that a perennial patron had endowed in the names of progress and estate taxes. Her office's inner wall was an ivy-scarred mosaic in shades of red and gray. The three other walls were half glass, half wood. Emma's name and function—acquisitions—both in easily removed black lettering, clung to the glass. Inside, there were mismatched cabinets, a battered side-chair, a computer-saddled desk, and an eye-catching dot of amber light blinking from her telephone.

Another morning had begun. She settled in quickly, fired up the computer, and pushed the blinking button. There was only one message in the queue:

"Em? Matt here. You in yet . . . ? No, I guess not. Listen, if you've got a minute—Shaunekker's down again and I can't find a clue in this mess.

Matt was the library's official Systems Administrator, the fourth in as many years. Like his predecessors he was a bright young man with a freshly minted master's degree and, like them, he had plans to bring the library's creaky computers into the modern era. Unlike his predecessors, Matt might stick around long enough to finish the job. One week into it, he'd had the sense to realize that someone kept the network alive between administrators and had found his way to Emma's office before she'd had to find her way to his. She gave him credit for that, and for paying attention each time she showed him where and why the bodies were buried.

Emma's monitor awoke with a pulsing, psychedelic display while Daffy Duck announced that she had mail. The mallard's voice removed some of the urgency from Matt's message. If Daffy had found her e-mail, then the whirring box beneath her monitor was connected to a functioning network. The last time Eugene Shaunekker's desktop died, it had taken the whole network with it.

Em could see her mail appearing on the monitor screen, but she couldn't read it. That wasn't through any fault of the computer. Watching her light brown hair grow streaky gray hadn't bothered Emma half as much as losing her near-focus vision—perhaps because she could hide the gray with hair dye but bifocals had only reminded her why she'd switched to contacts back in junior high. She compromised by wearing drugstore glasses over her contacts and kept extra pairs in her desk drawer, in her purse, beside her bed, in the bathroom, and next to her favorite chair. She grabbed the pair from her desk and squinted at the screen.

Half the messages were shared bits of Internet humor, most of the rest were purer junk. Four actually dealt with library acquisitions—better than average. Emma skimmed them, decided they could wait an hour, and gulped coffee before leaving her office, cup in hand.

"Betty, I'll be with Matt Barto," Em told the secretary she shared with the four other offices that backed onto the old brick wall. "Shaunekker's down again."

Betty nodded knowingly while her fingers continued their flight over her keyboard. The Director's ability to contort his computer was legend throughout the library.

"What's the problem this time?" Emma asked when she reached Matt's basement office.

"He stayed late last night, working on the budget," he replied, keeping his eyes on the columns parading down the screen.

Em moved ragged manuals and dissected hardware from a chair to the papered floor. "And?" She set her coffee a safe distance from his mug of faintly green tea.

"He was sure he knew what was wrong when he lost his notes. He said he remembered what I'd done to get them back the last time—"

Groaning sympathetically, Em asked: "How much did he manage to lose?"

"Nothing," Matt complained, looking at his guest for the first time. "It's all there. I can see every file—valid lengths, valid time-stamps. I even checked for new viruses. The files look healthy, but I can't open them. They're stuck in the Twilight Zone."

Matt was a compact young man who kept himself in shape without making a fetish out of it. He had dark, wavy hair which, unfortunately, had started to thin and recede. Matt joked that he could pass for forty and it was the truth. Hairline notwithstanding, Matt had an intelligent face—an attractive face, as Emma had measured attraction throughout her life. She had to remind herself that he was only a few years older than her stepdaughter.

Em held Matt's eyes just long enough to feel uncomfortable, then looked at his monitor screen. "So, Gene's locked himself out . . . and locked you out, too. Let's figure out how the miracle man did it this time."

Matt hadn't moved; she felt him looking at her. The ordinary gaze of one human being watching another? Emma couldn't say. The world had changed while she was a stepmother. She'd felt like Rip Van Winkle after separating from Jeff. Six years later and the feeling hadn't gone away. Emma Merrigan tried not to think about men, attraction, or romance. Sometimes she succeeded.

"Passwords, Matt," she decided, grasping at the first straw to rise from the phosphor mire. "Old Gene's gone and clobbered his own passwords."

"No way! All the passwords are over there—" Matt pointed at the rack of cream-colored boxes sharing his space. "Besides, Shaunekker doesn't use passwords. Can't. *Won't.* You know that; you're the one who told me he's allergic to them. This system's bastard-patched to hell and back just so he doesn't have to enter his password."

"All too true, but he's clobbered the patch and locked himself out. Or locked himself in."

She'd glimpsed a suspicious entry marching across the

monitor screen. Her grasped straw became a redwood spar of certainty.

"He couldn't have."

"Matt Barto—" Em reached across to hammer pre-emptive commands on his keyboard. "*Never* tell your boss what he can't do." The screen froze, cleared, reformed. She tapped the glass-covered culprit with an unpolished fingernail. "Says here it's got a zero-length file and it's had it since the nineteenth century. He clobbered it. Didn't you say you checked for zero-lengths and bogus time-stamps?"

"That file's not supposed to be in his box!" Matt flopped back in his chair long enough to sigh, then scootched forward. He was a classic two-finger typist: unorthodox, but fast and accurate. "It wasn't there a minute ago, Em. You put it there, just to make an idiot out of me."

"Trust me, if I had that kind of power over computers, I wouldn't waste it making you crazy, or Gene either. Sysadmins are a dime a dozen—cheaper in June—but a good director's worth keeping, with or without his passwords."

"What would you do with that kind of power?" Matt asked, giving the keyboard a final, authoritative tap.

His screen crackled like nylon in winter, went blank, and boxes all around them began chattering.

"I'd hide behind a firewall the likes of you couldn't see or break."

Matt laughed. "Still don't like networks?"

"The idea's fine, so long as it doesn't work too well. Call me old-fashioned. This—" Em gestured at the monitor that mirrored what Gene Shaunekker might be seeing, if he were in his office and watching his screen—"This messing with the guts of someone else's machine from a windowless room in the basement—even to save them from themselves . . . *especially* to save them from themselves, reeks of *1984*."

"You *are* old fashioned, Auntie Em. Get with the program: *1984*'s ancient history. There is no privacy."

Em swallowed coffee. "*I'm* ancient history, Matt," she said, intending to be funny but sounding just a shade bitter and regretful.

"You know this system better than anyone. You should have had this job ten years ago."

"I know this system because I was here when this system was two student-keypunchers and a computer the size of a refrigerator that did one—count it, *one*—operation per pass. I don't have the credentials for today. I never took a computer class in my life, just picked it up as I went along. Hell, Matt, when I started, a million-dollar system wasn't as sophisticated as a cheap watch is now."

"And only dinosaurs had the wrists to wear them."

"Damn straight we did."

"So, go back to school. Get the damned degree and get out of here! You're wasting your time, Em."

Emma shook her head. She wouldn't admit the truth she heard in Matt's words, but wouldn't deny it, either. Coffee cup in hand, she headed for the door. "Times change," she conceded at the threshold. "If you need me, call."

"Count on it."

Emma found the last dregs of the morning's mail on her chair when she returned to her office. She opened envelopes with catalogs printed in languages she scarcely recognized and handwritten requests that defied translation. Fortified with another cup of coffee, she began the daily challenge of adding titles to the library's collection. Soon, she was chasing down the source of a new East European political journal.

She ate lunch at her desk, a thermos of soup and a slab of machine-made bread, and switched her allegiance to tea, on the advice of the doctor who'd said "at your age, you shouldn't be taking in caffeine after noon." At ten after six, Daffy Duck reappeared on her monitor screen and reminded Em that it was time to go for a walk. She gathered her daily belongings; one more library chore and she'd be headed home.

Back in September, two weeks into the Fall term, a freshman evidently subsisting on a diet of pills and cola had died in the library stacks. Whether her death had been an accident or a suicide remained an open question, but no one had reported that the young woman was missing from her dorm and two student employees had discovered her body only after they'd noticed the odor. With solemn voice-overs and righteous indignation, the national media had jumped on the story. Satellite uplinks had sprouted like mushrooms and for nearly a week the plight of students away from home for the first time had been *the* crisis of the airwaves.

The university had needed to do something symbolic to atone for the tragedy. The head of campus security resigned. Students held a rally and promised to keep a closer eye on their roommates. And Gene Shaunekker announced that, effective immediately, library staff would inspect every nook and cranny of the stacks, not once or twice, but three times a day. He'd divided the 3-D maze into old-fashioned police-force beats and assigned them to his somewhat-less-than-eager staff.

Emma's beat ran from Archeology to Near Eastern studies. She walked it Monday morning and Thursday on her way home.

Overall, Emma approved of Gene Shaunekker. In his five-year tenure he'd protected the library's budget, made it a noncombatant in the worst of the chronic departmental turf-wars, and generally boosted staff morale, but sometimes he went overboard. The staff-as-police policy would peter out, probably in winter when weather took its toll on everyone's schedules. Until then, Em got extra exercise, just like everyone else.

A tiny, open-walled elevator—little more than a wrought-iron basket ratcheting on greasy, black chains—carried Em down to Archeology. Her beat took her through book-walled corridors and past individually lighted carrels with wooden desks into which bored students had been carving graffiti for the better part of a century.

The library was quiet: mid-terms were history, finals an eternal month away. Archeology was home-away-from-home for a single student, a displaced engineer by the look of his muscular laptop and the thick textbooks piled beside his chair. Their eyes met after Emma had switched on the area lights; she felt guilty for disturbing him.

Heading up a ramp into the Near Eastern collection, Em's thoughts were in her kitchen, trying to remember if she'd taken a chicken breast out of the freezer. Cooking had never been her favorite domestic chore and cooking for one was the pits. If it weren't for the consequences, she'd eat pizza every night. With a little bit of effort, she remembered setting a pale, frozen slab on a dish in the refrigerator before she'd left this morning. Her heart and waistline were set for another healthy night.

The Near East appeared empty: no lights, no noise. She was tempted to take a shortcut back to the elevator, but resisted temptation. A woman had died and no one had noticed. Emma Merrigan stayed her course, flicking light switches and thinking about supper. She'd decided to cook her chicken in tomato sauce with fresh mushrooms when something caught her eye.

Against all expectation there was a student slumped face down on the desk in an unlit carrel. Falling asleep in the stacks was nothing extraordinary; Em had done it more than once a generation ago. Staying asleep was another matter. The chairs and desktops were too uncomfortable for more than forty winks at a time. Any longer and one risked a seriously stiff neck or sore back. Unless one had died.

"Oh, God," she prayed, in the manner of agnostics everywhere, before taking another step toward the carrel. "Please don't let it be a body."

Two

"**E**xcuse me?"
   Emma wasn't a loud-voiced person. Her voice didn't carry past her own ears.

"Excuse me . . . ?"

She didn't know what words to add. In the dim light she still couldn't tell if her slumped-over student was male or female or possibly a prank. The students knew that the library staff was patrolling the stacks and students got bored very easily. They'd larded the stacks with theater-department corpses for Halloween and broadcast the results live over campus television.

Em glanced around, checking for cameras. On the Merrigan scale of fear and dread, she'd sooner walk down a dark, urban alley than face televised embarrassment. Seeing nothing suspicious, she moved another few steps closer to the carrel. At that distance, her contacts-corrected vision was sharp enough to spot the difference between a real hand, such as the one she glimpsed through tousled hair, and any theater-school prop. Sharp enough, also, to see that the dark blotches on the white object clutched in that hand weren't flowers printed on a handkerchief.

Blood? Em asked herself and her heart began to pound. The hand was slender, the fingernails were long and carefully coated with dark polish. Em took a chance on gender and hoped she was wrong about the rest.

"Miss?" She was an arm's reach from the carrel but didn't recall moving her feet. "Miss? Wake up—"

The tissue disappeared into a clenched fist. The student's head began to rise.

"I must have fallen asleep," she said. Definitely *she*: that voice could sing soprano. The tissue disappeared into her lap. She raked her hair away from her face.

Em's heart beat normally again. "Take it from someone who's sat at these desks before, you're better off—"

The light was poor, but moonless midnight wouldn't have been dark enough to conceal the young woman's swollen, bloody lip or the bruise that spread around her right cheek and eye like an open hand . . .

"My God," Emma whispered.

The young woman flinched. "I'm sorry," she murmured, touching her face, then casting about for the missing tissue.

She pressed the back of her left hand against her lip. Blood seeped slowly between her fingers.

"You're hurt." Em proclaimed the obvious. "Let me help you—"

Sniffing back tears, the young woman said, "I'm okay."

Finding the tissue with her right hand, she blotted her lip and her hand. Em noticed that she held her left thumb at an odd angle.

"You're not," Emma said, resorting to the mother-voice she hadn't used in years. "Did you fall here, in the library?" She wouldn't believe a denial, but that wasn't important; she'd accept any excuse to get the girl the care she needed. "Student health—"

"No. No, nothing's broken. I'm okay."

She looked too young to be a student and wore the ragged, baggy, all-in-black look that had been a fixture on campus for the last several years. The style had become even more popular in the high schools and downtown. Bower attracted a steady stream of suburban runaways. It was the most cosmopolitan city in the state and nowhere near as dangerous as Detroit. Nowhere near as safe as home, either—

Emma caught herself making an assumption that couldn't survive the front page of any day's newspaper and retreated to more obvious truths: "You can't stay here. You've got to go somewhere. Home . . . the dorms?"

The girl shook her head again, reinforcing Em's suspicion that she was a townie, not a student. She fussed with the tissue and her bleeding lip, both without bending her left thumb. Em dug a paper napkin—leftover from lunch—out of her tote bag.

She took it with a soft "Thank you," and a softer "I'll be okay."

"Of course you will." Emma's dusty but trusty mother-voice took command. "What's your name?"

"Jennifer. Jennifer Hodden."

Em might have guessed as much. The university—and the town—swarmed with Jennifers, Megans, and Heathers.

"Yours?" Jennifer asked.

It was a question Emma answered neither often nor well. "Em. Emma. Emma Merrigan," she stammered, and supposed she could have added a Miss, Mrs., or Ms to the mix, if she'd ever made a choice among them.

With the napkin and her left hand pressed against her lip, Jennifer gathered her books and papers. She got as far as a blood-smeared notebook. Disbelief, more than pain, seemed to freeze her in place.

"Let me help," Em offered and took silence for permission to close the notebook, hiding the offensive pages.

Jennifer stared into space and memory. "You can't." She shook her head. "No one can. It's gone too far."

Emma knew something about despair and hopelessness

and the tendency to think the whole world was dark when it was only the room you were sitting in. She'd looked at Jennifer's face and seen a boyfriend's abuse; that was the easiest, closest assumption, but there were others more dire. The mother-voice spoke directly to her for a change: *Beware of biting off more than you can chew,* it said.

The mother-voice was right. Em was wary and all the more determined that she had to intervene.

"I can listen, if you can tell me what happened."

Jennifer shook her head more decisively. "You wouldn't understand."

The true curse of the middle ages—Emma Merrigan's middle ages, anyway—was experiencing the generation gap from the older side of the chasm. "It doesn't matter if I understand," she said, drawing on the lessons her stepchildren had taught her, "when you hear yourself, *you'll* understand."

"Yeah," Jennifer said after a moment's thought. "Maybe I need to talk to myself."

"And," Em continued, consciously pushing her luck, "I can make sure you get those cuts and bruises taken care of."

Another moment's hesitation with a less positive result. "I'm okay," Jennifer insisted, retreating from her chair to the back of the carrel, leaving the scrunched and mottled paper napkin behind. "I don't need to see a doctor." A look of animal terror had settled across her face. "I'm not hurt."

"I've got eyes." Em sharpened her tone. "And I see that one of yours is black. Your lip's busted, your cheek's got a bruise on it that I'd call hand-shaped, and you're dripping blood all over yourself."

The wide-eyed woman looked down at her sweater front and sleeve. She lunged for the napkin and pressed it against her mouth.

"What happened, Jennifer? Who hit you? When? Did it happen here in the library?"

"No," Jennifer snarled with sudden, unexpected hostility.

She tugged right-handed on the backpack zipper. When the zipper snagged she clamped her left hand tightly behind it and yanked hard. Emma took that as a good sign regarding Jennifer's physical injuries, less so for her state of mind. She stood in Jennifer's escape path and trusted that the saner part of the young woman's mind wanted help more than the rest of her wanted to run.

"Where will you go? Home?"

Jennifer shook her head tentatively.

"Where did you get hurt, if not here? At home? In a dorm? If you won't help yourself, think about everyone else. You know that a person who hits one person *always* hits another—"

Emma's stepchildren had had the commandments of abuse drilled into their grade-school heads the way she'd learned the multiplication tables. Jennifer would know them, too.

"You *know* I'm right, Jennifer."

"Bran wouldn't. He didn't mean to hit me." The words burst like a ragweed sneeze. In the space of a heartbeat Jennifer's expression went from embarrassment to shame to guilty relief; a drama coach would have given her an A.

"What did he mean to do—if he didn't mean to hit you?"

Jennifer sank into the chair. "You wouldn't understand. It's not what you think." The way her eyes darted, a half-dozen fictions must have played out in her mind's eye before she said, "He didn't hit me."

"You're the one who said he did. Look, Jennifer, what your boyfriend's done to you isn't just stupid or an accident, it's a crime." Em didn't mean to sound like a public-service ad, but she wasn't about to apologize for it, either.

"I said you wouldn't understand," Jennifer shot back. She wrestled into a long black coat.

Unfurled, the wool released an aura of mothballs. In Emma's day, it would have been called a maxi-coat—and she'd swear it could have been the one she'd worn so proudly when she'd been an undergrad. But her coat had had big, satin-covered buttons; Jennifer's had three-inch safety pins which she linked awkwardly to similar bits of steel beside the thread-bare buttonholes. The Sixties style of coat, which had been romantic and Edwardian, had become industrial and goth.

Emma had been a good mother to her stepchildren; at least that's what they told her and she believed them because it would have been easy for them to tell her nothing at all. With them, the hard years had been the early years. By the time they were teenagers, it had been smooth sailing; neither had gotten into trouble or masked themselves in fashion's extremes. Jennifer, with her dead-black fingernails and mutilated coat, was a breed apart from anyone Emma had known.

Or could the transformed black coat be a sign that she would have worn black nail enamel herself, if black nail enamel, instead of patchouli oil, had been for sale in the tiny stores ringing the campus? The stores, after all, were still there. Only their names had changed with the decades.

"Talk to someone," she said when the last safety pin was closed and Jennifer raised her bruised face. "Someone who knows you. A friend, but not Brian."

"Bran," Jennifer corrected. "There's only Bran. We'll talk. We'll work past this." Mindful of her left thumb, she threw the backpack onto her shoulders. "Thanks, anyway."

Jennifer strode forward, head down and clearly expecting Emma to step aside, but Em stayed put and when Jennifer raised her head to scowl, Em stopped her with an icy glance. It was a trick—her own private body trick, like wiggling her ears or raising one eyebrow, both of which were beyond her. She'd done it a lot, until the fifth grade when the boys started calling her Snake-eyes.

Emma had grown more careful since then, and more confident.

"*Find* someone you trust and talk to them about what happened with Bran."

With her ultimatum delivered, Emma stepped aside. She expected Jennifer to brush past, but that didn't happen.

"Can we go somewhere, Emma? I don't want to talk here."

Emma savored her victory. "Dinner?" she suggested; the chicken breast would hold overnight in the refrigerator. "Hokkaido?"

The campus restaurant served a blend of Korean and Japanese cuisines in a jumble of basement rooms that were never too bright for bruises. It was only a few blocks from the library and cheap enough for student budgets, though Em intended to pick up the tab.

"Yeah, Bran and I—" Jennifer stopped short. "Hokkaido's fine."

Emma led the way, expecting her companion to change her mind at every step. Once they were free of the building, she tried small, neutral questions. Jennifer—to Em's astonishment—was a senior, pre-law, and a Bower native.

"I wanted to go East; but the tuition!" she said, with a frustrated growl. "So I stayed home. *Lived* at home my first two years. Now I'm in a house east of campus—"

Her voice trailed, leaving Em with the guess that the battering had occurred in the off-campus house.

"Bower High?" Em asked, changing the subject by mentioning the high school she'd attended.

"No, River."

Which told one native quite a bit about the neighborhoods where another's parents might dwell. River High served both the old red-line districts and the post-modern minimansions sprouting up in what had been pumpkin patches and apple orchards. Despite the safety pins—or because of them—Em guessed a mini-mansion and guessed, too, why Jennifer hadn't taken her battered face home.

At lunch, Hokkaido was awash with round-eyed faces chowing down on what the owners called "rustic Asian" cuisine. (Since when had "rustic" Asians eaten meat with every meal?) After dark the restaurant got closer to its improbable roots, serving rice and spicy noodles to homesick students. But the lunch menu remained available for supper-time refugees from the library. Emma ordered Number Two, which was Number One with chicken instead of beef; Jennifer asked for Number Three, which was Number One without any meat. Em paid for both over a solitary, soft-voiced objection and got a numbered, torn-paper receipt in return.

They made their way to a corner table. Jennifer shed her outer layers and swept her hair forward, hiding much of her boyfriend's damage in a single, apparently reflexive move. Em made two more assumptions: this wasn't the first time Jennifer had sported bruises and her hair wasn't anywhere near its natural color.

"You didn't have to do that," the younger woman chided as she sat down.

"Think of it as reflex. I'd do the same if my stepdaughter were in town."

"You have a stepdaughter?"

So they talked about Lori and her two-steps-forward, one-step-back quest to wrest a living out of ceramic sculptures. "Mostly she does the boring, clean-up work for designers who don't have half her talent," Emma said as the counter-chef called the number written on their receipt. "She says she'll give it another few years, then quit."

"I'd never give up."

Lori had said the same thing—until last summer. Instinctively, Em had never argued reality testing with her stepchildren. Life had its own way of teaching lessons; parental nagging only prolonged the agony. Keeping her mouth shut, that was the secret of Emma's success with Lori and Jay-Jay. Oddly, instinct counseled otherwise with Jennifer.

"Tell me about Bran. Brandon? Just the whys, leave out the whos, whats, and wheres, unless you think they're important. You're right about one thing: it doesn't matter if I understand anything, so long as you hear what you're thinking."

Jennifer began at the beginning: the eternal scramble for housing at a university with over thirty thousand students and less than ten thousand on-campus beds. A friend-of-a-friend had known of a house that needed fresh blood to make September's rent. She'd fallen in love with one of the two vacant rooms, judged the quartet already in residence no worse than her former housemates, and was unpacking her books two days later when Brandon "No-T" Mongomery arrived straight from off-campus housing.

No one knew him; he was a grad-student refugee fresh in from a small school in the East. Grad students and underclassmen in one house, Em and Jennifer both knew that was as chancy as a Japanese and Korean restaurant, but he'd had cash in his wallet.

"Do I take it that Bran wasn't housebroken?" Emma asked, coding her suspicions in ambiguity.

Jennifer spun her fork "Yes. No—the other guys, they'd been together since sophomore year. We were, you know, just the rent, and he didn't know the town. I guess there's orientation for grad students, but Bran didn't go. I showed him around—being a townie and all."

Emma nodded. Living off-campus and knowing the town cold was the best of both worlds.

"His car died, really died; cost more money to fix than replace. I guess that's when it started—him and me. We were together a lot, looking for one he could afford—Kind of funny, isn't it? I wasn't looking for anyone. I had—have—

plans: law school, passing the bar exam. I want—wanted—
to be settled before I got involved with anyone. We thought
we were looking for a cheap car; we found each other instead. Almost like a movie."

"So Bran lives where you live, and has a set of keys to
your car?"

"You make it sound like he's got control of me! It's nothing like that, Emma; if anything, Bran waits for me to tell
him what to do. He just loses it, sometimes." She stared at
the tines of her fork. A good thirty seconds passed before she
added: "We both do."

The vacant-eyed gesture sent a chill wind through
Emma's preconceptions. "Lose it how?" Ninety-nine times
out of a hundred, women were the victims, but there was
that hundredth time.

"Last night we were listening to music, his music, his
room, his bed—"

Jennifer raised her eyes, looking for a reaction, but Em reserved judgment which wasn't what Jennifer expected. She
showed her frustration by dabbing at her lip with a paper
napkin until it bled.

"This isn't working," she decided. "Talking isn't working. There aren't any words for Bran and me that don't make
him sound like a monster and me like some stupid high-
school kid. I'm twenty-one; I'm not a kid. I know he loves
me, and I love him."

"Except—?" Em prodded.

"Except nothing! Look, you're not the only one doing the
storm-warning bit. I've got friends who say the same thing
and my mother's sure Bran's not *good* enough for me. Well,
my life isn't a slogan, all right? Yeah, we've got problems.
Things happen that I wish didn't happen, but they don't
change anything. Yes, it all happened too quickly. We've put
the fall back into falling in love. It's different, even scary;
we both know it but the longer we're together, the more it

seems that we've always been together and we'll always be together. Forever."

Emma took a breath. "Until one of you kills the other?"

She'd planned to say, Until one of you gets hurt, but the words slipped out stronger than she'd intended. When Jennifer began silently, frantically shredding her napkin, Em judged she'd done more harm than good.

"Bran has dreams—nightmares," Jennifer said, raining paper bits onto her unfinished dinner. "He says there's someone else inside him. He says he's always been afraid when he first wakes up because he might not be the same person he was when he went to sleep."

"Are you telling me that Bran beat you up while he was asleep?"

"No. We were listening to music; I told you. I was looking at him, thinking how lucky I was that he loves me so much, and suddenly—Oh, God—this sounds *awful*. Suddenly I was thinking how much power I have over him because he's in love with the *idea* of me—because my friends have to be right: there hasn't been enough time for him to know me well enough to love me—the real me. And then I thought, when I looked at him, that my mother's right, too, and he's not good enough for me and I don't love him; I love the power. Which isn't true, I love Bran. I know I do. And I'm not *that* kind of woman. I don't know what makes me think those ugly thoughts."

A glimmer of maturity? Emma thought, but kept that strictly to herself, asking instead: "Bran hit you because you were staring at him?"

Jennifer shook her head emphatically. "No, I poked him. I stuck my finger between his ribs." She made a stabbing move with her fork. "I—I remember thinking, if I'd had a knife, it would be so easy to kill him. He's big and strong; he'd never think a *woman* could hurt him." The fork fell from Jennifer's finger and she hid her face behind her hands.

"What's wrong with me, Emma? I love Bran; I want to be with him forever . . . and I imagined killing him. It was so real, like a movie."

"But you *didn't* kill him?" When movies became the measure of reality, Em had to reassure herself, and possibly Jennifer. "You stabbed him with your finger?"

"I *poked* him with my finger, that's all. He looked at me and he read my mind. I saw it in his face. Bran knew what I'd been thinking—how I'd thought it would be easy to kill him—so it was self-defense, really, what happened next. If I could face him now—If I had the courage to face him, I'd tell him it was all my fault."

Emma knew that pattern from her last years with Jeff, when she'd joke that heroine was the feminine form of heroin, but Jennifer's blame-game had hers outclassed.

"At the very least, Jennifer, you'll have to admit he overreacted to a poke between the ribs."

She disagreed. "If I'd had a knife, I would have used it. I know I would have. What's wrong with me? I've never had thoughts like that. Never. I like black and goth and I got a tattoo last summer, but so what? I'm not a down-on-myself, morbid geek-freak. I don't do drugs and I'm not suicidal.

"Last night—afterward—when Bran started asking me Why? Why? Why? I ran downstairs and got in my car. I drove around, trying to figure out what had happened, and I thought: I must be sick—like I've got a virus and it's messed with my brain. There're viruses like that, aren't there, Emma? I've heard people talk about people's personalities changing when they get real sick.

"I got delirious once, when I was kid and had the flu. I thought I was at my grandmother's house and she was taking care of me while I was sick. It wasn't *bad* or anything, but Nanni was dead and I'd caught that flu at her funeral. So, I know what I remember didn't happen, but it feels real. I don't remember being sick with the flu; I remember being with Nanni. It's a *good* feeling, even though it never happened."

Jennifer leaned across the table. She lowered her voice. "I get that feeling with Bran sometimes—that I'm remembering things that didn't happen, but it's not a good feeling."

She'd reclaimed her fork, clenched it in a white-knuckled fist and plunged it repeatedly against the vinyl tablecloth as she spoke. Emma thought Jennifer wasn't aware of what she was doing; that only made the gesture more disturbing.

"Do you want to know the worst?" Jennifer asked as her hand fell yet again and the tines pierced the vinyl.

"What's the worst?" Em countered, bolder than she truly felt.

"Last night, I was so sure Bran's done terrible things that I knew killing him would be justice, pure and simple."

Emma sat back in her chair and took a moment to choose her next words. "You said Bran has nightmares. Did he say something that upset you while he slept?"

Jennifer sat back in her chair—leaving the fork upright in the tablecloth.

"He doesn't talk, at least he's never woken me up talking, and he says he doesn't remember his nightmares—except that he wakes up feeling he's done something terrible. He likes to sleep with a light on, so he can look in a mirror as soon as he's awake. He used to be afraid that he'd turn into someone his mom wouldn't recognize."

A psychiatrist, an old-fashioned Freudian psychiatrist, would have a field day, but Emma didn't know what to make of Jennifer's tale. Virus wasn't a bad analogy; there was something about Jennifer's logic that was both fevered and infectious.

"Do you think I've got a cancer growing in my brain that's making me crazy? Maybe I have these fantasies about killing Bran because a tumor's killing me?"

Em reached for the fork and was dismayed by the force

she needed to detach it from the table. "Anything's possible. Have you been having headaches? Seeing double? Do you seem to be looking at the world through a gauze curtain?" Those were the questions the doctors had asked while Dad was in the emergency room. He'd had a stroke, not a cancer, and he hadn't had any of their suggested symptoms.

Nor had Jennifer.

"I feel fine. Well, on the inside I feel fine. But there doesn't have to be pain, does there? I mean, people die from cancer all the time and they never knew they were sick. They call cancer the silent killer, right?"

That was hypertension. But Em was hardly surprised that Jennifer had her public-service ad campaigns confused. When she'd been in college, blood pressure and cancer had been equally remote from her life. "Do you want to die, Jennifer?"

A knowing smile curved the unswollen parts of Jennifer's lips. "Sure sounds like it, doesn't it? Patient fantasizes about tumors and killing her boyfriend; stabs table with restaurant fork. Table and fork both survive. Me, too. Maybe I think about *death* too much, Emma, but I don't think about *dying*, not me, personally."

Em couldn't have put it better herself, though she might have included the boyfriend among the survivors. "Then you've got plans for the future. You know what you've got to do about Bran, and where you're going to sleep tonight."

Jennifer's smile faded. "He's the one, Emma. You said listen to myself, and I have. I know how crazy I sound, but I'm not crazy. We're right for each other. It's fate; do you believe in fate?"

"Sometimes. When I was twenty, I believed in endless possibilities."

"Well, I believe in fate; my fate and Bran's fate are together. We're *not* going to die. I know how it sounds, even how it feels, but we'll find a way to stay together."

"Do you believe in fate, Jennifer, or are you just stubborn? And if stubbornness is the only thing keeping you from getting out of what you *know* is a bad situation, then you're not talking about fate. It's plain old foolishness. I speak from experience."

Jennifer looked at her long and hard. Em held the stare without flinching. She believed the young woman wasn't crazy, though she didn't know what to make of the rest. It took a good imagination to come up with the tale Jennifer told. Generally Em liked imaginative people; she certainly liked Jennifer.

"I wish you could meet Bran and talk to him. You'd know we were both telling the truth. We do love each other."

"I don't for a moment doubt that," Em assured her companion. "But real as love is, sometimes it doesn't bring out the best in us. Or it just comes at the wrong time. You said you weren't looking to get involved. Have you considered that you need what we hippies used to call 'your own space'?"

"Like, close my door? Sleep in my own bed? When we do that, we're so close I can hear him breathing through the wall."

"Maybe one of you has to move."

"Nobody plays house-chess in November," Jennifer laughed, and raised her hand quickly to her lip. "There's nowhere to go. I've tried crashing with friends already—they're not half as polite as you when it comes to telling me I've got my head up my ass. And I can't go home-home, not looking like this. My mother will call the police. I had to plead with her just to invite Bran to Thanksgiving dinner—he can't afford to go home for Thanksgiving *and* Christmas. It's just him and his mom; I think that's what bugs my mother. She says she's not prejudiced, but she kind of is. And I can't go back to the Blue House—that's what we call it, the Blue House. It's *very* blue; you've probably seen it, or tried not to."

Emma caught her eyes widening. "On the corner of East Reynolds and Pine?"

There'd been a town-wide ruckus a few years back when students had painted an architecturally significant Queen Anne mansion cobalt blue and turned it into a rooming house.

"That's the one."

"Very blue," she agreed.

"I can't go back. Not until I'm sure what I'm going to do."

"You have to go somewhere."

"I left my car back at the Blue House after dawn—no place else to park it. I can get it. I can stay at a motel. It'll be a month before my dad gets the bill."

Emma swallowed a sigh. "I don't make a habit of doing this"—she'd never done it before—"but I've got clean sheets on the guest bed. If you want, you can spend the night with me."

"That'd be a lot better than a Holiday Inn," Jennifer said so quickly that Em wondered if she hadn't played into the girl's hand. Her suspicion seemed confirmed when Jennifer added, "You won't be sorry, Emma. I promise."

Three

Bower's *weather had* changed while Em and Jennifer were eating. Raw wind blew down from the north. The picket fence in Ontario had blown away; winter was crossing the Lakes.

Jennifer's backpack didn't contain gloves, a scarf, or a hat. The young woman swore she was *tough* and never needed them, but she started shivering a block from Hokkaido. Shivering had become bleeding, and though the car's heater tried, it couldn't work miracles in the ten-minute drive to Em's home.

"The Maisonettes! I've been by here a million times," Jennifer chirped as they passed between the purely decorative brick columns. "I always wanted to meet someone who actually lived in the Maisonettes. They're so different."

Not, Em hoped, as different as the Blue House, though she knew what Jennifer meant. The clusters of two-story townhouses with their common gardens had been aggressively modern when they were built back in the Twenties. Inspired by a Paris suburb and funded by a university magnate who lost the mortgage and everything else after the Crash, the Maisonettes had matured into a quaint community with notoriously inadequate parking.

There were rules at the Maisonettes: one car, preferably a

compact model, per townhouse. Guests and second cars were supposed to fend for themselves on the neighborhood streets. The Maisonettes had a very active residents' association—Em was its secretary—which distributed discreet bumper stickers every January to separate the wheat from the chaff. Usually that was enough, but they weren't the police; they couldn't hand out tickets.

Both spots in front of Em's home were occupied by vehicles, minus the distinctive sticker: the true price of eating out. There wasn't an empty stretch of curb in sight.

"Better hope it doesn't snow," she laughed as they passed between the columns a second time.

Life at the Maisonettes required a sense of humor. Residents either laughed at the quirks and called them charming until they were wheeled out on a stretcher or they admitted defeat and sold at a loss. Em had bought her townhouse from one of the latter types and expected to become one of the former.

Weaving through the adjoining one-way streets eventually brought Em abreast of a curbside gap at least three feet longer than her car.

"I couldn't live here," Jennifer admitted moments later when the car was legally tucked and centered. "Parking on the street is too much for me."

"Parallel parking isn't bad, once you get the hang of it."

Jennifer shook her head emphatically.

"Parking's just as tight over on the east side around Reynolds."

Another head shake as they headed back to the Maisonettes. "There's a lot around the corner," Jennifer explained. "Some old guy rents out spaces in what used to be his back yard. One night, back in September when there was a party, all the spaces got filled while I was out, and I wound up ten blocks away in one of the campus lots!"

A walk across campus, alone and at night? Emma thought

that sounded harder, not to mention more dangerous, than parallel parking; she kept her thoughts to herself. There *was* a generation gap, not as broad, perhaps, as the one where Em's generation had confronted their parents, but all the more treacherous for its subtlety.

They passed between the Maisonettes' gates for the third time and, naturally, there was a parking space two doors down from her own. Em let that pass in silence, too.

Dinosaurs, she thought, wriggling the key as she slipped it into the lock and giving it a quick clockwise twist. Another few years, and only us dinosaurs will know the meaning of clockwise.

The cats, Spin and Charm (people either chuckled when they heard the names or wondered who'd taught Emma how to name her pets) were there to greet their delinquent goddess. One look at *company* and they bolted for the basement, tripping over each other in their desperation.

"Cats." Em acknowledged the obvious. "I forgot to mention them—they won't be a problem, I hope. You're not allergic?"

"Not me. My dad is. Mom got one of those little dogs— the kind that aren't supposed to shed—but it barked all the time and peed on the carpet, so she got rid of it."

Emma fished empty hangers from the closet. "Too bad," she commented without being more specific.

Like most of Em's infrequent first-time visitors, Jennifer had gotten as far as the living room and stopped. Em kept her home clean and tried to keep it tidy. She hadn't set out to be a collector of either books or odd objects, they'd simply arrived on tides of holidays and vacations, and the great sea storm when she sold the house where she'd grown up, the house on Teagarden Street, after Dad died. Em knew for a fact that she'd sold far more than she'd kept, but the aftermath filled both shelves and walls.

If she'd added tassels and removed the more indiscreet

objects (or draped them in musty velvet), the effect would have been Victorian. Without tassels it was—

"Home," Em stated from the doorway. "I wish I could say I found it like this, but it's all mine. I'm not a big believer in boxes; if I'm going to own it, I want to see it every day."

Jennifer replied with an indecipherable murmur. Her hands were locked behind her back: a well-behaved child determined to resist temptation. She needed two invitations before surrendering her coat.

"Let me show you upstairs where the bedrooms are, and the one bathroom."

In silence—the questions would come later—Jennifer followed Em into what she called the backroom, even though it was at the front of her townhouse. The backroom was home to the guest bed, her computer, and piles of plastic storage boxes, all neatly labeled. Here, there were tassels, attached to the mound of pillows Em had embroidered over the years. She dumped the pillows behind a chair to expose the bed.

Jennifer stared at the Amish-style quilt Em had made for the bed she'd shared with Jeff. The young woman's expression slowly changed from wonder to panic.

Emma broke the silence. "Jennifer—?"

"I can't stay. I've got nothing with me. No clothes for tomorrow. Not even a toothbrush."

"Lucky for you, I bought a new toothbrush last week. It's still in its box. And I can offer you a choice between an overgrown T-shirt and a flannel nightgown . . ."

She let her voice fade, waiting for a signal from her stranger-guest and asking herself—yet again—if she hadn't taken leave of her senses. Jennifer's stare was fixed on one of the several pre-Raphaelite reproductions Emma had scattered across her walls. It wasn't one of their more famous paintings of Arthur and Guinevere as they never were and always should have been, just a woman in a long, blue gown, standing beside her embroidery frame, rubbing an aching back. Between her hobbies and her work, Em knew the feeling well, but couldn't guess why it had so captured Jennifer's attention.

She called the girl twice before getting a reaction.

"I know her," Jennifer whispered.

"From a thousand calendars and cards, no doubt. That's where I got this one: January, I think—otherwise known as *Marianne*, by Millais."

"No, I know her. I've seen her before."

"That too—Millais and his buddies painted the same women over and over."

"Maybe." Jennifer wasn't convinced but she made peace anyway. "I'll like sleeping in the same room with her."

If there was a common element among Em's pictures, it was the sense of magic, from photographs of ancient wonders to Victorian fairy paintings. The cumulative effect could be branded "New Age," which Em resisted mightily. She'd surrounded herself with images she liked, but only as patterns of color and mood. Merrigans didn't believe in magic. At her most religious, Emma was agnostic and didn't want anyone thinking otherwise.

"It's just a picture—" She began to set the record straight, then retreated. "I'm sure I've got a copy of it somewhere around here, a note card or another calendar. I'll give it to you."

"I'd like that," Jennifer agreed. Her backpack slid from her arms to the bed. "I like this room, I really do. Thanks for finding me and bringing me here. I'll get my head together. Figure out what I'm going to do next."

Next included taking the backpack into the bathroom and fumbling with the old brass-key lock until the bolt thunked into the frame. There was another key in the kitchen junk drawer. At least, there was supposed to be another key. Emma hadn't needed to use it since her stepson's first visit.

She and Jay-Jay had laughed their way out of that embarrassing moment.

Em didn't need to believe in anyone's god when she prayed that the lock wasn't up to its old tricks and that she'd replaced the key in the junk drawer. Retreating behind her rarely closed (never locked!) bedroom door, Em got comfortable in sweatshirt and jeans.

She gathered a choice of T-shirts and flannel gowns— Emma had never been one for frills at night, even when married. Adding towels and a virgin toothbrush from the linen closet, she laid the pile in the middle of the guest bed.

Jennifer lingered in the bathroom, running water in the sink, but not loudly enough to mask her sobs. Em thought about knocking, but didn't.

"I'll be downstairs when you're done," she said to the closed door, not expecting an answer and not getting one either.

There were occasional advantages to being a creature of habit: the spare brass key was in the drawer where it belonged. With that anxiety at bay, Em thought about a glass of iced wine and decided on tea instead. Water was heating in the microwave when she heard the bathroom door open and footsteps on the stairs.

"I'm making tea—" Em began before catching sight of her houseguest in the kitchen doorway.

Jennifer had sobbed and scrubbed herself red. Her busted lip had the look of an overripe grape with a dark parasite clinging to its skin.

"Want some ice for that lip?"

"Something cold to drink? Pop, maybe? Asian food always makes me thirsty."

"Diet cola all right?"

Jennifer nodded and disappeared into the living room while Emma poured the liquid over a generous portion of ice.

Once again Jennifer had become transfixed by something hanging on the wall, one of Em's few photographs and the only portrait: her mother and father's wedding picture. It was among the last things she'd brought out of Teagarden Street. She'd debated long and hard before hanging it behind the chair where she usually sat. Come Christmas decorations, there'd be an embroidered Santa Claus hanging there; come January, and the portrait might well remain up in the attic, too precious to sell, too fraught with loss to contemplate daily.

Some things had to be kept in boxes.

"Your grandparents?" Jennifer asked after a long drink.

"Parents." The portrait was a bit old-fashioned—the black and white figures fading into a plain white background—but didn't Jennifer know the difference between World War II and World War I uniforms?

"They're very . . . *distinguished.*"

No argument there. Dad, in his Army officer's uniform, was the epitome of tall, dark, and handsome, and Eleanor—

"She looks like you."

Em couldn't recall that anyone had spotted similarities between her mother and her. Eleanor was a glamorous woman, in that hard-line, soft-focus Forties way—

"But younger, of course."

Jennifer innocently delivered the most unkind cut of all. Emma didn't know how old Eleanor had been when she married Dad, except that she'd been decades younger than her daughter was now.

"I never knew her." Em moved to end an increasingly uncomfortable conversation. "She was gone before I was a year old."

Usually Em kept a tighter rein on her bitterness; this time she'd let it escape in full measure.

"I'm sorry." The younger woman sucked down the rest of

her cola. "Did you—? No, I'm sorry; no questions. I should know better. I take too much for granted."

"I hung the picture there," Em conceded, deciding then and there that the portrait was indeed destined for the attic. "Do you want more to drink?"

"No—well, yes—a little more. The ice helps. My lip's not throbbing anymore." Jennifer followed Em to the kitchen. "Can I use your phone?" she asked cautiously, eyeing the cordless model on the counter. "For a local call. I've got to call home."

Em guessed Jennifer meant the Blue House and Bran, not her parents, but also the place where her absence should have been noticed first.

"Go ahead."

Like a frightened animal, Jennifer snatched the phone and retreated to the farthest corner of the living room. Emma couldn't have overheard Jennifer's whispered, hunched-over conversation if she'd stood two feet away, but she stayed politely in the kitchen, sipping her second cup of tea and humoring the girl's need for privacy until the phone had been returned to its charging station.

"Everything's under control?" Em asked, as she might have asked Lori or Jay-Jay.

Jennifer shook her head quickly. She'd gone pale and anxious "Michelle answered—she's one of my other house-mates. I told her I was spending the night with a friend—that's the truth, isn't it?"

Emma nodded, thinking Michelle had nothing to do with Jennifer's new distress. "Sounds truthful enough to me. Did she want the phone number? You could have given it to her. I should have suggested it—"

"He's not there, Emma. They thought we were off to-gether making up. He left last night—right after I did—"

Jennifer drew her swollen lip between her teeth; when her mind hurt, as it so clearly did, she instinctively redirected that pain to her body. Hoping to distract her, Em touched Jennifer's wrist lightly.

"Don't borrow trouble. He could have found a friend to talk to."

"No," Jennifer insisted, releasing her lip. "Bran's new in Bower. He doesn't know his way around town yet. He doesn't have friends here except me."

Em withdrew her hand. "He's a man, Jennifer, not a child; being alone with his conscience for a while won't hurt him—"

"You don't understand!" Jennifer shot back, a breath short of shouting.

"I understand that you're trying to live Bran's life, not yours and—believe me—I know that's a recipe for disaster. What would you do if you saw him right now—tell him that it was *your* fault and that *you're* sorry?"

"I told you: I started it." She'd lowered her voice, but not its intensity. "I had those thoughts; *I* poked Bran between the ribs. He wouldn't have lost it if I hadn't started it."

"Then I'm wrong and you're right: what happened is absolutely your fault." If she'd learned nothing else during two failed marriages and the rearing of another woman's children, Emma Merrigan had learned how to finesse absurdity. "Forget about what happened to you last night. For Bran's safety, *you* best stay away from him until you've calmed down."

Two women glowered in silence. Em wouldn't be the first to break; thanks to her most recent ex-husband, she'd been tempered in hotter fires than this one. She waited, hoping Jennifer wouldn't bolt into the night, but having no intention of stopping her if she did. Jennifer had surprises of her own.

"What's happened to me?" she murmured. Leaving the ice-filled glass on the counter, she made her way to the living room and curled up beside, not on, the sofa. "Lock the doors, Emma, and throw away the keys. Don't let me out of here. I don't know what I'll do next."

"I exaggerated," Em sighed. "I don't think you're a danger to yourself or Bran. If you want to go looking for him . . ."

"I don't want to," Jennifer replied without drama. "I *am* listening to myself—just like you said—I don't like what I'm hearing. Something's wrong with me . . . maybe with Bran, too." Resting her face against the cushion, she wrapped her arms over her head. Her body rocked slowly.

"Is there pain, Jennifer?" Em asked, revisiting the notion that the young woman needed a doctor. "More pain than cuts and bruises?"

"No—it's like when you want to cry and shout, but you can't. The tears won't come 'cause it's not the right time or place. I could cry, if Bran were here, but—probably—I'd shout instead. In my head, my thoughts are pulling in different directions. I don't know what I want to do; I don't want what I want."

"Don't think about what you want; what do you *need* right now?" Em asked from the chair beneath the wedding portrait. "How about a nice hot shower? Twelve hours of sleep? You didn't sleep last night, did you? Napping on a table at the library doesn't count."

"I want to stay here, Emma. If I can. If you'll still let me. If you're okay with having a crazy person in your guest room."

"I don't think you're a crazy person." There was a line between troubled and crazy which Jennifer hadn't crossed. "Whatever's been going on between you and Bran got out of control last night. Your emotions ran a marathon and your body's paying the price now. You need rest: down time, time to let the dust settle."

"You think so?"

Em shrugged. "That's how it's worked for me."

Her memory flashed to a time when she'd been younger

than Jennifer. Women's dorms were fortresses then, locked at midnight to insiders and outsiders alike. The memory was jagged, like a page torn carelessly from a book, but one night her dorm-room walls, for reasons Em couldn't recall, had seemed to be curving inward and she'd needed to escape. She'd wound up in the glass-bound lobby, hammering the locked doors with her fists. Security had taken her to the infirmary—another forgotten relic of undergrad life—where someone had given her a big white pill.

Em remembered crying herself to sleep and nothing about waking up. But that was the point of the memory: by morning, there'd been nothing worth remembering. Sleep had encapsulated the whole episode. In retrospect, the frightening part was that she'd taken an unknown medication from someone—the memory didn't recall gender—who hadn't known her from Adam.

Forget the black nail polish and the safety-pinned coat. The real difference between her and Jennifer was a change in trust. She'd never offer Jennifer so much as an aspirin and Jennifer should know better than to swallow anyone's big white pill. A safe place to rest, though, the need for that, and its restorative power, couldn't have changed very much in thirty years.

"It's fine to get back on the horse after you've been dumped the first time, but when falling is getting to be a habit, it's a good idea to give yourself a rest before you climb up again."

Jennifer nodded with a smile made ironic by her swollen lip. "A rest. That sounds good. I'd like a rest. I'd like to fall asleep right now and wake up feeling like myself again— but I'm not tired. I don't know what else to say: I want to stay here, but I don't want to talk about Bran. I don't want to talk about anything."

"Then we won't," Em agreed, which created a delicate awkwardness between them.

They weren't old friends or family who could be comfortably silent in a living room. Nor were they strangers in a waiting room. A television's glass eye stared at them but even to suggest a program for viewing seemed a violation of their pact, at least as Em measured its constraints. Jennifer might have had other reasons for her silence, but those were even further out of bounds. The evening newspaper was their sole salvation.

Four sections—five, counting the inmost classifieds—lay on the door-side table where Em had deposited them with her purse and canvas totebag. Generously, she began with the local section, leaving the world, sports, and features for her guest, who chose features first. The cats, beguiled by the sounds of paper and the certain knowledge that there were *laps* for the taking, emerged from the basement. Emma was unaware of their presence until Charm stuck her gray-furred head under one corner of the newsprint wall and oozed into her lap.

By ten, between a sleeping cat and the lackluster desperation of the personal classifieds, Em, though not particularly tired, was ready for bed.

"You can stay up—" she began.

"No, I'm ready to head down, too," Jennifer agreed quickly, as if she'd been waiting for the opportunity to escape.

The young woman was in the backroom with the door shut and the lights out before Em had loaded the coffee maker for a seven AM drip and finished her other downstairs chores. She slipped down the hall to the bathroom as soon as Emma had turned off her light.

"I leave at seven-thirty, get up at seven, no breakfast. I'll wake you?"

"I'll be up before then. Can I get a ride to campus?"

"I figured you'd want one. Sleep well."

"Yeah. Thanks."

The door clicked shut. Em rolled over in her bed, a double bed, not that she needed a double bed, just that she was used to it. Just as she was used to being alone at the Maisonettes. With her eyes closed, she was aware of the flash as Jennifer opened the bathroom door before flicking the light switch. She was aware of Jennifer breathing behind the backroom's closed door.

The door to Em's bedroom was open—the cats wouldn't have tolerated anything less. Spin hit the mattress with an "I'm here" bound and staked his claim to the valley between her feet. Charm, the oozer, was simply *there* at the back of Em's neck between one breath and the next. She purred softly, a sound Em felt more than heard and which usually lulled her to sleep.

Usually she went to bed after midnight and alone. Ten-fifteen was too early and, try as she might, Em couldn't shake her awareness of Jennifer. The blue digits of her alarm clock were too bright. She dialed the light back and changed her mind about the alarm, resetting it for six-forty, to give her time for a shower. Then she remembered there was a going-away luncheon tomorrow: the card and gift were in the backroom. The gift was wrapped, but unbowed, and Emma was more awake than she'd been since dinner.

Disgusted, she flopped on her stomach, scattering the cats, and began factoring sequential integers and counting prime numbers. Somewhere after 113, but before eleven-squared, she stopped counting.

Em slept better now that she was older. Until she'd hit thirty, sleep had been a crap shoot. Between night terrors and insomnia, she'd been lucky to get one decent night in three. It had been years since a night terror had launched her out of bed, none here at the Maisonettes. She'd forgotten what it was like to be suddenly awake, with her heart pounding in her throat and no notion where she was or who.

Who surfaced first, while Em was still gasping for air.

Where came next, with the knowledge that she was in a familiar place, her own place—and that she was not alone. There was a girl, Jennifer Hodden in the next room . . . not this room.

Emma was not-alone in *this* room.

She remembered her cats and bravely dragged a hand across the blankets. No cats, but still—not alone. Her eyes were open, her vision was attuned to the patterns of light leaking past the drapes. All was quiet, exactly as it should have been, so quiet she *could* hear Jennifer breathing behind the backroom door and one of the cats scratching litter in the basement.

The terror faded. Terrors were like that: over before she was completely awake. They weren't nightmares; they had no content. Other than the sense of terror itself, they left nothing behind to scar her memory. Emma could roll over, pull the covers up tight, close her eyes, and fall back to sleep. Or, she could have if the nagging sense of not-alone had faded with the terror.

Jennifer! Em thought firmly to her restless imagination. *I brought a stranger home. Impulsive, foolish—but no reason to lose sleep, for Pete's sake!*

It was useless; she was awake and might as well turn the light on for reading, except that reading might awaken Jennifer, because, truly, she wasn't alone. Sighing, Emma rolled over again, to look at the clock.

She might as well see the full measure of her punishment—

There was no clock, no inch-high numbers changing slowly, silently. Em recalled dialing down their glow. She propped herself up on one elbow, reached, and hesitated.

There was no clock, no bedside table, no lamp, no shadows. The rectangular glow seeping past the drapes which had been there a moment ago was gone. *I'm having a stroke,* Em thought, thinking of her father. But she could move both sides

of her body and see nothing with both eyes. That wasn't a
stroke or heart attack. Nothing wasn't inside her skull; it was
outside, and it wasn't *nothing*. Her eyes began to perceive
light—faint and ambient—without an apparent source.

Fog then, or *smoke*?

Before common sense could intervene, Emma breathed
deeply. None of the myriad scents of burning touched her
nerves, nor those of dampness. Yet there was a scent. Her
mind labeled it *old, ancient*.

But not empty.

The textures of Em's bed, the soft, almost suede-like
sheets, wool blanket, polyester pillow with the extra-firm
ridge along one edge to support her computer-abused neck
while she slept, they were all very real, likewise the over-
long T-shirt twisted loosely around her thighs and the birth-
stone ring she wore on her right hand. It was everything
beyond the bed that had gone unfamiliar—

No, not unfamiliar. Em *knew* this place, if it could be
called a place. A sense—call it her body's memory, rather
than her mind's—recognized it. The sense said *flee. Wake
up!*

Emma shook her head. She was already awake and didn't
want to run. After fifty years of waking up afraid, she'd
come to the place where the night terrors were born. Em
wanted to confront whatever it was that had terrorized her
younger self.

Clinging to the covers, Em sat up. Cold touched her back;
the pillow had vanished. She should have been frightened,
but her anger was stronger. Echoes of old black-and-white
movies and television episodes warned Em to stay in contact
with the familiar, lest she lose all hope of returning to full-
color reality. She rose to her knees on the mattress.

The shadow contracted around her.

Emma's eyes had fully adjusted to the faint light: she saw
more, but she still saw nothing. If east remained east and all

else were equal, there was someone else nearby. She pointed herself toward the backroom and called Jennifer's name.

Em might have made a sound. Air had passed over her vocal chords and her mind registered the proper word—but did she ever truly hear her own voice? Wasn't she always surprised by the sounds a tape recorder captured?

For a moment, Em's attention had been all inside her head, absorbed by electronics and philosophy. In the night-terror realm, a moment was a meaningful slice of time. When Emma's attention focused outward again there was something in the space where Jennifer should have been.

Not a shadow, but an ember, a good-sized ember. The palm of her outstretched hand didn't quite cover the ruddy glow, yet it cast no light into the darkness. Did it mark the place where Jennifer slept, or was it something else? If it were Jennifer, then Jennifer's presence was quite different than her own; and if it weren't Jennifer—?

If the ember hovered above Em's sleeping guest, then tonight's terror wasn't hers.

The sphere of me-and-mine had been violated. The protective anger Emma felt toward her own remembered self was itself an ember compared to the rage a threatened guest roused in her heart. She dropped the blanket and stood on her bed.

"Leave her alone." She mustered all the authority of her mother-voice.

The ember shimmered. It had no fixed shape, nothing to suggest that it was anything but a dancing bit of flame. But what should its appearance suggest? Human beings looked first for faces. They saw faces in clouds, rocks, and tree trunks. Emma didn't see a face in the ember, yet she sensed something in the ruddy light.

"Leave *me* alone!"

She added a thought of repulsion, of a force radiating outward from her spine. The ember intensified, growing brighter, but not larger.

"Get out of here—"

Em imagined a dog skulking in her garden: an anonymous stray, brindled like a wolfhound. Green plants obscured its feet, green vines rose some short distance above its head. Only its eyes retained the ember's glow. Its teeth were ivory and slick with anticipation.

Sound did exist in the night-terror realm: Em heard it growl.

"I *said:* Get out of here!"

She imagined a rock and coordination much better than her hand and eye usually possessed. Her arm never moved, but the dog whined and then ran. Green faded to gray and black. Emma sank to her knees. The not-alone sense was gone. She'd driven it away but doubts, rather than triumph, rose to take its place.

When she'd been a child, awakened by a terror and afraid to close her eyes ever again, Dad would take her into the living room and they spent the rest of the night in his easy chair. When she'd been old enough to read, he'd shown her books from the Med School library: research texts about dreams, nightmares, and night terrors.

There's nothing to be afraid of, Em. She heard Dad's voice as clearly as she'd heard her own. *It's just your brain doing what it needs to do while you're sleeping: getting rid of all those daydreams you have in school.*

Emma found hems of her sheet and blanket, found the edge of the bed and her pillow, too. She settled down with her eyes wide open.

Not a chance, Dad. Not a chance. I never daydreamed any of this.

Four

The alarm went off with its blue digits flashing 6:40 and predictions of rain, possibly sleet, changing to snow coming through the speaker. Em stared at it, remembering Jennifer in the next room before she remembered resetting it from 7:00. Weather predictions became an annoying commercial for one of those chain restaurants where no self-respecting Boweran would ever eat. She tapped the *Off* button and pointed herself toward the shower.

No signs of life in the backroom, not that she expected any. There might exist college students who told the truth when they claimed to rise before dawn, but she'd neither met nor been one.

Emma was in the shower with shampoo lather streaming down her face before she recalled the night terror and its aftermath. She stood in the warm rain, reconstructing events, and convincing herself that all of it, from the waking in terror to the snarling dog, had been a dream. Vivid, multisensory dreams weren't unprecedented, though usually they confined themselves to the spring allergy season when she relied on antihistamines to ward off the tree and early grass pollen.

Allergy-spawned dreams didn't require pop-psych intro-spection, thank God. One spring Em had dreamt a raging argument with President Nixon; he'd blown up the world rather than eat Szechuan food. Who'd dare look for meaning in that?

Emma had more important things to occupy her thoughts: possibly sleet, possibly snow, and a wrapped present sitting on a table three feet from Jennifer's head. She turned the water up and adjusted the nozzle to direct the water against the molded fiberglass walls. In the backroom, it should sound like rain falling on a drum. Em let it pelt a good while, confident in the water heater's capacity. When even the dead should have been disturbed by the racket, Em shut it off and finished her water-based rituals.

There was neither light nor sound coming through the closed door when Em emerged in a fast-dissipating mist. She tapped the closed door, not hard, and called Jennifer's name.

Nothing.

Em had a problem. Her husbands and stepkids had learned better than to drop problems in her lap before she'd made herself sane with a cup of coffee—which she could smell brewing in the kitchen. Jennifer's ignorance could be excused, but that didn't solve anything. Emma turned lights on, pushed clothes around in her closet, opened and decisively closed every dresser drawer. It was all meant to rouse her guest naturally and, naturally, none of it worked.

Em was dry, dressed, and standing in the hall. The backroom was as quiet and dark as it had been when the alarm went off. She gave the door a determined *thump*.

"Jennifer! Jennifer! It's after seven and I left something in your room. I've got to come in to get it—" Continued silence. "Okay? I'm coming in. Jennifer?"

Em turned the knob, gave a shove, and light from the hall fixture flooded the room. Jennifer lay on her side, one arm thrown up to shield her face.

"Jennifer?"

The girl burrowed slowly into the pillow but that was it. Jennifer was either asleep or very good at deception. And Em was going to leave a stranger alone in her house.

Teeth clenched in frustration, Em retrieved her gift. Retreating to the kitchen and a cup of the elixir of coherent thought, Emma got a handle on her emotions. She'd accomplished her purpose—if yesterday's impulsive invitation could be said to have a purpose. A frightened human being had found a place to reflect and rest. If there were justice in the universe, Jennifer, and only Jennifer, would be gone at the end of the day.

"Take care of yourself," she whispered from the foot of the stairs. "Good luck."

She scribbled a note offering the contents of her kitchen as breakfast and repeating her hopes for the girl's future, then taped the note to the bathroom mirror.

November was waiting when Emma opened the front door. Trees that had been gold-crowned yesterday were naked beneath today's mottled gray skies. Blustery winds found the seams and gaps in Em's raincoat before she reached the sidewalk. It was her own fault that her winter coat, with its weatherproof layers of synthetic down and arctic-tested nylon, still languished in summer storage. She wished she could pick it up at lunch rather than go to the luncheon.

And she'd forgotten, until she didn't see it in any of its usual spots, that she'd parked her car three chilly blocks away. By the time she'd completed the walk, Em had succumbed completely to November's magic and her mood was as bleak as the sky. She made it into her office without making eye contact with anyone.

No crises, computer-generated or otherwise, awaited her. Fueled with coffee from the office machine, Emma closed her door and buried herself in the latest batch of requests from Slavic Studies.

The U had gone cherry-picking as the Soviet Empire dissolved and snared itself a batch of scholars with impeccable credentials and implacable rivalries. If they didn't come to blows with one another or the original faculty still clinging to their tenures, Slavic Studies would mature into a world-class department. In the meantime, her desk had become a departmental battleground. The weapon of choice was the lengthy, annotated wish-list, written in an unholy mix of Cyrillic and Roman characters. There were days when Em thought she should simply make an offer for Moscow University's library and the entire KGB archives.

Fortunately, it was the detective aspects of acquisitions that most intrigued Em. She'd had to cede the Oriental titles to immigrants but if the requests were written with basic Roman or Greek alphabet, there was no request too obscure—or too badly misspelled—for her to handle. If it was already *in* the library—and after a few years of purchase-order warfare many of the wish-list titles already were—she'd send back a polite note, and if it wasn't, she'd find a source and a price for the budget committee's approval.

The search went slower than usual this dreary Friday morning; Emma's concentration was shot. Her thoughts wandered away from the scrawled lists. Twice she started to dial her own phone number only to hang up before it rang. What could she say—? Hi, Jennifer, how are you this morning and, by the way, don't be there when I get home?

Worse than fretting about home, Em's memory was churning. She'd look at a screen filled with transliterated titles but see Dad, or Eleanor, or that damn dog she'd dreamt about last night.

By midmorning, Emma's divided attention had spawned a migraine. She had medication for the torture, but the capsules came with so many warnings about overuse that she preferred to tough the headaches out instead. Em gathered her wish-lists and headed to the reference room for some old-fashioned paper research beneath its high, drafty ceilings. It proved a good choice, at least for her headache. Still, she hadn't gotten much done when the campus bell tower let her know it was time for the luncheon.

Fifteen women assembled in the back room of a campus eatery. After four years as Gene Shaunekker's assistant, Sarah, their guest of honor, was headed for California, following her husband who had nailed down a nose-bleed salary at a private genetics lab. She was radiantly pregnant and confident that the hard days of school and scrambling were behind them. Em hoped Sarah was right, but of the five women at her table, four of them, including herself, knew better.

Two of her table companions were married, one to the same man for nearly thirty years. When Em looked at Geena she saw all the paths she hadn't managed to take. Two others were divorced, single, and actively dating, unlike herself.

The five of them talked library politics and town politics, and the possibility of a movie next Friday. Tracy, one of the divorced women eagerly confessed that she'd met a man—

—"At the grocery store, of all places. In the coffee aisle. Something clicked from the start; we both felt it. He said maybe we should drink coffee, not just buy it. I thought, what the hell? At least he wasn't *wearing* a ring . . . So we met for coffee and it went well. He says he's divorced, two kids—doesn't want any more, so I didn't mention Buddy. What's the point, right? He's older than I thought—forty-five. Maybe that's too old? But we decided we'd try dating. We're going out for dinner tomorrow night—I feel like a kid again. I don't know what to wear—or what to tell Buddy.

The other women had suggestions, not Emma. She wasn't opposed to dating, coffee, kids, or a younger man, but likely suspects hadn't crossed her path. Apparently, she didn't buy coffee at the right time or in the right place.

Her headache had returned before dessert arrived.

When the eating, gift-giving, and socializing were over, Em sealed herself in her office. Her computer displayed the stock of a London book-broker, but what she saw on the monitor was her own reflection. Jennifer had said she looked like Eleanor, but the face Emma saw had none of her mother's glamor—none of her father's handsome ruggedness, either. Hers was not, and had never been, an arresting or beautiful face, though it didn't look like she'd seen a half-century's worth of sunsets. Em Merrigan's problem was weariness, not wrinkles.

Weariness, and an aversion to romance based on French Roast versus Espresso.

"Em?"

She bolted upright in her chair, looked around and saw Matt standing in the doorway.

"Got you?" he asked, giving her a necessary moment to gather her wits.

When she struck the space bar to save her place in the data file, the screen went blank: her connection had timed out. Her eyes had been open but her mind had been elsewhere for at least ten minutes. "Got me cold," she conceded, rubbing her eyes.

"You missed the Internet Group this morning."

Em's heart sank. In a day of random stumbles, that was a real fall. She'd fought to get on that committee to play a significant part in shaping the library's place in the electronic future. It was inconceivable that she'd forget the group's biweekly meetings, yet it had happened.

"I tried calling you, to remind you—but you were away from your desk. I called again, after lunch."

She glanced at her phone; the amber light blinked back. She hadn't noticed it—hadn't looked—before lunch or since her return.

"I'm not myself today, Matt. What did I miss?"

"Nothing much. The latest design specs. I got your copy—" From the doorway, he frisbeed a report across her desk. "Next meeting's in three weeks, not two, and bring refreshments. We're doing the holidays. I put you down for homemade chocolate-chip cookies."

"Thanks," Em replied without enthusiasm. "I'll change my calendar."

She put the Internet report in the totebag for at-home reading and summoned her calendar to the monitor screen, a not-so-subtle way of ending the conversation. Matt was a canny enough young man; she expected him to take the hint. But his canniness had left early for the weekend.

"Is everything okay?" He cleared her side chair and sat down. "Are you okay?"

"One missed meeting isn't Alzheimer's."

Matt blinked as if she'd splashed him with cold water. He cocked his head rather than leave. "When I walked up, you were staring at your screen. It was a bad-news stare, Em. Do you want to talk?"

Em shook her head. Matt wasn't a meddler, but she'd learned over the few months that she'd known him that he took his friendships, even his office-casual friendships, seriously.

"Are they going to shake everything up again? I haven't heard any rumors this week, but I wouldn't have known about the last reorg if you hadn't told me who'd won and lost."

"Not this time." She tapped a few more keys.

"Personal, then? Okay, I get the hint." He started to stand.

There was nothing like cooperation to bring on a guilt attack. "No, not personal, either. I didn't sleep well last night—and I did something stupid."

"You?" Matt exclaimed with exaggerated disbelief. He'd sat down again.

"Yesterday. My turn sweeping bodies out of the stacks . . . I found one."

"No way! I didn't hear anything; I would've heard *that*. So, what—you didn't tell? You're keeping it a secret?"

"Well, not a *dead* body. A girl, asleep. When I went to remind her that this is a library, not a dorm . . . she'd been beaten up."

"Hiding? Afraid to go home?" Matt asked. "Shit, what did you do? Call security? Take her to student health?"

"Neither. I wound up taking her home with me."

"You did *what?*" Matt covered his eyes. "Jesus, Em— that *is* stupid. You took her home! You live alone. You know that's not the safest thing to do. What happened next? How bad did it get?"

"Not bad at all, Matt. Give me some credit for knowing a dollar from a doorstop. Jennifer's got bruises and a busted lip; she's not a criminal. I took her out to dinner and heard her side of the story before I invited her home."

"If you knew what you were doing, why'd you say you'd done something stupid?"

Em shrugged. "Because, if I'd thought about it, I'd've had the same reaction you're having. But I didn't. Instant karma."

"Wasn't that a Beatles song?"

"They'd broken up by then; John wrote that one with Yoko, not Paul. Anyway, it seemed like a good idea—and I think it was. We talked some; she was calmer, more rational when she went to bed. I was the one who spent the night haunted." She hadn't, of course, dreamt about being beaten by her boyfriend, but something about Jennifer must have stirred her subconscious.

"So, what did this Jennifer say? Who beat her up?"

"Her boyfriend—"

Further words waited in Emma's throat as Matt's face hardened and he became a stranger. He didn't talk much about his family life, but she'd gathered it had been pretty raucous. She considered that he might have had a front-row seat for something which she, despite two failed marriages, could only imagine: a man striking the woman he claimed to love.

"Bran and Jennifer apparently fell in love at the deep end of the pool. They're bringing out the worst in each other—each of them—"

Em caught herself: of whom and to whom was she speaking? The moment was ripe for a logical jab from Matt. Their friendship had two roots: the library computer network and the tendency of clever individuals to use one truth to obscure another.

But Matt had a different surprise: "Bran? Her name's Jennifer and his is Bran?"

"Very Seventies," Emma agreed. "Just like Matthew. It was a good decade for pseudo-Celtic and Bible-based names."

"I guess." He didn't meet her eyes. "I know a Bran and Jennifer—I know the Bran half, anyway. I haven't met his Jennifer. Grad student. New in town. He put his name on the Intermural list for handball partners. We've played about once a week since early October. We usually go out for beer afterward."

"He didn't strike you as the girlfriend-beating type?"

Matt started to nod, then stopped. "Ah, maybe. If my Bran's your Bran. He didn't talk about her much—we're not friends, just've played handball a few times. But when he did, he had it bad."

"Jealous? Possessive?" Em threw out a pair of the more common motives, but Matt shook them off.

"He did things like buy her flowers and gifts."

"O-o-oh, that's a bad sign, for sure."

A shrug. "It was the way he did it. Okay, he's new in Bower, and lonely. He's into materials science—high-tech engineering, but he says he doesn't have much in common with the rest of his department. Doesn't want to spend time with them. So, he's got time to kill and he kills it on her; I can follow that, but there was something more. I figured if she didn't dump him, he'd wind up carrying her shoes around on a pillow."

Matt's record with women wasn't lustrous. By his own admission, he dated rarely and only women who weren't interested in long-term relationships. But pillows and shoes? Em had never heard that one. Times had definitely changed.

"So, what happened with Jennifer?" Matt asked, recapturing Emma's attention. "You bought her food, took her home, then what?"

"We talked. I wanted her to listen to herself; I think that much helped. Then we went to bed. She said she'd leave with me this morning, but she slept through—"

"You left a *stranger* alone in your house, Em? Now that *is* stupid."

"Risky," Em corrected, despite having put the other word in play. "Not something I'd ordinarily do, but it seemed right at the time."

"Except now you've got to go home and you don't know what you're going to find there. I could follow you, just in case."

"That's not necessary. I'm not worried," Em insisted. She was, though not about robbery.

Matt scowled. "You should be."

"I'm sure she got up and left. I half-suspected she was awake when I left, but was too embarrassed to say anything."

"Not too embarrassed to rob you blind. Let me follow you home."

What did he think she was? An old woman who didn't have the physical—or mental—smarts to take care of herself?

Em picked up the phone and punched in her own number. It wasn't on the auto-dialer. Why should it be? The phone rang three times before the answering machine cut in. She waited out her message.

"Jennifer? If you're there, Jennifer, pick up. This is Emma—"

No response and after ten seconds of silence the connection ended. Emma hung up.

"That doesn't prove anything," Matt challenged.

"The stupidity wasn't choosing Jennifer. She's no worse than young and naive. Maybe I helped her get through a bad day; I can hope. The stupidity was choosing *anyone* and what that says about the state of my life—or my lack of a life!"

She'd taken the advice she'd given Jennifer and put her thoughts into spoken words. The act had revealed their absurdities.

"You have a life if you're helping people: changing the world or raising kids," Matt replied, without a hint of irony. "Otherwise, you're marking time like the rest of us."

Em didn't know what to say, except that she regretted the entire discussion. "Don't you start getting all despaired and nihilistic."

Matt took that advice with laughter. "Get home before dark and walk around your house once before you go in— just to make sure. If it doesn't look right, don't go in; call someone. Call me. I'm here for you."

He'd never been to the Maisonettes and didn't realize they were rows of townhouses. She had a backyard with a tiny garden and a seven-foot-high fence all around it, but unless she walked through her living room, she'd have to walk several hundred yards down an unlit, grassy lane to reach it. Gesturing toward the November weather visible through the layers of windows between her office and the real world, Em said: "I'd have more trouble with mud than with Jennifer at her worst, or Bran 'no-T' Mongomery, for that matter."

"Mongomery with no 'T'? Then it's definitely the Bran I know. I wouldn't mess with him. The guy may be an engineer, but he played football at some eastern school."

"Can't beat him at handball, eh?"

"Not without a four-by-four in my left hand."

"So, you're not really surprised that he'd give a girl a black eye?"

"No—in that sense I am. I'm the one who'd have to think about cheating; he can win without hedging the rules. But if he did hit someone, there'd be damage. You be careful."

Emma caught herself before saying she was always careful. "If I'm not here come Monday morning, you know where the police should start looking. Any plans for the weekend?"

"Football!"

He described his hopes for a Saturday at the stadium, if the weather improved, or one spent glued to the television, if it didn't. The U's team had lost a game back in September, dimming its championship chances. But week by week, the team had improved its record. With two more games to go, there was a three-way tie in the conference and a good chance that the championship wouldn't be decided until the last quarter of the last game.

Tickets for tomorrow's game would be in short supply. Em wished Matt, and the team, luck before he left her office.

It was nearly dark when she left the library and though the sidewalks were merely wet, not icy or slush-covered, the wind-driven precipitation had an ominous, clumpy feel when it struck her face. She headed straight for the cleaners where she produced a wrinkled, dog-eared ticket from the depths of her wallet.

The hired help entered the number in a computer and announced: "It's in storage. Come back next Friday."

Emma protested that she'd paid extra to have the coat moved from the warehouse to the local cleaner after Labor

Day, precisely to avoid the week's delay in delivery. The help, clearly a high school student by the generous cut of his clothes and the length of his hair, explained patiently.

"If the boxes don't get picked up before November first, the owner sends 'em back. They ain't here. You gotta wait until next week."

Em wanted to complain that a *considerate* cleaner would know better than to send bought-and-paid-for boxes back to storage, but she wouldn't have her coat one minute sooner. She swallowed everything except, "You're sure my coat will be ready next Friday?" and left after the boy assured her that it would.

Nearly dark had become a low-slung night blanketing the treetops. Bower wasn't Alaska; it didn't get all thirty-five varieties of Eskimo snow, but November snows were different, and a November snow had begun to fall. A few swipes of the wiper blades took care of the splattering that clung to windshields, bushes, and branches like so much soggy cotton. November snows weren't pretty, not the way January's powder snow would be, but traction wasn't a problem.

The parking space at the end of her walk was empty and waiting. A plastic-sleeved newspaper lay on the stoop and Christmas catalogs filled the mailbox to overflowing. The front light was on, courtesy of the timer Em had installed herself two years ago, but the windows were dark. No Jennifer, no company: her home was hers again. With purse, totebag, and damp paper cradled in her left arm and the storm door against her shoulder, Em put her key in the lock and shoved the door open.

"Spin!" she called as she stepped across the threshold, all habit, no conscious thought. Her armload fell into the hall chair. With her freed left hand, Em hit the light switch and, with her back to the living room, closed the door. "Charm!"

"Emma?"

Jennifer. She recognized the girl's voice—timid, even

fearful—but not before her heart raced and the floor seemed to fall away from her feet. Light from the hall cut sharply across the living room. Jennifer was tucked up on the sofa, a study in shadows and four luminous cat eyes. Charm sprang from Jennifer's lap with a leap that took her halfway to the cellar door. Two more bounds and she was gone, but Spin— the traitor—yawned mightily and stayed put.

"I'm sorry—I'm *really* sorry," Jennifer insisted, though she, like Spin, stayed put on the sofa. "I didn't know what else to do except stay here."

The floor had reappeared beneath Em's feet. She made her way to her chair but left the lamp unlit.

"I called." Emma looked at her answering-machine's flashing light. "Didn't you hear me call?"

Jennifer shook her head. Her lip was scarcely swollen, even her bruises had faded, though that might be a trick of the shadowy light. She wrapped an arm around Spin who, most unusually, endured the hug. "I didn't know it was you. I took a shower; I thought it would help. I saw the light when I came out, but·I didn't want to touch it. I'm sorry, Emma, I really am."

Em had to ask: "What happened?"

"I overslept. It was after ten o'clock when I got up. I never thought I'd sleep the clock around . . . I really meant to get up but—well—I was kind of relieved that I hadn't. Everything was settled in my mind, like you said it would be. I wrote a note—" She pointed to a sheet of notebook paper on the table beside Em's chair. "And called my housemate Michelle again. She's usually home in the mornings and has a car. I thought she could come get me."

"But she couldn't," Em interrupted, trying not to mentally measure the distance between the Maisonettes and Reynolds Street. It couldn't be more than three miles; not a too-long walk, even in November.

"She could've, but—right after I called last night, Bran

got back. Michelle said he looked weird, like he hadn't eaten or slept for days—longer than he'd been gone—and crazy, too. His eyes, she said his eyes were weird."

"Drugs?"

Jennifer released Spin. The cat jumped down and began grooming himself; the girl curled up with her chin resting on her knees.

"Who knows?" she said, as if she didn't care. The act wasn't convincing. "Michelle said the first thing he did was to ask where I was. Michelle said I was staying with a friend; she said she was real glad she didn't know your name or where you lived. It must've been like a bad movie. Bran didn't believe her, or the guys. While he stormed around looking for me, they thought about calling 9-1-1. But Sam—he's kind of the guy in the house who makes decisions when they have to get made—Sam said they should try to calm Bran down first, 'cause of the lease. They had some trouble last semester; that's why there was space for Bran and me. The owner said something about kicking everyone out if there was another complaint with the police. I don't know if he could do that, but Sam didn't want to take a chance—according to Michelle. She always goes along with whatever Sam says—"

Em didn't want to know about Michelle or Sam. "Did they get your boyfriend calmed down?"

"Yeah. Kind of. He stopped yelling and said he believed Michelle. They talked him out of calling my folks, thank God, an' he shut himself up in his room, which everyone thought was a pretty good idea, until around two AM, when they were all in bed, and Bran started storming around again. Sam told him to get the hell out and he did.

"He hadn't been back when I called Michelle. She didn't think I should come back until, like, Bran and I had gotten things settled between us. That's Sam, probably, but Bran scared her, too; I could hear it in her voice. I don't think I want to see Bran right now."

Jennifer focused her attention on her toes. "I called home—I'd looked in the mirror and decided I could make out that I'd fallen or something. There wasn't an answer— not even after three. My mom's *always* home when my brother gets home from school; it's like this big thing with her. Suddenly, I got worried. Maybe he'd gone there, look- ing for me; maybe something real terrible had happened. So, dumb-shit me, I called my dad's office—they've gone out of town for the *whole* weekend; they left *yesterday*—with my brother, visiting colleges. They didn't even tell me!"

Another milestone on the road to adulthood: the moment, after you'd moved out, when you realized that it's more than you not telling them where you are; it's them not telling you either. Another time, Em might have commented on the oc- casion; this time she remained silent and still, except to wel- come the fully groomed Spin into her lap.

"I've got a key and all," Jennifer continued. "Like it's still my home, right? It's the address on my driver's license. Then I thought, suppose Bran did come there looking for me? He doesn't know I'm here. But my folks' number is in the book, with their address. We'd be alone, if Bran came . . . if some- thing's really wrong and I really shouldn't see him right now.

"And I felt safe here." She met Em's eyes. "Your cats came out and played with me. I thought I could stay here, at least until you got home. Then, when it got dark and started snowing and getting late, and you weren't here, I thought maybe you'd gone away for the weekend, too, and I didn't know what I was going to do."

Em heard echoes from her conversation with Matt and squelched them as she said: "You can stay here, Jennifer."

"I don't have any clothes—I mean, thanks, Emma, I want to stay with you, but I need stuff, my stuff." Jennifer wriggled her toes, not making eye contact, not directly asking for help. "I've got a paper due on Monday. My notes an' everything are in my room. My computer, too—unless I can use yours. I saw it there in the room where I was sleeping, the phone wire, too. I didn't turn it on! I've got a U-account." Jennifer's voice rose, turning a statement into a plea. "I'm no good with computers. Bran's good. So's my Dad. They get along okay. They both try to teach me, but I'd rather let them fix things when I foul them up."

"Let's go get your stuff," Em suggested as she pushed Spin off her lap. "I can tap your account from here, if you remember your number and password."

And possibly even if Jennifer didn't.

Five

C lots of snow slid down the warm windshield. The first clots melted completely before reaching the bottom but after several minutes of sacrifice a small beachhead of slush had formed against the wiper blades. Emma considered starting the car and the defroster.

A change of clothes, Jennifer had said, the notes for a paper on some obscure nineteenth-century novel, her toothbrush; those were the only items she needed. She'd be in and out in five minutes.

Conversations took time, especially after the previous day's drama. Outside the Blue House, Emma figured fifteen. There was a light in every downstairs window and several more on the second and third floors. That was a lot of housemates, a lot of conversation. Fifteen minutes was probably optimistic.

Snug within her car, confident in its technology, Em could indulge the sensations of isolation and cold feet while she waited, eyes closed, for Jennifer to reemerge. Neither snow nor night nor Em's eyelids could hide the Blue House. Its hidden walls radiated color like an old furnace leaked heat. Privately—not for sharing with her more preservation-oriented acquaintances—Em liked the color, though if it had been up to her—if she'd been the sort of person who'd *own* a wedding-cake house—she wouldn't have stopped with the walls. The fanciful lathe-work clinging to every eave and window cried out for more color, not less. The stark white trim against the cobalt blue was a visual failure, as if the Blue House had lost its nerve.

Behind her closed eyes, Emma imagined the house at the height of summer, blooming in perennial scarlet, purple, and deep green; not a pale petal or shingle in sight. She could hear the civic uproar, too, and was smiling when the passenger door opened.

"Can you come inside? There's a problem—"

That much was evident from Jennifer's face, illuminated by the dome-light. Em agreed to go inside. A moderately tall young man with black-wire glasses and severely slicked hair stood inside the front door, not quite blocking Em's path to the stairs. As a welcoming committee, he made a good rottweiler.

"Look, Jen," he said in crisp, patronizing tones, "none of us heard anything. This is as much a surprise to us as it is to you. If Bran trashed your room last night, we didn't know it. What did you expect us to do, anyway? You're the one who gave him a key."

Em surmised that she was in the presence of Sam and took an instant dislike to him.

When Jennifer shot back, "I gave *you* a key, too!" she was pleased with her companion's spirit, though she knew a name-calling argument wasn't going to resolve anything, if Bran had finished on Jennifer's possessions what he'd started on her face.

"For emergencies," Sam countered. "There were no emergencies. I checked the house last night, same as I do every night. The second floor was quiet. You weren't here; we knew that, but your room was locked tight; I rattled the knob to be sure. Bran's room was quiet, too. I hoped he was sleeping it off and didn't take the risk of waking him up by rattling the knob."

"We all *thought* Bran was up in his room," another housemate amended. A black woman with lacquered braids, she probably wasn't the Michelle who followed Sam's lead.

That started a competition of opinions. Emma had nothing to add as housemates flung their thoughts at one another, more interested in being heard than listening. For all the noise, there was substantial agreement: those who'd witnessed Bran Mongomery's last—and possibly final—appearance in the Blue House wouldn't soon forget it. To a man and woman, they had been unnerved by his appearance. No one doubted that Jennifer's boyfriend was responsible for whatever had happened in her room.

"Could we *go* upstairs?" Em asked, catching Jennifer's attention during a lull.

Sam struck quick: "It's *her* responsibility, Mrs. Hodden. Jennifer signed an agreement when she moved in."

Mrs. Hodden? Ah, Jennifer had felt the need for parental authority in this crisis. There might be consequences down the line, but for the moment Emma played along.

"Aren't you getting a bit ahead of yourself, Mr . . . ?" She cocked her head, waiting for him.

Wire rims and slicked-back hair retreated toward the stairs, fairly defying Em to climb them. "It's the security deposit," he explained—a clear appeal to maturity.

In a university town where four out of every five students lived off-campus, there was always friction between landlords and tenants. Em didn't want to guess the dollar amount of the deposit that preceded the lease on the Blue House, garish exterior walls notwithstanding. If Sam's name was on the lease, he had a legitimate concern—which was all the more reason not to cultivate hostility.

"Let's see what's where first," Em suggested, taking a short stride toward the stairs.

This time Sam retreated and "Mrs. Hodden" ascended behind her erstwhile daughter. Jennifer's room was at the end of the L-shaped hallway wrapped around the stairs. Its door was open and several lights were lit, enabling Emma to assess the damage before she crossed the threshold.

For sheer chaos, her stepson's room had often looked worse, yet there was a sense of suddenness to the disorder with little of the geological sediment that accompanied Jay-Jay's clutter. *All* the drawers were open and overflowing. *All* the shelves had been swept bare of books. Books and paper lay atop clothing; there were no garments draped over books.

"What might he have been looking for?" Em asked gently.

Jennifer shook her head. As she collected a handful of underwear and deposited it in an open drawer, something made her stiffen and grow pale. If a person's space was an extension of personality, then ransacking it was akin to rape and though she wasn't one for casual hugs, Emma—Mrs. Hodden—trod carefully through the ruins to put her arms around her purported daughter.

"Why?" Jennifer asked, too soft for her peering housemates to overhear. "Why would anyone do *this*? They didn't take anything—"

Not *he*, not Bran, but *they*, the nameless, shameless, and unknown. Em could feel Jennifer trembling. It wasn't a good moment for challenging her conclusions.

"You can hardly be certain nothing's missing. Just because your computer and stereo are still here—" Facts which, in Em's mind, tended all the more to incriminate Bran. "Something smaller could be gone. A piece of jewelry? Letters? Some other keepsake?"

"Stop blaming Bran! This wasn't him!" Jennifer wrested away. "Bran wouldn't do this to me, no matter how angry he got."

Em let her go. "He'd know, wouldn't he, how to hurt you? Is there anything he's given you? Or something he knows you cherish?" Jennifer's face was becoming a hostile mask; Em hastily added: "If those things *are* here—the things only you and he would know about—then maybe it wasn't Bran—"

There was, as the police would say, no sign of forced entry around the windows and the door had an intact deadbolt lock worthy of an urban apartment. If Bran hadn't done the ransacking, Em's suspicion shifted toward the housemates, including Sam. Framed in the doorway, they were as ordinary a collection of students as the U accumulated and though she knew appearance was simply another word for prejudice, Em couldn't believe any of them were responsible for the ravaging of Jennifer's room.

Jennifer took Em's suggestion. She sorted through the disorder around her night table until she found a small latched box. The box was open and empty, jack-knifed between a dictionary and a rolled-up pair of socks. Jennifer cradled it in her hands as if its worth were beyond measure, then set it on the dresser.

"They're gone. Nanni's earrings, they're not here." Jennifer took a backward stride toward her bed, forgetting the clutter. She was falling when the mattress caught her. "I can't remember. I can't remember when I wore them last, or if I put them away. I should have; I think I did—I don't know where else I would have put them, but I don't remember. I *can't* remember. I'm sitting here, and it's as if none of this is mine. It all belongs to someone else."

Raking her fingers through her hair and across her face, Jennifer flinched as she touched a still-sensitive bruise. Em cleared a space beside Jennifer on the bed.

"Do you want to call the police?" She wouldn't have offered her stepdaughter the choice.

Jennifer hesitated before shaking her head. "I want to

leave. I want to pretend this is all a bad dream. I know it's not, but I want to pretend."

The mother-voice in the back of Em's mind advocated an immediate restoration of order: fold those clothes, stack those books, papers, and knickknacks; check for broken glass and get rid of it, *now*.

Sometimes the mother-voice expected miracles from ordinary mortals. What was the harm in walking away? No clean clothes tomorrow morning, for one thing; an incomplete English paper for another.

"Find what you came for."

Mechanically, Jennifer packed a magenta duffle bag, then, over Sam's protests, she pulled her room's door shut and locked it.

"You can't just *leave* a mess like that!"

Sam exercised his mother-voice well; Em was curious about *his* private space.

But Jennifer was moving. The young woman had mastered the art of zooming through a crowd. When she lowered her head and started for the stairs, her housemates cleared a path wide enough for Em, too. At the bottom, Jennifer took a sharp left to the kitchen. She caught Em's eye.

"My hands are full, Mom, could you put Auntie Emma's number on the refrigerator?"

Not a bad recovery and improvisation, Em thought, looking for paper.

"I'll be at my aunt's until Monday morning," Jennifer told her housemates while Emma wrote her phone number on an outdated pizza coupon and stuck it beneath the feet of a Mickey Mouse magnet. "I'll be back after my Monday afternoon class. I'll deal with my room then."

"And if Bran comes looking for you?" Sam demanded.

"Tell him to call. There's the number."

With no more than a phone number it was unlikely that Bran, or anyone else, would appear at the Maisonettes. Of course, Emma had been committed to playing host for the whole weekend with no opportunity to object, the same way she'd been summarily transformed into a parent.

Jennifer might not be able to manage her relationship with Brandon "no-T" Mongomery, but she wasn't a stranger to getting her way. She deposited her duffle in the back seat before Em could suggest the trunk.

They pulled away from the Reynolds Street curb in silence. The temperature seemed to have dropped several degrees in the short while they'd been inside and the small clumps of snow on the windshield had congealed over the wipers. A prudent Bower native had to wonder if this might not be one of those years when winter arrived with an overnight *thud.*

Em glanced at her passenger, but never turned her head. A veteran of raising stepchildren to adulthood, she recognized a rigid profile as an omen of confession. There was something about a darkened automobile that loosened tongues.

"His demons won," Jennifer said as they joined the herd in pursuit of green lights along Main Street.

A moment passed while they slowed for a mistimed light. Two cars up, brake lights flashed and fish-tailed. Em seized the steering wheel then relaxed as her winter-driving instincts awakened. Em maneuvered into her preferred lane for the retreat to the Maisonettes and recalled last night's supper when Jennifer had described her lover as a demon-haunted man. Personally, Emma wouldn't accept demons as an excuse for bad behavior.

"That's too easy. If Bran's got demons, he made them and he can control them."

Emma saw Jennifer shake her head curtly. The confessional moment had passed. There was no further conversation. Spin and Charm greeted them with the suspicion they reserved for any suitcase-like object, whether it was coming or going. Two-part yowling followed the women upstairs.

"Can you show me how to work on your computer?" Jennifer asked, a palpable chill in her voice.

A weekend with a hostile near-stranger loomed in Em's imagination. Disparaging Bran's demons had not been a winning idea. Into what, she asked herself, had she become entangled? But she pushed the buttons to bring her home machine to life. Daffy Duck spoke from the speakers and cracked the indoor ice.

"My dad does stuff like that," Jennifer said with patent approval. "Bran, too. Can you really get to my account from here? My dad says it's illegal."

Père Hodden was right, too, but he didn't know the network's underbelly the way Em did. She had an electronic tunnel to the blinking boxes in Matt's office which, if he'd discovered it, he'd left undisturbed. Once she'd convinced the network that the Maisonettes were within the library walls, it readily accepted her perfectly legitimate account and password. From there it was only a few commands before a waving banner invited another user to log on.

Jennifer spiraled into the vacated chair. "I'm impressed. I'm calling you the next time I nuke myself."

Em bypassed both the compliment and the invitation with an inquiry about supper. "Will chicken and broccoli be all right?"

An expression Em was beginning to recognize as mild embarrassment tinged with shame slackened Jennifer's face. "Supper. Yeah. Chicken and broccoli sounds great. I forgot about food, Emma. I should give you some money for feeding me. How much? I've only got about twenty dollars on me."

"Don't worry about it."

Jennifer visibly relaxed and asked how long before dinner. When Em said an hour—she had to thaw a second chicken breast—Jennifer said an hour would be fine.

Downstairs, it was almost like having Lori home for a

visit: a palpable yet somewhat detached extra presence in the townhouse. And a reminder to Emma that she shouldn't start discussing the evening news with Spin and Charm. Not that she'd been paying much attention to the outside world recently. She hadn't cracked the folded newspaper or caught a weather-radar impression of Bower on the TV. It was too late for the news but according to the Weather Channel, the snow wouldn't amount to much.

Em hadn't checked her nonprofessional e-mail for over twenty-four hours either. These days most of her significant friendships and all of her family communications were touch-and-go's across the Internet.

Upstairs, keys *were* clicking; it would be unsporting to re-claim the computer, possibly until Monday. She'd best phone Lori before she forgot. Em touched a button on her auto-dialer. Fifteen years ago she'd kept dozens of phone numbers, area codes included, in her head. Thirty years ago, she'd actually *dialed* them.

Dad had talked about his first radio, first television, first time he looked up and saw a plane flying overhead. With changes like that—progress, he'd called it—Dad knew that time was churning away. Boomers like Emma Merrigan measured Progress in smaller steps: rotary phones, touch-tone phones, and auto-dialers. They deluded themselves into thinking there was lots of time.

Lori's answering-machine message, a cautious recitation of digits and unavailability, completely impersonal and recorded by her brother, broke Em's reverie.

"Just checking in," she told the tape. "I'm off-line for a few days. If there's anything important, use the phone."

They kept in touch, she and the kids; Em was justifiably proud of that, but it had been at least a month—no, much longer than that, more like August—since she'd heard Lori's voice. The computer had changed so many things in such subtle ways. Em's typing had never been better or faster, and the knowledge that *her* machine had become someone else's companion for the weekend was like one-too-many cups of coffee on her nerves.

The microwave beckoned before Em could slip further into a generational funk. She concocted dinner with the flair of a cook whose highest priority was minimizing the number of dirty dishes. Had she been alone, there'd only have been one, but she ladled the chicken and broccoli mixture onto a pair of plates and summoned her guest.

Emma had to admire the speed with which Jennifer ate and hurried back to her paper. Her stepchildren had never hit the books with that kind of diligence, though Em had. When you poured yourself into your grades, you couldn't think about missing mothers . . . or violent boyfriends. When you poured yourself into e-mail and the occasional nonprofit organization, you could think you had a life.

At loose ends once she'd cleared the dishes, Em phoned her best friend, Nancy Amstel, who'd moved down to southern Ohio last spring to nurse her widowed mother through what every one had assumed was terminal cancer. Nance's phone was busy, and so was her husband John's. He was still in Bower. Emma caught herself hoping that Katherine had finally died and they were making the arrangements. It wasn't an entirely selfish hope; Nance herself had said the same thing: disease and treatment had stolen her mother's personality along with her ability to care for herself. As these things were measured—and there was scarcely a Boomer who wasn't measuring them—Em counted herself lucky: Dad was active and lucid until his stroke, and dead forty-eight hours later.

This time last year, they'd had no idea the end was looming. Friday was their night. They'd have supper at the Tea-garden house and then talk or watch movies until midnight. They'd rarely missed a Friday, even when she'd been married to Jeff.

Fridays were still hard.

Em turned the television on and turned it off moments later. Desperate without her computer for distraction, she braved the basement. Her Christmas decorations spilled off a battered table. Emma hadn't gotten them stowed before Dad died and there really wasn't a rational reason to tackle the mess now. She was an early decorator; her tree went up on St. Nicholas' Day and stayed up until Twelfth Night. She was only a few weeks short of hauling it all upstairs.

But she sorted, boxed, and sniffed back tears until after midnight when she came upstairs to find everything quiet and the lights out in the backroom. Emma thought it rude, then she imagined Jennifer poised at the top of the basement stairs, listening to the sounds of mourning.

After checking the locks and turning out the lights, Em bedded down herself. The cats had scattered while Em puttered about in their basement domain. Charm made a reappearance, lured by the familiar *click* of an electric-blanket control. With the gray cat purring beside her, she turned out the light.

Em fell asleep easily. She'd already decided that last night's terror had actually been a dream, and she'd never been plagued by recurrent dreams. Then, suddenly she was awake and shivering, despite the heated blanket clutched around her shoulders. Mustering courage, Emma hooked a finger over the blanket hem.

A blue 2:43 filled her vision rather than a glowing ember. Em let out a sigh. She was awake and coherent enough to appreciate the irony: Jennifer was here for safety and she was the one who couldn't sleep.

Her mouth tasted like week-old fish. Despite being born in Bower, Emma had never developed a taste for city water. If she wanted something to drink, she'd have to go downstairs. The terror was gone—this time it had been a terror and not a dream. Em moved without fear—or the need for light. She'd be awake all night if she turned on a light. Even the one in the refrigerator was a risk. She extracted the juice with her eyes closed then carried a bottle of cranberry juice into the living room.

A headlight glow came and went around the drapes. There'd been no sound. Em pushed back the cloth, expecting snow and seeing it. The streets remained mostly clear, but the sidewalks had started to disappear and the grass was blanketed. It was a beautiful sight after a terror. She watched a moment, then took a long drink from the bottle. When Em lowered the bottle the scene had changed: a man approached along the sidewalk. His head was down, his shoulders up.

If he'd had a dog, Emma wouldn't have given him a second thought. The Maisonettes' residents balanced their love of pets and lawns with leash rules that mattered, even at three AM. But the walker didn't have a dog and as he strode closer, Em failed to recognize him. That was odd. After two years as the owners' association secretary, she knew just about all her neighbors by sight.

Emma lowered the drape by half and kept watch as the stranger came closer. His pale hair was plastered against his head; his jacket—a light windbreaker—hung limp from rounded shoulders. Em imagined that his car had broken down a few hours ago and he was on a long, miserable walk to a neighborhood beyond the Maisonettes.

Having provided him with sad circumstances, Em felt sorry for him, until he stopped at the end of her neighbor's walk. The stranger was young, far younger than her neighbor, Mrs. Borster, whose only daughter was nearly Em's age. Home invasions and the rape of elderly women were not unimaginable at three AM. Setting the bottle on the sill, Em glanced at the phone. It was a good ten feet away and the cordless one was back in the kitchen. She didn't want to turn her back on the window.

A wispy cloud formed around the stranger's face: the November sigh of an agitated man. He walked past Mrs. Borster's. He stopped at the end of Emma's walkway and stared at *her* upstairs windows, at the backroom windows where Jennifer slept.

Or didn't sleep.

The stranger had no sooner stopped than Em heard noise overhead: the rustle of blankets, then there was light upstairs. It illuminated the stairs and the stranger's face.

"Turn off that light!"

Jennifer obeyed, but the damage had been done.

"It's Bran, Emma. That's Bran out there!"

He came up the walk. Jennifer came down the stairs. Em let the curtain drop and headed for the front door. She heard the unlocked storm door swing open and the *clunk* of metal against metal as Bran had the gall to try the latch. The inner door was painted steel, locked, bolted, and pierced with a peephole, nothing more. Em peered out. At this hour and with the outside light turned off, the portico was pitch black.

"What are we going to do, Emma?" Jennifer asked. Her voice was shrill, anxious, nearly hysterical.

"Stay calm and quiet," Em advised as the brass door-knocker struck the door.

"We have to do something! Did you see him, Emma? Did you see how he looked? He's not himself."

The knocker struck again, harder, louder than the first time. "Jennifer!" He'd heard and recognized her voice.

"Bran!"

Emma spun on her heels. "Be quiet—unless you want to go out there with him and *stay* out there with him. You said it yourself: he's not himself."

"But he's cold and soaking wet! We've got to do—"

"Jen! Jennifer, I've got to see you!"

The knocker hammered the door. Em was grateful that the steel door had been her first capital improvement after buying the place, but the hollow metal amplified sounds. The

Maisonettes' residents didn't take kindly to midnight distur-
bances. Someone would call the police.

That someone might be her.

"Go away," Emma warned in her mother-voice. "I'm
going to call the cops if you're not walking away from here
in ten seconds."

Her mother-voice didn't always work with grown men.
Bran struck the door with his fist or arm. The impact made
the door jump against its hinges.

"Jennifer! I know you're in there."

Another hinge-rattling blow. The door would hold, and
the walls. The Maisonettes were old-fashioned and solid.
But the windows were ordinary glass and accessible behind
evergreen shrubs. After Bran struck the door a third time,
Em imagined that he would come after the windows. She
went for the phone.

"No!" Jennifer pleaded. "You can't call the police. He'll
get in trouble. He'll get thrown out of school."

Emma shook her head. "He's dangerous, Jennifer. Dangerous to himself and to you."

"Maybe if I talked to him . . ."

Bran struck the door a fourth time; a slower *thud* followed
by a sigh of slick fabric, as if he'd hoped to shoulder his way
in.

"That could be *you* he's hitting, Jennifer."

"Jennifer!" Two *thuds,* two fists hitting the door and more
sliding. "Help me! Help me, Jen."

The sliding moved down the door, shifting, changing. Em
guessed he'd turned and had his back to the metal as he sank
to the sill.

"The police won't help him. They'll take him to *jail,*
Emma. Bran doesn't belong in jail. None of this is his fault."

Before Em could summon the outrage for a proper lecture
on responsibility, the young man outside her home began
banging his head against her door. She couldn't see him, of

course, couldn't be absolutely certain the sound wasn't made by a fist, elbow, or foot, though her sense of certainty was boosted when each *thud* was followed by a hurt-dog whimper.

Bran Mongomery *was* responsible. All people were responsible, especially for their most stupid, self-destructive acts. If Bran was cold, wet, and battering his skull against hollow steel, then he'd made all the choices that led him to his present misery. Emma Merrigan did not believe in fate, luck, or the collusion of malign deities—

"It's not his fault," Jennifer insisted, wringing her hands in the charcoal light. "I'm not arguing with you: Bran is dangerous right now, and I don't really want to go out there, but he's not a criminal. You can't call the police."

"I'll ask for an ambulance."

She understood Jennifer's objections. Her fifty-year-old mind phrased itself in responsibility, not to mention concern for property, but the ageless part of her mind understood that an ill-timed encounter with the police or emergency-room doctors could turn a bad night into a bad life.

"What about your housemates?" she asked. "Would they come to get him?"

Emma thought of wire-rimmed Sam and had rejected her own notion before Jennifer shook her head. The banging and moaning continued. No longer loud enough to disturb her neighbors, the sounds had become pathetic.

"Is there anyone else who'd brave the middle of the night to get him off the streets? Other grad students? He's a grad student. He must have a faculty advisor." Though in terms of consequences, contacting Bran's advisor could be worse than turning him over to the police.

"I don't know," Jennifer said with a sniff. "He's mentioned a few names, but I don't remember them. Once our paths crossed . . . it's been, like, *total* involvement. Bran spends his time with me when he's not in class."

That couldn't be completely true, not if Matt had been telling the truth—and Em trusted Matt over either Bran or Jennifer. "He plays handball—"

"Handball?"

With a hidden groan, Em scolded herself for forgetting to censor herself—a mistake she'd rarely, if ever, made with Lori or Jay-Jay. Use it or lose it. It was time to exercise another bit of advice she'd given the kids: when deceptions start to unravel, swift confession is all-around better than slow exposure.

"I mentioned Bran last night to one of the men I work with at the library. He plays handball with a grad student named Bran who's got a girlfriend named Jennifer. I made an assumption."

Em couldn't see Jennifer's face in the faint light. She didn't need to; the silence was awkward enough.

"Bower's a small town, you know that. The U's even smaller. No six degrees of separation for us: people know each other. Matt knows Bran."

"Bran's never mentioned anyone named Matt."

"Maybe they're not friends, but they've been playing handball for a month and going out for beer afterward." The slow thumping and moaning continued outside her front door. "We're wasting time, Jennifer. Does Bran have any other friends? Anyone at all in Bower, or I'm calling 9-1-1."

"No, no one, but please—please don't call 9-1-1. That's so *final*. Why not let him come—"

"No!" Em hadn't realized how adamant she was until she'd heard her own voice.

"Listen to him! He needs help—he needs *me!*"

"Then get dressed and leave, Jennifer. I'm not keeping you here, but I'm not letting Bran inside my home. It's your choice."

Em stepped aside, expecting Jennifer to bolt, perhaps for

the bedroom where she'd stashed her belongings, but just as likely for the front door.

With a defeated sigh, Jennifer said, "Call this guy Bran's never mentioned to me."

"All right! Bran has no friends except you. Matt and Bran aren't friends!"

"Neither are we!" Jennifer shot back, and silence reigned again, until she added, "I didn't mean that, Emma. Honest. Right now, you're the best and only friend I've got, and I don't want to fight with you, but please, *please* don't call the police, or 9-1-1."

If it doesn't look right, don't go in, Matt had said yesterday, *call someone. Call me. I'm here for you.*

Em had made similar offers over the years to friends and family. Only Dad had called: *Em, I've got a tingly feeling in my arm, and my eyes aren't right.* Everyone else got along without Emma Merrigan's intervention. She'd gotten so she made the offer easily, knowing the odds of anyone accepting it were small.

Surely Matt didn't expect to hear from *her* at—Em glanced at the VCR—a quarter after three in the morning. At least she knew his phone number or, more accurately, had included it in the printout she kept under the phone.

What was the worst that could happen? Matt could get angry, refuse, or laugh with acid scorn, and she'd have to face him Monday morning. Much as Emma hated embarrassment, she had survived worse. She turned on the light, found the paper, and tapped the unfamiliar number.

Matt answered on the first ring.

"Matt?" Em asked before he'd uttered a word. "This is Emma Merrigan. I hope you meant what you said yesterday—"

He said he did, once he found his voice, and promised to come as quickly as he could dress and drive. Em's hand was shaking when she dropped the receiver in its cradle.

"He's coming," she said, assuming—incorrectly—that Jennifer was right behind her.

The young woman had returned to the hallway and the door.

"He moved when you turned the light on. I think he's gone."

Em's heart skipped. She'd dragged Matt out of bed and across town to save a poor soul who wasn't there.

"Wait . . . It's been snowing, sticking to the sidewalks," she said to herself and Jennifer. "If Bran's gone, there'll be tracks in the snow."

Emma turned on the outside light then returned to the living room to draw back the drapes. Yellow light spilled out of the portico, but there were no footprints in the fresh snow and no sign of anyone moving anywhere.

"He shouldn't be out there alone," Jennifer said unnecessarily. "We should have opened the door."

Em looked at the phone. *Sorry, Matt, false alarm. He's wandered off* . . . "I don't believe this."

"Don't believe what?"

Emma didn't answer, just grabbed her keys from the hall table, searched her coat closet for the fleece-lined boots and ratty coat she wore for snow shoveling. The boots were loose and lumpy around her bare feet, but she wasn't of a mind to find a pair of socks.

"Emma?" Jennifer protested as she zipped the coat and headed for the kitchen.

Each Maisonette kitchen had a pantry, each pantry had a door leading to a fenced-in backyard. Each fence had a door: a panel of slatted wood too flimsy to warrant a lock. Beyond the creaky door, a narrow path ran north to a shed where residents stowed their yard tools and south to the street. Feeling young and foolish—she'd left the kitchen without a flashlight—Em headed for the street.

She was halfway there and giving most of her attention to

uneven, slippery ground when she heard a growling dog—a big dog—or not a dog at all. In an instant Em's thoughts had returned to last night's dream which, perhaps, hadn't been a dream.

The classic mortal dilemma—fight or flight?—failed to resolve itself. Emma was petrified, unable to lift a foot or scream until the growling became a slushy lope fading away from her. Even that wasn't enough to get her moving. She needed another moment of leaning against the fence, asking herself if she'd gone mad before she could continue.

The street with its sidewalks and lamp posts returned a sense of security. A few steps farther and Em was at the curb end of her own walkway, peering into the portico where her storm door was held ajar by a shadowed hulk. Bran didn't move or otherwise acknowledge Emma's approach. With her right hand in her pocket and her keys bristling between her hidden fingers like claws, she hailed him from twenty feet away.

"You there in the doorway, what do you think you're doing at this ungodly hour?"

A pale face appeared in the shadow. "Who—?" he began, then changed to a different thought. "Jennifer? Where's Jennifer? She's with you? She's okay?"

"No thanks to you." Em wasn't in a mood to be generous.

"But she's okay?"

She didn't bother to answer.

Bran stretched and stood. Measured against the door, Em judged him to be a bit over six feet tall, broad-shouldered and brawny. She remembered Matt's assessment: a small-school football player who didn't have to cheat to win and wouldn't go down to anything less than a four-by-four.

He closed the storm door carefully. A dog was barking, a big dog. The mother-voice whispered something about too many coincidences; it advised caution.

It was a little late in the game for caution.

Clutching her keys tight enough that the jagged metal hurt her fingers, Em marched up her walk.

"Who told you she was here?" She conceded that bit of information in hopes of getting something in return.

"No one."

"No one?" Emma put a scornful edge on the words. "You just happened to find this place? You just stood up and said, Jennifer's at the Maisonettes on McKinley Street?"

"McKinley Street? Is that where I am? I thought I'd walked north of campus."

In her gut, Em sensed deception and cunning. "North, yes—about three miles from the Blue House. Who told you to look for Jennifer in the Maisonettes?" She imagined that Sam had tailed them.

Bran's head swiveled. His ear was against his shoulder when he repeated: "No one."

Her stepkids had squirmed that way when she'd caught them telling lies. "You've got to do better than that, Bran Mongomery."

In silence, Bran smeared his hands over his face. "I knew," he moaned through his fingers. "I know where she is. I can feel it . . . I followed it, but I can't explain it. All right?" He sat down hard on the cold, wet bricks.

"Try to explain it."

More squirming and finger-twining that had to hurt, then his hands fell. "Do you believe that a man's spirit can come back?"

Em heard a sound: a door closing. Not the door behind Bran, nor Mrs. Borster's, neither of which had opened. It might not have been a door, nor even a noise, but the sound of her mother-voice giving up on her as she asked:

"You mean reincarnation?"

"Yeah, maybe."

Bran's hands, broad like his shoulders and short-fingered, covered his face again and pulled his head down. His forehead rested on his knees and he spoke to the ground. Em had to strain her ears to hear him.

"Jen's the piece I didn't know was missing, except, in a way, I did. There's always been this hole inside me. I've been looking to fill it as long as I can remember, but I didn't know what I was looking for until I met her. Me an' her have been together *before;* I was *born* missing her, and now she's part of me again, where she belongs. I didn't need to ask anyone where she was. I just knew."

"Nonsense," Emma retorted. "Jennifer's been here since yesterday—after you'd slapped her around. Is that your idea of belonging, Bran Mongomery—bruises and blood? There's no excuse for that, no 'hole inside' you can blame it on. The devil didn't make you beat her up or wreck her room."

When Bran's hands dropped and his head began to rise, Em wanted—needed—to see a monster sitting on her steps, but beheld an ordinary man.

"I don't know what you're talking about, lady. I was steamed when I went back to the Blue House last night, so I left. I didn't go near Jen's room. There's a hole inside me and it aches when she's not close. I could've found her last night. I could find her any time or any place. All I gotta do is follow the pain. I want to tell her I'm sorry about what happened. It won't happen again."

Emma had relaxed her grip on her keys; she tightened it again as she said, "I don't believe that."

Bran began to shiver. He tucked his bare hands inside his sopping jacket, up under his armpits. An act, Em decided, a plea for sympathy she'd never give to a man who pummeled women. She stood silent, fighting the shivers herself. The weather had changed from a quiet snow-drizzle to a northerly breeze since she'd left the kitchen. Soaked as he was, Bran needed warmth and dry clothes. Em's conscience twitched: it was wrong to keep him sitting on her steps, but Matt had to be on his way by now.

Another minute or two, five at the most and the standoff would be history.

"I need help," Bran said when half that time had passed. "I'm losing it. I remember getting here, but it's like a movie—like something I saw, not something I did."

A word rose in Em's mind: schizophrenia. The passage out of adolescence could be dangerous. Every semester the U lost a student or two, usually freshmen or sophomores, but a late-blooming grad student could fall prey to madness. "You need to see a doctor before it gets worse."

"Yeah, some kind of witch doctor."

Headlights flashed at the corner. Matt double-parked at the end of the walk. He turned out the lights but left the engine running.

"Hey, big guy, kinda far from home, aren't you?"

Bran squinted and gave Em the impression that he'd parted company with a pair of glasses.

"Barto? Matt Barto? What the hell—?"

Matt stopped alongside Em. "I'm here to give you a ride home."

Shaking his head, Bran said, "Jen? I didn't think—?"

"You're in no shape to be thinking, big guy. Just come on down to the car and I'll get you home."

"Can't go back there. Left. Got thrown out."

"Yeah, well, you can't stay here. The ladies don't want you blockin' their door. Up on your feet. We'll figure that one out in the car where it's warm. You could use some warm, big guy."

"I found Jen. She's here. I can't lose her again."

"Em'll take good care of Jennifer. C'mon, stretch those legs. This'll all seem like a dream in the morning."

Matt held out his hand but Bran stood up on his own. "You know him? You called Matt?"

She admitted they worked together at the library.

"I'll be damned," Bran muttered and started to walk toward the car.

"I owe you," Emma whispered to Matt before he followed Bran.

"I said to call if you needed help. He needs help, that's for sure. He's not drunk and if it's drugs, it's none of the usual suspects."

Em didn't ask how he'd reached his conclusions. "Jennifer started to panic when I suggested calling 9-1-1; I didn't want two crazies on my hands. I'd take him to the emergency room. He might go quietly. He said he knows he needs help."

Matt grimaced. "I'll take him home and put him in a hot shower. The guy downstairs from me's a cop." Bran hesitated; he seemed to be looking at the driver's side of Matt's car. "Talk to you Monday," Matt said and bolted down the walk.

Em waited until they were gone, then let herself into her house.

Six

Emma heard the backroom door close as she came through the front door. Jennifer, it seemed, didn't want to discuss what had happened. At four AM, Em wasn't much interested in talking either. Leaving her boots in the kitchen and her coat draped over a dining-table chair she headed upstairs, where the cats and her electric blanket were waiting. She snugged the covers around her, but it was a lost cause: though her body was cold and weary, her mind was racing.

She couldn't tear her thoughts away from growling dogs, troubled youths, and disconnected coincidences. When her clock read 4:27, Emma gave up the fight. Wrapped in her warmest robe and slippers, she made tea—not coffee—in the microwave and returned to the basement. She'd packed enough suitcases and hatchbacks over the years to convince herself that there was room on the shelves for both her Christmas decorations and all the boxes she'd brought out of the Teagarden house—but only if she cleared the shelves first and started over.

Dust billowed from the Teagarden boxes as Emma moved them. She should have gone upstairs for the vacuum, but cut corners with an old, stiff towel instead. A thorough-going mistake. The box dust was worse than all the ragweed of

August. Em started sneezing and didn't stop until she was sitting on the floor with tears running down her cheeks.

She wasn't wearing her contact lenses—a wise move considering the dust—but that left her squinting upward at a box, one of the last on the topmost shelves, that she didn't recognize. It was an old box, paler than the rest and slightly less than two-feet square. Em guessed it weighed about twenty pounds as she lifted it down.

A label and ancient cellophane tape sealed the upper flaps, a handwritten label bearing a first, last, and middle name that stopped her cold. The names were her names— her real names—written in lush calligraphy that hadn't faded with the years. She never used the first and middle names on her birth certificate. People knew her as Emma Merrigan; institutions from the university to the bank and the IRS knew her as Emma Merrigan.

Dad called her Emma. She'd never suspected she wasn't Emma Merrigan until kindergarten roll call. She'd known the alphabet, known that M came between L and N. She'd waited, tense and eager, but the name Miss Bryce called was Merle Acalia Merrigan. Such an odd and ugly name! The other kids had laughed, and she'd laughed with them because the ugly name wasn't *her* name. At the end of the roll, after the Williams twins and Raymond Young, there was one student who hadn't said Here! and one name no one else had claimed.

Em was the student and Merle Acalia Merrigan was the name. She'd gone home in such tears and despair that Mrs. Carbone had summoned her father. Gently, he'd explained to her that Merle Acalia was the name her mother had chosen for her and they couldn't change it because it was printed on her birth certificate. Dad said he called her Emma because her initials were M and A, and that she could continue to be Emma, if she preferred, or she could become Merle or even Acalia.

Emma didn't prefer Merle or Acalia.

Dad had escorted her to school the next day. He'd exchanged a few soft words with Miss Bryce and Merle Acalia vanished from the Bower public schools. Such was the power of a tenured professor in those heady days at the start of the Cold War.

Her stepchildren didn't know the names from hell. Her husbands hadn't. But there they were, in India ink and inch-high letters, for the whole world to read. And written on a box she'd swear she'd never seen before.

As angry as she was curious, Em carried the box to the washing machine. Brittle cellophane tape splintered when she touched it. The flap with the florid label detached from the sides when she lifted it. The other flaps did likewise. The box was disintegrating; it wouldn't survive the unpacking.

Without its flaps, the box revealed a layer of crumpled, yellowed newspapers. Like the cardboard, they crumbled when Em touched them and were too fragile to flatten. Scattered words, though, were legible. The pages were from the January 24, 1949, edition of the *Bower Tribune*.

She'd been nearly six months old and Eleanor hadn't left yet, but she'd probably been thinking about it.

The newspaper layer was some two inches thick. Beneath it, Em discovered a black, wooden box lacquered in an Oriental style and fitted with tarnished brass. An unimpressive brass padlock clasped the lid shut; a stained brass key was ribbon-tied to the padlock. With little effort and a few drops of penetrating oil, Em opened the padlock.

Faint aromas of spice and citrus bloomed above the washing machine as Emma raised the lid. The lining was bright crimson silk, undimmed by time. The uppermost object was an envelope, subtly old-fashioned, like the cardboard and the newspapers. It blocked her view of the remaining contents, but she probably wouldn't have noticed diamonds or gold coins, not after she read the words, *To my daughter, Merle Acalia / When she needs me and the time is right.*

A pair of silk ribbons supported the lid after Em released it. The mother-voice sang in her mind, urging her to open the envelope, but she folded her arms over her heart instead.

"The time's not right. I needed you years ago."

Lies, the mother-voice countered: You *wanted* her. You wanted what everyone else took for granted, but you didn't *need* Eleanor. You did just fine without her . . .

More lies. She'd wound up alone and lonely, busy but without purpose, bereft of two ill-chosen husbands. That wasn't her definition of *doing just fine.*

Em picked up the envelope. It was sealed with glue and a lump of wax a few shades darker than the box lining. There'd be no opening it without damaging the paper. A black book of unknown thickness and contents lay below the envelope. Bound in morocco leather, it had the look of a Bible, but bore no title nor religious symbol. She guessed it was a diary and was tempted to read it before she opened the envelope.

Resisting temptation, Em rummaged among her tools until she found a flat-blade screwdriver with which she slit the envelope. A single unfolded sheet of plain, high-quality stationery slid out. It was covered, one side only, with elegant script.

Within this box I have placed your inheritance. I awaken the gift of power that sleeps within. You stand revealed by the stars and moonlight. You have received your wyrd. It is time for you to claim your place among your near and distant kin. Do not lose heart or succumb to darkness.

A shiver shook Emma's spine, leaving her dizzy. The sensation passed quickly, but she sat down on the basement steps before she tried reading further.

Your childhood has ended. I hope it was happy. I did what I could to make it happy. Your father is a good man. I would

*not have married him otherwise. Bower is a suffocating lit-
tle town with too many dusty books and gossips, as I'm sure
you've learned. It is a bad place to stay, but a good place to
be from. As the years pass, you will be glad for what you
learned there, little as you may believe it at the moment
when you read this letter. Your exile has ended, Merle
Acalia. It is time to take your place in the world.*

Your childhood has ended.

*You were born with the power to walk through time. It lay
sleeping within you. Perhaps you suspected it for many
years and explored it as you now explore your crib and
playpen. But now you have been challenged by the enemy
you are destined to defeat. Do not be afraid of the dark,
Merle Acalia. In this box you will find everything you need.
May your light shine bright, Merle Acalia. When the time is
right, we shall meet as equals—*

The stationery slipped through Em's fingers—and just as
well; if she'd kept hold of it, she'd have torn it to shreds.

Had her father known what sort of a madwoman he'd married? Had he accepted Eleanor's disappearance so calmly because he'd considered himself lucky to be rid of her with so
little scandal? And had he taken that guilty, secret knowledge
to his grave?

Emma could believe that the answer to each of her questions was *yes,* but that left her with more troublesome
questions: if her father had known what Eleanor was, why
had he kept this boldly labeled box for half a century?
Where had he kept it? And, most troublesome of all, how
had it gotten to her basement?

After he married Eleanor and moved to Teagarden Street,
Dad had never moved again, never been forced to confront
or discard the past. After Dad died, Emma had personally
laid hands on everything in the house. She would have noticed a box emblazoned with *that* name. She couldn't have
failed to notice—

But she had failed. She'd done the winnowing by herself. No one else could have carried that box from the Teagarden house to her car and from her car to the basement.

Boxes didn't move themselves.

Em picked up her mother's letter. The words swam before her.

Within this box I have placed your inheritance . . . I awaken the gift of power that sleeps in your spirit . . . You were born with the power to walk through time . . . You have received your wyrd.

Wyrd?

If any one word convinced Emma of Eleanor's madness it was "wyrd." It had meant fate, back when sensible people believed that life couldn't be explained except through magic. Once fate had fallen out of fashion, it had become simply *weird*. Weird couldn't be inherited, wasn't a gift, and as for the power to walk through time—well, try *not* walking through time! Try to make time stand still.

Em folded the letter with its writing to the inside. She was the daughter of a university professor and a certifiable nutcase. It was, after so many years of wondering who Eleanor Merrigan might have been, a bitter disappointment. But despite disappointment, she'd gone too far not to return to the washing machine and investigate her inheritance down to its red silk bottom.

The black book was about an inch thick, with flexible covers that curved gently over gold-edged onionskin pages. A rainbow of bookmark ribbons protruded at the bottom edge. After tucking Eleanor's letter inside the front cover, Emma pulled the purple ribbon.

Curses of the third order are called persistent curses. They have concluded themselves at least once and are sustained by their own malevolence. A persistent curse has both a root moment when it was conceived and a shadow through which it seeks and corrupts new pawns.

Eleanor had written the words large in the same calli-graphic script she'd used for the label and the letter. She'd written other paragraphs on the page also, though Em didn't waste time reading them. She riffled the entire book, assuring herself that Eleanor had written every page—at least every page that wasn't blank. All the left-side pages were blank, and perhaps a third of the right-side pages as well.

Whatever Eleanor had begun to write in the black book, it seemed she hadn't finished that either.

Em pulled other bookmark ribbons. She saw references to curses of the first and second order, and "effective" dreaming, transference, and a variety of bonding techniques—which Em initially misread as bondage, a measure, perhaps, of her own disillusion. In the front pages of the book, where no ribbons were stretched, she found the sort of chants and recipes she associated with witchcraft.

A sleeping draught, useful for "effective" dreaming, listed "Two dr. Tincture of Poppy" among its ingredients. Drams or drops, the result might well put someone to sleep, but it was illegal, not magical.

Emma snapped the book shut and set it on the washing machine. It would have been better never to have discovered the box and its sorry contents. She'd be months—years—undoing the damage the last few moments had done to her sense of what-might-have-been. An hour ago, the worst behavior she'd ever attributed to Eleanor was running off with another man to the bright lights of New York City.

When her second marriage gave up the ghost, Em had forgiven Eleanor for New York City. Recklessness was an impulse she'd learned to recognize in herself, but "effective" dreaming and tincture of poppy crossed the line.

Em stared into the box, trying—and failing—to sustain a sense of outrage. Her anger sputtered and died along with anything that might be termed hate. What remained was bleak, gray emptiness. Fatigue caught up with her; she was ready for bed. If there were such a thing as effective dreaming, she'd pull the blankets over her head and effectively dream this night to oblivion.

Emma was ready to let the lid fall when she noticed the objects the morocco book had concealed. They pricked her curiosity; curiosity had always been Em's strength and downfall. Her fatigue evaporated as she lifted from the box a pair of brass soup bowls, one plain, the other enameled with mythological beasts from the Orient. Then she removed a silver plate about five inches across, etched, embossed, and utterly untarnished; a miniature school bell with a wooden handle; a leather sheath that held two table-sized knives, identical except for their black and white handles; a separate leather-bound box for a set of silver demitasse spoons and a satin-covered one that held a single lead-crystal goblet. Piece by piece, Emma lined the objects up on the dryer.

The box wasn't empty yet. Beneath the loose objects another layer appeared: a wooden tray tightly packed with bottles, each a bit over an inch square. According to their many-colored caps, each bottle had once held colored ink: India, midnight, and royal; peacock, purple, and green. Hand-written labels—Eleanor's script again—advised that the inks had been replaced with saffron, dragonsblood, and "Tincture—Poppy."

Em lifted the ominous bottle into the light. The tincture had become a residue. She thought of washing the bottle in the kitchen sink, but returned it to its place near the center of the tray. The tray itself refused to budge when Emma tried to lift it out of the box. She probed its underside and encountered a waxen blob.

Candles. Melted candles. What witchcraft assortment would be complete without candles? She'd already found a bell and book.

A few *thumps* and the tray popped free. Emma left it balanced atop the brass bowl. Her suspicions were confirmed;

Eleanor's ultimate legacy was candles. At least three wicks snaked through the block of milky-dark wax that clogged the box bottom. A spiked, wrought-iron candle holder rose out of the wax and also, to Em's sincere disappointment, the stamped corners of a nearly submerged packet of letters. Excavating with her thumbnail, Em brought an address— Eleanor Merrigan on Teagarden Street—to light.

Would the letters transform her mother into a human being?

Em could only hope. Her fingernails weren't up to the job of freeing the packet from the wax nor the wax from the box lining. Eleanor should have known better than to store candles for any length of time. Michigan summers were short, but over fifty years Michigan attics got hot enough to melt wax.

Fifty years.

Emma Merrigan's childhood had ended thirty years ago. She was easily twice the age Eleanor had been when she packed the box.

Yawning, Em replaced the bowls, the bell and the rest and lowered the box's lid and locked it. The black book she tucked under her arm before turning out the light and going upstairs. November nights were long here on the western border of the eastern time zone. It was six AM according to the glowing clock, but her bedroom was midnight dark.

Em's body believed it was midnight too. She was sleepy now, not interested in her mad mother's notions about cooking or curses. The book slipped to the floor as Em snugged the blankets.

It would be there in the morning . . . or afternoon.

* * *

Night still reigned when Em rolled over and stuck a foot outside the blankets. She didn't remember waking up, but most people didn't, did they? The air was pleasant. Her nightshirt was enough to keep her comfortable. She could take a barefoot walk, if she wished . . . and Em did wish to take a walk. There was something she had to do, something waiting for her just out of sight.

Usually that something was coffee, but not now, not here. This was different, very different. Emma wondered if she was, in fact, awake, or if she was dreaming again. Everything was strange: her eyes weren't seeing, her ears weren't hearing, and her nose wasn't smelling. She must not be awake; she must still be asleep and dreaming.

The mother-voice said, no, she wasn't dreaming.

In the corners of her consciousness, Em knew there was something *significant* about hearing her mother-voice, but she couldn't remember what and, anyway, she had a job to do. In this place of nothing there was something that did not belong. She strode forward, confident that she could vanquish it.

Emma climbed a little hill. Her quarry was apparent from the summit: a glowing, blood-colored whirl in the darkness. It noticed her and grew brighter, stronger, and moved toward her.

"This place is mine," Em told it. "Return to your own place. Leave mine alone."

The whirl put forth swift fireflies and embers. She raised an invisible hand. The sparkling bits stopped, then flowed more slowly in her direction.

"Don't be silly," she said sternly in the mother-voice she used with cats and stepchildren, and which was different from the one she heard.

The whirl puffed up. Its minions flowed toward her again. Em stamped her foot. Invisible cracks formed in the unseen ground. The minions fell into the cracks and disappeared.

"My place."

Sizzling, the whirl grew larger . . . or came closer. She

wasn't sure; it didn't matter. Calmly, Emma stood *her* ground.

"Don't," she told the whirl, not in the mother-voice but like the soft warning one adult gave another before all hell broke loose.

The whirl was unimpressed, undeterred. Em had known it would come to this. Sighing, she closed her hand into a fist and filled herself with an old-fashioned nemesis—righteous indignation—down to her fingertips. It simmered there for several ordinary heartbeats while the whirl made a foul-smelling sulphurous display.

Emma had been fair and more than generous. Beyond doubt, Em had generously given the whirl several opportunities to leave the place she claimed as her own. But it was only a whirl and not nearly bright enough to save itself. She released a different sort of darkness from her fist.

The whirl vanished.

Em waited another few moments, to be sure the delinquent didn't resurrect itself. She studied the dark and silent horizons. Nothing stirred her senses—a proper nothing, *her* nothing. She turned around and walked down the hill.

Seven

There was light when Emma awoke. Sunlight seeped through the bedroom drapes. It flooded the hallway, which faced west. Em couldn't remember the last time she'd slept past noon. Then again, she could barely remember which nerves and muscles moved her feet. Sitting up brought waves of pain and nausea. Along with a puzzle box, Eleanor Merrigan had bequeathed her daughter one hellacious migraine.

Pain-dulling bags of blue gelatin waited in the freezer, if she could drag herself that far. And she could. The all-over head throbbing quickly localized. As long as she didn't focus her right eye, the migraine was bearable. Picking up the black book before she tripped over it, Em made her way to the bathroom where the cats were waiting.

Charm danced figure-eights around Em's ankles: the source-of-food was moving; righteous order had been restored to the universe. Spin was slower to forgive lapses in divine etiquette. He sat in the hall with his back resolutely turned. Watching his tail twitch, Em almost laughed aloud, but laughter would rekindle the throbbing. She ran cold water instead and splashed it against her face.

Emma heard a sound as she patted her face dry. The television was on—

Jennifer!

The wide-open bathroom door!

She dashed into her bedroom with more haste than was wise. Quickly dressed and still seeing double on account of her right eye, Em kept her hand on the rail as she hurried down the stairs.

Her guest was curled up on the sofa watching football.

"Who's winning?"

"We did: thirty-one to eighteen. Now State's clobbering Notre Dame."

Any Saturday when the home team won and Notre Dame lost was a better-than-average day even if it hadn't started until three in the afternoon. Em headed for the kitchen, filled a mug with yesterday's coffee, and plunked it in the microwave.

Jennifer followed her. "I was starting to get worried about you."

"By the time I got to sleep, I'd've been better off to stay awake." The microwave beeped; Em retrieved her mug of bitter, steaming brew. "A little coffee and I'll be good as new."

"I felt bad, running upstairs like that when you came inside. Your friend looked like a nice guy—a lot, well, *younger* than I expected."

Ah, the many meanings of *friend.* "Matt got his master's in June," Emma explained, while waiting for Jennifer to say what was really on her mind.

"It's just . . . I listened while you and Bran were talking. I could hear him pretty clearly. That stuff about reincarnation and knowing where I was. Maybe it's just the way he talked. It's like he's got problems I can't help him solve."

No similes need apply. Bran *had* problems but Emma kept that conclusion to herself. "You did your best."

"I know," Jennifer agreed. "But I've got my own life to live. Bran sounded . . ."

Em suggested, "A bit over-possessive?"

Jennifer nodded.

Em pushed her luck: "Bran needs to make some changes before any woman gets serious about him."

Another nod. "I do love him. I'm not going to look for anyone else—I wasn't looking for him, you know. But everything's on hold until he gets himself together. *If* he gets himself together . . ."

Once again Jennifer left her thought unfinished, reminding Emma that her guest was still young and caught between a need to do what she wanted and to have her choices approved before she acted upon them. Em could be generous with her opinions—she had so many of them—but not this time. She sipped scalding coffee until Jennifer said, "I'd like to go home. Home-home, not the Blue House. I need you to drive me over to Reynolds, so I can get my car. I've got too much stuff to walk. Would you mind?"

Emma took another gulp from the mug. She was visualizing giant coffee molecules marching toward her throbbing headache. Brain chemistry didn't work that way, of course, but the mind did and while the coffee molecules didn't win a swift victory over the Migraine Army, they did contain its rebellion.

"Not a problem. We'd have heard from Matt if things hadn't settled out between him and Bran. We didn't hear from Matt, did we?"

"No calls, not even when I was in the shower. God, you were sound asleep!"

"Snoring?" Em asked, willing herself not to blush or otherwise reveal embarrassment.

"Not that I heard, but your cat, the black one—"

"Spin. The gray one's Charm. She's a quark. Spin's intrinsic momentum."

Jennifer cocked her head; obviously she hadn't grown up reading *Scientific American*. "I stepped on his tail. Between the two of us, I was sure you'd wake up. We were right outside your bedroom door, but you didn't twitch. That's when

I started worrying whether you'd gotten sick or something while you were outside with Bran."

"No, I'm fine," Em assured her, though she'd been a light sleeper all her life and within a very intimate circle was renowned for her ability to rise from bed with a single, whole-body twitch at the slightest noise. It was disconcerting to think she'd slept so soundly with a stranger in the house. "Let me put my contacts in and we can get going."

Em had left Eleanor's black book on the bathroom floor when she'd raced back to her bedroom to get dressed. She'd left her bed unmade as well. Routine, however sterile, had been the core of her life since Jeff took off. Disorder, randomness made her anxious. It was time to be alone again, safe again.

After hastily smoothing the covers and tucking the book beneath her night table, Emma popped three ibuprofen pills into her mouth and two gas-permeable lenses into her eyes. Notre Dame was down by 21 in the fourth quarter when she and Jennifer left the townhouse.

Last night's snow was gone from all but a few protected nooks, vanquished by a clear sky and a pale sun already sinking in the west. The smell of the air had changed. Autumn was a memory now. Em buttoned her coat's topmost button and tucked her gloves into her sleeves.

"Got everything? No disks left in the floppy drive?"

Emma would have said the same to Lori or Jay-Jay and the words wouldn't have sounded so final. She and Jennifer hadn't become friends. They wouldn't likely reconnect.

"Nope, I've got everything right here." Jennifer shook the magenta bag for emphasis before tossing it into the back seat. "Floppy disks, underwear, even my toothbrush."

The university stadium could seat more football fans than showed up in Bower's official census and after a late-season victory, they tended to stay around and celebrate. To avoid them, Em wove through a maze of back streets and connected with Reynolds via an unpaved alley.

It had long been said that Bower natives had only three abiding passions: football, weather, and routing. Jennifer hadn't known about the half-block alleys that dated back to the horse-and-buggy era when houses like the Blue House had a stable out back. The young woman was clearly impressed.

They exchanged the proper platitudes as Jennifer got herself and her bag out of the car. Emma waited—stepmother habits—a moment. She wouldn't have been surprised if Jennifer had gone into the Blue House, but she climbed into a late-model, fire-engine-red, and too-powerful car—hardly the sort of vehicle Em expected a young woman with dyed-drab hair, black fingernails, and a safety-pinned coat to drive, but very much what a River High parent might bestow on their morbid daughter in hope of luring her toward brighter lights.

Jennifer waved and Em put her car into reverse. She retraced her route down the unpaved alley. Em knew the campus warren well enough to drive it on reflex while her conscious thoughts recalled Eleanor's black book. The danger, though, in reflex navigation, was that sometimes a driver fell into very old habits: Em turned right where she should have turned left and turned right again two more times.

She was headed home, all right; straight down Teagarden Street where she hadn't driven since May. Emma hadn't needed to sell Dad's house. Its mortgage was long since paid off and her income was adequate to cover the maintenance. She could have left the Maisonettes and gone home again but the nine-room house had been too big when she and Dad had lived there.

Two Realtors had referred to its brick Tudor style as "quaint" and "charming" and advised Em to be patient; it might be Christmas before they found a buyer whose peculiar needs it met, and—by the way—the house would never sell unless she knocked ten grand off the asking price. A third Realtor sold it for the asking price the first week it was on the market.

So, Teagarden Street had become a memory before she'd had a chance to reconsider or regret the sale. Emma had met the buyers just once, at the closing. He was an American-educated Japanese who'd gone home but couldn't stay there. His wife never said a word during the exchange of papers and signatures. Em hadn't met a more invisible woman.

All summer Emma had refused to consider how they might have changed the house. Now she sat too long at the last stop sign, asking herself: did she want to know? The car lurched forward.

The changes were subtle: an elegant harvest wreath hung on the front door, a child-sized bicycle dropped in the drive-way, a new mailbox. Yet those changes were enough. One, two driveways past the house, Em pulled over. Her hands were shaking; she couldn't hold on to the steering wheel. She couldn't stop the tears.

In the natural order of things, all children became orphans. The loss of a parent was tragic only if the child was young. Old children—children with gray hair and reading glasses—were supposed to get on with their lives. Em thought she'd been getting on pretty well; suddenly she wasn't sure.

Another car drove toward her. Em recognized the driver and hoped the woman didn't recognize her. Swiping her sleeve across her face, she restarted the car and drove cautiously through a blur of tears.

"Maybe I'm coming down with something."

Emma changed course again, looping to a grocery store for fresh lemons, hot black-bean soup, and a bottle of yellow syrup sworn to diminish all twelve major flu symptoms. Afternoon had become twilight before she got home and after nearly twenty-four hours without food, her stomach was growling loud enough to earn suspicious glances from the four-footed welcoming committee.

With a warning word to stay off the table where her soup was steaming, Em went upstairs to retrieve Eleanor's book. She opened it to the first written page—*The Moon's Phases and Seasons of the Sun*—but though Emma wouldn't take her mother's writing seriously, she felt awkward exposing a biblical book to black bean soup. There'd be time enough for mockery after dinner.

She sipped her soup in decorous silence and wondered instead if Eleanor had ever slipped back to Bower, ever driven down Teagarden Street. Had she seen the big Christmas tree through the windows? Or Em's toys strewn across the front yard?

It pleased Em—Merle Acalia Merrigan—to believe that Eleanor had come back to Teagarden Street and shed bitter tears before continuing on her way. Then Em wondered if her mother might still be alive. Odd, but true: the notion had never before crossed her mind. She'd grown up believing Eleanor had died before she turned one. Learning that Eleanor had driven out of Bower in an Oldsmobile hadn't changed that fundamental belief. Mother-died had mutated into Mother-left-before-she-died without a conscious effort on Emma's part.

She was familiar with tales of intrepid Web surfers who'd traced their roots on the Internet. How quaint, she'd thought, though sour grapes might have been more accurate. Dad had been the only child of elderly parents who'd died—truly, indisputably died—before Em was born. There was someone Dad had called Uncle George and his wife, Margaret—who was probably a second wife, because Dad never called her Aunt Margaret—but they'd both died before Em was ten.

Emma knew more about her stepchildren's ancestors than she knew about the Merrigans and nothing—nothing at all, not even a maiden name—about Eleanor's family. She could change that. When the need arose, Em could find addresses for obscure Ukrainian publishers; surely she could rustle up Eleanor Merrigan's maiden name.

The computer beckoned; its call went unheeded.

If Eleanor had kept Dad's name or gone back to her maiden name, the Bower police would have tracked her down fifty years ago. If Eleanor had wanted her daughter to come looking for her, she'd have left broader hints than the phases of the moon. Mostly, Emma didn't want to find Eleanor. Tragedy, even madness, was more easily borne than rejection.

She wished that she'd never found the old box, never brought it home, never opened it. But she'd done all three, so call it Eleanor's box, instead of Pandora's, and accept that once she'd seen it, she'd had to open it. Once she'd seen the morocco book, she had to curl up in her chair and read it, cover to cover, no matter the nonsense it contained or the damage it wrought.

Emma was, after all, Eleanor's daughter. The resemblance wasn't physical, no matter what Jennifer thought she'd seen in the wedding portrait. But she saw the world in ways Dad had never quite understood and she knew restlessness in a way he'd never shared. She'd come back to Bower and made her peace with the town, but it hadn't always been easy.

A moment later, she opened the black book.

The introductory pages had all the excitement of a cookbook for a cuisine she'd never tasted or a repair manual for an appliance she'd never seen. Overlooking the illicit ingredients, Eleanor could have been writing a How-To-Get-Even column for a supermarket tabloid. It was hard to imagine that a woman who'd had the wits to attract Em's father could have believed a word of what she'd written on the sleek, onion-skin paper.

Then Em turned a page and found the *Incantation for Charming Strangers*. The ingredients were innocuous: citrus oils and spices: a simple but possibly alluring perfume. The incantation itself was burdened with nonsense syllables and a warning that it worked only when the moon was full and the incantor stood naked in the shadow of an evergreen tree.

Dad, the scientist who believed in good works but not God, would have been appalled.

Closing the book, Em went upstairs to the computer. She waded through her accumulated e-mail, answering chatty messages from Jay-Jay and Lori, and Nancy's grimly humorous update regarding the downhill race between her mother's kidneys and her mind. Jennifer's account passwords were still in Em's system. She was tempted—she'd have been lying if she'd pretended otherwise—to peek into her erstwhile guest's files, but after an hour with the morocco book, Jennifer belonged to another life.

Emma was feeling feverish when she finished her e-mail and reassured the cats that she loved them more than she loved the computer. She stopped at the medicine cabinet and took her temperature with an old-fashioned mercury thermometer—sub-normal as usual. It wasn't her body that was making Em feel fragile; it was her thoughts of Eleanor and that damned black book.

Emma made tea, sweetened it with honey, bleached it with lemon—a sure cure for any ailment, real or imagined, especially when she drank it from an antique, bone china cup. *A Teacup for Curing Colds and Soothing Nerves?* Not perhaps as outrageous as Eleanor's nostrums, but not altogether different either.

With the scent of tea and lemon surrounding her, Em reopened the book near its middle, where the practical gave way to the theoretical. In her mind, Em had labeled Eleanor a witch. Bells, books, and candles taken together equaled witches, but Eleanor wasn't about covens or Halloween. Eleanor Merrigan was about one thing: curses, and not the creation of curses, either. None of her handwritten pages promised to dump misfortune on someone else's head. Without exception Eleanor wrote about unraveling curses, laying them, and mooting them.

According to Eleanor, curses came in a bewildering variety: natural, accidental, casual, actuated, sacrificial, and, most potent of all, persistent. Each broad category had its examples, its countermeasures and a few blank pages. The bureaucrats who prepared the library's budget forms would have recognized a kindred spirit in Eleanor Merrigan, but for her daughter, as she skimmed page after tedious page, there was only waste and delusion.

The mother-voice whispered: be grateful you never knew her. Be grateful she never had a chance to warp your mind.

Saturday had become Sunday when Em reached the last handwritten page, marked by a black ribbon through which Eleanor had drawn a pair of gold threads. The stitching was uneven: another disappointment. Emma hadn't inherited her thread-bending knack from her mother.

The clumsily stitched ribbon wasn't the only difference revealed in the final section. A crimson border, the only splash of color in the book, surrounded a single, India-ink paragraph:

If a curse is not unraveled, then it might wither or it might persist. A persistent curse is a thing unto itself. Like a parasite, it moves from pawn to pawn, recreating its doom and growing stronger. Unless destroyed, it will escape the substance of its origin, and root itself in the Netherlands, where it can more easily find new pawns across the breadth of time. A persistent curse cannot be destroyed directly. It must be tricked into revealing its moment of conception, which is the one place where it is vulnerable. No two such curses are the same. No two will succumb to the same deceit and some, to our lasting shame, have outwitted us for generations. They terrorize our nights. Their danger to the too-proud and unwary cannot be exagger-

*ated. They are our greatest enemy, but we will defeat
them, each and every one of them . . . You, my young
daughter, will defeat your share of them. I am sure of it.*

"Nonsense," Em sputtered and the cats took refuge in the
basement. "Ridiculous." She closed the supple covers. "Inane
. . . madness!" But bitter words couldn't keep the memories of
countless nights of terror from rising in her mind.

Suppose the night terrors were her true inheritance. Even
worse: suppose that the terrors weren't the mind's understanding of the brain's chemistry. Suppose, for just one
breath or heartbeat, that everything Eleanor had written was
the literal truth and that Em's dreams were visions into a
cursed world. Suppose that this morning, she'd actually battled and defeated a persistent curse.

More nonsense of the highest order.

If she'd owned a fireplace, Emma would have burnt the
book right then, but the Maisonettes had been the modern
marvels of their time. No dirty fireplaces for them, but coal
furnaces, one per basement, upgraded in the Fifties to gas.
She put the book on the hall table beside her purse. Tomorrow, she'd drive down to the river and *drown* the thing!

Em turned out the lights. In her mind's eye, as she
climbed the darkened stairs, Eleanor's book floated on steel-
gray currents. Its onion-skin paper would not absorb water.
The India-ink words would not smear. It would not drown.
A persistent curse had entered Emma's life and its name was
Eleanor Merrigan.

She had been falling asleep until her head hit the pillow.
Insomnia was nothing new; it went hand in hand with migraines, but apprehension, a plain-old fear of the dark, hadn't
plagued Em's nights since college. Without permission, her
senses went on heightened alert. One cat was in the kitchen,
crunching through a late-night snack; the other was coming

up the stairs. Next door, Mrs. Borster's furnace was on; and in the backroom, the clock ticked steadily.

There was no sound that Em couldn't pinpoint and name, none she wouldn't hear. If one sound was the wrong sound, there was a jack-knife wedged between the mattress and box-spring, and a phone set to dial 911 at the touch of a single button. The outside doors were locked, ditto the windows. Short of an electronic alarm system, Em was safe.

She lay between the sheets, straining her awareness, knowing full well that nothing, nothing at all, was keeping her awake.

And nothing was doing a good job.

Without witnesses, Em was ashamed of her failure to outgrow a childhood fear. Spin came to her rescue. When the heavy-footed cat marched across the blanket, Em raised her arm to create a warm cave for him in the curves of her body. He flopped solidly against her stomach. His cat's eyes weren't much use, of course, covered up with layers of cotton and wool; that wasn't the point. The presence of something alive and unafraid was what she'd needed.

Emma battled her misguided instincts. She breathed deeply and regularly. She calculated factors and prime numbers. She heard something in the alley behind the townhouse.

It whined and scratched at the wooden fences. Sounding too big to be a raccoon, Em guessed it was last night's dog. There were leash laws in Bower and stricter rules in the Maisonettes. People couldn't let their pets run loose night after night.

Her backyard gate, the one Em had used last night, rattled as the dog pawed it. She hoped the hinges would hold, hoped she'd remembered to relatch it. Hope died with a slam. Beside her, Spin stretched his neck across Em's arm. She felt a growl brewing in his throat.

The dog leapt against the back door.

Fear of nothing might paralyze Emma, but once nothing

became something, she could be brave. Without thought, she swept the covers aside. Her eyes were on the drape-shrouded window, a rectangle of faint light in the darkness. She'd *deal* with that animal, identify it, and track down its owners. Spin exploded away from her as she began to rise. He raked her ribs and arm before he vanished. Emma blinked from surprise. When she opened her eyes again, the faint rectangle was gone, replaced by darkness, by nothing.

This was neither the aftermath of a night terror, nor the illogic of a dream. She was awake, with a stinging, bleeding arm, and blind . . . but not deaf. The dog was off to her left, about where the back door should have been.

Time for a reality check—

"Spin? Charm?"

She felt the words in her throat, heard them and the dog with her ears. The cats didn't respond—but the obedience of cats was no reason to bounce a reality check. Em patted herself down: her arm was palpably scratched. There was a familiar ring on the correct finger, a flannel nightshirt hanging from her shoulders.

The dog laughed. Did she really think this was a *dream*?

Em took a deep breath. The air was dry and still and about as warm as her bedroom had been. It didn't smell like her bedroom, but it was air. She was standing: there was gravity and substance beneath her bare feet, but not the blue-gray carpet of her bedroom. Her toes kneaded a breakable substance, like dried mud. Squatting, Emma confirmed her suspicions with her hands. A network of crumbling cracks revealed themselves to her fingertips. She ground a clod to powder and sniffed the residue; it had no odor. Wherever she was, nothing grew here. Nothing lived here.

Her nightshirt had no pockets. Em knotted a clod into the flannel. The lump bumped her thigh when she stood up.

The dog howled, closer than before. She stared futilely at the sound.

Dreams, terrors, reality—which was which? Thursday night, when she battled an ember, had that been a dream? When she'd banished the blood-red whirl, had that been the aftermath of a night terror? Or were they both as real as the howling dog? Could she banish the dog with words or smother it with darkness she made with her hand?

She tried words first. "This place is mine. Go away. Leave my place . . . *Now*!"

Manic laughter grew louder. Claws scrabbled the parched mud; they sounded longer and sharper than a dog's claws. Em imagined the beast had halved the distance between them.

If Eleanor were mad, Emma thought, *then I have inherited every drop of her madness, and if she wasn't mad, then this is real and that dog-beast is a persistent curse.*

"Show yourself. I want to see what I'm up against."

A breeze pulled Em's hair forward. Something swelled in the darkness. She waited, looking a bit away from the place where the breeze had blown. At night, peripheral vision was keenest. Moments passed; Eleanor wasn't mad.

The curse had two holes in the darkness above a smaller one in the middle and an irregular, larger one at the bottom. Call it a face. The human mind was predisposed to faces. The face laughed.

"Do you think you can vanquish me?"

Emma hesitated. She'd always thought herself a fast learner, but she'd never had to learn a new reality. No, not a *new* reality—if Em accepted the reality of this wasteland, then she had to accept that she'd been here before.

"I'll vanquish you, if that's what I've got to do."

Her calm crumbled: Emma Merrigan no more knew how to unravel a curse than she knew how to return to her bedroom.

"Catch me!"

The curse-face loomed closer. Em looked through its gaping mouth. She'd had magical powers the first time she'd come here; she'd thrown off sparks and flames as if they were a natural part of her. Her second time she'd cast darkness. Before the mouth closed around her, Emma conceived an explosion radiating from her body. She made blinding light and deafening sound. The curse retreated, still laughing, not at all unraveled.

"Catch me!"

It taunted her, disappearing and reappearing, now in front, now behind. Wisdom rooted in the reality Emma knew best, advised her to let it go: she didn't have the wherewithal to challenge the denizens of the wasteland. Another voice, no less wise in its way, counseled that if she didn't know where she was or how to get home, she might just as well give chase.

If she'd pursued the curse as it flashed around the wasteland, Emma would have worn herself out in no time. She walked, instead, toward the place where she'd first sensed a dog's whining. Eleanor's book said the only way to destroy a persistent was to attack its point of origin. Any assumption was inherently dangerous, but once she'd begun walking, the curse taunted her primarily from behind. It was tempting to think that she had chosen the direction it did not want her to go.

Out of the frying pan, into the fire? Em asked herself. She left tracks in the crumbling dirt . . . like Armstrong's on the moon? Or, Emma *assumed* she left tracks. Though she'd made an explosion, she'd failed to conjure a steady light.

God knew she tried.

The curse-face gave up its rear-guard harassment. It hovered, beacon-like, before her.

"You cannot catch a curse by walking. You cannot unravel one with thoughts. Didn't they teach you anything?"

Emma ignored it. She considered herself a healthy woman, dead-on average for her height, weight, and age. She didn't run or jog, but she walked regularly. She averaged three-and-a-half miles per hour, hour after hour, year after year in the university's charity walkathon. She'd never outwalked herself.

Maybe the air *wasn't* the same as the air in her bedroom, or maybe walking barefoot was that much harder, or maybe the utter darkness—the fear that her next step might be over an edge or into a wall—sapped her energy. Whatever the reason, Emma hadn't walked more than two miles before she was gasping.

She had to sit with her head resting on her knees as she massaged her aching calves. The curse mocked her, whirling fast and close. Emma felt its wind against her hair and felt the stirring of despair as well. Head down, she wondered if she was doomed . . . or already dead.

Unbidden, an image of Emma Merrigan sprawled within a yellow-tape outline formed in her mind's eye. She raised her head. The curse had multiplied into an encircling ring of silent faces. As if they'd been waiting to seize her attention, the curses began to rotate. They gathered color: a bilious yellow, a color from which Em had always recoiled.

Perhaps she'd been born knowing that this day or night would come.

Emma was trapped. Even if she'd believed she could escape through the ring, it was unlikely she could have reached it: gale-force winds flowed from the curses toward the ring's center. Viselike, the wind folded Em against herself and squeezed the breath out of her lungs. Her fingers went numb, then her toes. Within a few heartbeats, she felt nothing at all, including the parched ground.

She was falling.

Eleanor's black book had warned that there was no exaggerating a curse's danger and it appeared that Mother was right. The warnings, though, could have been a bit more explicit, a bit less poetic, her daughter thought before thinking itself became difficult.

There was laughter—lewd, triumphant laughter—and hunger.

A hand, or maybe jaws, clamped down on Em's neck, hard enough to pierce the numbness. As a mother cat carried her kittens, Em felt herself lifted away from the laughter.

Who taught you the ways of this world?

It was the second time a voice inside her head had asked that question. *No one,* she confessed. *I'm here by mistake.*

Obviously.

Her captor flung her away. Moments earlier Em had believed she was falling; now she was rising, pushed by an invisible rocket. She imagined friction flames belling around her: the final injury. Thank God, there was no pain.

✳   ✳   ✳

The phone was ringing. Em lifted her head; something was terribly wrong. She was cold. She hurt in every living place. She was on the floor.

Her answering machine took the call. Fine. She'd unreel it later. In the meantime, Em took inventory and tried to remember. There'd been a noise—a dog scratching at the door. She'd gotten out of bed to investigate; Spin had carved racing stripes on her arm.

He'd gotten her good. There were three bloody gouges on the inside of her left arm.

She must have stepped on him, fallen, and knocked herself unconscious. All things considered, Spin could be in a lot worse shape. Em pushed herself up and looked around for her cat. The effort left her dizzy. She sat back on her heels and didn't try to stand. Downstairs, the answering machine date-stamped the message that had just ended. Her head was clearing; maybe she didn't have a concussion after all. The rest of her felt battered, but not broken, as if she'd struck a multitude of objects on her way to the carpet.

She couldn't have, though—she'd awakened with nary a chair or bed-frame in reach.

Emma wanted to reach something before she tried to stand. She crawled to the bed and hauled herself onto the mattress.

"I'm losing it," she muttered, trying to impose order on her mind. "Losing it big-time."

Her legs felt strong enough to carry her to the bathroom, where normal days began with normal rituals. She'd gotten as far as brushing her teeth. The face in the mirror was her face with a faint bruise above her left eye. *That* was an ache she could account for, *that* was where she'd knocked herself silly against the carpet. The rest?

The back of her neck hurt like absolute hell.

Emma swept her hair aside. Swollen bruises reached forward like fingers from her spine. She remembered the last moments of her dream. She noticed she was naked. Her second-favorite nightshirt was gone, and with it the knotted pouch of wasteland dirt: the one chunk of tangible evidence she might have taken as proof of her sanity.

Em searched the whole house, not merely the bedroom. The nightshirt, and only the nightshirt, was missing. There was a nasty bruise on her neck that couldn't be explained if she'd tripped over Spin but which made perfect sense if her dream hadn't been a dream.

The phone rang again: John Amstel, Nancy's husband, calling back to see if she was up yet, to see if she wanted to share a four-egg omelette at Rafaello's and the winter flower show at the botanical garden afterward. Emma wasn't much for omelettes or greenhouse flowers, but they sounded good, compared to the alternative of staying home by herself. She told him to pick her up in twenty minutes.

After sloshing down cold coffee and three ibuprofen pills, Em dressed, waited, and left. She hoped she'd have the courage to return.

E*ight*

S*unday breakfast at* Rafaello's was a Bower tradition, meaning that there was a line to get into the restaurant. Emma and her best friend's husband waited twenty minutes to get a small, wobbly table close to the fogged-over windows. By then, she'd told John about the howling dog, her stumble into unconsciousness, and shown him the bruise she'd found on her neck. She left out the other, more embarrassing parts about nightmares, dubious legacies, and missing nightshirts.

Those were omissions, not lies. She could have added them anytime during breakfast or afterward without endangering her overall honesty; at least that's what Emma told herself as John nodded and absorbed.

He was a patient man, renowned as a good listener in the small circles through which he, his wife, and to a lesser extent Em herself traveled. Acquaintances said that knowing John Amstel was better than paying ten psychiatrists, psychologists, and social workers together because when John was done listening, he'd sit back and give you his opinion.

Em practiced patience herself while John dosed his coffee with sweetener and whitener. When it was just right, he leaned back in the fake bentwood chair and told her to make an appointment with her doctor.

"Stress, Em. We've reached the age where stress kills: heart attacks, strokes, you name it. The loss of a parent, Em, that ranks up at the top of the list. The library's not the place it used to be: Shaunekker's had more visions than a gypsy. And you're alone with no one to talk to. Everything stays bottled up."

Em didn't argue, especially about John's last points. When she envisioned the future, she foresaw twenty, perhaps thirty, years of living at the Maisonettes with all the comforts of home except the living warmth only a man could provide. Forget the sex—not easily done, but possible—and the subtle tension of romance, Emma missed the casual touches, the thoughtless familiarity: reaching for the ketchup bottle and not pulling her hand back when he reached for it at the same time.

That kind of loneliness was stressful, and stress did kill.

Had she lit a slow fuse for self-destruction? That wasn't a question for Rafaello's. Em let her subjects drop as they talked about Nancy, Katherine, and John's own loneliness. When push came to shove, Emma could be a good listener, too.

The winter garden show was small and poorly attended. Winter gardening in Bower consisted of reading catalogs and knocking off the snow before tree limbs snapped. The University's bonsai and orchid clubs had other ideas for long, dreary days. Succumbing to the allure of miniature trees, Em bought a ten-year-old maple growing in a soup bowl.

John became entranced by a contorted fig—a compact sphere of coiled and tangled branches, especially handsome against snow, or so the grower claimed. John thought it would be "interesting" outside the Amstel windows. Em looked at it and saw the swirling faces of her nightmare.

"It looks diseased," she said, then added, "It looks cursed."

Times had changed in Bower. After decades of civic secularism, going to church was fashionable again. Grocery

stores sold angels for every occasion and Rafaello's had a
sign above the daily specials offering a discount to patrons
who could brandish a timely church, synagogue, mosque, or
Buddhist temple bulletin. But *cursed* wasn't a word that John
or Em would have expected her to use to describe a tree.

They maneuvered past the conversational pothole. John
bought his twisted tree. Emma helped him wrestle it into the
trunk and out again in the Amstel driveway. Jokingly, John
offered to help carry her maple into the Maisonettes. Without hesitation, she accepted the offer. She couldn't dwell on
curses with a sane man at her side as she opened the door.

"Give Nancy a call, if you get a chance," John suggested
after she'd made a home for the soup bowl on a living room
windowsill. "This thing with Katherine is wearing her
down. She needs to get away. Katherine's not Katherine
anymore, but she's not dying, either."

"I'll call her tonight and warn her about that tree you're
planting in her yard."

"Call after nine. It takes that long to get Katherine into
bed. Nance needs help, Em. She shouldn't be doing this
alone. I don't think she should be doing it at all, but she
doesn't hear me."

They hugged, same as they would have done if Nancy
were in the doorway with them, or Jeff, back in the days
when they'd been a foursome. It was an over-learned, mean-
ingless ritual that did nothing to lessen Emma's isolation.
She slumped against the door after she'd closed it. Her neck
hurt; it hadn't bothered her all day, only now, when she was
alone again.

Calling Nancy gave Em a focus for her thoughts. She was
planning what she'd say to her friend while she fed flour,
water, and yeast into the bread machine and when she went
downstairs with a basket of laundry. Eleanor's box atop the
washing machine took her by unpleasant surprise.

Emma was ashamed for allowing her life to sink to such a

low ebb that dreams, old letters, and books of nonsense had seemed more important than Nancy's ordeal. If she'd been a better friend, she wouldn't be wasting her weekends fretting about her long-lost mother, she'd drive down to southern Ohio and give Nancy the help she needed and deserved.

A moment of shame reinvigorated Emma Merrigan. While her sheets and towels sloshed through the rinse cycle, she attacked the mess of boxes. The shelves were neatly packed when her laundry was ready for the dryer. Upstairs, she found other chores to occupy her until a few minutes after nine.

With a cup in one hand and a steaming pot of tea in the other, Em approached her chair. She'd left Eleanor's black book on the table beside the phone. It wasn't worth the work of unpacking and repacking to put the book back where she'd found it. She shoved it onto the bookshelves behind her chair, appropriately onto a fiction shelf filled with fairy tales and myths.

The phone rang seven times before Nancy answered. It had been a bad day in south Ohio. Katherine had had a tantrum for breakfast. She'd broken a juice glass and gashed not only herself, but Nancy too. While Emma and John had enjoyed a leisurely Sunday, Nancy had been in the Emergency Room.

"The doctor told me everything has got to be plastic from now on. But that wasn't the worst, Em—"

"What was the worst, Nance?"

"When we got to the ER, Mother was a horror. She screamed and swore the air blue for five hours—my mother! The doctor treating her came behind *my* curtain and said he wanted to admit her for observation. *Psychiatric* observation."

"What did you say?"

A two-hundred mile silence, a sigh, and then: "She's my mother, Em. I couldn't leave her there like that. She'd never have left me."

Of course not. The mystic bond between mothers and

daughters which Emma Merrigan could never know. She dug deep for empathy. "If you were the one in trouble, she wouldn't have taken care of you herself, not for this long. She'd have gotten help; your dad would have seen to it—for *both* your sakes."

A liquid sniffle came through the line. "The doctor gave me the name of a place that does respite care. I'm going to call them tomorrow. I feel so guilty, Em. It's not right . . ."

Em didn't—couldn't—argue and retold the tale she'd told at Rafaello's—parity was always a good idea when you were friends with both husband and wife. This second time, Emma told it for laughs. Both she and Nancy felt better when their conversation ended.

An hour later, Emma sat in bed, working the Sunday crossword puzzle. An hour after that, she turned off the light. Em didn't manufacture her terror: it was either there, or it wasn't. Saturday night it had been; Sunday, it wasn't. She found a position that didn't hurt her neck and fell into an unremarkable sleep.

Em was in her bed, in her nightshirt, surrounded by cats when the alarm went off. She felt refreshed, as she hadn't felt for a few days. Her morning routine was routine. Traffic was light, she found a good parking place, and encountered absolutely no one on her trek through the stacks. Everyone was smiling, talking about football and the team's chances for a January First bowl game as Em made her way to her office.

The message light was dark and Daffy Duck awoke uneventfully from his weekend nap. She checked her e-mail, expecting to see something from Matt, at least, but everything was business, junk, or jokes. She handled one query from France before shutting everything down. Gene Shaunekker might indeed have seen many visions of the library's future, but they all included Monday morning senior-staff meetings. Em refueled at the coffee station and headed for the elevator.

Three hours later, with her stomach churning from neglect and her eyes glazed over from yet another onward-and-upward presentation from bright-eyed consultants who'd never done anything but give high-priced advice, Em returned to her office. There were memos scattered in the seat of her chair. The message light was blinking angrily and her monitor was fringed with pink "While you were out" notes.

Em read, listened, sorted, scribbled, and signed until she'd cleared enough space to eat lunch. None of the messages or notes had been from Matt; she dialed his extension and got his voice mail.

"This is Emma," she told the machine. "Give me a call when you get a chance. Nothing urgent."

Mondays were busy days for everyone—witness what had happened to her desk. Still, memories of Bran on her front steps flashed in her mind's eye and were not easily laid to rest. After lunch, Emma sent Daffy out to look for mail. The mallard brought back a short-sentence message from Matt.

A vendor meeting had turned into a free lunch. The weekend had gone quietly. Bran wasn't a bad guy, just old-fashioned where women were concerned. He'd decided to move out of the Blue House and let it go between him and Jennifer. The two of them were going to go car-scrounging to free Bran from his dependence on Jennifer's wheels.

Matt's message finished with a three-word paragraph: *After work? Dinner?*

Dinner—with a single man who was closer to her stepchildren's ages than hers? Was this how men stumbled into their second childhoods?

Emma typed, *You're on,* in the reply window and clicked the *Send* button.

Time passed. There was a foul-up down in receiving: a crate of books without the necessary paperwork. Emma scrambled to figure out who might have ordered it; she was certain from the start it hadn't been her. Her quest had gotten nowhere when the phone rang.

"You'd better come down here."

"Matt—this isn't a good time. I'm up to my eyeballs here."

"This is important. Serious. Real serious. You'd better come down."

You didn't have to believe in telepathy or magic to know that human beings could convey information without words and Emma didn't need to look at her monitor to know Matt wasn't talking about problems with the network.

"I'm on my way."

She heard Bran Mongomery before she saw him—

"I can't wait, Matt. If she says no, I'm goin' anyway. I *can* find Jen, same as I did before."

Quickening her pace, Em crossed the threshold and said, "If I say no to what?" before Matt said anything.

"Jen's in trouble. I've got to get to her; she needs to be with me."

The light was better in Matt's office than it had been on the Maisonettes sidewalks early Saturday morning, which made Bran's wild blond hair and wilder eyes all the more disturbing. Em turned to Matt, who'd surrendered his chair to Bran and was standing, protectively, in front of the network hardware racks.

"What's going on here?"

"Bran thinks someone's hurt Jennifer—"

"Not someone!"

"Not someone," Matt repeated, condescension seeping into his voice. "Bran thinks that some*thing's* hurt Jennifer."

"You don't believe me!" Bran swept a heap of paper off Matt's desk. "Damn it—I never should've come here. It's a waste of time. She's in danger! Jennifer *belongs* with me. She's not safe when she's by herself."

Red-faced and shouting, Bran had risen from the chair.

His overly bright eyes fastened on Em. She'd backed into the doorjamb before she was aware that her feet had moved. Security had an office nearby. Emma thought if she screamed they might hear her and was one breath short of testing her theory when Bran squeezed his eyes shut.

Bran collapsed, grimacing with some inner agony, to his knees. He beat his forehead against the edge of the metal desk. Matt recovered first, half-wrestling, half-guiding the bigger man out of harm's way.

Emma had her eye on the phone and circling both of them, Bran's fit ended, as suddenly as it had begun. His body relaxed and after a pair of deep sighs, his breathing settled into a normal rhythm. Emma picked up the phone, only to have Matt intervene before she could summon help.

"Give him another minute."

"He's done this before?"

Matt nodded. "On the way home Saturday morning."

"You took him to the emergency room?"

"No. He wouldn't go. Says it's nothing medical, just his demons going out for a walk. Apparently, it used to happen a lot, but he thought coming to Bower had cured him. I guess it didn't—or it took them a few months to find him."

"You don't believe that, do you?" Emma challenged.

Before Matt could answer, Bran's eyelids fluttered open. Emma knew that look of panic from the inside. She'd never blamed it on demons—then she thought of Sunday morning and the ring of curses. In the absence of science, one woman's curse could be another man's demon.

Forgetting the phone, Emma knelt beside Bran. "How do you feel?"

Bran ignored Em's outstretched hand. He sat himself up without assistance. "Better."

"You had a seizure. Do you remember?"

His upper lip curled. "Yeah, I *remember* just fine. The ants were chewing my brain to little shreds." The weariness in his voice was matched only by contempt. "And you weren't listening to me."

Bran reached for the desk chair which spun away from him. Matt offered an arm and nearly lost his own balance getting Bran upright. Bran swayed on his feet before landing heavily in the chair. Matt perched on the edge of his desk; Em retreated to the doorway.

"How can Jennifer be safe with you when you've got ants chewing up your brain?" She wasn't as unsympathetic as she sounded, but patterns were emerging and she didn't like any of them.

"Because when they're chewing on me, they aren't chewing on her. Now they've gone out looking for her. I've got to find her before they do."

"You don't know where she is, then?"

Another lip curl. "I know, Miz—?"

After a weekend with Matt, it was inconceivable that Bran didn't know she called herself Emma. Perhaps he didn't want to be on a first-name basis. That suited Emma.

"Merrigan," she snapped back. "Merle Acalia Merrigan."

Matt's eyes went wide. He'd never heard the name Eleanor had given her and Emma didn't know herself what had possessed her to blurt it out. Possession might not be an inappropriate metaphor when Bran was talking about demons and she was thinking about curses.

"Yeah, Miz Merrigan, I know she's at your house. I could've gone straight there, same as I did Friday. I came here instead . . . to tell you first, 'cause if I'm going to your house, I'd just as soon have you with me."

"You're not going to my house. Jennifer's not there. The last I saw of Jennifer, she was driving down Reynolds, headed for the By-Pass."

Bran deflated: his shoulders fell, his nostrils unflared, his lip uncurled. He wound his hands together; the contortions

spread up his arms. Matt plopped a hand on Bran's shoulder.
It didn't help.

"No, Miz Merrigan, she's there and she's in trouble. I can
hear her screaming." Bran closed his eyes. He seemed on the
verge of another fit. "I can see her: she's hiding in a corner,
behind a sofa, and things are flying past her. She's holding a
little gray cat—" Eyes open again, he met her stare. "There
aren't any cats at Jennifer's parents' house, Miz Merrigan."

A lucky guess about where Jennifer had been headed and
Emma's cats? At eight pounds, Charm wasn't what Em
would have called a *little* cat, but compared to Bran—?

No!

She wasn't going to believe Bran Mongomery and there
was no space between Emma's living room sofa and the
wall.

"You need to forget about her, Mr. Mongomery—" If he
was going to treat her like a high-school teacher, she'd play
the part. "And you need to stop thinking about women as
your possessions. Jennifer doesn't *belong* to you."

"You don't know what you're talking about," Bran
snarled back. "Jen doesn't belong *to* me, she belongs *with*
me, 'cause it's not safe for her to be anywhere else. I warned
her—sometimes I'm not myself. She didn't care—and I
didn't know what was going to happen until it was too late.
They're my demons—always been my demons. Last
Wednesday—Did she tell you about last Wednesday, Miz
Merrigan? How she came into my room 'cause she'd had an
argument with her mom—probably about me—she didn't
say. We listened to music, like we usually do, an' I dozed
off—that's pretty usual, too. Out of nowhere, she's jabbing
me between the ribs an' tellin' me that if she had a knife,
then I'd be dead. I look at her an' I see all my demons
lookin' back at me. They've got her surrounded. They were
going to make her crazy, if I didn't get them back with me.

"So I did what I had to do. I hit her to make them let go.

Only she didn't want to let go. Everything's been different since then. The demons—they're like a mean dog that won't bite me, but they've bitten Jennifer. I'm tellin' you, Miz Merrigan: we've got to go to your house, 'cause Jen's scared now. She knows they're real, but she can't fight 'em and I can."

Emma wished, as she'd wished few things in her life, that Bran hadn't compared his demons to a mean dog. The image made his words all too believable. She retreated into bare facts: "Jennifer's not at my house, Bran. She left Saturday and she doesn't have a key to get back in. It's as simple as that. If she's not at her parents' house and she's not at the Blue House, I don't know where she is."

"Maybe you could call your house?" Matt suggested softly. "Just to settle things."

"People don't answer other people's phones when they're attached to answering machines."

But she tapped the number and held the receiver away from her ear so the men could hear the ringer. Once, twice—the machine usually cut in around the third ring. The fourth came and went, the fifth . . . the tenth. She hung up.

"I have cats."

Spin had scrambled her phones more than once since she'd rescued him and Charm from the animal shelter. But an off-hook receiver produced a busy signal, and there was an override message that cut in when the tape was full or otherwise not working.

"I can find your place from here, Miz Merrigan. I can find Jen the way I did on Friday, but it'll take too long. She needs me *now.*"

Em stole a glance at Matt. His face was a mask of concern without opinions—not that Matt Barto's opinion really counted in this. The demons were Bran Mongomery's, the dog was Bran Mongomery's, the curse was Bran Mongomery's, and the last safe place for Jennifer Hodden was near Bran Mongomery.

"I don't know what I can do to stop you, Bran, but I'll think of something, and if I see you hanging around my house—if I think for one moment that you've tried to break into my house, I'm calling the police and demons will be the least of your problems."

Bran lurched to his feet. He cussed Emma out soundly, if unimaginatively, and halved the distance between him and her. Fists clenched and muscles bunched, Matt pushed away from his desk. He was a solidly built man. Pound for pound, he might be Bran's match—but he was giving away fifty pounds and, besides, Em wasn't about to have some champion fighting her battles. She met Bran's glower with her snake-eyes stare. He swerved through the door without touching her.

"I'm not joking, Bran," she called. "You're looking at uniforms if you hassle me."

He walked backward to say: "You're nothing compared to what I'm afraid of," then hurried down the corridor to the stairs.

Em let him have the last word with her and took the first with Matt. "I'm terribly sorry I got you involved in this."

"No problem, my life's been pretty dull lately. I don't know what's with him—maybe it's drugs. Once he'd had his little fit in the car, he was clean and sober all weekend. Maybe he loaded up after we left this morning. Whatever he's doing, he's got symptoms I've never seen before."

"And you'd know?" Emma asked.

"Yeah, more than you." He made a sour face. "I don't think it's drugs—nothing from the street anyway. He's making his own, right in his brain."

"The mind is what the brain does."

"Yeah," Matt nodded, "something like that."

"Bran doesn't have a key to your place, does he?"

"Do I look like an idiot? I told him to come here if he finished up early. I was thinking if he didn't find a place, I'd let him crash with me. I've got the room, splitting expenses would give me extra money, which never hurts, and it's not as if having a roommate would cramp my style."

They'd come to the awkward part of the conversation. Matt retrieved the papers Bran had swept from the desk. Em let her young friend off the hook.

"Don't worry about dinner. There's not much left to talk about."

Matt dumped the paper on his desk without squaring it. "Sez who? I want to know who this 'Merle Acalia' is. Where'd *she* come from?" His voice caught; he stared at her with his mouth open. "Em. Emma. Em-ah." He repeated the syllables twice more. "'M' and 'A.' Not bad. If your name's Merle Acalia, Emma's a definite improvement."

"On a scale of one to ten, it was definitely an eleven."

"Or a minus-one. How'd you get stuck with a name like Merle Acalia? Grandmothers?"

Em shook her head. She didn't know. The black book had raised more questions than it had answered.

"Okay, tell me over dinner."

"There's nothing to tell, Matt. It's my name, but I've never used it. I don't think Rob or Jeff ever knew. You've become part of a *very* select, *very* small group."

"Me and Bran Mongomery. He must've struck a chord."

"He struck something," Em agreed. "I wasn't planning to tell him . . . or you."

"Weird. I'll forget I ever heard it—if you'd like. We don't have to talk about it over dinner."

Long-dormant pathways shuddered to emotional life. For months, Emma had assumed she was the only one with an attraction problem. Her instincts, if she trusted them, advised otherwise. This was not the moment any sane person would choose to re-enter the romantic world after a long absence. At the very least, a wise person would wait for a better moment.

Emma Merrigan aspired to wisdom but frequently fell short.

"As long as I don't have to cook or clean up afterward, I'll talk about anything."

"Apples and Oranges?" Matt rattled off the name of a trendy hamburger joint out near the Interstate.

Em nodded.

"Fine. I've got a couple of things to do right after work. I'll meet you there at six-thirty?"

"Six-thirty's fine," Em replied. At least they didn't have to negotiate transportation.

Emma returned to her office, but not to work. Her mind had become a raucous playground for her past, present, and future: Eleanor, Bran and Jennifer, and Matt Barto. Twice she reached for the phone: six-thirty, she'd decided, was impossible. She made up a reason. The books on the loading dock belonged to a Japanese book-broker and she needed to talk to him real-time. They didn't, but similar situations *did* arise.

Twice her hand had begun to move to the telephone before she stopped it with the question—had she sunk so far into middle age that *appropriateness* dictated her happiness? Become so lonely that a dinner—a mere dinner at a restaurant noted for its student-friendly prices, not its intimate decor— could set off a school-girl frenzy in her imagination?

"Get a grip," Em scolded herself.

She attacked a stack of requests from the high-energy physics group. Nominally in English, the titles might well have been Chinese for all she understood of the subject matter. Her co-workers poked their heads into her office to say good-night and remind her that it was time to go home or get a life. She laughed and said she would, any day now.

Daffy burst out of background processing at five-forty-five with an important announcement: "Rabbit season!"

Em replied, "Duck season!" and shut everything down.

Bower didn't have a rush hour so much as it had a twice-a-day traffic jam as everyone tried to get to the opposite side of the city. Forty-five minutes from center campus to Interstate was about right. Em pulled into the restaurant parking lot five minutes early. A handful of office types, mostly smokers, waited outside the faux antique door. She scanned them quickly and recognizing no one, reached for the door without breaking stride.

"Hey, Em! Wait up!"

Matt's voice. He was sprinting across the lot and he wasn't alone: Bran Mongomery loomed behind him like a grizzly bear. Feeling betrayed, Em let the door slip and intercepted them at the edge of the cloudy crowd.

"Bran still can't find Jennifer—"

"I can find her," the big man corrected. "I know exactly where Jen is. She's hiding inside Miz Merrigan's house."

In the grip of sudden, wild anger, Em could only reject Bran's conclusion and everything else with a blunt, "I'm out of here."

She had taken a couple of steps toward her car when Matt—not Bran, but Matt!—caught her arm.

"We should drive by and make sure."

Em lashed out with the old snake-eyes stare. Her arm was free as Matt tucked his arm close against his chest. It was more reaction than Em had intended, a bridge-burning reaction, but at that precise moment she didn't care if she roasted the world.

"Don't even *think* of following me," she warned.

Emma's car was about fifty feet away—fifty feet behind Bran. She aimed her wrath in his direction, expecting him to step aside. Bran folded his arms. He became the immovable object to her resistible force.

"Jen's not at her parents' house. She's not at the Blue—"

"Jennifer could be anywhere, Bran—except at my house."

Matt chimed in, "If we drove over there, we'd know once and for all."

"What changed your mind?" she demanded, an honest question despite the harshness in her voice.

"I told him I'd go to a doctor if I'm wrong," Bran answered for him. "I'll get out of your life, his life, even Jen's life. If I can be this sure, and be wrong, too—then I gotta accept that there's something wrong with me."

On the surface, it was tempting. There was no way Jennifer was holed up in the Maisonettes; Bran would seek the help he obviously needed. Matt said nothing, though he could easily have reminded her that she sucked him into this mess. She owed him; she owed herself to try the easy way.

"All right. This is it, though. The last step. She's not there and, Bran, you're gone, you're history."

"She's there," was Bran's reply.

Parking was, as always, impossible. She found a space; Matt double-parked on her flank. Her townhouse was dark except for the outdoor light in the portico; the mailbox bulged with catalogs. Bran followed Em up the walk, Matt followed Bran, and no one said a word as she propped open the storm door. She turned the key to the right and felt the usual resistance as the deadbolt retreated. Switching keys, Em attacked the lower knob-lock.

Most times the door opened of its own weight, but sometimes it needed encouragement. She gave the knob a jerk and a shove; the door opened a scraping inch and stopped. Spin and Charm were out of their kitty-Olympics years; they didn't knock things over while she was at work and, short of the hall table or chair, there was nothing near the door that could have blocked it. Em shoved a little harder. Bran reached over her head and put his weight against the steel.

"Jen!" he bellowed and pushed. "Babe—?"

Whatever he might have added was lost in a *bang!* They all leapt back. Em thought "gun" even as some more acute part of her consciousness analyzed the sound as a good-sized wooden rod snapping in two. The door swung wider. In the yellow light, she watched a broken leg from the hallway chair roll past. Twin sensations of violation and rage thrust Emma forward, into her dark, quiet home. For the second time in as many days, she felt a hand close around her neck. The pain was intense; she couldn't fight free as Bran swung her out of his way, couldn't stay on her own feet when he let go.

"Jen? Jen! Where are you, Babe?"

Matt caught Emma before she collapsed. They followed the sounds of Bran crashing through unfamiliar terrain. Em hit the light switch and staggered a second time: her home had been ransacked.

"Jen!"

"Bran!"

There was no mistaking that soprano voice. Em clambered down the hall and gaped at the silhouetted couple in the middle of her living room.

"How?" she sputtered, not loudly enough for them to hear. "How did she get in? Why?"

Matt tried a lamp left upright near the television. Nothing happened. He traced the cord, plugged it in. Sudden light left them all blinking, Em most of all.

It's only stuff, Em told herself as she absorbed the overturned furniture, swept-clear shelves, and downed pictures. *I'm insured. I'm safe. The cats are safe.* Spin marched right up to her, complaining about the disorder in his universe while Charm emerged from behind the displaced sofa just long enough to make a run for the basement. *Stuff can be replaced*—which wasn't completely true, not for the objects whose values were measured in memories.

Em's attention fell on bits of blue-green pottery, pieces of a vase she'd owned since freshman year in college. She picked up the largest pieces and fitted them together. The vase might be repaired if she could find the pieces. There were so many pieces. She set the ones she'd gathered in a little heap beside the lit lamp.

"Why?" she asked again, addressing the back of Jennifer's head.

The rest of Jennifer was hidden by Bran's gently rocking embrace.

"I tried to help you. I didn't hurt you. Why did you do this?" Em despised whiners, but couldn't keep a tremor from infecting her voice.

She spotted the bonsai tree she'd bought yesterday amid the wreckage. Matt caught her hand as she reached for it. Their eyes met; he shook his head.

"Don't touch anything else," he warned softly. "You need to call the police."

The word police was sure to get Jennifer's attention. She unwound partway from Bran's arms.

"I didn't do this."

Jennifer's tears flowed more easily than her words. As the girl blotted them with her sleeve, Em noticed fresh cuts on her hand. She looked around: the living room windows appeared to be intact.

"How did you get in?" Em demanded, heading for the kitchen and its more vulnerable door.

"I found a set of keys while I was here and kept it."

Em turned slowly. She was not at heart a violent person, else blood would have flowed. Even so, Jennifer paled and flattened against Bran whose arms tightened protectively around her.

"I'm sorry. I'm sorry! I wasn't thinking—I didn't remember I had keys until I needed them."

Jennifer cowered in Bran's embrace, the very image of terror. Emma was not impressed, but her stiff-lipped indignation was wasted on the girl whose eyes were tightly shut. She raised her voice instead.

"What did you need my keys for?"

"I thought I'd be safe here, that they couldn't touch me here the way they were touching me at Mom and Dad's."

"They? What *they*?"

"*Things*. Dark *things* with empty eyes. Bran's demons—"

"Don't give me that demon nonsense!"

Matt appeared beside Em; she'd momentarily forgotten he was in the room. He put his hand over hers, which she'd clenched into a fist. With a bit of pressure, he tried to guide her into the kitchen where she wouldn't be able to see Jennifer.

"Call the police," he urged.

Emma knew just enough about martial arts to know what Matt was trying to do. She freed herself by pretending to move where he wanted her to go. She would call the police; that was the right thing to do, but she wouldn't grant them the privilege of extracting Jennifer's confession.

"Why?"

"I didn't do this! I didn't!" Jennifer broke free of Bran and faced Em on her own strength. "All night last night at my parents' house, things were crashing around me. I was so scared . . . so scared. When the sun came up, I found my keys . . . I tried to get away in my car . . . but I couldn't. I couldn't drive my car; it wouldn't start. I didn't know what to do next, then I remembered seeing the keys to here in my duffle bag. I didn't remember picking them up; I just remembered how safe I felt when I was here, so I found them and started running. When I couldn't run anymore, I walked. I didn't stop until I got here—"

For Jennifer to walk that far, something had seriously frightened her.

"I let myself in. I found that note you left before—the one with your phone number on it? It was still in the bathroom. I knew I should call you, but I thought, somehow, if I made any noise, any noise at all, they'd find me again. I fell asleep, I didn't mean to—I meant to keep awake, but I was tired; I didn't sleep at all last night. I woke up when they found me. I hid over there—" Jennifer pointed at the sofa. "The gray cat came and hid with me. We held onto each other. It was like that Spielberg movie with the little girl and the television. *'They're here!'* They were here until a few minutes ago. They must've known Bran was coming."

Right.

Bran had described Jennifer hiding with Charm. He'd insisted that she was here at the Maisonettes. Which meant what? That both he and Jennifer were telling the truth? That they'd made Em the butt of a monstrous practical joke? That her home had been savaged by poltergeists?

"I don't believe you," Emma decided. "I can't."

Jennifer sobbed in Bran's arms.

"What more do you need, Miz Merrigan? You were wrong about everything. It's all the way I said it would be. Even the little cat."

Feeling suddenly weak, Emma sat down gingerly on the arm of the de-cushioned sofa. She took a slower inventory of the living room—the glass on her parents' wedding portrait had been shattered. Dad's face was intact, but Eleanor's had been blackened. And on the chair, sparkling with broken glass: her missing nightshirt.

She started to shiver and couldn't stop. For the third time, Matt suggested calling the police.

"Leave," Em whispered. "All of you, please leave now . . ."

Matt protested, "I can't leave you like this. You're shaking, your house is wrecked, you've got to call the police."

Emma clasped her hands together to stop the shaking. "There's nothing here for the police, Matt. Bran's wrong: there are no demons; he's been cursed instead. Please, *go.*"

She shouldn't have said that. They wouldn't leave—not until she'd explained about Eleanor's box, the book it contained, the dreams she'd had after reading it, and the missing—now found—nightshirt. She held it up while they watched. The dirt she'd so carefully preserved was gone as if she'd never tied a knot to hold it, but other, older stains were there. It was the proof she needed, but didn't want.

Bran hung on her words, nodding emphatically and muttering: *I knew. I just knew.* Matt asked questions, endless questions. She couldn't tell if he believed in curses or demons—he did stop insisting that Em call the police—but his curiosity had certainly been fully engaged. She'd never have gotten rid of him—or Bran Mongomery—if Jennifer hadn't made it abundantly clear that she wanted to be anywhere but in Emma Merrigan's living room.

Even so, Jennifer couldn't leave until Bran and Matt had righted the furniture and piled the books back on the empty shelves. Emma drew the line when Bran had tried to shake the broken glass out of her nightshirt.

"This is *my* home!" she complained from the verge of tears. "And I'll take care of it!"

It was after ten before the three of them had driven off. Em waited until the taillights disappeared, then bolted the door. Standing in the doorway between the hall and the living room, Em confirmed a growing suspicion that the disorder had been far greater than the damage, as if Bran's demons—Eleanor's persistent curse—had merely fired warning shots.

Em found Eleanor's black book—one of the men had shoved it back on the shelves without realizing what it was—and started reading.

Nine

Thirty-plus years earlier, in the depths of her sopho-more year, Emma had fought a desperate battle against Calculus 103—Differential Equations. She'd known from Day Two that the course would be the swan song of her math and science career and she'd claimed a C- victory only with the help of her roommate's boyfriend, Art Weiss. These days, Em doubted she would recognize a differential equa-tion, her roommate, or her roommate's boyfriend if any of them had leapt in front of her car, but Art's advice had stood the tests of time.

Read the problem, then put everything you think you know in one column beneath it and everything you don't know in a second column. Stare at it awhile, then read everything again, including your notes, and write down some more stuff.

Repeat until solved.

Sitting in the middle of the dirty carpet, Emma drew a line down the center of a blank sheet of paper and prepared to give Art's advice a try.

She'd have been more comfortable in her favorite chair. Spin and Charm weren't going to give her a moment's peace while she sat on the floor and her back wasn't too happy ei-ther, but three passes with the vacuum had failed to remove the glint from the chair's upholstery. The mere thought of sitting there made Em's legs itch through her jeans. She'd restored the bonsai tree to its unbroken soup bowl; she could glue the broken vase back together, take the damaged wedding portrait to a photographer for a restoration that would remove Eleanor entirely, even get new legs for her hallway chair, but she didn't imagine she'd ever get fear of broken glass out of her once-favorite chair.

Shoving Spin off her lap, Em wrote "What I know" atop the right-side column. Beneath it she listed what Bran called his demons and Eleanor would have called a curse. She added that he claimed they—or it—had been part of his life as far back as he could remember—as Emma's night terrors had been a part of hers.

Em knew as well, from both Bran and Jennifer, that she'd poked him between the ribs as he lay quietly on a bed. Jennifer had used a finger, but she'd been thinking about a knife. The young woman had blamed herself for the attack and wondered what had provoked her to thoughts of violence. Bran claimed he knew: he'd seen his demons swarm around her and had driven them off by beating his girlfriend up.

Emma had gotten involved nearly a day later when she'd found Jennifer sleeping in the stacks and, in an act as uncharacteristic as Jennifer's attack on Bran's ribs, brought her home. That night, Thursday night, Em had endured a night terror for the first time in many years and in its aftermath had dreamt of a wasteland and an ember that she'd first envisioned as a dog, then had driven away.

She drew a box around the word "dog." Did it belong in the "What I know" column or on the other side? The last few days made more sense when she subtracted reason and reality from the equation, but once she started doing that, was there any turning back? Did she have to accept what Eleanor had called her *wyrd*? Emma drew a horizontal line across the "What I know" column and labeled it "Friday."

Friday she'd taken Jennifer to the Blue House where the girl's room had been ransacked. Bran had seemed the logical suspect, though he'd denied the damage when he'd shown up outside the Maisonettes. And, of course, that brought Emma back to dogs. She'd heard a dog when she'd gone out to confront Bran Mongomery. Reason said it was a real dog, a mere coincidence, but she'd already removed reason and reality from her analysis.

There was something else about Friday. Emma made her first entry in the "What I don't know" column. If she hadn't had a second night terror at just the right time, she wouldn't have been downstairs, peeking past the drapes as Bran came down her street. What had sparked her terror? Were night terrors a weapon used against her, or were they her early warning defense against dogs, demons, and curses?

Em opened the black book and retrieved Eleanor's letter. *You were born with the power . . . It lay sleeping within you.* If, after subtracting reason, a daughter made a leap of faith and considered her mother an honest woman rather than a lunatic, then that daughter could think of Jennifer Hodden and Bran Mongomery as trip wires.

Until she'd crossed their paths, Emma hadn't done anything to attract unwanted attention. Meeting Jennifer had triggered the first night terror. Meeting Bran after the second had produced the box in the basement. A stubborn fragment of reason wanted to put the blame on Eleanor and her box, as if opening it were the root of Emma's troubles, but Eleanor's letter pointed in the opposite direction: *now you have been challenged by the enemy you are destined to defeat.*

Emma wouldn't be sitting on the floor making lists and rereading a letter from her mother if she hadn't gotten between that dog—that persistent curse—and its prey: Jennifer Hodden.

Em picked up her pen and made another entry in the "What I don't know" column. Who or what had grabbed her by the nape of the neck early Sunday morning? She underlined the question several times, then thought of another one: her nightshirt.

She'd examined it thoroughly as soon as Matt had driven off. There'd been no dirt, no stains, not even creases to mark where she'd made the knot. Try as she might, Em couldn't remember if she'd lost the nightshirt before or after her bruising rescue. Eleanor had written, *When the time is right, we shall meet as equals.* The time hadn't been right for a meeting between equals, but if her mother hadn't rescued her, then who had? It seemed, as Emma fine-combed her memory, that the voice she'd heard wasn't a woman's voice. But, again, neither was the mother-voice that had advised her—rescued her?—as far back as she could remember.

Em sat back to study her sheet of paper. It occurred to her that Art Weiss's method worked best when one knew from the start that the problem under examination had a single, correct solution. That wasn't the case with curses. Writing in the left-side column, Emma added: what else besides Bran's curse exists in the wasteland? She circled the question again and again, until her pen carved through the paper.

The black book was a handwritten book, deliberately organized, with many blank pages. Eleanor had taken great care with the India ink she'd used. There were no cross-outs, insertions, or other errors that Em had noticed and, as she flipped through the pages, it was tempting, if not reasonable, to think that Eleanor had transcribed it from some other book.

Where was my grandmother? Em wrote beneath the ink-rimmed hole of her previous question. If Em had inherited a *wyrd* from Eleanor, from whom had Eleanor inherited her dubious gift?

Eleanor's past was a complete mystery. When inevitable "Mother's Maiden Name" questions had appeared in doctor's offices and college application forms, Dad had said the answer was Smith; and he'd said it in a way that forbade additional questions.

Smith was a common surname, but odds were that it wasn't Eleanor's. There was an equally good chance she wasn't American. Dad had served as an artillery instructor. He spoke without affection about the long, hot Oklahoma summers, but he'd been stationed in Washington, D.C. and overseas, too. He'd taken pictures in Paris a week after it was liberated.

Up in Em's dresser there was an exquisitely monogrammed handkerchief. When he gave it to her, Dad said he'd bought it from a hungry woman on the Champs Elysees. The embroidered initials were "E" and "R." Years ago, Em had convinced herself that Dad and Eleanor's marriage had begun as an Audrey Hepburn-Cary Grant romance after he bought her a handkerchief.

Em remembered the wooden box in the basement and its wax-imprisoned letters. She remembered seeing stamps, but not whether they were American or French. Hoping that the letters would answer her left-column questions, or at least illuminate the empty pages of the black book, Em pushed Spin off her lap (again).

She was stiffer than she should have been—for some reason, sitting on the floor bothered her bruised neck—and latched on to the arms of her favorite chair to pull herself upright. Em's rump was at half-mast when insight stormed her thoughts. She fell back to the carpet with an embarrassing *thump.*

In the most trivial sense of the word, Em's chair had been

cursed. She couldn't look at the chair without thinking of broken glass.

Taking up the black book, Em pulled ribbons and riffled pages in search of a heading—*To Make a Safe Place*—she'd glimpsed before. The nostrum, once she'd found it, was simple: take a gold coin, Aqua Regia, and mercury; put them in a glass sphere and seal the sphere with pitch; then let the sphere absorb all the malign influences until the gold disappeared.

"No way," she muttered. She'd come perilously close to believing in magic, but thoughts of acid and toxic metals rallied her skepticism.

Even if she'd owned the ingredients she'd never combine them in a sealed glass sphere, unless she'd needed to make a bomb. But the *idea* of making a safe place had taken root in Emma's mind; she let her imagination play with it. Vampires weren't curses—at least vampires weren't mentioned in Eleanor's book—but garlic figured in some of the other nostrums and was surely safer than mercury. Silver, too. In fairy-tale magic, silver was often more valuable than gold.

Em found an old silver spoon in the junk drawer and polished it for the first time in years. Then she opened a jar of processed, minced garlic and carried both it and the spoon to her chair.

The cats watched closely and through their eyes Emma Merrigan saw herself. Nothing destroyed magic more completely than reflected silliness. She returned the garlic to her refrigerator and washed the spoon. The key to making a safe place wouldn't be found in Eleanor's book or kitchen rituals.

Em had found her own way before, through childhood, school, and marriages. She wasn't good at finding the easiest route or the shortest, but she usually got where she needed to go and she'd always survived.

Standing in front of the chair, she announced, "Mine. My chair. My home. My safe place," before sitting down.

It occurred to Emma, as she sat down, that there wasn't much difference between a safe place and a prison when you didn't know how to get out. She filled one sheet and then another of divided paper. It seemed that she'd used up all her insights. After an hour of frustration and futility, Em retrieved the wooden box from the basement and faced the challenge of extracting her mother's letters from their wax cocoon.

When Eleanor's candles had melted, their dark waxes had penetrated the stationery. The sheets were fused and tore more easily than they separated. With fingernails and kitchen knives she slowly freed the topmost letter. Its postage stamps were clearly American but most of the written words were lost. Here and there a sentence survived in an unfamiliar hand:

> *Pay no attention to the young woman's name. Once created, a curse is timeless. It persists in the soul, not the blood. . . .*
>
> *You will know the root when you find it, but, I caution you: a damaged mind cannot give rise to a curse of the third degree. If the woman you found in that village is as deranged as you describe, then look somewhere else for the root. She was only a pawn. Her death freed the curse; it did not create it. . . .*
>
> *The curse may be timeless, but its root is not. . . .*
>
> *It is well and good to follow your heart, my dear, but you must know something about the past!*

The word *Nonsense!* in her mother's hand stretched across one margin and *the heart knows!* filled the other. Mother and daughter had one thing in common: they'd been difficult pupils.

Em went up to the backroom in search of a jewelry box as old as the letters. She'd just found it when Spin rocketed up the stairs, yowling all the way. He usually reserved that amount of rage and terror for visits to the vet.

"Knock it off!" she shouted as the black cat vanished into her unlit bedroom.

On the off chance that he'd hurt himself, Em went to investigate. She'd just turned the light on when Charm shot between her legs. At least Em thought it was Charm who disappeared beneath the bed—she'd never seen her gray cat move so fast or fluff out so large.

"What's wrong with you two?"

Spin and Charm chased ghosts and got chased in return, but not both at the same time and not upstairs. When her cats hid, they hid in the basement.

With the jewelry box still clutched in her hand, Em returned to the living room. There was no earthly reason for her heart to be doing double-time. The lights were on. The house was calm and quiet. The wax-saturated letter was where she left it, the book, the wooden box, even the open newspaper where she'd whittled the wax were each exactly as she'd left them. Her bookshelves had not miraculously restored themselves into alphabetical order, nor did any of the books launch themselves as Emma stood at the foot of the stairs gaping at them.

She thought she felt a draft at the center of the room. She checked the doors—front and back; closed and locked. A draft no worse than usual flowed out of the cat-sized opening in the basement door. Em tapped the thermostat for a shot of heat. The furnace rumbled to life and sent warm air wafting.

False alarm.

Cats could stay under the bed, sleeping off a bout of temporary insanity. Humans—cursed with consciousness—were left to pant and wonder when the next panic attack would occur. Tomorrow, Em promised herself, tomorrow she'd call her doctor. If she wasn't losing her mind, maybe she was having a heart attack.

In the meantime, it was nearly midnight. Her cats had tracked wax flakes across the carpet. She hadn't finished cleaning up from the early-evening excitement. And it was still Monday, with four more workdays lined up like an obstacle course.

Em picked up the phone. She had hours upon hours of personal time banked with Human Resources and while a messy house and vague anxiety probably weren't on the university's official list of emergencies, she had sufficient seniority to burn a Tuesday without giving any explanation at all.

After identifying herself to the Human Resources voice-mail system, Emma recited her name and employee number before explaining, "I won't be in tomorrow, Tuesday. Put me down for personal time. I'll be back on Wednesday."

A robotic voice advised her to wait for a confirmation number. Em took a deep breath and noticed her distorted reflection in the brass table lamp. She also noticed a layer of dust on the lamp and that the metal needed polishing.

Then she noticed something large moving behind her.

Out of nowhere, a strange man had entered her living room. Dark-haired and unshaven, he was costumed for one of Shakespeare's muddier histories, complete with a knee-length chain mail shirt and a yard-long sword hanging at his side.

"Who—?" she began and he drew the blade from its scabbard.

The sound of sliding steel was breathtakingly real, as was Emma's view of the sharp, shiny blade her unwelcome visitor leveled at her heart.

You're out of time, he said without moving his lips.

The sword came closer. Em took a step backward. She

should have tripped over the telephone table; instead she found herself in unexpected but not unfamiliar twilight darkness. The stranger lunged after her and in the grip of instincts she hadn't known she possessed, Em dove sideways. She eluded the sword, rolled across her shoulders, and—miraculously—back onto her feet.

For a moment they stared at each other, would-be murderer and would-be victim. Instincts seized Emma Merrigan a second time and she ran for her life. The chain-mail shirt clattered and must have slowed the stranger down or she couldn't have stayed ahead of him. Em was a walker, not a runner, never a brawler—though something very like the mother-voice told her to stand her ground and strike back.

The first time she'd come here, whether in reality or a dream, Em had fought a whirling curse with fire. She imagined a wake of flames flowing from her hair, engulfing her pursuer, but the magic didn't work that way. This time she had no magic, no light whatsoever. The light by which Em ran, cast her shadow in front of her. That shadow grew darker as the man and his sword cut her lead.

He swung the sword; the sound of a steel wind, though Emma had never heard it before, was unmistakable. Like a runner at the finish line, she threw herself forward. She was still alive when she hit the ground but that wouldn't last long. The luminous warrior with his stubbled chin and bowl-cut hair towered above her with his sword in both hands and straight up over his head.

There wasn't time to plead for her life—and perhaps that was for the best. As the sword descended, Em surrendered not to fear, but to outrage. The magic that had failed moments earlier burst out of her with sound and force. White fire enveloped the warrior; his screams were pleasing to Emma's ears and she expected him to fall in char-broiled pieces to the ground. But her fury did not consume him. He turned and ran, as she had run from him.

Em was in darkness as she got to her feet. In this place, she realized, doubt and fear were darkness, so she told herself that she wasn't afraid. Her belief was thin, and so was the light that flickered around her, but it was enough to get her moving again. With each stride she took along the warrior's retreat, Emma's belief grew stronger, her light grew brighter, and the distance between them shortened. He cast away his sword. Em heard it bounce, then it was lost in the darkness. She wouldn't have known what to do with a sword anyway. In an environment where thought became action, Emma Merrigan put her faith in a simple desire to annihilate the enemy who'd tried to kill her.

She believed that lightning could pass from her fingertips to his metal-sheathed torso and it happened. She imagined him spinning around to face her as raw destruction danced over his metal shirt and that happened too.

Em imagined that she'd vanquished a persistent curse and a new force arose in the wasteland between her and her enemy. Suddenly, it was like being north-pole to north-pole with a world-sized magnet. One moment their eyes were locked—she'd know that face forever—the next they were flying away from each other.

Em heard a single word, *idiot,* which might have come from her own mouth, the instant before she landed on her back. She didn't lose consciousness; no gaps erupted in her memory and she never lost a sense of who she was in her mind. It was her body that Em had lost touch with. She could see puffy clouds and blue sky overhead and tall, leafy green trees—not Bower, at least not Bower in November—but when she turned her head, she saw only grass and dirt, nothing at all that looked like her arm or hand.

Her mind's sense of her body was intact. Emma could feel the weight of her arm when she swept it through the grass. The grass, though, didn't ripple and she couldn't feel it either. And as clearly as Em remembered landing on her back—as much as her view of the sky confirmed that impression—she couldn't feel the ground and had no leverage for sitting up.

She closed her eyes, thinking that might sharpen her other senses, and quickly realized that she'd made a mistake. Without visual cues, her mind was lost in total vertigo. If she'd had a body, she would have turned it inside out with vomiting. A seeming eternity passed before Emma got her eyes open again.

Her perspective had changed in ways both subtle and profound. All her bodily sensations had returned—the problem was that the body wasn't hers. Em found herself surrounded by the thoughts and flesh of an Eddie-weese or Eddie-war or Eddie-win; and Eddie-whatever was a young man. His mind was the ultimate nightclub—all flashing images and over-amped lyrics. She caught his mood, which was both fearful and murderous, then recognized the dark-haired face that dominated his thoughts.

As Emma steeped in a stew of thoughts and emotions, she pieced together that Eddie was hiding, waiting, and planning a deadly ambush against the same warrior Em had confronted in the wasteland. Did that make Eddie the man who uttered the curse that put the dark-haired man in Emma's living room or was he the curse's first prey?

It wasn't easy but through concentration Emma could keep her own thoughts collected and recall the black book pages where Eleanor had written about bonding and killing curses at their root. Her determination to destroy the wasteland warrior had somehow transported her into a young man's mind. Em couldn't begin to explain how such an exchange might have happened. Then again, she couldn't explain how flour, water, and yeast became bread and that had never stopped her from loading up her bread machine each Sunday night.

She concentrated on the book and letters she'd left behind, trying to extract greater detail from her memories. *The curse is timeless; the root is not . . . the root is not . . .*

Insight seemed within Em's grasp when the disco-chaos grew deadly quiet. Eddie didn't open up a thousand eyes or shoot bolts of mental lightning through his mind; nonetheless, he'd become aware of an invader—of her—and meant to oust her. Emma didn't blame him; she would have done the same thing.

Em imagined herself back in her own body, her own living room, and remained enmeshed in Eddie's thoughts. She imagined herself small and harmless, but the harder she tried, the more hostile Eddie's mind became. There must be a trick to unbonding and the trick must be written on another page. Emma vowed to find that page when she got home—

Thoughts of her Maisonette's living room were the most toxic imagery Emma had yet generated in Eddie's mind. He deafened her with words she couldn't quite understand and blinded her with images of bearded, axe-wielding men.

Emma had braced herself for catastrophe when a twig snapped.

Eddie's attention refocused between heartbeats. His mind became leaves and branches, and he had the feel of a trusted weapon in his right hand. The young man—Eddie *felt* young—might banish doubts and invaders with images of men armed with long-handled axes, but he planned to kill with a sword.

Moments after the twig had snapped, the woods echoed sound that even Em recognized as horses and clinking metal. A painfully bright sphere took shape in Eddie's thoughts and a dark-haired man, with a familiar face, took shape within the sphere. This time there was a name— O'dough or O'days; Em couldn't be certain and not merely because Eddie's thoughts blared in a language that wasn't twentieth-century English. The dark-haired man was a for-

eigner as well as an enemy. In Eddie's mind, O'days was a
word to curse with.

A second figure loomed in the light of Eddie's mind: a
woman, blonde and beautiful; a sister, a whore, and a traitor.
Em had barely begun to sort out the nuances when riders
hove into view.

Not O'days . . . Not O'days . . . The first rider wasn't
O'days, but another man of the bastard . . .

Eddie seethed with hatred for the bastard who had destroyed everything that Eddie cherished, especially his sister. Emma assumed that O'days was the bastard in question.
Her assumption seeped into Eddie's awareness and was ven-
omously rejected: the bastard himself had never come to
Sheepsie—the best rendering Em could give to the name
Eddie gave to his home. The bastard had sent a man whose
name eluded Em completely and that man had sent O'days.
She saw them all, like flashbulbs firing at night.

O'days was the one Eddie hated most of all. O'days was
the one who'd ruined his sister. And O'days was the one he
intended to kill, any moment now, once he emerged from the
woodland shadows.

And emerge O'days did, looking exactly as he'd looked
in Emma's living room. Inevitably, irresistibly, she made another assumption: Eddie would get the vengeance he craved
for his sister's dishonor and, in the process, spawn the persistent curse that tormented Bran Mongomery.

Shouting an oath that had something to do with dogs and
the devil, Eddie burst out of the bushes. He'd drawn his
sword and held it before him. The blade was horizontal, not
vertical, the better, Em supposed, to pierce between a man's
ribs.

She was appalled by that bit of inspiration, and also inspired—if she could hijack Eddie's muscles she might not
only change the course of history in a forest clearing, she
might change it in a Midwestern university town. She didn't

need to seize control of Eddie's arms or legs; a wrist, or even a few fingers should be sufficient.

If she could seize control of anything.

Eddie had already halved the distance between his hiding place and O'days. The dark-haired man's jaw hung open with disbelief. Emma believed her intervention was O'days' only possible hope for survival—and a faint hope at that. Try as she might, she couldn't take control of Eddie's weakest finger.

Then, as she and Eddie watched through his eyes, O'days drew his sword and swung it down to meet their charge. Emma screamed and there was a chance—things happened so fast that she couldn't be sure—that Eddie had hesitated when she did. Steel circled steel without contact and Em thought the fight was over.

She was wrong.

Eddie sprang back then thrust again, beneath O'days' motionless sword, and it seemed to Emma that the dark-haired warrior was doomed. All around her Eddie's mind celebrated a victory. The young man didn't see what Em saw through his eyes: a move of unthinkable strength and agility as O'days beat Eddie's sword aside with a leather-gloved fist and swung his own like an axe at Eddie's unprotected neck.

Em—far calmer than she had any right to be—knew what had to happen next, but knowledge wasn't enough when Eddie's mind darkened swiftly. There were no bursts of pain or regret: Eddie's eyes were fixed on O'days' horrified face when his vision, and life, came to an end. He'd used his last breath for a curse.

Emma had no time to digest what she'd experienced. She was falling through darkness again and praying that she'd land in her living room. It would be a hard landing. To the extent that Em was aware of her speed, she seemed to be accelerating. Then she began to spin and the spinning, too, grew faster until she couldn't hold onto her thoughts.

*   *   *

One moment there was nothing, the next Em was herself again. She lay in darkness, but not utter darkness. A faint glow surrounded her, as if her body produced light as well as heat. A brighter but gentle light shone near her feet. With neither thought nor effort, Em sat up to get a better view. She recognized the wasteland, but not the self-illuminated man sitting in front of her. Like O'days, he was dark-haired and costumed for Shakespeare, but the resemblance ended there.

"You are no wiser than before, madame, but bolder still. That is very foolish." He spoke English with a faint, unplaceable accent. "Do you think I have nothing better to do than rescue fools?"

Em wasn't fool enough to answer that question. He looked at her with evident dismay and she replied with her snake-eyes stare, taking his measure, inch by critical inch.

As her inspection progressed, Em changed her mind: he'd stepped out the pages of Dumas' *The Three Musketeers* where he'd been playing the part of elegant Aramis. Only the heights of fashion could have produced such an absurd appearance. The musketeer's shoulder-length dark hair fell in tangled corkscrews that were too thick to be entirely natural. His coat was an extravagance of cuffs, colors, gold braid, and yards of lace. His pants were best described as baggy, beribboned shorts worn over dark stockings that were rolled and gartered around his knees. His hat, which rested in his lap, had the better part of a peacock spilling from its wide, lacy brim.

"Well, madame? Have I met with your approval?"

"If you rescued me, I'm grateful. But I don't recall asking

for your help and I imagine I'd have landed somewhere sooner or later."

He smiled, a pleasant smile without malice. "Yes, yes—everywhere is somewhere, sooner or later, isn't it? The challenge is to find the right where, the right when. I think you are not ready for that challenge, madame. You should stay closer to your home until you know how to find it again."

Emma wouldn't argue with good advice, but beyond that, she was speechless. Eleanor's black book hadn't mentioned allies, only curses and enemies. She could believe the glowing man had rescued her without for an instant trusting him.

"I do what I have to do. I haven't had the luxury of doing what I should." Em stalled for time. Recreating the rage she'd felt as O'days had chased her across this bleak landscape wasn't easy, but she'd do it, if she had to, and—just to test herself—Em summoned up a bit of anger.

Aramis narrowed his eyebrows and Em was locked in fire and stone. The sensation lasted a moment, or less, and left only a faint impression in her memory. But that was enough to warn Emma that her rescuer was both more subtle and more powerful than O'days had been.

"It is of no great concern to me, madame, that you cannot distinguish a friend from an enemy. I have no wish to hurt you, but do not imagine that you can hurt me. Your ways are crude, your means are weak; you would not have a prayer of success."

Em found her voice: "What are you?"

"Easier to say what I'm not: I'm not what you'd call a curse and I'm not quite what you'd call a man."

Wonderful. In that case, it scarcely mattered whether Emma believed or trusted him. She tried a different question. "You say you rescued me . . . why?"

He shrugged and seemed very French. "A little mouse chases a lion. Why aid the lion? Why not aid the mouse?"

Em thought of the black book, which supposedly contained everything she'd need to know. She wondered if Eleanor had encountered anyone like Aramis. "So, I'm a mouse. And a fool."

"Also bold and brave. That is more important. We fear so much to lose our battles, we forget that we are only supposed to win them, not survive them. You . . . do what you have to do. I salute you, Madame Mouse."

Emma felt her cheeks grow warm—God only knew what that meant here. She turned away. "Don't get your hopes up too high. You were right the first time: I have no idea what I'm doing here. I really can't distinguish a friend from an enemy—" She forced a laugh. "I don't even know who 'we' are. And, to be honest, I'm not too sure about 'them' either. I think I came in through the back door."

"There is no back door for au-delà, madame."

Em dusted off her French to translate au-delà as the beyond, the outback, the frontier, or no man's land. She was pleased to have deduced something on her own. Her gut instinct was that she could learn more about us, them, and au-delà from Aramis than she'd ever get from Eleanor's book, though that was certainly damning them both with faint praise.

"I sure didn't get here the way I was supposed to," she said after Aramis said nothing for several moments. "If I was supposed to come here at all. I've got one lousy book at home, a lifetime of night terrors, and a couple of kids with big-time problems. Some costume-drama warrior showed up in my living room and tried to kill me—he was the lion this mouse was chasing. Next thing I knew, I was inside the head of another mouse who thought he could kill the lion, but got himself killed instead—" Without intent, Emma relived the moment of Eddie's death. She remembered only what had happened, not how it had felt. Even so, she shuddered and lost her voice for a moment. "If you can explain that to me, then I will be forever in your debt."

"This is not a place to speak of forever, madame, but I can explain a little: It is written that God created man in His own image—"

Em recoiled; she couldn't stop herself. Never mind that she'd been chasing curses, an explanation that began with Genesis grated on her Darwinian nerves. She stifled the reaction as quickly and casually as she could, but the damage had been done.

"I see you are not a believer. Very well, the truth does not care what you believe. For me, it is enough to know that we are the very image of Our Heavenly Father and that hidden deep within our souls is the moment of Creation. We are meant to use that power to seek His grace, but we are weak. Sometimes we mistake His power for our own and sometimes—never wisely—we let that power escape and a curse is created."

"And where do you or I fit into this divine plan?" she asked caustically.

"You and I are no part of His plan, madame. We are *here*, in man's Creation, trying to undo what man has done."

"Vanquish all the curses, go to heaven, sit somewhere near the right hand of God, the Father Almighty? I know the tune, I can fake the lyrics, but I'm afraid I don't believe a word of them."

Aramis succumbed to one of those *You'll learn* smiles parents should never bestow on their children. "Madam, I do not—"

Summer lightning brightened the wasteland beyond his right shoulder; a roar like thunder followed close behind. The man in lace, feathers, and excessive embroidery sprang to his feet in an apparently effortless bound. He offered Emma his hand.

"Come, madame. We cannot remain here."

With thoughts of frying pans and fires echoing inside her skull, Em grasped his hand. She expected him to stand firm while she hauled herself upright, but he pulled while she pushed. Excess momentum carried her into his chest. For someone who'd described himself as "not quite a man" he had all the usual attributes of manliness: texture, warmth, pulse, and an eminently believable gasp of surprise as he backed ever so slightly away.

"Quickly, madame. We must find your back door. I do not suppose you know which way it lies?"

"Not a clue," Em agreed. "What are we running from?"

"We have attracted attention—or say that I have attracted it. I have more enemies than I can count."

He took Em's hand and led her away at a jog-trot that seemed effortless for him, despite those ridiculous shoes, but proved exhausting for her. They'd heard two more thunderbolts at the beginning of their flight, nothing since. Em pulled free and staggered to a halt. She bent at the waist and let her head hang.

"I thought I was in decent shape," she complained between heaving breaths.

"Better than others of your time."

Remember that, Em told herself. One would think she'd be unable to forget a single moment in this dark environment, but it was bizarre, like a dream, and just as elusive.

"Quickly, madame. They still have our scent in their noses."

Dogs again, the wasteland was filled with dogs. Em straightened, felt dizzy, and slumped again, shaking her head. "Not another step."

"Are you quite certain?"

"Quite." Her exhaustion was getting worse, not better.

"Then we have come to your proper place in time."

Em looked questions at Aramis rather than waste breath with words.

"Poor shadow that it may be of His creation, au-delà is also timeless, limitless in all directions. But we are His creation, not our own. For every living man, there is a time and limit, a direction in which you can go just so far and not one step farther. We have come to that place which, I devoutly hope, is yours. Make a hole here, and you will pick up the strands of your life, exactly as you left them."

"Wonderful. Sounds great. So, where's the shovel?"

Her attempt at humor fell flat as a third thunderbolt thumped the dark ground behind them. The flash was intense and the sound nearly simultaneous. Em figured she knew what that meant and so did Aramis.

Without warning, he wrapped Emma in a passionate embrace—if sheer surprise were all she needed to return to Bower, odds were that she would have been there before her eyes popped open. But it had been too long since a man had swept Em off her feet. Trust him or not, she didn't want to let go.

If she'd felt any resistance, any hesitation, then she would have backed away. There was only a similar, cautious opportunism: arms tightened, fingers spread apart and pressed inward, heads turned slowly until cheeks, then lips, were together.

When the lightning came again, it tore them apart.

Emma screamed, "Who are you? What is your name?" but by then she was alone, on the living room carpet, staring at a sunlit ceiling.

Ten

Cautiously and methodically, Emma tested her muscles. This business of falling—literally—asleep and waking up on the floor was getting to be a habit. She'd been lucky, except for a bruised neck which, strictly speaking, hadn't been the result of a fall. She was lucky still: although she'd landed in a twisted awkward sprawl on the living room carpet, Em hadn't damaged either the furniture or herself. And her clothes were intact, seriously wrinkled, but each in its customary place, right down to her shoes.

The phone handset lay beside Em's head. It was dead silent. She remembered calling in for personal time and O'days appearing behind her. Raising her head, Em checked for whatever damage *he* might have left behind. Given that the room had been a mess before, it wasn't worse by sunlight.

Spin and Charm, who had a sixth or seventh sense about such things, trotted out of their hiding places to see if the order of the universe—in the form of breakfast—was about to be restored. Em sat up and gave them both a good ear-scratch before she tried standing. Her stomach churned, reminding her that she'd never gotten her Apples-and-Oranges supper. Simple hunger, nothing more or less, set the room spinning when she stood, and it passed quickly.

The VCR clock read 10:17. Emma guessed she'd lain on the floor for about nine hours. Whether she'd dreamt her most recent misadventures in the wasteland and beyond, or if they'd been what the psychic fringe called "Out of Body Experiences," she should have had time for a decent night's sleep in between them. Em didn't feel particularly rested but maybe that would change after she'd eaten.

Em returned the handset to its cradle, fed the cats, and stood in front of the open refrigerator. She drank the last of her cranberry juice. Sugar was nice, but her body craved complex carbohydrates and protein. Breakfast wasn't a meal Emma usually ate. She found a dust-covered jar of peanut butter on the top shelf of the pantry and smeared a chunky-style layer on a slice of Sunday's robotic bread.

Her tongue was firmly glued to the roof of her mouth when the phone rang.

Emma was never home on Tuesday mornings so the call couldn't be from anyone she wanted to talk to. She let the answering machine deal with it while she took another bite. Peanut butter—food in general—had never tasted so good.

"Hi, Em—"

She recognized Nancy's voice. Her friend sounded cheerful, without the solemn undercurrent that invariably accompanied bad news.

"I know you're not there. I wanted you to know that I called respite-care. They must get lots of calls like mine; they knew just what to say to handle my guilt before it got out of control . . . And they said they'd have a bed for Wednesday night through Monday. I'm taking Mother over this afternoon and driving up tomorrow morning—"

That made no sense. Em abandoned her balanced breakfast. She grabbed the phone during Nancy's suggestion that they meet for lunch.

"Sounds great, Nance—but today's Tuesday!"

They laughed and Nancy confessed that the last few

weeks had been more exhausting than she'd admitted on Sunday. Katherine was confused most of the time.

"It's gotten so I don't know who I am half the time. Sometimes Mother's so convinced I'm her sister Mary that it's easier to just go along with her. This morning she thought it was Sunday and wanted to know why we weren't going to church. I'm afraid, Em: if I'm gone for a week, I won't come back . . . I don't want to put her in a home."

Nancy's dilemma was a bucket of cold water on Emma's overheated imagination. Curses, ghosts, and musketeers with extravagant hats seemed unimportant—*were* unimportant—when parent and child exchanged roles.

"You do what you can, then you do what you must," Em said—as Nancy had said to her in February when Dad, not Katherine, had been the parent in decline.

The line carried silence until Nancy asked the obvious question: why was Em at home on a Tuesday?

"It finally happened: I lost my grip on reality," Em joked. "And I needed to take a day off to find it again."

Nancy wasn't fooled and Nancy remembered Em's careful abridgement of the weekend's events. "Did you black out again? You need to be more careful, Em—especially around this time of year."

It occurred to Emma as she sat in her chair, staring at Eleanor's black book, that her best friend thought she'd started drinking. God knew she wouldn't have been the first woman who solved the what-do-I-do-with-the-rest-of-my-life problem with alcohol. In many ways, that would have been simpler. She could have stopped drinking or taking pills.

"It's not the time of year, at least I don't think it is." True, Em had found Eleanor's box while putting away her Christmas decorations, but the pending holidays and mournful thoughts weren't the reason she'd been in the basement. "I've been having trouble sleeping; my life's gotten strange."

Emma wouldn't lie, not to Nancy; their friendship went deeper than that. She confessed that the strangeness had started when she discovered a young woman sleeping in the library stacks. But when Nancy echoed Matt Barto's assumption that compassion was dangerous and inexcusably reckless, Em began editing again. She omitted Bran entirely and attributed her close encounters of the irrational kind to the box she'd found in the basement.

"This isn't about Dad being gone," Em concluded. "This is Eleanor. And the wonder of it is: I didn't think I cared."

There was wisdom in the advice Emma had given Jennifer: sometimes you really didn't know what was on your mind until you put it on your tongue. She'd let herself go angry with anger and grief because she did care. Em had never stopped caring and she was glad there was no one to see her blotting tears with her sleeve.

Nancy didn't need eyes. "How can you say that, Em? I'll never forget the day you found out she hadn't died when you were a baby. You were so angry! I've never seen you like that. You told your dad to take their wedding picture off the wall or you'd never go home again."

Em grimaced in astonishment. "I don't remember that. I remember going to Dad's office and asking him if it was true. I was angry with him—that was only natural, but I don't remember saying anything about that picture. He never took it down. I thought I realized pretty quick that Dad wasn't to blame."

"Maybe he wasn't to blame, but you were furious with her. You called me up and we tore your house apart looking for anything Eleanor might have left behind. And you started talking about moving to New York City. You wanted to transfer to Columbia. Your dad was worried; he agreed you should get out of Bower, but Columbia was way too radical for his taste. I always thought that's what you saw in Rob—he'd get you to New York."

"Dad talked to you about me?" Bad enough she didn't remember the tantrum, but Dad and Nancy conspiring about her, and Nancy thinking that about her and Rob for all these years?

"He talked to my folks, and Mother talked to me—you know, one of those 'we wouldn't ask you to break a promise to a friend, but this is very important' conversations. The kind I swore that I'd never have with Katy or Alyx, and you know I did. God, the things we pass along . . ."

And the things the closest of friends didn't share until thirty-odd years after the fact. "Did Katherine say anything about Eleanor? They must have known each other."

Nancy chuckled. "No, but nothing was enough. If you can't say something nice, say nothing at all: that was Mother's motto and no one could say nothing louder than her—"

Em abandoned the increasingly uncomfortable subject. "When will you be getting in on Thursday?"

"If I get away by seven, and I should be able to, I'll be in Bower a little after noon."

"I'll take the afternoon off. Where shall we meet?"

"Apples and Oranges? John says they've got a new menu that everyone's raving about."

"Apples and Oranges it is." Maybe this time she'd get to eat.

They talked a bit longer, until Emma heard Katherine swearing a blue streak in the background. It would be good to have her friend-sister back in town, if only for a few days. They each needed someone to talk to.

Peanut butter beckoned. Em opened the drapes on a bright, windy morning and finished her breakfast while the sun chased clouds through the sky. She concentrated on Nancy's problems and what consolation or advice she should be prepared to give, but her thoughts wandered back to Eleanor, the black book, the wasteland, and the forest where she'd felt a man die.

Could even that be hung on some psychologically twisted variation of post-traumatic stress? Some need to punish herself with mystery and terror? Could hysteria account for Aramis, too?

Em remembered his impulsive kiss. If hysteria had invaded her life, why couldn't it be exciting and romantic? Emma could think of several reasons, most of them rooted in the notion that when a middle-aged woman became infatuated with her own imagination she also became the most pathetic stereotype under the sun.

It was high time, Emma chided herself as she washed the dishes, to pull herself together, to seal the last few days behind a "do not open" door in her memory. There were clothes wrinkling in the dryer and wax shavings cat-tracked up the stairs. Her backyard could do with a few bags of winter mulch. The cats' litter box needed cleaning and so did her computer's hard drive.

Em took care of the litter box—the most critical chore on her list—but breakfast hadn't filled her with energy. Picking up the threads of responsibility would have to wait until she'd had a nap. Taking a long, steamy shower before she took that nap sounded delightful and felt even better.

Emma was damp, naked, and thoroughly relaxed when she crawled into bed. In the quiet, drawn-drapes darkness, she relived that last moment in the wasteland. Everything else, even Eddie's death, was flat and sterile compared to Aramis. If she'd dreamt him, she'd never dreamt a more vivid or tactile dream.

Charm stomped off in feline disgust as Em rearranged her pillow for the fourth or fifth time, but no amount of fussing pushed her over the line into sleep. She'd rather lie there, like some schoolgirl mooning over her first kiss, and was deep in fantasy when the phone rang.

Em was naked and the downstairs drapes were wide open. No way was she going to race downstairs to intercept the message. No way at all. The ringing stopped; a hang-up, she thought, someone trying to sell her something . . . but no, she heard a voice, faint but clear—

"Em! Are you there? Are you okay?"

A man's voice . . . Matt Barto's voice. She hadn't left a message for him and he, bless his pointed little head, didn't know anyone on her floor well enough to ask if she'd called in sick. Well, a little frustration was good for the soul.

"Em! Pick up your phone, Auntie Em. Pick it up or I'm coming over to see if you're dead or alive. Do you hear me? Pick up the damn phone! Merle Acalia Merrigan, pick—!"

Emma reached for the emergency phone by her bed. "Don't—" Electronic feedback fried her ears. Matt shouted something about the star key. She tapped it and the squealing stopped.

"Em? Em is that you?"

"Yes, it's me. Nothing's wrong. I was up way past midnight and I decided to take the day off!"

"That was yesterday, Em. Tuesday. Today's Wednesday! It's past noon and we're about ready to send out the Saint Bernards."

"It's Tuesday," she protested, but with fading conviction. Could she have been out that long? And Nancy. She'd convinced Nancy that it was Tuesday. Dear God, what had she done to Nancy and Katherine?

"Em? Are you still there?"

"Yeah, I'm still here. You're absolutely certain it's Wednesday?"

"It's Wednesday, Em. Turn on the television, your computer, check your mail, or look for a newspaper, if you don't believe me. What happened? What *else* happened? You don't sound so good."

"I'm okay. I lost a day, that's all—"

That's all? What was she saying? Healthy people—sane people—didn't lose a day out of their lives. Amnesia was a myth of movie directors and novelists. It didn't happen to real people unless something was seriously wrong. It didn't just happen once and go away nicely as you please.

"Tell everyone I'll be there in a half hour. If I don't keel over from embarrassment first."

"You're sure? You don't sound good. What do you mean 'lost a day?' "

Matt's parents were both drinkers. His meaning couldn't have been clearer if his tongue were a neon light. Emma didn't have the energy or time to waste in an argument.

"I seem to have slept the clock around and then some, so, naturally, I'm dead tired right now."

"Easy there! Look, we can talk at lunch—"

Matt wasn't going to back down; he wasn't a gentleman. A gentleman would have said *As you wish, madame.* Em covered her face with her unoccupied hand: her French musketeer was all over her imagination.

She shivered violently and realized she was frightened—not the pumped adrenaline fright of her night terrors or intrigue of magic, but a cold fear rooted in guts and organs. Staying alive, staying healthy wasn't just a question of taking reasonable care of herself anymore. Natural causes had entered the picture: tumors, cancer, toxic waste and poison. An exotic virus eating its selective way through her brain . . .

That had been Jennifer's fear too.

"I'll be working through once I get in." A single slice of bread with peanut butter wouldn't be enough. She'd have to make lunch . . . and deal with her damp hair. She didn't want to face her co-workers looking half-dead or hung over. Embarrassment again. "Look Matt—there's really nothing to talk about but if you're going out for lunch, pick me up something—a sandwich, a burger, whatever and leave it on my desk. I've got to get moving. Thanks for calling. God knows how long I would have slept."

Of course, Em hadn't slept much at all, that was her problem . . . the least of her problems. Her judgment and concentration were shot, to say nothing of her self-confidence.

"You the BLT type or ham and cheese?"

"Ham and cheese."

The conversation ended with Matt's promise to leave a ham-and-cheese sandwich on her desk. Em tugged the bed into shape on her way to the hall. Double-mint toothpaste and a blast from her hair dryer worked miracles. Except for weariness and a fading bruise on her neck, she really didn't feel too bad for a person whose mind was rotting away.

Emma scuffed yesterday's—*Monday's*—clothes out of the way and belatedly noticed the stains covering the back of her blouse. Closer examination revealed a fine, black powder ground into the fibers, consistent—as the police might say—with her memory of the parched-mud soil of the wasteland. In moves that were equal parts recklessness and caution, she sniffed, then touched the tip of her tongue to the largest stain.

It wasn't cocoa; it might have been charcoal; and more than that she couldn't say. The university had a materials science department and it had the equipment to analyze anything down to its subatomic structure. Em ordered their books, knew their names, and might be able to negotiate some tests. Careful to protect the stains, she folded the blouse and left it beside the computer in the backroom. Then, with time wasting, Em grabbed fresh separates from her closet.

Spin and Charm sat on the wax-chip covered newspaper in the middle of the floor. Their identical expressions warned that they did not approve of the mess she was leaving behind and that they'd make it their own before she returned.

"Behave!" she chided before fleeing to her car.

Emma had hoped to slip into her office without fanfare; she should have known better. Co-workers she scarcely knew accosted her on the way to the elevator. Matt hadn't been kidding about the Saint Bernards—he must have hit up everyone in the library when she hadn't made it in this morning. Her reception was worst with the people she knew best, starting with Betty who'd already fielded the first round of calls with Human Resources.

"I forgot to turn the alarm back on," she explained to Betty, knowing that others were listening. "So it didn't go off and I overslept and overslept. I must've had a twenty-four hour virus without knowing."

"Likely story!" Betty laughed. "The only virus you had was in your computer. You can't fool us, your line was busy. You were surfing the Internet the whole time."

Em didn't argue; the Internet was better than alcohol and they'd never guess the truth.

Then Betty handed her a form emblazoned with the university seal. "I need that back before you go home tonight."

She scanned it: The Friends of the Library were collecting donations for this year's holiday bazaar. Every year, for more years than Em cared to count, she'd made patchwork animals for the children's table. Usually she had a half dozen done by now; this year she'd forgotten completely. She wanted to say no, that she'd skip this year's festivities, but everyone would think she was depressed. They'd point to today as proof. Betty's face already wore *the look*.

"No problem." Her stomach tied itself in a knot. "I'll get them to you by—" she scanned the letter, looking for a date. "The fifth."

Dear God, her fingertips would be hamburger if she tried to make a dozen patchwork animals between now and the fifth, but all the other options were worse. Emma folded the paper between her fingers and forged ahead to her office.

There was no sign of Matt or a ham-and-cheese sandwich when she got there. If she was honest with herself, Em missed Matt more than the sandwich. As discomforting as her fascination with the much younger man could be, it was a lot better than catching herself thinking about Aramis . . . again.

Thoroughly disgusted with herself, Em sipped stale, cold coffee from a half-empty mug and fired up her computer. There were messages everywhere. She started with the ones stuck to her monitor. When the largest fires were out, she mended fences with Human Resources and made arrangements to take Thursday—tomorrow!—afternoon off. Betty offered to walk the stacks for her when she explained that she was meeting her friend Nancy for lunch; Em accepted the offer.

Matt was waiting in her side chair when Em returned from Betty's desk. He brandished two objects wrapped in white wax-paper..

"Westphalian ham, Swiss cheese, mustard, mayo, on a Kaiser roll—for that vaguely German taste. But, for the *real* ham-and-cheese experience: prosciutto and provolone, bell peppers, and a splash of olive oil. Take your pick."

Em took the Kaiser as she sat. "How much do I owe you?"

"In dollars, nothing. Your phone was busy for thirty-four hours and, contrary to popular opinion, you *weren't* online."

"I might have another account, Sherlock." She was flattered by Matt's diligence, also annoyed.

"It had nothing to do with computers, Em: your *phone* line was dead." He unwrapped the Italian sandwich. "I was worried about you."

"In case you haven't done the arithmetic, I've been taking care of myself since before you were born."

Em couldn't blame him for looking puzzled. She couldn't have said whether that last remark was a joke or a warning shot.

Matt chewed and swallowed before asking, "How about poltergeists? Have you been taking care of poltergeists that long, too? I thought getting your living room trashed was something new."

He was, Emma reminded herself, a competent young man. No, age had nothing to do with it. Matt was a competent man, period; that and a somewhat edgy sense of humor was what made him attractive. She'd gotten in trouble twice before with edgy men.

She ate a bite of sandwich herself before asking, "Have you heard from Bran or Jennifer?"

"Not a peep. Our lovers have gone to ground. Tuesday's been handball night; he wasn't there."

Tuesday. Handball and her night to meet with the other officers of the residents' association. She was surprised no one had come banging on the door—or perhaps they had and she'd been too far gone to notice. The message light would be flashing when she got home. Emma swallowed another mouthful, but her stomach had lost interest in food.

"Maybe Bran had something else to do," she said, thinking of O'days and Eddie.

If her shirt was stained, then she'd been in the wasteland. If the wasteland was real, then so were O'days and Eddie. They'd both worn chain mail and fought with swords. If they'd been real, they'd also been dead for centuries. It hardly mattered whether Eddie killed O'days or O'days killed Eddie—unless one or the other of them held the key to Bran and Jennifer's curse.

"Maybe," Matt agreed. "What do you think? You must think something; I see it in your eyes."

So she told him. Despite the messages still waiting to be handled, the unopened mail, and everything else that had piled up on her desk, Em told Matt about the armed-and-armored apparition in her living room, her two-part plunge through the wasteland to what might have been another place, another time, another mind. Finally she described the feel of a sword in her hand, and one slicing through her neck.

"I died with him. I think that's how I lost the day: recovering from Eddie's death, recovering from changing the course of history—the *curse* of history."

She didn't mention Aramis. Aramis was different. Aramis was a fantasy . . . with dirt stains. They finished their sandwiches in silence which Matt broke first.

"If only there was a way to prove there really was an O'days and he killed a guy named Eddie. As I see it, proof's a two-fold problem: on the one hand, you've got to have the details of the past so clearly in your mind that you can see whose head is on a dime or penny, or remember what the headline was on some newspaper you saw lying around. But that leads to the second problem: if you're not reliving the specific life of someone famous, it's not going to matter what you remember, 'cause it's not part of history anyway. From what I know, the psychics and such who go on about regression or reincarnation stuff, they can do the details, but not the specifics."

Details without specifics: Emma could have picked O'days' sword out of a museum line-up. She remembered the blade nicks that well. But she didn't know the year when Eddie had died. "It was old—the Middle Ages with swords and chain-mail armor." She let her mind's eye roll inward. "There'd been a war—a nasty war, and Eddie's side had lost, O'days was there as a conqueror. Eddie wasn't stupid, but I'd say he didn't know how to read. What would he have read, anyway? The Bible? There were no newspapers."

"And nobody named Eddie or O'days."

"Catching his thoughts was a lot like like watching a foreign movie, or being in some club with a bad sound system and worse video." Em defended herself. "Eddie's just the closest I can come to what he called himself. Same with O'days. It wasn't. Half the time I wasn't sure what was real—" She didn't believe she'd used that word—"and what was bubbling out of his memory. He had a sense of himself—maybe we all do—and it sounded like Ed-de-with-es or Ed-de-was." She gave up after the two failed attempts. "I can't do it. I can almost hear it, but the sounds slip away when I try to pronounce them."

"Like nailing jelly to a tree." Matt offered the classic programming analogy.

Em agreed. "And O'days is even worse. Eddie *hated* O'days. He mutilated his enemy's name as a matter of principle." She let her thoughts slip again. "When I see O'days myself, the way he was when I saw him with my own eyes in my living room, he was a hard, brutal man. I thought of him as a warrior, but I've seen that look on cops and soldiers. It's what they do; what they become. I was frightened, but I wasn't thinking *evil*. To Eddie, O'days was a monster, an offense against God. And it was personal between them, somehow, on account of the sister."

"Sister? Sibling sister or nun-type sister?"

"Sibling." Em nearly felt a name, and lost it just as quickly. "Hypnosis," she muttered. "That's what I need: hypnosis to recover lost memories."

Matt scowled. "You can't trust that shit," he said with unexpected passion. "You wind up remembering things that never happened."

"I was joking," she soothed.

And Em had been joking when she made the remark, but the notion had merit. There was a thirty-hour-plus hole in her mind to fill. A little self-hypnosis couldn't hurt. There was more than the name of Eddie's sister floating just below her consciousness.

Her silence had given Matt the chance to reflect. "Yeah," he said, shrugging his shoulders. "Hypnosis couldn't hurt. Close your eyes, start counting backward from ten and tell yourself that when you get to zero, you'll have gone backward in your own time and become an observer in your own memories."

Em guessed that Matt's notions of hypnosis didn't stem from parlor games and regretted that she'd blundered onto a delicate subject. On the other hand, memories of events that hadn't happened, at least not to her, were precisely what she was looking for. And considering the way things had been falling lately, it wouldn't hurt to have a pair of hands nearby to catch her.

"I can give that a try right here and now."

Matt shrugged. "Whatever."

Eyes closed, Emma tried to relax. She'd tried meditation back in the Sixties, when it was the rage, and given it up as hopeless. Empty wasn't a natural state for her mind and detached meant she was looking down on all her flaws.

"Ten . . . Nine . . ."

This wouldn't work. Her face was starting to turn red; she could feel the heat around her ears.

"Six . . . Five . . ."

Life was random. No omens gave it meaning, no mysticism gave it a pattern. There were no curses, especially no persistent curses. Life only appeared to have patterns . . . stains on the back of her blouse.

"Two . . . One . . ."

Nothing. Nothing at all. Emma Merrigan—Merle Acalia Merrigan—was a fool looking for patterns in her life while she was losing her mind. She'd dreamt about a random spring day, decorated it with bits of movies and Shakespeare, then embroidered her dreams with cheap romance.

God knew from which corner of her memory she'd dug up Eddie, the fool who charged a mounted warrior in the middle of his war-band. And it was foolishness compounded to think Eddie's dying thoughts had created a curse, or to believe in curses persisting from one century, one life, to the next.

Emma heard a word—

"Em!"

—That wasn't the word.

"Em! Em—snap out of it! C'mon, Em—back to the land of the living!"

She was shaking and dizzy. Her vision came in black and white rather than color, but she had the word:

Graun-mes-nil.

Matt. Matt Barto. She recognized him leaning over her chair. His hands were around hers.

"Say something, Em!"

"Graun-mes-nil."

He sprang back, releasing her wrists and very nearly sitting on her computer keyboard. "You're okay?"

"Of course I'm okay." Em was still a bit dizzy, but nothing worse. "It worked—by God, Matt—it worked! I recovered a lost memory: Graun-mes-nil."

Matt shook his head decisively. "You scared the shit out of me, Em. Do you—? This isn't easy to ask, but, like—do you—? Have you had, well, like—*fits* or something?"

"No," she answered, then added, "not that I know of." She felt fine, but Matt was dangerously pale. "What happened? Did I start speaking in tongues or something? What's got you so upset?"

"You, Em. After you got done counting, you froze up and started trembling. Your lips were turning blue. When I grabbed you—I'm sorry; I didn't know what else to do—you were cold as ice."

Emma rubbed her hands together. They were cool, but that was normal for her: cold hands, warm heart. "I'm fine now, honest."

"Now," Matt agreed reluctantly. "A minute ago . . ." He cast judgment with another shake of his head. "I'm no doctor, Em, but whatever was happening to you just now, it wasn't hypnosis. You weren't conscious. You said you lost Tuesday, well, you lost a piece of today, too. If I was you, maybe I'd think about checking in with a doctor."

"I've already thought about it," she assured him.

Thought about it, yes, but made the call? Not yet, and not today. She'd found two lost memories: Graun-mes-nil, and another, Blaze, which went with Aramis. It was his answer to her question: "Who are you?"

Blaze. Fire. For a person who hadn't had a life for the last six years, Emma was getting quite a taste of risk.

"That word, Graun-mes-nil, that's what O'days shouted as he killed Eddie." Em wrote the syllables phonetically on the back of a memo. "Some sort of war-cry, I guess. Martial arts and all—shouting focuses their thoughts. Anyway, Eddie knew it; he heard it as a word, not just a noise." She wrote the syllables again, this time as one word with a capitalized first letter: Graunmesnil. "That looks French—" Insight rattled her thoughts. "Mongomery's French—or at least *Mont*gomery is. I remember reading that: Montgomery, in World War Two, as British as a bull dog, but his name was French. If we're going to make all this real, we look for a French connection between Graunmesnil and Montgomery."

Matt took the paper when she offered it. "You want me to look this up, me—the guy who never cracked a B in history or English?"

"What about French?" Em teased.

"French? Is that a dialect of Fortran?"

"*Old* Fortran." She took the paper back. "I thought you were interested."

"To tell you the truth, I'm more interested in that soft-cover black book I picked up off your floor Monday evening. The one that's all handwritten. Where'd *you* get a grimoire?"

Em's heart skipped a beat. "A what?" she asked indignantly, though she knew the word described a witchcraft book and had resolutely refused to apply it to Eleanor's legacy.

"Book of Shadows. The guys I hung around with in high school, the geeks, the freaks and losers, a few of them were into the whole black magic, Antichrist, Satan thing. They all had books like that, or said they did. Black candles, goats' heads, blood, and shit like that. I didn't figure you for that crowd."

"Nor I, you," Emma replied without answering.

"I was in it for the music." He mimed a few chords on the air guitar.

"But you spotted my mother's book. You believe in witchcraft? You know something about it?" She didn't know whether to be relieved or doubly anxious.

"Your mother, eh? No, I don't believe in that crap. Not believe-believe, anyway. My ma, she's big on horoscopes and lucky anything—if it's in the National Enquirer it's gotta be true, right? She checks the serial numbers on every dollar bill she gets; if it's got her lucky number then—*BAM!*—she buys herself a lottery ticket with it—"

There were, Em thought, some mothers whose children might be better off without them.

—"If she got a bill that had her lucky number backwards—her *unlucky* number—then she'd give it to me. So, yeah, I was a big believer every time she checked her wallet. Couple of times she gave me a twenty. That was hard for her, a twenty was a lot of money for us, but Ma takes her luck seriously."

"So you don't believe there's any connection between Bran and me and something that maybe happened hundreds of years ago?"

"You tell me, Em." Matt snatched the paper back. "If it's not drugs, food poisoning, or mass hysteria—and not some conspiracy you guys put together to make me crazy—then a curse is as reasonable as anything else. Something strange *is* going on, right?"

"You looked at the book?"

"Glanced at it before I put it on the shelf. I didn't want to say anything, not in front of Bran and Jennifer. They're crazy. Tell you what: looks like you're going to be too busy to play on the computer today—" He gestured toward the messages still fringing her monitor. "I'll surf around for our French guys—if the network behaves itself."

She forced a smile, watched him disappear down the hall, and felt very alone.

Eleven

Emma left the library hours after sunset. A fine, cold rain was falling. Clouds hung lower than the roofs of the departmental fortresses ringing the quad and muffled the bell-tower clock as it chimed the half-hour. There was a particular beauty to late autumn nights when the trees were skeletal and spheres of amber fog wrapped around each sodium lamp.

The lamps were too bright. The astronomy department complained that light pollution had rendered their observatory worthless. The forestry school called the bulbs "murderers" because they tricked the trees into believing the long days of summer never ended. Astronomy and forestry had truth on their side, but ordinary people liked the bright lights and both the city and the university liked what ordinary people liked.

Emma had dutifully signed the environmental petitions. She appreciated the stars and the trees, but when her conscience was her own, she appreciated the ruddy glow as well. There was something beautiful, even magical about the rows and webs they traced across the campus.

As recently as a week ago, she would have described the walkway scene as one of timeless beauty. The last few days had given her a new understanding of timelessness. She wondered what Eddie might see or think if he were a hapless fly on the walls of her mind. He'd probably agree that the lights were magical, but magic would mean something quite different to him. Eddie might consider that the identical lights with neither flame nor flicker were the tools of Satan, though Emma hadn't noticed much Christian freight in his thoughts while she shared them.

Eddie's world, where death came with a sword thrust and medical care was somewhere between primitive and nonexistent, had struck Em as unacceptably dangerous, but her world might seem far more frightening to him.

And her musketeer rescuer? If Aramis had been real, he'd seemed a little more sophisticated, a little more recent than Eddie and O'days, but still pre-industrial. The sights she took for granted would have beggared Dumas' imagination.

Tires squealed as someone raced down the parking structure's tight-spiral ramps. Emma turned toward the noise, half-expecting to hear a glass-and-metal crash. As impressive as it was, the beauties of modern technology weren't half as awe-inspiring as its destruction. It wasn't hard to imagine that Aramis would prefer the wasteland to Bower.

She drove home safely—a minor miracle. Between lack of real sleep and an excess of excitement, Em couldn't have said whether she'd stopped for any red lights along the way. The red light on her answering machine was blinking and the tape was loaded with one long message from the residents' association president and another from the treasurer who'd taken notes at last night's meeting. By the sound of things the Maisonettes were gearing up for another abuse-of-parking-privileges brouhaha. She'd have to return the calls—but not just yet. There wasn't room in her mind for parking and curses.

Food might help. Matt's taste-of-Germany sandwich had left a strange flavor in her mouth. She stood in her kitchen, staring at the refrigerator and cupboards, hoping for inspiration. Everything that came to mind required at least two ingredients or, worse, the stove. She settled on a box of nuclear food that pretended to be ravioli. After the requisite time in the microwave, the fake-ricotta filling was icy, the tomato sauce was rubbery, and the pasta had the taste and texture of a vinyl raincoat.

But it was food—energy pellets—and Em ate it down to the waxed cardboard while turning the pages of the newspaper. She checked her personal e-mail after that and found two-day-old messages from her stepchildren. Both reported the same bit of news: Jeff, their dad and her ex-, had been back in Bower last weekend. Business, he'd told them, which meant, she hoped, that he'd finally found a job but—Emma's fingers froze—but not one in Bower.

The mere thought that she and Jeff might once again find themselves face to face on a downtown corner was more horrifying than all the curses in Eleanor's black book. Em dearly wanted to know if the kids knew more about the visit, but asking would have violated her self-imposed rules for dealing with the divorce.

She'd planned to surf the Web for *Graunmesnil* but by the time she'd composed replies to Jay-Jay and Lori that avoided all mention of their father, the clock read ten PM and Emma was an hour past exhausted.

In the dark, Em's mind unraveled with thoughts of problematic men. It was her own fault; she knew better than to bring conundrums to bed. As she felt her chances for sleep slipping away, she retreated into factors and primes, but Aramis' face kept getting in the way of arithmetic. Habit beat out novelty somewhere after midnight and the next thing Emma knew, a radio voice was telling her that if the rain didn't stop before noon, the streets would be skating rinks after sunset, because temperatures were headed for the basement.

Spin, purring louder than any November rainfall, had

taken over the middle of the pillow. Em had a corner and a twisted neck. She was aware of her bruise, but the rest of her felt better than it had. For the first time in days, she'd gotten through the night without a misadventure. Regardless of the weather report, the storms had finally cleared out of her mind.

Showered, dressed, and fortified by coffee, Em arrived at the library with time to spare. There were two messages from Matt, one in her e-mail queue, the other a paper-and-pen scrawl propped up on her keyboard:

Come see what I found!

Em tossed the paper note into the university-sanctioned recycling box beneath her desk. Yesterday, she'd worried about losing her mind, today she had it back. Someday she'd have to deal with the events of the past week—maybe she'd make a start this afternoon when she had lunch with Nancy, but not right now, not with Matt.

She typed a reply to Matt's e-mail: *Busy right now. Catch you tomorrow!*

Maybe.

Matt Barto had become part of last week. She might have to let him go, lest he bring Jennifer, Bran, and all the rest back into her life before she was ready to face them. She'd regret that. Matt hadn't chosen to get involved in the strangeness; she'd made that choice for him.

She clicked the *Send* button. The two-sentence reply disappeared from her monitor screen and largely from her mind, replaced by Acquisitions details until Matt himself appeared in her doorway with a sheaf of paper in his hand.

"I could really get into this." He spread his paper through the borderland between Em's keyboard and the monitor.

A casual glance indicated he'd spent last night harvesting information from the Internet. One word—*Grandmesnil* (rather than *Graunmesnil,* but Emma knew the joys and pitfalls of transliteration) bold-faced in a web of genealogical lines—caught Em's eye. She was spared closer examination when her phone rang. The greeting voice belonged to one of her peers at a private university, a man from whom she'd begged no small number of favors over the years, and whose requests couldn't be ignored no matter when they arrived.

Em shot an eloquent look in Matt's direction; he quickly scooped his papers out of her work space, then sat in her side-chair, thumbing through them. He should have left. The effort of ignoring him while she did her paying job had heated Em's temper to dangerous levels by the time she hung up.

"That was *work*, Matt. Do—?"

Matt cut her off before she got up to speed. "Look!" He brandished his papers again, spread them out wider than before and pointed to the very word that had caught her eye. "Look at that!

"I didn't have any luck with Eddie. Half of Anglo-Saxon England had names that started with 'E' or 'A' or that funky 'A-and-E-together' letter, and half of those have 'd' for the second letter. But when I took that word you heard at the end of your fit and searched for it and Montgomery, using wild-cards for the vowels, I found the mother lode! These two families have been around for a *thousand* years. You can make your reservations for vacations in French villages named after them, but the best stuff took place centuries ago. Would you believe the Grandmesnils fought a war with the Montgomerys back in the tenth century? *And* the Grandmesnils—but not the Montgomerys—were part of the army that invaded England in 1066 with William the Conqueror—who was also known as William the *Bastard*.

"You know how you said Eddie couldn't think of the O'days guy without making him out to be a bastard or a bastard's man? Well, maybe O'days was a son-of-a-bitch, and illegitimate, too—but probably they were all William the *Bastard's* men. That's what William the Conqueror was called by his friends and enemies before he made it into the history books. Supposedly his father never married his mother, or couldn't marry her because she was only the undertaker's daughter. A lot of people called him Bastard, it was an insult, even then, but he made jokes about how he'd learned how to sew up a wound from his grandfather.

"I never thought about it. Shit, the Norman Conquest, 1066—it was maybe a two-point, fill-in-the-blank question back in the 10th grade. Some guy named Norman conquered England. What did I know? It's not like he *changed* anything, right? Like we didn't fight the *Normans* in 1776, we fought against the *English,* same as he did. Wrong!"

Emma willed herself not to listen. "Matt—didn't you get my e-mail? I'm up past my eyeballs here and I'm taking the afternoon off to visit with a friend—"

If she'd punched him in the gut, or pierced him with a sword, Matt couldn't have looked more wounded. "But I thought you'd want to see this, Em. All that stuff you talked about—You weren't making it up. It could have happened. *Think* about it Em!"

That was just about the last thing she wanted to do. She squared Matt's printed sheets. "I don't have time. I've got *work* to do."

"Forget work! You and Bran could be onto something: reincarnation . . . time-travel . . . who knows what? You two could be famous, win the Nobel prize for something. You could make history—you could *change* history."

Their eyes met over the paper. His were wide with excitement. Hers? Emma could only imagine what she looked like. She'd been thinking about proof and truth to ease her own mind, but proof on a larger scale? *Please, Miss, Mrs. or Ms Merrigan, tell our audience how it feels to wreak havoc with history, religions, and everything else that humanity holds dear . . . ?*

"You haven't told anyone, have you?" she asked urgently.

"No." He flashed his hurt, astonished look again. "It's not my story to tell; and it's got to be done right. I wouldn't do that to you, Em—turn your life into a media circus."

Emma couldn't hold his honest, injured stare. "I appreciate that," she said after a moment. "Don't breathe a word. I'm not cut out to be that kind of famous."

"Yeah," he agreed. "I thought about that, too. Like—who knows? Maybe there are lots of other people just like you and Bran who've made the same decision. Well, not Bran— From what he told me over the weekend, he just gets headaches and fits, not flashbacks with knights and armor. But there might be others like you, who do things and keep quiet about it. It's not like the world fell apart when you switched bodies and made Eddie die instead of O'days."

The pleasant sense of peace with which she'd awakened had been completely overwhelmed. "I don't know if that's what I did. I don't know if I changed history; the more I think about it, the more—to tell you the truth—I hope I didn't. There are things mankind was not meant to know or do."

Unwillingly, Emma thought of Eleanor. How many times in the last week had she cursed her own mother? A media circus raging was the worst fate that Emma could imagine for herself, but there would have been other, far worse, fates in the past. Heresy, witchcraft, and burning at the stake sprang swiftly to mind, followed by the more "modern" solutions of lobotomies and mental institutions.

If Eleanor had met a 1950's Jennifer . . . If a big, shaggy dog had started scratching on the back door . . . If a chain-mail warrior had appeared in the Teagarden living room . . . Suddenly there were reasons for Eleanor's disappearance that weren't so easy to condemn.

"I really do have work to do, Matt," Em said honestly enough, though she hadn't a prayer of being productive before she headed off to lunch.

"Right, but I've got to tell you the best part: there's this book—William the Bastard wanted to know what his new kingdom was worth, so he had his people go out and ask questions and write down all the answers: who lived where, who owed what, and everything. It was the first real census since the Roman Empire. The English called it the Doomsday Book, 'cause it was supposed to be the final word in taxation, like the Last Judgment, and—get this—the book still exists—"

Emma clutched at a straw: "Maybe I'm remembering scenes from a book I don't remember reading in high school."

"It's not a reading kind of a book. Really, it's more like the Bastard built himself a database a thousand years before anyone thought of a computer to access it. It's only been in the last few years that they've gotten the whole thing loaded onto CD-ROMs—and you, Emma Merrigan, Acquisitions Officer Extraordinaire for a Major University Library, can get us a copy of it."

Matt pulled a folded piece of paper out of his shirt pocket.

"I can't, Matt. That's not the way Acquisitions works. I don't decide what the library buys; I don't have a budget."

"Oh, come on, Auntie Em—" Matt took her hand, and laid the folded scrap in her palm. "You can do it. Even if we never tell anyone, you know you've got to know if what you thought happened, really happened. And, I'm telling you, this Doomsday book is the key. It puts everybody together in the same place: William the Bastard, a whole bunch of Grandmesnils, and lots of guys who might be named Eddie." He paused, frowned. "Well, almost everybody. I didn't find any Montgomerys, but they're probably there. And no Irishmen. Did you know Dublin wasn't Irish? The Vikings founded it when they set up colonies in Ireland . . . about the same time they were pounding snot in France and England, too. The Vikings—the Northmen—when they parked in France, they changed their name to the *Normans*.

Hell, Em—if the English King Harold hadn't had to fight a battle against the Viking King Harold two weeks before he had to fight William the Conqueror, old Eddie and O'days might never have met."

Emma had seen that look of wonder and excitement once before—the day Lori came home from summer camp with a box of ceramics. Now, and then, her feelings were mixed. Ceramic art wasn't rewarding in the traditional monetary way and Matt's sudden affection for history was doomed if it relied on her.

"There's a lot more to this history stuff than I ever knew," Matt rolled on. "It's like football season: you've got to track the whole conference if you want to know who's going to make it to the Rose Bowl."

Em stared at the paper. She could read Matt's writing through the fold. If he hadn't transposed a decimal point when he wrote down the price, his Doomsday Book had been burned onto solid gold CDs, but she could get it into the library without endangering her job security: she routinely alerted departments to potential acquisitions and they just as routinely accepted her recommendations. For that matter, the library might already have a digital copy of William the Bastard's Doomsday Book. According to Matt's note, it had been published in the '80s.

Forget the Middle Ages, the '80s were ancient history for electronic media. Having the CDs was no guarantee of having a machine that could read them. The whole thing was probably moot.

"I'll look into it," she promised, "*when* I get time. Which isn't right now. Whatever happened the other day with Eddie and O'days, it was the end of the crisis. Bran and Jennifer have gone off on their own; they're not my problem anymore. I'm curious about what happened, but, Matt, I need some time, some distance, and I've got to get back to work, okay?"

Matt was disappointed, but game. "You want to keep that stuff I printed off?"

"No, not really. I won't have time to look at it and it'll just get lost here on my desk. It's all Internet stuff, anyway, right? I'll do my own searches, get my own copies—when I'm ready." She was pulling the wings off fairies; if Matt's face dropped any lower, she'd knuckle under and keep the paper. "Don't do this to me, Matt."

He got the message. Tucking the paper under his arm, Matt retreated to the doorway.

"Have a good lunch with your friend. I hope you and he have a good time together."

Em almost called him back to explain that her friend-in-question was a woman she'd known since kindergarten, but that might have opened the door to rooms she'd decided she didn't want to enter. She was pleased, though, to think that he assumed the friend on whom she'd blow her personal time was a man, not another woman. A random spark of jealousy, however mistaken, had the power to brighten her morning. With the extra light, she could see the humor as a middle-aged woman coped—not well—with a last gasp of schoolgirl hormones.

Karl Marx and his friend Groucho had gotten one thing right: everything occurs twice, the first time as tragedy, the second time as farce. She taped Matt's folded note to the side of her monitor, sipped coffee, and got back to work.

Twelve-thirty found her driving to the restaurant in a cold rain. Emma pulled into the parking lot ten minutes early, but wasn't surprised to see that Nancy's car was already there. Nance had a thing about promptness and it didn't pay to interfere with her need to be first on the scene or they'd have been eating dinner at dawn years ago.

Nancy waited at a corner table on the glassed-in patio, watching the rain, not the door. She'd lost weight since

March, and Nance had never needed to diet. Emma felt bones when they hugged.

"It's so good to see you," Nancy said as they sat down and it seemed to Em that there were tears in her friend's eyes.

Tears certainly fell before they'd finished eating—before Em finished eating; most of Nancy's lunch went into a Styrofoam clam-shell. Nance had done most of the talking, but that wasn't the reason she pushed her food around on the plate. She said she was tired from the drive, headachy, just a bit nauseated; neither one of them believed a word she'd said. Em couldn't say the words her mind shouted: if you can't put Katherine in a home, at least bring her up here to Bower where your friends can help you . . . where *I* can help you.

They watched the coffee cool while the waitress prepared their checks, sharing a silence that grew long enough to be uncomfortable.

"How are you doing with the holidays coming?" Nancy asked.

Em gave her coffee cup a slow quarter-turn. "Not bad. I don't think it's really sunk in. Lori suggested that I fly east and spend a week with her, but—in the back of my mind, I guess I'm in some sort of denial. I've been doing a pretty good job of keeping myself distracted."

That was an understatement.

"Distracted! When I realized you were the one who didn't know what day it was, I wanted to get in the car right away. I've been worried about you, Em."

"That's what friends are for: you worry about me, I worry about you. It's so much easier that way. We don't have to take care of ourselves."

Nancy smiled, her first honest grin since they'd sat down. "Ouch—that hurts," she conceded. "I've been thinking about that box you found. Not just how strange it was that you didn't remember bringing it out of Teagarden, but that your mother would have packed it for you in the first place—and filled it with such strange things." She lowered her voice to a whisper: "I asked Mother about your mother—"

"And?"

"Nothing—at first. She said I was trying to trick her again—she's convinced I'm out to have her declared incompetent—but later on she asked me if I remembered that 'nice Dr. Merrigan whose wife ran off and left him with a baby girl'? I said of course, and asked if she knew why Mrs. Merrigan left. I shouldn't even repeat this. Mother gets confused. When the television's on, she thinks she knows everyone. I don't believe her, and you shouldn't either, but Mother said there was another man—she called him a 'foreigner.'"

Something—guilt or the downdraft from one of the overhead fans—made Em shiver.

"I can't imagine any woman leaving your dad," Nancy added quickly. "He was always the perfect gentleman."

But Eleanor had left Dad. "He was older than her, a lot older. Dad was thirty-five when I was born. Think of that wedding picture—sure it's glamorous and retouched, but Eleanor couldn't have been more than twenty when she married him."

"You think there could have been another man?"

Emma shook her head and sipped coffee before answering, "I've started to wonder how well they could have known each other, period. I mean, if Katy had gone off with a man fifteen years older than herself when she was twenty—how perfect of a gentleman would he have to be before you wouldn't worry?"

Nancy's eyebrows shot up. "*What* was in that book you found? Those letters? Did you dig them out of that melted wax yet?"

"Only the one, and it wasn't a love letter. I told you,

Eleanor was into the occult. She had a teacher, a mentor. The letter's about magic—about undoing curses, really. I couldn't make anything out of the signature, but I thought it might be from Eleanor's mother, my grandmother. There's nothing *personal* in the box, nothing more than that letter from Eleanor to me, and even that's formal like a last will and testament. I can't imagine Dad marrying a woman—a girl—whose family tradition was chasing curses and changing history!"

"Is that what she did?"

"Nan-cy! Maybe it's what Eleanor *thought* she did, but we both know better than that—and so did my father. Dad would have had no time for any of that. Science was his religion. He sent me to Sunday School, but I knew better than to *believe* anything I heard there."

Another silence and Em realized she'd admitted something shocking. She tried to backtrack. "It sure would be easier right now if deep in my heart I didn't think there were only two choices: science or insanity."

"You think your mother was . . . well, mentally ill?"

Emma rolled her eyes, "Insanity *does* run in families. I know so little about Eleanor, it's almost like being adopted: I've no idea what time bombs she might have slipped into my genes, but actually, no, it's the other extreme that's keeping me awake. What if Eleanor wasn't crazy? What if science parts company with these curses she wrote about? There's a lot I haven't told you."

"Well, *tell* me!"

Their waitress appeared with the checks. Em stopped her with a snake-eyes glance. "Sorry, we've realized we're not finished. We're going to have dessert."

Nancy protested, but Em held firm: the three-for-one price of Eddie, O'days, *and* lace-trimmed Aramis was a slice of strawberry cheesecake, or its equivalent in chocolate. This time, perhaps because she was the listener, Nancy ate every last crumb of her chocolate cake. The rain had ended, too, and the waitress had collected her tip before Em came to her conclusion—

"Either I met a ghost or I've become infatuated with a figment of my own imagination! Matt's standing in my office, radiating ambiguity, and I'm daydreaming about some guy who accessorizes better than I do. Can you blame me for thinking I'm losing my mind? If this is the infamous *Changes,* I want my money back."

"Why does everything from measles to menopause sound so much more interesting when it happens to you?"

"What was so interesting about my measles? I'd waited all year to go to California with Dad and I spent the whole week cooped up in a hotel room, sick as a dog, with chambermaids taking care of me because Dad had to lecture. I never got to Disneyland; I *still* haven't gotten to Disneyland!"

"I just live my life from one day to the next, but you have adventures going to the grocery store. I'm down in Ohio, trying to deal with my mother who's afraid to die, when, lo and behold! *your* mother turns out to be some kind of witch and you've inherited her powers. With anyone else, I wouldn't believe it—but you—with you, I can't honestly say I'm surprised. All the signs were there."

"What signs, Nance? What signs? I never saw any signs. I promise you, if I'd seen signs I'd've turned myself around and gone the other way."

The Apples and Oranges staff was putting up signs that lunch was over and dinner wouldn't begin until five PM. Emma and Nancy were the absolute dregs of the lunch crowd. A small horde of employees lurked in the main dining area, armed with carpet sweepers, fresh tablecloths, and watering cans for the hanging ferns.

Sensing that they were holding up the wheels of progress, the two women left the restaurant in a belated hurry. Nancy wanted to browse the bookstores; there were none near Katherine's Ohio home. Em offered to drive. No sense taking two cars; campus parking was almost as bad as the Maisonettes and with her staff-parking tag, she could get them into a better class of parking structures.

Driving also gave her a chance to repeat her question.

"What signs, Nance? Why aren't you surprised? You've been waiting for me to lose my mind all these years?"

"Not your mind. Your judgment, yes—I told you that when you married Rob *and* Jeff—but never your mind. You see things differently. Books, movies, music—I'd come away with the same reactions everyone else had, but you'd come away with something different. You were, by far, the strangest kid in our class."

"Gee, thanks—"

She eased up to an electronic gate and waited for the California parking system to recognize her car.

"If there'd been a yearbook vote for most likely to see ghosts or chase curses, we all would have chosen you."

"Double thanks. And here I've gone through my life thinking I might be normal."

The arm flew up and they began the spiral search for parking.

"Emma—you brought a *snake* to show and tell!"

"It was just a garter snake. It wouldn't hurt anyone—it couldn't. There was no reason for anyone to get upset."

"Our teacher—what was her name?—didn't think so once you'd turned it loose on her desk and it vanished into her drawers. I'd never seen an adult cry. She ran from the room."

Em found an empty stall. "That was . . . memorable, wasn't it?" She'd wound up in the principal's office with the principal, the teacher—she couldn't remember her name either—Mrs. Carbone, and eventually Dad. In retrospect, she supposed she could understand their concerns. At the time, she'd only felt injustice. "I knew there was a rule against bringing *pets* to school. I hadn't brought a *pet.* I'd brought a *wild,* completely undomesticated snake; I'd caught it myself. If they *meant* no animals, then they should have *said* no animals, not no pets!"

"I rest my case: different. And, to top it off, you were a *girl* with a snake. Back in the Fifties, that was worse than different."

"The Wild Seed," Emma said in her deepest voice. "A girl with no mother to civilize her." She sighed dramatically as they got out of the car. "Imagine the uproar if Eleanor had stuck around. I might have brought her books, candles, and curses in for show and tell—" The thought stuck in Emma's throat. "They knew. Mrs. Carbone, the principal, the teachers—they must have read what had been written in the paper. Every time I did something, it must have been awful for Dad—and he managed to keep me from ever suspecting a thing."

"It's enough to make you glad you grew up in the Fifties when people kept secrets."

"I don't know as I'd go that far," Em said with a laugh. "At least this way, I'm old enough to handle it."

When Nancy didn't reply, Emma shot a glance over her shoulder. Her friend had stopped and was gazing into the distance. "Curses couldn't be much worse than what Mother's become. I dread what she'll be like when I get home; I really do."

Emma seized the opportunity she hadn't thought she'd get. "You *are* home, Nance. If you're going to dread Katherine, why not dread her here in Bower?"

"I'm going to think about it. Seriously think about it. John's been a saint, but his patience is wearing thin and her doctor said the damage's been done, but she could go on for another year or more."

"I won't nag," Em promised quickly. "I won't spoil your

visit. It's too good to see you. I've missed you; I've missed not having you here to talk to—especially this last week."

"If I'd known what was going on! I wish you had a picture of your gentleman ghost. I'd love to see that box and the black book. Don't get me wrong, but they sound like something straight out of Mother's bodice-rippers. I've been reading them to put myself to sleep."

Privately, Em thought her wasteland adventures had more in common with horror than romance, but the mood of any story lay in its telling and in trying to cheer her friend, she'd emphasized absurdity over terror. "Come over any time while you're here. We'll hack the wax off another letter—"

"I don't know what John's got planned, but I'll try. I'll make time."

They roamed the bookstores and other shops that made Bower unique in the Midwest. Em watched with satisfaction as Nancy seemed more like herself with each threshold they crossed. She had no intention of buying anything until Nancy spotted a book on a remainder table.

"Domesday," she read from the cover. "King William and the Conquest of England."

Emma gave the huge book a professional appraisal: under-texted, over-pictured, and reduced to a small fraction of its publication price.

"You said you knew next to nothing about the eleventh century. How can you resist?"

In the end, Em couldn't. If the Domesday Book didn't sate her curiosity, she could always take it to a second-hand bookstore, or screw legs into the corners and use it as a coffee table. Her only regret was not waiting until they were on their way back to the car to purchase it.

Nancy used a cell phone to arrange her evening hook-up with John. She assured Em that she was welcome to join them for dinner. The invitation was probably sincere— they'd been a threesome when she first came back to Bower, a foursome while she was married to Jeff, and a threesome again for the last few years—but Emma demurred. She waited with Nancy until John drove up, then lugged her version of the Doomsday Book—the back cover of her purchase assured her that when William's scribes had written Domesday, they'd meant, and said, Doomsday—to her car.

Arriving home, Em collected her mail—bills and Christmas catalogs—greeted her cats, and pushed the playback button on her answering machine.

"Emma? Emma? Are you there, Emma? Please be there, Emma. This is Jennifer—Jennifer Hodden. You remember me and Bran? Yeah, you probably want to forget us. Emma—something terrible's happened. Bran's real sick. He's got a fever, and something else. I took him to the hospital. They gave him something for the pain, but it made him delirious crazy. He started talking about demons and killing people. The doctors gave him something stronger but it didn't work right and now he's in, like, they say, a coma. The doctors don't know what to do. They've called his mom in New Jersey, and I called my folks. They're real upset with me— even Dad. I didn't tell them about the demons. I can't; I don't know how. They want me to come home *now,* but I thought—maybe—you could stay with him 'til his mom gets here? Maybe? My mom's picking me up in an hour. Please, Emma, if you get this message, could you come to the hospital? Please?"

Twelve

Courtesy of the university and the Catholic Church, the not-large city of Bower had two hospitals. Emma replayed the message to confirm her initial impression that Jennifer hadn't mentioned either of them. She started with University Hospital. Bran was a student and, if Jennifer hadn't been exaggerating, mysteriously ill. University Hospital tended students by default and mysteries by desire. Their admissions nurse had never heard of Brandon "No-T" Mongomery. Em called Bower-Mercy and heard the same thing:

"We're sorry, ma'am, but we have no patient by that name. Can I transfer you to Emergency? His records might be there."

Emma had nothing to lose except time, and she lost about fifteen minutes of it listening to insipid background music before the ER nurses told her that they had no Mongomery, with or without a "T."

If she weren't so sensitized to the notion, Emma might have loosed a small oath in Jennifer's direction. She pushed the cats away and went mechanically through the motions of changing out of her work clothes and fixed herself a dinner, most of which she scraped into Spin and Charm's bowl. When the dishes were washed and drying, she called both hospitals again. She got the same admissions nurse at Bower-Mercy.

"If you'll give me your name and phone number, I'll look into this for you. You know, not everybody who comes through the door gets admitted. There are other places I could check and then have someone call you."

Bower-Mercy was the Catholic hospital. The other places included the morgue and someone was likely to be a priest. Emma wasn't up to a discussion of her religion, or lack of it.

"No, that's not necessary," she temporized. "I'm just a friend. I'll find someone in the family who knows the whole story."

The nurse blessed Em anyway and she hung up the phone knowing she'd made her last attempt to track down Bran or Jennifer. More than ever, Emma wanted to forget every moment of the past week and needed serious distraction to make that happen. She remembered the patchwork pets she'd committed herself to making. The box of patterns, buttons, fabric scraps, and stuffing was on the top shelf of the backroom's shelf-lined closet. It felt suspiciously light when she brought it down, and indeed it was. Lifting the lid, Em found her stash of paper patterns, a nearly empty jar of buttons, and a note she'd written last December listing all the supplies she needed to replace.

Emma couldn't remember writing the note. She couldn't even remember which of the well-used patterns she'd made last year: cats, dogs, or rabbits. If Nancy had been there to ask how she was handling the holidays, Em's answer, just then, would have been *badly, and getting worse by the minute.* She closed up the box and brought the note downstairs. She put it in her wallet, next to the receipt for her winter coat.

A bath with fragrant oil and mounds of bubbles softened Em's despair into lethargy. There was nothing on television and the novel she'd been reading was too intricate to hold her interest for more than a paragraph. The new Domesday book beckoned from the hall table, but after Jennifer's message, she'd lost interest in the eleventh century. Crawling into bed with a book on investment strategies, Em hoped to learn something useful about municipal bonds or fall quickly asleep. After reading a chapter without accomplishing either goal, she turned out the lights.

No terrors disrupted Emma's sleep and her dreams evaporated the instant the radio jolted her awake.

Winter had arrived. The furnace blew full-bore through the vents and the bathroom tiles were ice against her bare feet. In the kitchen, the outdoor half of the indoor-outdoor thermometer read twenty-five degrees. Emma tied a bit of string to her keys, reciting, "*Don't* forget the damn coat," as she knotted it several times. The idea was that she'd remember to visit the dry cleaner when she pulled out her keys for the drive home.

Across the street, a neighbor had raised a banner in university colors, reminding Em that tomorrow would be the last home game of the season and a very good time to stay indoors. She put another knot in the yarn as she thought about patchwork pets: "*Stop* at the Hobby House!"

Near the central campus the marching band had their throttles out and were filling the air with school spirit. A competing version of the university fight song chimed from the bell tower above the administration building. A visitor might marvel at the coincidence; residents knew the brassy discord was tradition. Like so many traditions, it couldn't bear close examination, but succeeded in lifting Em's mood before she reached the elevator. Inside, the fight song had replaced the usual piped-in music and a pair of school-colored carnations sprouted from plastic vases on every desk, including her own.

Emma was smiling as she thumbed through the papers slid beneath her door—even after she realized Matt had paid an early-morning visit. Bright yellow streaks highlighted the two sheets of paper he'd left on her chair: *King William's half-brother, Bishop Odo of Bayeux . . . William's half-brother, Otho . . . Bishop Eudo of Bayeux . . . Bishop Eudes commissioned . . .* In the margin near the last highlighting Matt had scrawled, "Eudes = O'days?"

She considered the transliterative possibilities as her computer whirred to life. It was possible. Anything was possible when nothing was real. Armed with a fresh cup of coffee, she headed for the basement to tell Matt, as gently as possible, that he was wasting his time.

He greeted her with, "I'm sorry about yesterday."

"No problem. Nancy and I had a nice lunch—" which she didn't want to talk about.

"I'm glad. I was worried that you thought I was going overboard on this curse stuff. And you were right, I was. I'd always thought history was like looking something up in the phone book and about as interesting—but, hey, *normal* people would say that about a crashed computer. And the idea that you could slip through time—that's just stupid, right? You probably paid better attention in your world-history class and held onto the names like I never could. I slipped the last of what I found under your door. It's interesting—the whole history thing's been an interesting ride. We both got taken for a ride by Bran and Jennifer."

"You've heard from them?" she guessed after a sip of coffee.

"From Bran. He left a message on my answering machine. He told me to leave him and Jennifer alone—to stay away from Jen in particular. He was pretty blunt about it, and drunk. Real drunk—at two o'clock on a Thursday afternoon. Loser," Matt concluded with a dismissive shake of his head. "Sometimes I can spot them from the beginning. Sometimes it takes a little longer."

"Interesting. When I got home there was a message from

Jennifer on my machine. She said Bran was in the hospital—"

"He must've kept on drinking."

"She said something about a fever and a coma. According to her, he'd been ranting about demons before the doctors put him out. Jennifer wanted me to come to the hospital."

"Did you go?"

Em frowned. "I would have—it's a small enough gesture to hold someone's hand when they ask, but she didn't say which hospital and when I called, neither Bower-Mercy nor University had any record of a Brandon Mongomery. I didn't know what to think. I gave up."

"Jen conned you the way Bran conned me. Too bad you didn't call the police."

"I don't think they conned us, Matt. I don't think any of it was deliberate. I admit I can't figure out what's been going on, but adding conspiracy to the mix doesn't solve the mystery. Jennifer's no actress. She thought Bran was dying. I got to thinking, while I was talking to Bower-Mercy the second time, that hospitals don't admit dead people. You can go from the ER straight to the morgue. I'll read the paper closely tonight."

"Jesus—" Matt slumped back in his chair. "The big guy could've been dying while he was talking to me and I thought he was drunk. Doesn't say much for me, does it? He talked about his 'demons' and I thought mental illness, not physical. Bran must've had something growing in his brain and it made him crazy before it killed him."

"A tumor's better than my alternative."

"What's your alternative?"

Emma avoided Matt's eyes. "Some sort of disease, one of those 'hot' viruses or bacteria—something contagious. Jen caught it from him, then I caught it from her, and then you got it from me, or from Bran. Something's made all of us a little crazy."

"Shit. Contagious. I don't want to go there," he decided after a moment. "That can't be it. Crazy isn't contagious."

"No," Em agreed. "A fatal disease without physical symptoms, that's Hollywood. A tumor's more likely—or you were right with your first guess and Bran was into serious alcohol abuse. What happened to the rest of us—to me dragging you into this—that's hysteria. And hysteria *is* contagious."

"Yeah, just look at the way everybody's wearing the school colors today. But, damn—yesterday when he called and made an ass out of himself on my answering machine, I was blaming him for being stupid. It just never occurred to me that he could be dying."

"We don't know for sure that Bran's dead. It's a possibility, because I couldn't find him at one of the hospitals," Em reminded them both. "All we know is that you got a nasty call from him and I got an hysterical one from Jennifer."

"Jennifer," Matt repeated. "You know, Em—you say she's not an actress, but if there's nothing to Bran's demons, then *Jennifer* broke into your house, messed it up, and put on an 'I'm scared' act. How do you account for that?"

She couldn't, except to say, "You don't like Jennifer, do you?"

"She doesn't add up. She's got the street look, but none of the moves. Look at her and ask yourself what kind of guy is she going to go for? Same with Bran—the guy's a jock *and* an engineer. Put the two of them together and ask yourself: what's wrong with this picture?"

"Opposites *do* attract, Matt."

"Yeah, so they attract, then what? Bran told me how much he loved Jennifer and how they belonged together, but he didn't say a word about them doing stuff together—then I met her and knew why. You and I have more in common than the two of them. Once I started asking questions, that was the first: what kind of hold does she have over him?"

Emma censored the first answer—sex—that came into her mind. "It doesn't really matter. Our paths aren't likely to cross again. It's over. We caught whatever they had, and now we're immune, right?"

Matt hesitated. "Yeah, but I'd get my locks changed, if I was you. She said she had a key."

Em couldn't bring herself to argue or agree with him and changed the subject entirely. "Going to the stadium tomorrow?"

The tension that had built up during their conversation about Jennifer and Bran broke.

"You know it. The season comes down to this week and next. Win 'em both and we're bowling for the Mythic National Championship. You? You got tickets?"

She shook her head. "It gets too cold *and* too intense in the stadium. I'll watch the game on television—unless it's close, then I'll turn it off. When I was married to Jeff, I used to spend the fourth quarter in the basement. I didn't want to know until it was over. Just call me chicken."

Matt did, which reassured Emma that regardless of any other fallout Jennifer and Bran might have brought into her life, she hadn't lost Matt's friendship. "I said it before, but I've got to say it again: I'm sorry I dragged you into this."

"I'm not. No other way I could have learned your real name: Merle Acalia Merrigan!"

"I think I'd rather you stuck with Chicken. Even Auntie Em is preferable to Merle Acalia."

They exchanged good wishes for the weekend and, especially, for the football team. Back in her office, Em had better luck than usual with the morning's correspondence and fewer interruptions. She decided to press her luck with her "problem children," a file of requests she'd been unable to match with books for sale. Only a few years ago, her acquisitions horizons had been limited to a shelf of printed catalogs; now, she had the world on her desk and a new batch of potential suppliers hatched every day. The "problem children" had gone from futility and frustration to an excuse to probe the ever-expanding Internet.

She was doing what she did best when Daffy hijacked her screen with a priority message from the network administrator:

Bran's at University. Things don't sound good. Call quick.

She considered clearing the screen and later pretending she'd never seen the message. There was a downside to being Matt's informal mentor: he'd never believe her. If she wanted to ignore the message, she'd have to admit a conscious decision. That made picking up the phone the more attractive choice. Matt answered before she'd heard a ring.

"So what's wrong at University Hospital?" she asked with negative enthusiasm.

"Lots. I figured he'd have to be in University, so I called a friend in their shop and asked her to check yesterday's files. Seems that when Jennifer showed up with Bran around four yesterday, she handed them her med-services card. That put Brandon Mongomery into the ER system as Jennifer Hodden. Sher called it 'the fog of war' and that it usually gets fixed within a few hours, but Bran didn't get his own name back until after midnight. Sher says the big guy's already taking up a lot of real estate on their drives and she didn't recognize half the tests they'd ordered on him. Mostly, she said they've got him locked down in a converted fallout shelter, the part of the hospital where they'd put an alien, if they got one. She thinks it's got some kind of panic button where they could pump all the air out and replace it with CO_2. Your virus theory's starting to look good, Em. Pretty scary, eh?"

Daffy Duck reappeared on her monitor to announce that the Utilization Committee would convene in ten minutes. Across town, a young man was fighting for his life and she had a meeting about rearranging shelves in the stacks. Em knew where her priorities lay.

"Scary, but I've got a meeting upstairs in ten minutes, and my saner self is telling me that's the place where I should be headed right now."

Silence—disappointment?—came through the phone.

"Matt—I'm not the sort of person who gawks at accidents. If I'd gone last night—If I'd thought to mention Jennifer's name, yes, I'd have gone. But it's been nearly twenty-four hours. His mother's probably there by now, and from what I heard, Jennifer's parents would have made certain she wasn't. There's nothing to do—"

"Em-ma!" Matt exasperated her name. "They've got Bran in super isolation. He could have the *plague*. Remember *contagious?* We could have it, too. We could be spreading it all the hell over the place, and/or dying ourselves. I'm on my way over to the hospital and you should come with me."

"No," Emma said, hesitantly at first, then more firmly: "No, not the plague or anything close. Something strange is going on, I'll grant you that, but if anyone was thinking plague, the guys in space suits would be all over town. They'd be looking for us—for you and me, by name. Jennifer took Bran to the hospital. She called me from the hospital. She'd've been grilled like a steak if the doctors thought Bran was contagious. She'd be in that isolation unit with him and they'd have my name. And it's not like I'd be hard to find, Matt. If we were in any danger, or if we were a danger ourselves, we'd know it. There's been enough time. I'm not going to panic; I'm going to my dull, pointless meeting."

"But—"

She could hear him frowning, "Go to the hospital, Matt, if that's what you need to do. If I'm wrong, hey—you know I'm here or in that stupid meeting. Okay?"

"Yeah. I'm outta here," he replied and the line went dead.

Emma stared at Daffy emblazoned on her monitor. If she were wrong, she'd be wrong on an infamous scale. But Em couldn't be wrong; simple explanations worked best. When you heard hoofbeats, you didn't think zebras. She shut the machine down, gathered her gear for the meeting—including a fresh cup of coffee: no way she'd get through the afternoon without it. But she hedged just the smallest bit when she stopped by Betty's desk.

"I'm going to the Utilization meeting. We'll be in the fourth floor conference room—I think it's room four-sixteen. In case anyone comes looking for me."

Betty dutifully stuck a note on *her* monitor, but no one came looking for Emma Merrigan. She spent four hours in the airless conference room, listening to yet another scheme to cram more books into the existing building without cracking its foundations. The high point—or abyssal low—had come when one of her less luminous co-workers asked why they worried about floor-stress and shelf-weight when everything was going to be on the Internet in a few years. The insight that no one remembered Winston Smith or what he did for a living in *1984* triggered another migraine. Em was seeing double when she returned to her desk.

Her monitor was flagged with the usual array of messages. The phone light blinked, too, and there were almost certainly e-mails lurking behind Daffy's wild-eyed face. She figured another hour before she could go home for the weekend—not bad, even with a headache.

The phone rang about five-thirty.

"Em? Great! You're still there. I was afraid I'd miss you." She recognized Matt's voice.

"No rest for the weary. I'll be here until six, at least. Did you go to the hospital?" Her brain throbbed. She didn't want to be having this conversation.

"Still here. You said to call, so I'm calling: you should

come over here—now, if you can, but no later than on your way home."

"On my way home?" The throbbing intensified. Light hurt and her stomach soured. She wanted to curl up under her desk. "If it's not an ambulance-and-sirens emergency, why should I come to the hospital on my way home?"

"You were right: if anyone thought that what Bran's got was contagious, we'd all be locked up. They do think it's toxic—like he's been exposed to something, maybe a fungus. But we've been around him, so we might've been exposed, too. I've given 'em enough blood to choke a vampire. And, get this—maybe Jennifer's the one who did the exposing. She's been running around saying she poisoned him."

Emma massaged her unencumbered temple with her empty hand. "Dear God." That wasn't the story she'd heard on her answering machine last night, but almost from the start Jennifer had declared herself capable of murdering her boyfriend . . . and Em had dismissed every word. "Is Bran going to be all right?"

"Unknown. Jennifer may be saying she poisoned him but from what I've been able to pick up, nobody believes her because whatever she's telling them doesn't add up to Bran's symptoms."

"That sounds like something for the police. What good can you or I do? Other than give blood?"

"You remember that name: 'O'days'?"

Migraine throbbing sharpened Emma's recollection. "How could I forget?"

"And did you look at that stuff I left for you this morning?"

Massage wasn't helping. Em closed her eyes and saw the mounted warrior as Eddie had seen him. "Briefly. I can't remember right now. Don't play twenty questions with me, Matt."

"Okay—O'days isn't Irish, it's another Norman name:

Eudes. There are lots of Eudes and at least one of them worked for the Grandmesnils."

"O'days. Eudes. I get it. Eudes could be the guy's name. But what's that got to do with Jennifer poisoning Bran?"

"Real simple: Jennifer says she got the poison from Eudes. She's trying to finish what he started."

The migraine grabbed Em's stomach. She felt weak, flushed, and dizzy, but the vision of Eudes hung firmly in her mind's eye. "She's confused. Eudes killed Eddie. He won; there's nothing left for him to finish. Eddie died cursing Eudes. It's his curse; he's the one who didn't finish what he started."

"Em—you're watching the wrong hand! Where did *Jennifer* learn Eudes' name—unless she saw the same guy you saw? What is a persistent curse, anyway, Emma? Eddie wanted to kill Eudes, but Eudes killed him instead. Jennifer wants to kill Bran, but Bran pounds snot out of her instead."

"I don't know. I don't know what a persistent curse is. To be honest, I'm not feeling all that great right now."

"Then you better come to the hospital quick, 'cause whatever pixie dust is making Bran and Jennifer crazy, it sounds like you've been breathing it too."

Pixie dust! Em wanted to laugh but all she could think of was the dark powdery stains on her blouse, the stains she'd sniffed and tasted. She'd assumed the wasteland was sterile. Suppose it wasn't. Suppose it were toxic? She could take her blouse to the hospital for tests, but if the labs found something toxic . . . something *alien,* then there'd be no compromises with Eleanor's black book.

"Em? Are you still there, Emma? I can get out of here. I can come to the library and get you."

She shook her head, realized how foolish that was and said, "No, no—I've got a migraine. I've been getting migraines since I was a kid." The same way she'd had night terrors. "I'm used to them. I'll come to the hospital as soon as I can."

"When you get to the front desk, tell 'em you want to go to Section U. When they give you an argument, just tell them to call Security. That's the easiest way."

Easiest, Emma thought after she'd hung up. Easiest would have been going home and drinking enough wine to erase everything to do with Bran Mongomery from her memory. Easy wasn't an option.

The bright yarn dangling from her key ring caught her attention as she locked her office door: her coat and what? Em strained her aching memory. "Hobby House. Hobby House. Don't forget Hobby House."

Maybe tomorrow, if she lived that long, during the game, when the streets were deserted she could catch up with her chores. Patchwork pets sounded very good at that moment.

Emma moved her car from one parking lot to another and walked another suspended tunnel to reach the hospital lobby.

"Could you tell me how to get to Section U?"

Argument wasn't the word for the reaction at the desk. The way the two women scooted their chairs away from her, Em expected blaring air horns, flashing red lights, and layers of slamming metal to seal off the doors. She didn't have to ask for Security: two uniformed guards showed up by themselves. The bigger of the pair suggested she follow them into a windowless office.

If this were Matt Barto's idea of humor, he was going to die.

The hostility faded to bearable levels once her companions made a few phone calls.

"They're expecting you," the guard explained as he returned Emma's driver's license and university ID.

A woman escorted her into a locker room where she was given a locker and a pink garment midway between a bunny costume, minus the ears and tail, and a space suit. She could keep her underwear on, if she'd sign a waiver giving the hospital the right to confiscate it without remuneration in the event of an "incident." Emma figured that if there was an "incident," the last thing she'd need to worry about was her underwear.

The locker room and its attached downward sloping hallways were heavily and gustily air-conditioned. The bunny suit was about as substantial as a sheet of newsprint. Emma grew goosebumps the size of mountains, but cold, moving air broke the migraine and she was pain-free when she reached a series of doors at the end of the tunnel.

Red-lettered signs in English, Spanish, and Chinese warned that the doors were electronically controlled and any attempt to tamper with their safeguards would result in both fines and imprisonment. When Em reached the final door— the locked door beyond which she could see furniture and people—she noticed slots in the doorframe. After ringing the bell, she had time to examine them and decided that Section U could indeed be sealed off from the rest of the world. Its air could be pumped out and replaced with CO_2 or any other gas.

An hour, give or take five minutes, after Matt's call, a woman in a white bunny suit opened the door.

"You're Mrs. Merrigan?"

She nodded; this was not the time for a discussion of titles and feminism. The white rabbit led her into a larger room where other white rabbits sat at a cafeteria-style table and a pink rabbit fumbled with his mittens and the pages of a tattered magazine.

"Matt?"

"Em! I was about ready to call out the National Guard."

"What *is* this place? Where's Bran? Jennifer?"

Matt lowered his voice to answer. "It used to be the fallout shelter. Now it's the closed systems unit: recycled air, negative air pressure. Bran's in there—" Matt gestured over his shoulder at a door Em hadn't noticed. "In the lowest pressure. We're a little higher here. If his door opens by mistake, our air goes in, his doesn't come out. But we're still lower than outside. You noticed the doors as you came in?"

Emma nodded. Everything sounded like the national disease center labs, but the rabbit suits were distinctly second-rate. "Shouldn't we have masks or something?"

"They've pretty much stood down. I guess the place was pretty frantic last night when they wheeled Bran in, but it's looking more like a false alarm all the time."

"Bran's better? Is Jennifer with him?"

"No, not better and not with Jen—"

A petite woman in a white suit interrupted them. Her complexion and accent were foreign. Em guessed Asian, but not Indian or Chinese. The woman said she'd like to ask Em a few questions before she drew "the blood."

They went to a three-walled cubicle that faced the air-sucking door to Bran's room. Em sat in a chair especially designed for drawing blood from a victim's right arm. Matt had warned her about donating blood and she'd concede that it was a good idea, but the thought of needles always activated her fight-or-flight reflex. When the med-tech pulled a razor-blade knife out of her kit and reached for Emma's wrist with her gloved hand, Em folded her mittens beneath her armpits.

"You signed upstairs?" the med-tech asked.

"I agreed to a blood test, not a slasher movie!"

The med-tech—her name-tag read Imelda—laughed and pointed out that the pink-suit mittens weren't detachable. The suits had to be cut along the seam line before she could sample Emma's blood.

"Sort of defeats the purpose," Em commented when they were ready to proceed.

Imelda explained that the hospital had been two days into

a week-long dry run of the contamination unit when Bran showed up. They'd welcomed their first patient eagerly, though tests had quickly determined that whatever ailed the young man wasn't viral, bacterial, nor particularly contagious.

The needle pricked Emma's skin. Rather than respond to her tormentor, she stared at the square, chicken-wire window in the door to Bran's room. Giving blood didn't hurt; it was the idea of giving blood that set her heart racing.

Em tried to distract herself. "So, what *is* wrong with Brandon Mongomery—if it's not classified information?"

"It's still easier to say what's *not* wrong with him. His girlfriend didn't put drain cleaner in his coffee, no matter what she says about strangers giving the powder and threatening her parents if she didn't. I feel so sorry for her. Why tell such a lie? She must know something that frightens her very much, I think. The Fifth Floor—that's psych services—talked to her, but before they got anywhere, her parents took her home . . ."

Emma heard a *pop!* as Imelda attached a new collection vial to the needle. She took a deep breath and held it desperately.

"The doctors think it's a designer drug gone bad—something they tried to make from mushrooms and a recipe from the Internet. The boy's symptoms are *interesting* for a mycotoxin. It's different somehow—we don't know, but she does. He could be the first of many; we want to find out."

Em forced herself to breathe. "You think *I'm* doing kitchen-sink chemistry?"

Imelda laughed. "I don't believe a word the girl said." She removed the needle and folded Em's arm over a cotton ball. "Look through the window yourself," she suggested. "He won't see you."

Em extracted herself from the odd-shaped chair. The window gave her a clear view of a scarcely recognizable man surrounded by tubes and monitors and covered with dark, glistening sores. Most were a few irregular blotches inches across, but one on his neck was much larger.

"My God, there's something *growing* on him," she said, not censoring her thoughts. "He looks like something out of special effects."

No question why Bran Mongomery had been sealed in an isolation chamber. In addition to the disfiguring blotches, his face and hands were swollen to unnatural proportions while the rest of him seemed withered. Em guessed he'd lost at least twenty pounds since she'd seen him on Monday.

"What could it be? One of those flesh-eating super-bug bacteria?"

Imelda stood beside her. "The doctors say no, nothing like that at all. Nothing like anything they've seen before. When he came in yesterday, there was only the one mark on his neck. You see how much it's spread and you can imagine the rest."

Emma didn't want to imagine anything about Bran's condition. Instead, she remembered Eudes' sword biting into Eddie's neck—right about where the sores on Bran's neck seemed worst.

"What do you think he's got?"

"Don't tell anyone that I said this, but I don't think there's anything *medical* wrong with that boy. When I was a little girl, my mother told me about a boy who was wild, too wild, and he fell in love with the wrong girl. She was a *brujo's* daughter—*brujo,* that is like a witch, a witch-doctor—and he cursed that boy for stealing her away. This was not so long ago. My mother remembers that boy dying so bad— eaten away from the inside—that the priest wouldn't let his body be brought into the church. My grandfather, he was a doctor, so I asked my mother why he couldn't save that boy, and she said her father wouldn't go near him on account of the *brujo*. The *brujo* had that boy's soul in his fist and there was nothing more anyone could do.

"Some *brujo* has this boy's soul in his fist. I think you understand."

Em was neither pleased nor surprised that Imelda had faith in her. "It's so hard to understand or believe. You can't blame anyone for not believing."

"This boy will die like that boy did."

Imelda expected her to say something more, but there was nothing Emma cared to add about witches or curses or souls held in fists. Back in the larger room, she and Matt retreated to the corner farthest away from the poker-playing rabbits.

"You saw him?" Matt asked.

Em nodded. "Thank God for negative air pressure. I wouldn't want to get any closer. I gathered that Jennifer's parents raised quite a stink when they took her out of here."

"I told you she was here when I got here. I had a front row seat for round two."

"You believe the tale of the stranger who told her to put drain cleaner in Bran's coffee?"

"Okay, it sounded pretty far-fetched," Matt grumbled. "A stranger in a steel suit, brown hair long in front and shaved in back, and a nasty sword. I wouldn't have believed her at all, if I hadn't heard it first from you. It was like you and she were reading from the same script."

Em whispered, "I didn't have a script."

"Yeah, I know that. You didn't get Eudes' name right, either. I've gone back and forth so many times my brain feels like a ping-pong ball, but I'm convinced now—if you are."

She leaned into the corner. "I still don't know. It's not the same for me. If you believe, you're still on the outside looking in. If I believe, I might just as well be on the other side of that chicken wire."

"I don't have to stay outside. You could let me try your black book."

Emma stood straight as if all her strings had been pulled taut. "No," she said, a single word. The book was *hers*. She hadn't realized that before, at least not quite so emphatically.

"You're convinced, then?" Matt asked, as if his request had been nothing more than provocation.

Was she? "I'll go home and look through the black book and·I'll carve out the rest of my mother's letters. There's got to be more—"

"Emma, when you changed the past before, it made things worse here in the present. You must've stepped on a butterfly or something. You've got to go back to that clearing and try again."

It was easy for Matt to make declarations; he hadn't raced across the wasteland or lived another man's death. "Matt—I *lost* a day earlier this week playing around with ideas I don't half understand. I don't want to try anything again."

"Then stay here with the big guy and I'll give it a try. I promised Jen I'd stay with him until his mother gets here, but she'd approve, if you stayed instead. Or we could try waiting until tomorrow. She's supposed to get here around noon. Maybe it takes two people: one for Eddie, the other for Eudes."

So much for provocation. Emma wasn't looking for a partner. If she were, she realized with a sinking sensation, she'd be looking for Aramis.

"You're right about that. No broken promises," she agreed, and tried to sound sincere. "I'll go home, read the book, the letters, make plans. Maybe Eudes will show up in my living room again. You stay here and keep an eye on Bran. Give me a call if anything changes. Okay?"

"Yeah—I'll call."

Thirteen

The better part of another hour rolled off the clock before Emma, in all of her own clothes, left the hospital. Between the yarn knotted on her key ring and the bright snow-ring around the moon, she had no trouble remembering that she needed her winter coat, but the cleaner was long closed. And her patchwork pets would have to wait for another day.

Dinner, though, could not. If Em didn't want her migraine to resurrect itself, she had to ingest some high-quality protein and soon. She stopped at an upscale grocery where the deli sold pre-cooked meals. At nine PM, the pickings were slim. She settled on a withered Tex-Mex platter, mostly because she could crack the lid in the car and wolf down half a burrito without a knife or fork.

Everything, including the moon, looked better the instant food hit Emma's stomach. She was human again and confident that she'd get to the bottom of Bran's curse—especially when a parking space stood empty at the end of a neighbor's walkway.

Emma had wrapped her mind around Bran Mongomery's flesh-eating curse as if it were an Acquisitions problem-child. Her concentration was total and she was halfway up her walkway before realizing that someone was standing inside her portico. Her *dark* portico—the timer had cut off the light.

Clutching her dinner, Em studied the moonlight shadows and decided that her visitor was a woman.

"Jennifer?" she asked.

"Who's Jennifer?"

The answering voice was feminine and unaccented American, but not Jennifer Hodden's voice, not a voice Em recognized at all.

"Is this where Merle Acalia Merrigan lives? Do you know her? I'm looking for her. I'm—"

The shadowed woman hesitated, cleared her throat. Em thought she detected an apprehension equal to her own. With the possible exception of Jennifer and Nancy, there wasn't a woman alive on the planet who knew that name.

"Who are you?" Em demanded.

"I'm Eleanor Merrigan. I'm looking for my daughter."

Dinner slipped from Em's hands. She opened her mouth to insist that her mother was dead, but words failed her. The shock was too great. Her mind was empty—no thoughts of her own interfered with the echo of that singular name: Eleanor Merrigan.

"Are you Merle Acalia Merrigan?"

The woman descended the two brick stairs and took a step along the walkway. Emma found her voice.

"Stop. Stop right there."

"Merle—I know this must be quite a surprise. Quite ... difficult. I'm sorry." She continued forward.

"Stop. I mean it: *Stop!*"

And Emma did mean it. She brandished a fist with John Wayne bravado, as if she knew how to throw a punch.

The stranger claiming her mother's name had moved from the portico into moonlight. Emma had always been good at arithmetic. Her mother had been at least twenty when she was born. Fifty years later, that would put Eleanor in her early seventies. Granted that seventy wasn't as old, decrepit, or infirm as it used to be; still, the dark-haired, easy-moving woman standing some ten feet away wouldn't pass for seventy, nor sixty. Even fifty would be a stretch of the visual imagination.

"Merle—"

"My name's Emma Merrigan. No one calls me Merle."

The stranger stiffened. Emma judged her taller; then again, the stranger wore heels . . . in November. She couldn't be local. Em looked again and saw a suitcase by the door.

"Your name is Merle Acalia."

Em recognized the mother-voice when she heard it. Her wariness became outright hostility. "My *father* called me Emma."

"Arch—How is Arch? I thought—There was only one Merrigan in the phone book."

And that listing read simply Merrigan, no Em, Emma, Merle, or Archibald. She paid extra to keep it so simple.

"Dad died this past February. February twenty-third."

"Two days after his birthday," Eleanor replied, not missing a beat. "I'm sorry to hear that. May I join you inside? I've been standing out here since the taxi dropped me off at six-thirty and, frankly, Merle—*Emma*, I'm numb below the knees."

Em squatted to clean up the mess at her feet. The Styrofoam clam-shell had opened and dumped her dinner onto the cement. A lifetime of doubt, anxiety, and resentment grounded in a ruined supper. Emma's eyes glazed; she could scarcely see the lumps in the moonlight. She was hungry enough to eat off the sidewalk, but she did the right thing— and not merely because a woman claiming to be her mother cast a shadow over her shoulder.

A woman who against all expectation and appearance *was* her mother. An impostor might have been able to ferret out the three Merrigan names: Eleanor, Archibald, and—God help her—Merle Acalia. She could have found Dad's birthday at the same time. But why bother unless she *was* Eleanor?

From her knee-high vantage, she looked past her mother's legs and reconsidered the suitcase. High heels, no hat, a suitcase, and a taxi: Eleanor had come a long way for a joke.

"Why are you here?" she asked as she snapped the clamshell shut and stood up. "After fifty years, why now?"

Eleanor answered, without hesitation or apology, "Because now you need my help. You've—"

"Because I need your help!" Em sputtered. "I needed your help when I was learning to walk, when I was in school. That's when I needed your help, Eleanor."

"Eleanor." She pursed her lips and dipped her chin. "It's going to be Eleanor. Well, I didn't expect you to welcome me with open arms, but you do need my help, Merle. Your name *is* Merle Acalia. I regret that you don't like it, but it was the best I could give you and it cannot be changed. Cannot. I told Arch before I left, but obviously he didn't listen. I told him to remarry too; and he didn't listen to me there either. No matter. We were expecting you years ago. When you didn't show up—we assumed the worst. It happens sometimes. Then, three nights ago, you popped up in the Netherlands."

"The *Netherlands*? What on earth gave you the idea that I was in the *Netherlands* three nights ago? My passport lapsed three years ago."

With gestures worthy of opera, Eleanor stepped backward and raised her chin high. Her face was bathed in moonlight. At seventy-plus, it was wrinkle-free. She held her prayerful pose longer than necessary, then met her daughter's eyes.

"You haven't read the letters. Did you open the box I left for you? Did it come to you? Can we go inside your home to discuss this, or shall we stay out here in the dark and cold to exchange our *bona fides* where the whole world can over-hear?"

The box ... Of course, the box, the black book, the wax-sealed letters, and persistent curses. Nothing in Em's ordinary life had been important enough to draw her mother out of the woodwork, but a week to the day after she'd found and opened that damn box, here she was: Eleanor Merrigan, ready to assume her maternal duties.

Em decided that she hated her mother more after knowing her for five minutes than she'd ever hated her during her fifty-year absence. Then the curtains moved in Mrs. Borster's front windows.

"Inside," she agreed and led the way.

The portico reeked of cigarette smoke. Insult *and* injury, which made Eleanor's youthful appearance all the more inexplicable. Emma got the door unlocked and flipped the light switch. She let Eleanor struggle with her suitcase; she looked healthy enough to manage it.

Spin and Charm were waiting. By the kinks in their tails and the set of their ears, Em knew they didn't approve.

"What pretty cats." Eleanor made an attempt to be friendly. "What are their names?" She left her suitcase alongside the hall table and bent down, hand extended, to greet them.

"The black cat's Spin, the gray one's Charm."

Em's voice was as cold as she could make it, and the tone wasn't lost on Spin, who hissed and fluffed himself out. Charm took off, echoing down the basement stairs in two hollow bounds.

"Strange," Eleanor said.

Emma had waited since they were kittens for someone to feed her that line. "No, not Strange. I know I should have called him Strange. Strange goes with Charm, like Top goes with Bottom. But, as cats go, Spin's not at all quark-y. He's all movement and momentum. What kind of a name would Strange be for a cat anyway?"

On her head-down way to the kitchen, Emma handed Eleanor an empty hanger for her coat. In the kitchen, she dumped her dinner in the garbage and inhaled the flames of anger that were stronger than she expected.

I can do this, she told herself. *I can face her. Find out why she's here—How she knew to come a week after I found that damned box.*

Eleanor was coatless in the living room when Emma entered it. She was staring at the wedding portrait. Bits of shattered glass still clung to the frame and there was the dark smear across the bride's face. Emma wasn't ashamed of her anger but she hadn't vandalized the portrait, which would almost certainly be what Eleanor was thinking as she stared at it. She cleared her throat to get Eleanor's attention.

"That's new—" she stopped.

Eleanor had turned around. Forget seventy. Forget fifty. Eleanor Merrigan *was* the portrait Emma remembered. She hadn't changed. But if Emma Merrigan was astonished by her mother's appearance, Eleanor Merrigan was clearly horrified by her daughter's.

"My poor child! What's become of you? How could this happen? How could you—?" Then Eleanor's face hardened. "No, I know how it happened—the only way it *could* happen. You turned your back on your name. Your name was your power, Merle: your ticket through time. You denied yourself and look what's become of you. How could you be so *blind.*"

Blindness might have been a blessing at that moment. Emma knew what she looked like. "I turned fifty in April, if that's what you're getting at," Em snarled. She wasn't happy about starting her sixth decade, but it had happened, as it happened to everyone, except apparently Eleanor Merrigan. In deep, wordless parts of her being, Emma felt betrayal and loss; they surfaced bitterly. "You walked out of my life, Eleanor Merrigan. Did you think you left yesterday, or twenty years ago? I'm sorry you missed my peak years. I've put my fair share of miles on this body and I've got nothing to hide—" Except some gray hair—"Besides, I've got better things to do than live in a plastic surgeon's office."

Not that Eleanor's face had the drawn-tight rigidity that even the best cosmetic surgery produced after too many nips and tucks. Eleanor's hands were young, no liver spots nor spaghetti veins for her. Emma's mother had defied nature.

"Death and taxes, Eleanor, everyone grows old. It's inevitable. Time's arrow moves in one direction—" Insight shattered Em's anger. "My god," she whispered. She'd told Matt and Nancy that she'd lost a day chasing curses in the wasteland. She'd lost it in more ways than one. "It's more than changing history. It's more than getting rid of curses . . ."

"So—you *did* find the box? You've read the book—but not the letters?"

Mechanically, Em's chin went up and down. "Last week. Last Friday. I found it in the basement, here. I must have brought it here from the house on Teagarden after Dad died, but I didn't notice it. It must have spent fifty years in the attic, Eleanor." *Too long,* Em's mother-voice whispered, with both accusation and despair. "Too long," Emma repeated the words aloud. "Too late. The candles had melted. The letters are sealed in a block of wax. I hacked one out and read as much as I could. A few words here and there. If you had a plan, Eleanor, it failed miserably."

Eleanor covered her mouth and seemed genuinely distressed for a moment. Then she was all steel and attitude again.

"I gave you your name. I gave you everything, and you denied it. *You* denied it, Merle Acalia. Every time you look in a mirror, you'll remember you have only yourself to blame. It's not my fault. The box was always there for you, attached to you in the Netherlands, waiting for you to pull the string. It's not my fault you waited fifty years to acknowledge your wyrd. I gave you a powerful name and you chose Emma instead. There's no wyrd in Emma Merrigan. Whatever made you choose Emma?"

"My initials," she answered before she could stop herself.

"Initials? 'M' and 'A'? Ah—that explains it. Some part of you always knew who you were, who you truly were. The connection frayed, but didn't break—you lived without your wyrd all these years until—? Last week? You say you found the box last week. What happened last week? What awakened you?"

Emma started to say a night terror, but checked the impulse. She *would* tell Eleanor the whole story, from her walk through the Near East section of the library to the crud eating away at Bran's flesh, but she'd tell it in her own time, on her own terms. Little as she liked the idea, Em believed this unnaturally young woman was her mother. She planned to be the one who asked the questions, though, and collected the answers, not the other way around.

"We can talk about that after dinner. I'm starving and my supper wound up in the garbage." Emma Merrigan wasn't nearly rude enough to eat in front of a guest; her *father* had seen to that. "Shall I fix something for both of us?"

"Anything between raw and charred sounds good, great . . . awesome. My stomach thinks my throat got cut over Pittsburgh. Where's the john?"

Faster than a chameleon changing colors, Eleanor became a twenty-something like Lori, Jay-Jay, or Jennifer Hodden. It had to be an act—and a useful one if you *were* seventy but looked twenty. Oddly, it made Eleanor seem less a stranger, less an intruder, than she was.

Em's anger lost its focus. "Straight ahead at the top of the stairs," she said wearily. "Be careful, the door sticks. I wouldn't want you to get locked in."

They went their separate ways—Eleanor upstairs, Em to the kitchen where she contemplated her refrigerator as if it were an unexpected algebra quiz. No matter what she fixed for supper, she'd be baring her soul.

Should she throw nuclear lasagna into the microwave or get creative with rice and a can of stewed tomatoes? Add broccoli, a few days past its prime, but still edible, or peas frozen in a tasty but high-calorie, artery-clogging butter sauce? Allow herself to care what Eleanor thought, or pretend that she didn't?

Every choice was heartburn stressful but suggesting a trek to a restaurant wouldn't improve the situation. If she'd been alone, Em would have settled for nuclear lasagna, but she got out her cast-iron skillet. It was easier, in the long run, to do her best; Dad had taught her that, too.

And Dad had loved Eleanor enough to marry her.

Emma had rice swelling in a saucepan, chicken thawing in the microwave, and onions sautéing in the skillet when Eleanor reappeared on the border between the downstairs carpet and the kitchen tile.

"I needed that. What about something to drink?"

There was no specific reason for the wave of resentment that paralyzed Em's arms in mid-stir. Eleanor's request wasn't unreasonable or impolite; she hadn't set foot in the kitchen without an invitation. "There's the usual in the 'fridge: juice, pop, a couple of fancy iced teas in the door. Help yourself. The glasses are over the sink."

"Anything stronger?"

"There's a bottle of wine in the 'fridge, too, but it would go better on salad, if I had any lettuce."

"Nothing else?"

"Not a drop—" she began, then corrected herself. "Wait—I hauled a few bottles out of Dad's liquor cabinet.

They're in the bottom left of the cabinet behind the table, behind you."

Emma looked up from the stove. Eleanor had started to follow the directions, but something had caught her eye and stopped her cold. By the angle of her head and the expression on her face, Em knew exactly what it was: the wedding portrait . . . again. She turned off the gas and slid the skillet to a cold burner.

"I didn't do that, Eleanor. It happened Monday afternoon. I had a guest staying with me. She might have done it while I was gone, but she said she was hiding behind the sofa while things were flying around by themselves. If you *are* here to help me, that's what you're here for." Em was surprised that words had come so easily, so politely, and that her voice had held steady while she spoke them.

With neither eye contact nor detectable emotion, Eleanor softly said: "You left an open door to the Netherlands after you found my box."

Em remembered the stained script in her mother's letters. Not the Netherlands, the country in Europe, but the night-terror realm she'd christened "the wasteland."

"If there was a door, Eleanor, I didn't open it."

"You did, Merle. There's no other way. This world protects itself from accidents, but not from fools. What happened before you found my box? What *strange* thing happened?"

Emma dropped her spatula in the skillet. Weaponless, she halved the distance between herself and her mother. She'd promised herself she'd ask the questions rather than answer them, but her resolve had withered.

"I have night terrors, Eleanor—not nightmares, but moments when I wake up and think I've been in another place. Dad told me there was no other place, only the bed where I went to sleep and where I woke up. Anything else was imaginary. I believed him because I never actually *saw* the place that frightened me. Not until early last Friday morning—before I found the box. Or it found me—that's what you're trying to say, isn't it? The box wasn't in the attic; it was waiting for me in the wasteland, wasn't it? You should have stayed. You should have been here with Dad when I started having night terrors."

Slowly and without looking away from the defaced picture, Eleanor shook her head. "You were better off without me. You didn't need me."

"I need the truth."

"And you'll have it. The box was waiting for you, but not in the Netherlands. I put it in a railway trunk with my wedding dress. I thought you'd find it while you were still a little girl. I thought you'd be curious. I thought you'd be like I was."

Eleanor completed her interrupted journey to the buffet where Emma had stowed her gleanings from Dad's liquor cabinet. He wasn't a drinker, much less a drunk or alcoholic, but he'd kept bottles of the best brands in the dining room. It was part of who he was and the times that had shaped him.

Eleanor made a noise like she'd pricked herself with a needle. She sat back on her heels with a wax-sealed bottle across her thighs. Em covered her mouth—that unopened bottle of single-malt scotch had been in the Teagarden house for fifty years . . . like the wooden box.

"He remembered," Eleanor said softly.

"Dad loved you. He wanted me to love you—that's why, I think, he told me you were dead."

Eleanor's head swung around; her face was a mask of surprise. "Arch told you *that*?"

"He thought it would be easier if I believed that instead of thinking that you'd abandoned us. I was eighteen, a freshman right here at the U, when I blundered across the newspaper stories. I was looking for Bower's reaction to the

Berlin Airlift and there you were on the front page. The FBI was in town for a week."

Eleanor caressed the bottle. "I did the best I could. Believe me. Please believe me, Merle."

Em slouched against the door frame. "You know—against all odds, I do. All the same, I wasn't better off without you. Children *need* their parents. I needed you."

She scored a direct hit, a home run, and a hole-in-one. Eleanor hid her face and lost her grip on the unopened bottle; it slid harmlessly to the carpet. Emma tried to savor her triumph, but the taste was too sour. Retreating to the kitchen, she got one of her top-shelf glasses.

"Do you want ice?"

No answer. Em returned to the doorway.

"I'm sorry, Merle. What more can I say? I can't undo the past."

"Oh, I don't know, it looks like you've done a pretty good job of that." The remark, phrased more caustically than she'd intended, scored another hit. They both cringed and Emma took a deep breath. "I'm sorry, too. Sorry that I'm not overjoyed to see you, to know you're alive. Sorry I can't keep myself from wondering why the hell you look the same age as my daughter—"

Eleanor gasped. "You have a daughter? Your name? Your hus—"

"Isn't coming home. I'm divorced . . . twice over. I kept my own name—my own *last* name—both times. Lori's my second husband's child. And her brother, Jay-Jay, Jeff Junior."

"No children of your own?"

A mouthful of bitter words clamored for expression. Em gagged them all down. "No children. The first time, I was too young, and thank God, I realized it. The second time, Jay-Jay and Lori were there ahead of me: used kids . . . second-hand, pre-owned kids. We got along fine—still do. But there were times when they needed their mother, not me."

"You got wisdom from Arch." Eleanor brought the bottle toward the kitchen. "He saw everything so clearly." She took the glass from Emma's hand and poured herself three fingers' worth of single-malt scotch, neat. After a sip that would have left Em with watery eyes, she evened it off and recapped the bottle. "Arch was the best thing that ever happened to me, and my biggest mistake."

They were within reach of each other. It was easy for Eleanor to take her daughter's hand, hard for Emma to avoid the contact she instinctively dreaded. She fixed her mother with the snake-eyes stare and learned from whom she'd inherited that peculiar gift.

"Do you think I didn't love you or your father?"

"I *thought* you were dead—some horrible *Dark Victory* meets *Stella Dallas* sort of death. It didn't occur to me that you'd up and abandoned us until I was in college."

"Did Arch ever say that I'd abandoned him or you?"

"He said you'd promised him five years, and that's pretty much what he got. Nothing about running away. Maybe you were lying then, maybe you're lying now, maybe there's some grand unified-field-theory of Eleanor Merrigan's life. If there is, don't bother wasting it now. No matter how good it is, or even how true, this isn't the time. I've got more important things on my mind—"

She didn't. In a purely selfish and hopefully forgivable way, nothing was more important to Emma Merrigan than her own history. She wanted to fill every empty space in her memory, but knew she needed a layer of time and reflection to soften the impact.

Maybe she had inherited wisdom from her father.

Eleanor withdrew her arm. "That's fair enough, Merle. I can wait. Gods willing, there'll be time. You *have* grasped it—the reason I couldn't stay more than five years. I saw the light go on behind your eyes when you looked at me. We lose time in the Netherlands. We can't *reverse* the effect of the here-and-now on our physical selves—more's the pity for you, I'm afraid—but, judiciously, we can slow it to a crawl: a year for every ten or twenty. Take care of yourself, and you won't just see the start of the twenty-first century, you'll see the start of the twenty-second and twenty-third."

Em side-stepped and snapped the dial that controlled the large front burner. Her onions had gone wormy in the cooled oil. She didn't care. Undoubtedly she'd remember this meal for the rest of her life—however long that turned out to be— and not because of the food.

"I'll burn that bridge when I get to it. Right now, there's a young man in a contamination room at the University Hospital. I've read that book you left me—the one that was supposed to contain everything I'd need to know. Maybe you forgot a few pages, or maybe I misread them, but Bran and his girlfriend are tangled up in something that I think might be a curse, and might be rooted in eleventh century England—King William the Conqueror's cronies versus the English people they'd conquered.

"I've even been inside the mind of the hot-head who caused the curse. I was there while I was losing a day. I *thought* I'd taken care of the problem when he didn't kill Eudes, the Norman he was trying to ambush and murder. Eudes killed him instead. I'd *thought,* based on what I'd read, that would do it . . . or, undo it. Now, instead of beating up his girlfriend, Bran's got black crud chewing away at his flesh. And that girlfriend, she's running around telling everyone that Eudes—remember Eudes?—gave her the poison that caused the crud that's eating away on Bran's flesh. Before I left the hospital to come home, here, to find you— I talked to a nurse who as much as told me that it looked to her as if Bran had been cursed."

"Was she doing anything about it?"

"We weren't comparing notes from our respective little black books, if that's you mean."

While Eleanor's lips tightened into a line, Emma gave her attention to the onions. She didn't want to spar with her mother, but her emotions had the inside track to her mouth. Everything that came out was bitter and jagged. She hacked the chicken breasts apart and threw the pieces in with the onions. Eleanor said something that got lost in the sizzling. Emma could have asked her to repeat it, but didn't, and Eleanor walked out of the kitchen without saying anything else.

Setting the table, Emma saw Eleanor occupying her favorite chair, absorbed in a black morocco-bound book—a different black book than the one on the fairy-tale fiction shelf. Eleanor affected not to notice the clatter of knives and forks. Em wanted to say something conciliatory, but nothing would have been completely sincere, so she didn't take the risk. Back in the kitchen, she added stewed tomatoes, mushrooms, and her slightly wilted broccoli to stir fry and covered it for the final minutes.

"I can do this," she whispered. She wanted someone there in the kitchen beside her, someone with whom to share the moment's absurdity. "We'll talk," Em assured herself. "Eleanor can tell me what's been going on and how to put a stop to it. Then I'll deal with the rest. God! I wonder when she really was born . . ."

She spread rice over two plates, ladled the stir fry over the rice, and brought dinner to the table. Eleanor refreshed her scotch. Em considered, and rejected, a glass of her salad-dressing wine.

"It's delicious," Eleanor announced after a small forkful.

The meal was tastier than Em had dared hope, though perhaps pure, ravenous hunger improved their opinions of the food, if not of each other. Em managed a chokehold on her resentment. She asked simple questions without noticeable bite or edge and Eleanor answered them the same way.

Where did Eleanor live these days? A little town an hour north of New York City. Did she live alone? No, she shared a home with another curse-hunter, a man. Were they married? Legally, yes, in the here and now. And other than legally, in the here and now?

"It's all pre-arranged," Eleanor confessed with a grimace and a sip of scotch. "Harry's a good partner, and we've been together for five years. We'll divorce next year. It's all in the contract. Harry's going to Boston. Reward time: he's earned it. I've put in for a West Side apartment. Gods willing, it's reward time for me, too. If not, you go where you're sent. We used to be tribes, like the gypsies; now we're a global corporation."

Another sip of scotch. Eleanor's refreshed glass was nearly empty.

Emma pondered the obvious answer to a question she hadn't asked: Eleanor Merrigan was not a happy woman. Her global corporation brought to mind an unholy hybrid of the Mafia and a conscript army. Em didn't want to enlist if she could help it.

For her part, Eleanor's questions were about Arch— Archibald Merrigan, Em's father—and it was hard to escape the conclusion that Eleanor harbored regrets about the husband she'd left behind, if not about the daughter.

They cleaned their plates, then finished off the rice and stir fry that remained on the stove. Emma was loading the dishwasher when Eleanor asked—

"Where is the box? I'll mix the draughts while you finish up here. They need to breathe, like wine. We'll want them to be ready when we've finished laying out our strategy."

Em turned the water off. "After fifty years, there was nothing usable in those bottles."

Eleanor didn't bat an eye. "We can use mine, then; I

brought enough for two. We'll need the service, at least one bowl. And incense—any incense. Vacuum-cleaner pellets will do in a pinch. The draughts are what count. You can't move through the Netherlands without them."

"No, Eleanor, none of your potions, not for me. I looked at those recipes—I'm not drinking any homemade laudanum, thank you. I'd rather face a night terror."

"You can't control your dreams, Merle. The draughts are the only reliable way to do what has to be done. You've lived in the here-and-now all your life. You've got to let go of your prejudices. The rules you've learned don't apply to you anymore. They never did."

Objective truth about drugs was elusive. Eleanor's statement had the ring of propaganda to it, but then, most statements, pro and con, about drugs did. Emma stuck with her own subjective opinions.

"No opiates. No hallucinogenics. Period. I've read enough of that black book to know that it's what I believe that makes the difference. I believe I can do what has to be done, but I don't believe in drugs. If sheer determination isn't enough to free Bran from whatever's got a hold of him, at least I'll know I did my best, and my best doesn't include opium."

"Belief *is* what matters, Merle," Eleanor agreed after a moment's thought. "All the belief you can muster. And more. Harry heard you—*I* heard you on Tuesday. You've drawn dangerous attention in the Netherlands and you're teaching it our secrets. That's got to stop, Merle. I'm here to stop it."

Curses had begun to sound like bacteria always searching for new hosts and growing resistant to antibiotics—or perhaps she was merely thinking about Bran with his corroded skin.

"I don't see how I could be revealing anyone's secrets when I don't know what I'm doing—but that's not the point tonight. I left the hospital knowing I'd need something more than I had in hand if I wanted to save Bran—and there you were: the proverbial gift horse waiting at my front door. Well, I won't look in your proverbial mouth. I'll follow your lead—*if* you can tell me that Bran's going to be okay when we're done."

Eleanor nodded. "Listen to me carefully and do exactly what I tell you and we'll do what has to be done together."

Why did anyone ever make a deal with the devil? Why did a condemned criminal climb the stairs to the gallows or a sailor walk out on the plank? Because he knew for certain what would happen if he didn't and there was always a chance he was wrong about the rope or the ocean.

Emma got the wooden box out of the basement. Eleanor got a bottle of off-brand cough syrup from her suitcase. They lit incense that smelled like the inside of an old shoe and sat at the dining table.

"No need for circles or mystic incantations, Merle. This isn't religion." Eleanor uncapped the bottle and took a swig before passing it over to Em.

The syrup was sickly sweet, saccharin rather than sugary, and definitely not over-the-counter cough syrup. It burned Em's tongue and throat. She couldn't have managed a second swallow and didn't need to. The draught hit her heart like a batter hitting a fast ball. Em felt herself rise out of her chair—out of her body—for a home run.

Fourteen

E m *had barely* adjusted to the sensation of flying when she was assaulted by a blast of light, sound, and pressure from all angles. Instinctively, she pulled her floating self into a diver's tuck. Her opiate-afflicted senses left her conscious of little more than terror and vertigo. When those twin miseries faded, she was stretched out on a dry, solid surface.

Unclenching arms and legs, straightening her spine, and opening her eyes, Em was relieved to find herself face up in the wasteland's silent darkness.

This bleak place where time did not apparently rule supreme was subtly emptier than it had felt during her previous visits. A moment's thought offered an explanation: the other times, Bran's curse had preceded her. Whether it had lured her or she had chased it, the curse had, in Eleanor's phrase, opened the door.

Em called her mother's name. There was no response. It would be just her luck to have lost the elusive Eleanor along the way.

As a matter of pride and habit, Em had mastered the art of standing up without putting a hand down for balance or leverage. Rocking forward, she rose first to her knees, then shifted her weight and balance to her toes for what should have been a smooth, upward thrust to her feet. Should have been, but became instead a fish-flop onto her side.

The opiate-laced draught which was supposed to strengthen her perceptions had done the opposite. Whatever physics ruled the wasteland, ordinary human metabolism hadn't surrendered its power. Em was doped, stoned, seriously 'zoned. She needed both hands and intense concentration to get her feet under her again and keep them there when her head was a body length above her ankles.

Mother did not know best.

"Eleanor! Where are you?"

"Over here."

Em turned toward the sound and past it as well. In her wilder, younger days, Em had learned how to move with exaggerated caution, but Eleanor's draught was more potent than watered-down campus beer or the mostly oregano marijuana that made its way to the Midwest in the mid-Sixties. She rotated more carefully the second time and faced the life-sized column of shimmery white light that spoke with Eleanor's voice.

"I'm not enjoying this, Eleanor," Em complained. "It'll be a cold day in hell before I drink from your bottles again."

The column threw off a sparkling sigh. "Open your eyes, Merle."

"They *are* open. Everything's dark, except for you, and you're a white flame. I'm dizzy just looking at you. I've got to go back until this wears off, Eleanor. Show me the way back."

Another breath of glitter. "Your other eyes, Merle. Open your inner eyes."

Other eyes, inner eyes—it was nonsense, but so was the wasteland itself. With her teeth ground so tightly together that she had no doubt whatsoever as to her jaw's reality, Em imagined Daffy-Duck eyeballs hovering brightly nearby.

"Good, Merle—now make them your own and use them."

Emma obeyed reluctantly but successfully. Migraines had taught her the basic lessons of double vision; the combination of opiates and the wasteland provided an advanced course: a silvery Eleanor Merrigan hovered within the white column. A vaporous horizon of dawn pink over purple sage was visible behind her. Em looked down and saw that she, too, had become a quicksilver etching within a luminous column.

"I'm impressed," Em admitted, wriggling her fingers, "but the price is too high. I'll find another way to get here and avoid the side effects. I've lost more than I've gained."

"Suit yourself. The wisdom of the ages goes into our draughts, but feel free to ignore it."

Eleanor came closer. The parched ground crunched and crumbled. Squinting through her Daffy-eyes, Em saw lavender footprints.

"If you want to return to the here-and-now, look for a wall made from clear glass. I see it there—" Eleanor pointed to her right. "You may see it elsewhere. The Netherlands are real, but subjective. Do you understand that—the difference between a subjective reality and an objective one? The here-and-now is objective. The tangible past—the past that was created by the passage of time—is objective. The Netherlands are subjective. You must discover the truth for yourself; knowledge can't be received."

It was Em's turn to sigh. "I can grasp that—You say toe-may-toe, I say toe-mah-toe, but we're talking about the same thing."

"Close enough. Do you see the glass wall?"

Em turned slowly to the left. About a hundred feet away she saw faint reflections of Eleanor and herself on a black, yet also transparent, mirrored surface. She nodded. "I see it."

"Remember where it is and what it looks like! That's the threshold between the Netherlands and the here-and-now

236 * Lynn Abbey

world we left behind. Your body and your life are on the other side and you *don't* want to lose track of them. Wherever you are in the Netherlands, you should be able to see the threshold; if you're somewhere where you can't see it, you're in deep trouble. Pass through it, and you're home."

"But a day later than when I left."

"An hour, maybe two. A day is very long. No matter how long I've taken in the Netherlands, I've never spanned a full day in the here-and-now. I'm no scholar; can't explain why you lost so much time—unless it's that your approach and knowledge are so irregular. The subjective again."

Aramis had told Em to walk until she couldn't walk any farther. That was how he understood this place and, perhaps, how she'd lost a full day rather than a few hours.

"I can change my subjective, right? I can decide to say 'toe-mah-toe,' can't I?"

Eleanor wavered. "Yes, I think. The way it was explained to me, the Netherlands is the track of time. When you walk away from that glass wall, you're walking away from the border between here-and-now and the un-become future. Usually you're walking into the past—but it's subjective, worse than subjective. Don't even try to measure distances in the Netherlands, *ever.* You must move to get anywhere, that's bedrock truth—not subjective. Running *is* faster than walking when you're being chased, but last year isn't any closer than the last ice age, and unless you are being chased, running won't get you anywhere or any-when any faster. This whole place is a paradox; accept it and don't worry about it—that's my advice.

"And wherever you go, never lose sight of the threshold back to the here-and-now. The worst of what's here can't face the future's edge."

Em shrugged. Paradox was as good a word as any to describe a place that couldn't be explained, but wasn't all that difficult to understand—although perhaps her understanding would vanish when Eleanor's draught worked its way out of her body. "Take drugs to get here. Go home by jumping through a piece of plate glass that better be right behind me. Walk until you get where you're going, unless running seems smarter. Okay. Just one question? How do I find out which way to England between 1066 and 1086?"

"That boy's curse?" The white-column leaned as Eleanor cocked her head. "Don't think about place and time, Merle. You either know exactly and precisely where a curse is rooted, or you'll never find it. The usual way to lay a curse is to find a manifestation of one in the here-and-now. Those blotches you mentioned on his skin, those could be a curse's manifestation. Then, when you've fixed the manifestation in your mind, you enter the Netherlands and trace it to its root. You can leave the Netherlands at any time and any place— you already know that. Knowing where and when in the here-and-now is nice afterward for the reports and rewards, but useless beforehand."

"Needles, haystacks, *and* time—a mapping problem with an extra dimension. I get that, Eleanor, but what other way is there? Tell me, show me: how do I reconnect with that magic moment when Eddie got himself killed?"

"Eddie? That's not the name you mentioned in your living room."

"Eddie, Eudes," Emma complained. There'd been alcohol as well as opiates in Eleanor's draught; Em was reckless and disoriented. "Does it make a difference?"

Eleanor said it did, so Emma explained how she'd fallen into Eddie's mind and shared the last quarter hour of his life.

"You should have told me that," Eleanor chided.

"You didn't ask." Em supposed Eleanor would like to know about Aramis, too. She wasn't ready to hear her mother's opinion of the men she kissed.

"Never mind," Eleanor said with a shrug. "We don't have to search for the root. You've been there once already. Imagine those trees you saw are growing on the horizon and start walking toward them. I'll be right behind you."

They struck a steady pace, less than Em's three-and-a-half miles per hour exercise pace. They might have been on a giant treadmill for all the wasteland changed around them. Eleanor made several attempts at conversation. Each was innocuous and each died, stifled as much by the pervasive silence as Em's disinterest. When they'd trudged about two miles, Em put her head down and picked up the pace.

With her system burdened by drugs, it was a foolish, stubborn act. Her pulse rate rose, her breathing grew heavy, and she broke into an unhealthy sweat, but Em would have kept going until she dropped if Eleanor's white fire hadn't gotten in front of her and forced her to stop.

"Let go of your anger, Merle! It's getting us nowhere."

"Get out of my way, Eleanor. You told me to imagine trees on the horizon and walk toward them—and that's what I'm doing. If it's not what you had in mind—"

"Merle! Forget who I am. Forget that I'm your mother. Gods forgive me, someone else should have come to guide you through this. I misjudged your life; I thought you'd be glad to see me. I couldn't have been more wrong. We can retreat—I could call Harry. He'd come, but it would take time, here-and-now time. Can you afford to wait that long? Can that young man? Or can you put your mother out of your mind long enough to lay a curse to rest and save his life?"

Em had bent forward, bracing her hands against her legs. "I don't know," she answered between labored breaths. "I'm not as young as I used to be. No irony intended. I can't roll with the punches. It's been one outrageous thing after another since last Thursday. My world's been turned upside down. You showing up—that was the last straw, not the first. If he dies—" She paused. Her breath came easier and her stubbornness had burned out some of Eleanor's drugs. "If Bran Mongomery dies, I'm going to chew myself into guilty little pieces, but this idea that it's my damn destiny to risk life and sanity to save him sticks in my craw. It won't go up or down."

"I know how that feels, Merle—"

"*Please* call me Emma or Em. Maybe Merle Acalia's a better name for a place like this, but it's not me. I'm not ready to become someone else—No, I'm not *willing* to become someone else. Hearing you call me 'Merle' is like fingernails on a blackboard."

"Emma. All right, Emma. You're not the first woman who's been handed a wyrd she didn't want. You wouldn't be the first to turn her back on it either. You're right about the guilt, too. For my money, the guilt's worse than the risk, but the risk of letting anger get the better of you while you're marching across the Netherlands is the greatest risk of all. If you can't decide to go forward of your own free will, we'd better go back."

For Bran's sake, it should have been an easy decision, but it wasn't.

"You've done well so far," Eleanor continued in her wisest, most soothing voice. "We can do this together, Emma."

Em didn't need to see Eleanor's face clearly to know what she was trying to do. She would have encouraged Lori or Jay-Jay the same way.

"All right." She emptied her lungs. "There goes the anger. Let's start walking again."

They walked a mile and another. Em's resolve wavered. She tasted failure and looked to her right where the here-and-now mirror beckoned. Then Em had another Alice-in-Wonderland moment, tumbling blindly down an unsuspected hole. Unlike her previous plunges, this one ended after only a few top-over-teakettle revolutions. She was grateful for small blessings: there was sunlight, the dappled sunlight of a summer forest and the wild chorus of a young man's thoughts. She'd tumbled into a familiar mind.

His name was Edwys—she'd learned enough about the eleventh century now to decipher its more common names. His other notions were more comprehensible, also, like listening to lyrics over and over until the sounds became words, though there remained many words whose meanings Em couldn't grasp and many thoughts that were wordless emotion.

Em followed one thought that had eluded her before: the beloved sister, the beautiful, dishonored woman. She had extravagant blonde braids and radiant beauty. In Edwys's mind, his older sister was everything a woman should be. He'd loved her once with a boy's pure devotion, obsession; now he despised her.

Edwys's thoughts of O'days—Eudes, Em made the match—were not nearly so bitter as those that framed his sister. Eudes was one of *them;* no more than an animal, nothing good could be expected of Eudes. But his adored sister should have known better than to fall in love with a beast.

Emma.

The sister's name was Emma, after good King Edward's mother. Edwys had seen his king and the royal family in the better days of his early childhood. The memory was bright in his mind but without much detail, like an overexposed photograph.

Em recalled the Internet notes Matt had given her and the introduction to her Domesday coffee-table book. The Norman-born queen whose name she'd accidentally adopted was related by marriage or maternity to all the Conquest players. When Emma's last son, good King Edward, died without heirs, William the Bastard had claimed the English throne.

Em's thoughts about William the Bastard seeped out and set off a firestorm in Edwys's mind. Her knowledge came from words first written down by the conqueror's scribes and perpetuated by his inheritors. Edwys's knowledge flowed in blood and atrocity.

Emma! Emma, can you perceive me? Unbind yourself before it's too late!

Awash in another mind's memories, Em couldn't blame Edwys for hating Eudes enough to assassinate him. In a sea of grievances witnessed and inherited, the wonder was that civilization survived—

Emma Merrigan! Enough of this! I'm impressed; I've never seen such deep binding in another living mind. I'm awed by your skill, now detach yourself—please!

It took Eleanor's words, echoing inside Emma's intangible skull to make her realize that what she had done—falling from the wasteland directly into the core of Edwys's being—was not the normal way to bind with another personality or to locate a curse's root—if the word "normal" could be applied to any of this. But when it came to getting out, the only way she knew was death.

I don't know how. If she could hear Eleanor, perhaps Eleanor could hear her.

Be yourself and quickly. Someone's coming. This scene will play itself out soon.

Em heard the hoofbeats, too, the same as before. Edwys had his hand on the hilt of his sword. He crept forward.

Be myself, Em thought and willed herself not to move with him. She imagined them pulling apart, like DNA unwinding, and felt as if she'd been torn in half. But the image worked—the subjective became objective. Em was herself, apart from Edwys as the Normans rode into ambush for the second time.

Separated from Edwys, Emma had become a ghost, invisible and impotent. There was nothing she could do to influence events as they unfolded.

"Is this the time and place?"

Em heard Eleanor's voice but there was no Eleanor. They were both ghosts.

"Yes. The one in the center—Eudes—he's the curse, the curse-maker, Bran's demon. He came into my home Monday night and tried to kill me there and again in the wasteland. I fought him in the wasteland. At the moment when I thought I'd won, I wound up here, in Edwys's mind. That's his name, Edwys, not Eddie; just like I thought Eudes was O'days. I kept Edwys from killing him—though God knows, I'm sure he deserves it.

"Isn't that what I was supposed to do: make a little change to keep a curse from being born? Edwys died instead, and now Bran's got black spots all over him."

"Shhhh," Eleanor advised and the leaves around her voice fluttered ever so slightly.

Edwys lunged out of the bushes, sword in hand. His war cry spooked the horses of the men who had the best chance of stopping him before he reached Eudes, who was—by the manifestly greater quality of his horse and armor—the leader of these men.

Eudes needed no help from a twentieth-century ghost to save his own life. Em winced when she saw the Norman reach for his sword and when her vision cleared, young Edwys was mortally wounded.

"I don't understand—Eudes is the root of the curse!"

"When you change a thing, Emma—if you changed it— you change it for all time. More likely, you only thought you changed events and laid your curse."

Edwys had slipped to the ground. He lay on his side, with one arm up over the wound in his neck. Eudes's companions, who'd been caught by surprise, had their swords drawn, ready to prevent a miracle, though Em was confident that the young man was quite dead.

Two of the Normans objected when Eudes dismounted. The warrior who'd threatened Em in her own place and time thrust his sword into the ground and knelt beside Edwys. He rolled the would-be assassin onto his back. Cradling Edwys's head, Eudes clasped his hands together in fervent prayer.

Em assumed the Norman was thanking God for favoring him. She wouldn't have been surprised if Eudes had simply ordered his men to drag Edwys's body into the woods. But Eudes took a cloak from one of his men and commanded them all to help him wrap the cloth around Edwys's corpse. Eudes alone lifted the heavy bundle off the ground and secured it across his high, uncomfortable-looking saddle. Em caught a glimpse of Eudes's face as he took the reins to lead the animal along the path. It was not the face of a man who was glad to be alive.

"This turns interesting," Eleanor said. "Stay close, we'll follow them. Do you know why Edwys set out to kill Eudes? Were they caught in some wider net of honor? One vendetta can fuel a hundred curses."

"Every victim gets a death wish?" Emma asked as Eudes got the procession going.

"Rarely. Persistent curses are complex. Did you play 'pick up sticks' as a child? A death wish is a stick that falls outside the pile. You might score a point for removing it, but you haven't touched the hard work. Six ways from Sunday, your Eudes is going to pay for killing that boy and therein will lie your curse."

Emma nodded—a gesture that was lost on her mother. They were invisible in this eleventh-century here-and-now, apparently inaudible to the natives, yet oddly substantial as they kept pace behind the Norman horses. Having decided that she was a ghost, Em expected to hover above the cohort. Instead, she walked with her own natural weight and stride.

Neither she nor Eleanor left footprints, though the road was pocked with mud from a recent rain. The horses had no difficulty with the road, and Em wouldn't have had either, if she'd been able to see her feet. It was as hard to walk on her invisible feet as it would have been on a moonless midnight. Em fought for her balance with every step.

Out of respect for the dead—or for one of his men who limped along on a stiff and withered leg—Eudes set a slow pace. After about a mile and a half of the stumbling staggers, Emma got the hang of *knowing* where her feet were when she couldn't see them and was able to share the rest of what she knew about the eleventh century in general and Eudes in particular with her mother.

They were still walking and not in sight of anything interesting when Em ran out of knowledge. She asked a question of her own:

"Is this how I—we—have to travel or are you waiting for me to figure out how to fly?"

"If you can manage to fly in any here-and-now, all of us would be grateful," Eleanor replied, alluding once again to that greater and mysterious organization of which she was a part. "You can fly in the Netherlands, or swim for that matter. I don't myself—you don't gain anything by doing it— but you can, if that sort of thing pleases you. When you're tracing a curse to its root in the here-and-now, though, it's walk or hitch a ride—horses don't seem to mind and I've climbed onto more than a few broad shoulders. It's uncomfortable, though. Be glad everyone's walking."

"Let me get this straight: there's *my* here-and-now—the living room where, presumably, my body is keeping itself healthy—and there's the wasteland, which isn't here-and-now but is the Grand Central Station for the infinity of here-and-nows of the past. Am I right so far?"

Em glanced sideways. The only way she could see her mother was peripherally, as a reflection in the dark-glass mirror. It was impossible to read Eleanor's expression.

"Am I?"

"You're the one with all the education," Eleanor replied.

"When this is over and we've laid this to rest, you can come to New York with me. There are things you have to know—not just about the Netherlands and curses, but about managing money and keeping yourself above suspicion. You can talk to Harry while you're there. He thinks he's the Einstein of the Netherlands."

The bitter edge to Eleanor's words was unmistakable. Toward the end of their marriage, she and Jeff had talked that way about each other, though Em's gut feeling was that her mother's bitterness reached far beyond Harry. She remembered the letter with which she'd begun her exploration of the wooden box, the letter about gifts and greater causes that justified obligations. She wondered if Eleanor would write those words now.

Em wondered, too—no, *worried* was more accurate—how her own life would change now that she'd brushed up against a secret society of age-defying witches. She imagined that keeping oneself above suspicion was both individually and organizationally important. Especially for the organization. If the twentieth century was more tolerant of witchcraft than earlier centuries had been, it was only because the twentieth century was confident that witches were deluded.

It didn't take Einstein to theorize what would happen if word of competent witches with the power to change the past started getting out. Every segment of society, every philosophy, science, and religion would confront a sea change of fundamental proportions. At the very least, Em could forget about describing her adventures to anyone who couldn't share them. She'd already been dangerously indiscreet with Matt and Nancy.

That left an over-long life filled with Eleanor, Harry, and the rest of a nameless organization that sounded a whole lot less benign than a university library. The sailor on his plank or criminal at the gallows had no more optimism than Emma

Merrigan had at that moment. She swallowed hard and kept walking until Eudes and his cohort emerged from the forest into meadows and cultivated fields.

At first glance, the farm could be any farm, anywhere, glimpsed from the side of any road. At second glance, it was old-fashioned—the sort of living-history exhibit that bridged the gap between a museum and an amusement park. It wasn't until Emma was close enough to see faces and expressions that the full paradox hit home.

"This is real," she said, needing to hear the sound of her own voice speaking twentieth-century American English. "These men walked this road nine hundred years ago. I'm here. I'm watching them. It's not a dream. It's not a movie. It's real. This afternoon *happened* once upon a time."

"And apparently gave rise to a persistent curse," Eleanor added from a point on Emma's right.

Eleanor had been on Em's left the last time she'd been aware of her. The surprise, however momentary, served as another reminder that everything was not merely real, it was unpredictable and dangerous. Instinctively, Emma slowed and fell behind.

"Don't do that!" Eleanor chided, a warning that she was more attuned to Emma's movements than Emma was to hers. "Stay close to them. You can squeeze between them, if you have to, but there's no walking through walls and opening a door is more trouble than it's worth."

Em hurried through a palisade gate, just in case one of the Normans took a notion to shut it. She was shoulder to shoulder with Eudes when he lifted Edwys from the saddle. She'd managed to live for half a century without rubbing shoulders with an unembalmed human corpse, much less one with its mortal wound still dripping blood on the ground. No words, pictures, nor a handful of funerals had prepared her for the view.

Edwys wasn't the first young man to die a futile death,

and by the measure of Em's life, he'd been dead for nine centuries, but that didn't make the sight of him any easier to bear. If memory hadn't supplied a counterimage—Bran Mongomery's sore-encrusted flesh—she'd have run through doors, walls, and everything else in her effort to escape.

The memory of an ultra-tech hospital room and its solitary patient kept Emma glued to Eudes. He was younger than she'd first thought in her living room. Everyone was younger; in the eleventh century age seemed measured by scars, not wrinkles. Eudes had his share of scars. A part of the right side of his face was immobilized by a sharp-lined patch of once-burned, now-healed skin. From some musty science or history lesson Emma remembered that people cauterized wounds in the days before antiseptic surgery.

The scar gave Eudes a brutal expression that was, perhaps, not a true measure of his personality. Yes, he was part of a conquering army, and yes, soldiers of any era did things that scarred their consciences, and, yes—above all else—a man who resembled Eudes had nearly put an end to *her* in the wasteland. But Edwys had set this ball rolling because his sister had committed the unpardonable sin of loving the man who'd married her.

Eudes spoke quietly to the limping man who'd kept their pace comfortable on the road as they all walked past what had to be the main house with shuttered windows and a massive front door at the top of a flight of steep wooden stairs.

Emma couldn't understand a word. She was getting used to the "I'm in a foreign country sensation" and paid more attention to body language. Eudes's second didn't approve of following a laid-stone path across the bare earth yard and around a corner. She guessed why a moment later when they surprised three women and a gray-bearded man elbow deep in the business of butchering a sizable pig.

One of the women and the man dropped their cleavers immediately but the other two women held onto theirs. Of that pair, the younger appeared dumbstruck. The other leapt into a shrieking rage. Emma recognized Edwys's name out of the wrath spewing in Eudes's direction and while she didn't see a profound family resemblance among them, behavior alone suggested that the dumbstruck woman was Emma, Edwys's sister, and the older woman was his mother.

Whatever the blood relationships, the older woman clearly blamed Eudes for Edwys's death and when the Norman attempted to explain himself the woman came at him with her cleaver held high. Both the younger woman—the probable sister, daughter, and wife—and the limping man intervened, disarming the elderly woman without injuring her or curtailing her invective. While the limping man swept swine guts from the blood-sopped plank-and-trestle table, the older woman berated the younger one with what had to be a mother's fury.

Em would have laid odds that Edwys had confided his plans to his mother and had her approval when he laid his ambush for his brother-in-law. The mother's anger, then, was that the wrong corpse was stretched out on the butchering table.

Eudes appeared to share Em's conclusion. For him, perhaps, it wasn't a gut-feel guess. He stalked around the table with a predatory grace and purpose that Em remembered from her own living room. He spat out Edwys's name and other words that drained the color from Emma-the-sister's cheeks. The eleventh-century woman gasped a phrase that was either a denial or an apology, or a bit of both. Her hands lost their grip on her mother's arm.

The next moment the older woman was on the move. She scooped up a wicked-looking butcher's tool with a fifteen-inch wooden shank and a flat, crescent-shaped, iron hook fitted to one end. The hook dripped a viscous liquid as the woman flung it with admirable accuracy toward Eudes. The shank made half a cartwheel and dragged the hook across the Norman's already scarred cheek.

The third woman and the elderly man who'd dropped their cleavers when the Normans arrived raced off in opposite directions—she for the stone-walled house, he for the fields—both shouting their heads off. The wiser part of Em wanted to join them.

She could see disaster coming as Eudes scooped the meat hook up from the mud in which it had fallen. Matt's notes and her coffee-table book described the Norman conquerors of the English kingdom as warriors untempered by remorse or restraint. History books didn't capture individuals; Em had glimpsed considerable remorse and restraint in the way Eudes handled Edwys's corpse and bore his mother-in-law's initial attacks. But once blood was spilt a certain type of human being, regardless of the century, was apt to use violence for vengeance.

Emma-the-sister latched onto her husband's raised arm. Though she was a slender woman, when she jerked his elbow with all her strength and weight, her husband spun around to face her. Em's ears couldn't pick out the syllables for "Please" or "I beg of you" but the word for "mother" hadn't changed much in a millennium. Eudes struck his wife with the back of his hand.

Both Emmas reacted to the blow. Emma-the-sister lost her grip and stumbled backward until she tripped and collapsed in the bloody mud. Emma, who contributed time and money to Bower's battered-women shelter, wanted to fight back. She knew that would have been foolish, even if she'd had a body or a sword. In the Middle Ages, women were little more than property. If a man beat his wife to death, he'd committed a sin, not a crime.

Eudes *hadn't* killed his wife—that indicated he was in control of his rage, but it remained a murderous rage when he focused it on the old woman.

"He'll kill them both," Em gasped. "Eudes will kill her mother and her brother. It's not really his fault—they attacked him first, but he's a professional and they're amateurs. It's mice attacking a lion."

Em conceived a plan: grab onto Eudes's chain-mail lapels, get in his face, and yell as loudly as possible. If he couldn't see her, maybe he'd feel her, or maybe she'd manage to climb inside his head. Eleanor had complimented her for getting inside Edwys's head; obviously she had some talent for it, even if she hadn't any coherent idea how to use it.

She'd gotten one step toward her goal when Eleanor appeared in front of her.

"Let it play out! We need to see how the curse emerges before we intercede in its creation! We'll come here again to lay this curse to rest."

Eleanor's bag of tricks was deeper than Em had suspected. Not only was her mother clearly visible in her own untimely clothing, but she made herself felt when she tapped Emma on the breastbone. There was a trace of magic, or electricity, in Eleanor's touch. Em didn't stagger backward. She was simply standing in one place one instant and another, some three feet distant, a moment later.

It was worse than running an undocumented computer program for the first time. What were the commands? the rituals? the proverbial keystrokes? She didn't know the rules of curse hunting. Why was Eleanor suddenly visible? Could Eudes and the others see her? Could she, Emma Merrigan, make herself invisible to Eleanor yet visible to Eudes? With computers there was always a reset button. Here, there seemed nothing better to do than stiffen her spine and attempt to shove Eleanor aside.

This time Em found herself paralyzed as well as three feet back.

"Let this human tragedy play itself out!"

And play out it did.

The old woman hadn't been idle while Em sparred with Eleanor and Emma-the-sister pled with her husband. Butchering a pig required any number of tools that could double as weapons. Edwys's mother had picked up a nasty one that fit over her fist like a set of brass knuckles and, to judge by the stringy tissue attached to the narrow blade rising above her fist, was meant to separate meat from the hide of a pig. The old woman meant to separate Eudes from his life, but first she had to get within striking distance. That proved impossible. Eudes wielded the meat hook as expertly as he'd wielded a sword.

He dealt the old woman a flat blow along the forearm—which Em took as another instance of restraint until she heard arm bones breaking. If Edwys's mother had dropped her weapon then, she might have spared herself. But Edwys's suicidal tendencies came naturally and the old woman somehow kept a grip on the flesh-ripping steel. Eudes struck her a second time, another flat-weapon blow against her ribs. The old woman crumpled. She tried to break her fall with her broken arm.

Luck and fate were against Edwys's family that eleventh-century day. As the old woman's broken bones ripped her flesh, her clenched hand turned upward and her nasty little weapon sliced through her gown between her ribs.

Em closed her eyes and turned away. Her twentieth-century dinner went toxic in her stomach. When the nausea ebbed, she reopened her eyes. Emma-the-sister had moved to her mother's side and rolled the seriously—perhaps fatally—injured woman onto her back.

The old woman opened her mouth, but blood rather than words flowed from her lips. Like her son a few hours earlier, Edwys's mother was passing through unconscious on her way to dead. The composite fracture would probably have proved mortal in a few painful days, but the old woman had effectively slain herself when fate let her fall on her own filthy weapon. As Em fought the shivering dizziness of emotional shock, her namesake closed her mother's lifeless eyes.

Eudes said something grim. Emma-the-sister replied with words that were both tearful and shrill. Em Merrigan watched in helpless silence as her namesake opened the old woman's hand and withdrew the piercing weapon from her side.

"Now she's going to attack him and he'll kill her too, in self-defense. The whole family will have wiped itself out!"

"I believe you might be right." Eleanor had become invisible again, but her voice came from Em's right, where a better view of Eudes could be had. "Feel the air, Emma. Smell it. Taste it. Like a storm, there's a curse coming."

The air around them *was* charged. The silk shirt she wore but couldn't see or feel shot static sparks against her skin when she touched it. Her hair had lifted from her scalp.

Eudes's dark hair lay flat against his head and Emma-the-sister's braids hung heavy down her back. The storm wasn't part of the eleventh-century here-and-now; it brewed in the halfway place where Em and her mother stood.

"Should we be getting ready to do something significant?" Em asked.

"No. No, we'll let it play to its end. We can always come back—as many times as we need. Once we know what happens. Do you understand now that you changed nothing in the woods the other day? This curse has many parts. We don't yet know which ones are critical and which are merely fuel."

Eudes and Emma-the-sister continued their bitter exchange, gesturing now at Edwys's corpse on the butchery table, now at the old woman's on the ground between them. The choreography reminded Em of the verbal brawls in the early stages of the dissolution of her second marriage, when she and Jeff could still say honestly that they loved each other. Em wondered if she and Jeff could have fallen victim to a curse or, worse, given rise to one. To know the truth, she'd have to play the secret observer of her own life.

While Em pondered that question, Eudes shouted one of his own. Emma-the-sister stiffened and trembled but finally answered with a single word that had to mean yes. For a moment there was silence in the eleventh century and a sound like the swarming of a thousand angry bees in the halfway place.

Eudes wrapped his hand around the hilt of his sword. He withdrew it an inch or two from the scabbard, never turning away from Emma-the-sister's face. She was paler than either corpse but unbowed. She challenged her husband to slay her. *Morthor,* her word for cold-blooded killing, had scarcely changed in nine centuries. Eudes shoved his weapon back into the scabbard.

He turned his back on his wife and walked away. The limping man preceded him.

Em's breath caught as her namesake adjusted her hold on the crescent-shaped tool that had slain her mother. She wiped it in her mother's blood. The look she cast at Eudes's back shook Em to her insubstantial core.

"She said it would be easy to kill him," Em Merrigan whispered in horror. "Jennifer said he'd done things that deserved killing."

"What was that?"

Em couldn't answer. She could scarcely think for herself as her namesake threw herself at her husband. Eudes wore a mail shirt that descended from his neck to his knees and from his shoulders to a point several inches below his elbows. The nasty little tool was no match for hundreds of steel links and Emma-the-sister knew it. She aimed high, for her husband's shaved neck—for the same place where Eudes had struck Edwys—and hit hard with the cold purpose of a guillotine blade.

Eudes fell like an unstrung marionette. He could not have known what hit him.

Em felt a hot, gritty wind against her back. In no time at all it had reached howling intensity although nothing moved in the eleventh century. She began a prayerful litany: "Oh, God. Oh, God . . ."

"Hold steady," Eleanor advised. "We're almost done."

"There's more? What more could there be? How much more does a curse need to persist for nine hundred years?"

"We'll see."

The limping man spun around on his good leg, fumbling with his sword. Emma-the-sister uttered a dire handful of words that nailed the Norman to the ground while she got both hands on her husband's sword and yanked it free from the scabbard beneath his body. The Englishwoman's face was tear-streaked, though she made no sound that Em could hear above the swarming bees and stinging wind in the halfway place.

Eleanor's voice, however, was as clear as if her mouth were inside Em's head.

"Now we see what happened here. Now comes the moment when a curse is born."

Under the grim watch of the limping man, Emma, whose brother, mother, and husband were now dead, wedged the naked sword between Eudes's arm and body. The point stood some twenty degrees short of perpendicular.

Em realized aloud: "She's going to kill herself!"

"What else can she do?" Eleanor countered. "She's murdered her husband and made real the conspiracy to murder that her mother and brother began. The crippled man has seen it all, and heard her confession. It's kill him and keep on killing until someone kills her, or kill herself and put an end to it—or so she thinks. The strongest curses are unconscious, Emma. They're born from the heart, not the mind."

Before Em could reply, her namesake invoked God's

name and blessing, then threw herself down on the upraised sword.

It wasn't an easy death. Eudes had thrust his sword deep into Edwys's gut, but his warrior's strength was greater than his wife's weight and for a moment it seemed that her dusty blue gown was sufficient armor to keep the blade from piercing her. But Em's namesake slipped slowly down the blade.

This time Em lacked the will to close her eyes and she witnessed the ghastly process as the sword pierced her back. No doubt the Englishwoman had given herself a fatal wound, but not instantaneous death or even swift unconsciousness. As she lay suffering, the limping man clouted her skull with the hilt of his sword—whether through mercy or vengeance, Em wouldn't guess.

She'd become lightheaded from shock, and sank to her knees muttering—

"It's Hamlet. It's goddamned Hamlet! The play's not over until everyone's dead. Where do we intervene, Eleanor? Who do we stop? Edwys? Eudes? The mother? The sister before she kills her husband or before she kills herself? The limping man?"

"Soon," Eleanor replied. "Soon. Listen."

The wind had died. The bees had stopped buzzing. The sounds of the limping man's uneven stride as he walked away from the abattoir were the loudest sounds Em heard in the eleventh century or elsewhere.

"What happened? Where's this great curse? Where's the curse that reaches across time to make Bran and Jennifer destroy each other?"

"It's coming," Eleanor assured her daughter, and laying a palpable arm over Emma's, she pulled her backward a good twenty feet. "Pay attention, but quietly, too. It would like nothing better than to feast on us as well."

Though the sky was bright in the eleventh century, it

turned dark around Eleanor and Em. She heard a familiar sound: a dog that growled as it hunted, and saw a familiar sight: a pillar of orange fire rising from the wound in her namesake's back. It lingered there at least a minute, growing stronger before a flaming streamer reached out to envelop the old woman. Another minute and another streamer had reached out for Edwys. It took Eudes last.

By then it was tall and thick enough to have a face. Hollow black eyes focused in Em's direction.

"Can it see us?"

"Perhaps—but like any infant it doesn't know what it sees. Quickly, back to yourself, before it learns."

Before Em could ask how that feat of magic might be accomplished, her mother had seized her arm.

"Stay with me!" Eleanor commanded as the eleventh century disappeared beneath a blanket of thick gray smoke.

Emma tried, but it was Eleanor whose grip loosened as they tumbled through darkness. In an instant, Emma was alone. She thought of home in Bower, the Maisonettes, and her physical body. She thought of her musketeer, Aramis, though that wasn't his name, merely the label Em had put on his memory. He'd come out of nowhere to save her before, and warned her the last time that she shouldn't depend on him doing it again. That didn't stop Em from shouting,

"Aramis!"

There was no answer, no breathtaking rescue. Em was alone and losing consciousness as the tumbling intensified. The thought, *I'm going to die,* grew until it was very nearly Emma's only thought and she could feel it becoming truth. Her memories lit up: she was at school, with Dad, with Jeff, Lori, and Jay-Jay, on vacation at the Grand Canyon . . .

Em's panic faded, replaced by serenity. She waited for the light. Light was part of the American myth of dying. She believed in the light.

Belief mattered.

If she believed in something else . . .

If she believed this was a dream?

Panic threatened; Emma couldn't convince herself of that. She believed in the light again . . . the eerie lavender twilight of the wasteland when viewed through her "other eyes."

Belief mattered.

Em shut down her distant memories. She concentrated on the wasteland. Eleanor had told her how to get home from the wasteland—just find the black-glass mirror and walk through it.

Too soon! Too soon to believe in mirrors or walking again. But Emma was on the right track. She believed in the wasteland the way she believed arithmetic exercises would cure her insomnia. And, after about the same amount of time it would have taken her to fall asleep, the tumbling stopped. Em drifted gently downward until her hands and knees came to rest on the parched dirt of the wasteland.

"The black-glass mirror is right behind me. *Right* behind me," Em whispered before she opened her eyes or stood.

Belief mattered, and hers was potent enough. The mirror was where Em needed it to be. It took her three tries before she figured out how to walk through it. Immediately she felt the aches that came from sitting too long in her dining-room chairs and knew before she raised her head that Eleanor was waiting for her.

Fifteen

E *very light in* the living room was on, even the old-fashioned sconces left over from an era when electric fix-
tures still resembled candles. The old screw-switches were
tricky to operate; Em rarely bothered but Eleanor had found
the elusive sweet-spot where the power was steady and the
bulbs glowed without flickering.

Emma didn't smoke: never had, never would, and without
getting too fanatical about it, preferred not to be around
those who did. When she'd moved into the Maisonettes
she'd seized the opportunity to get rid of her never-large collection of ashtrays which left her wondering, even as she
stretched the kinks out of stiff, aching joints, what inappropriate object Eleanor had been using while she soothed her
nerves and stank up her daughter's home.

"I'd gotten worried," Eleanor explained once their eyes
had met. "You've been out too long. I can believe you lost
Tuesday. You were all hunched over in that chair. I tried to
make you comfortable, but I didn't want to move you. It
shouldn't make any difference, but I didn't want to take any
risk. Do you need a hand standing up?"

She offered the hand that wasn't leaking smoke. Emma
pushed away from the table without assistance and tried not

to be too obvious as she did a "what's wrong with this picture?" scan of her living room.

Eleanor's version of the morocco-bound book sat like a black roof in the seat of Em's favorite chair. A shot or two of liquor filled the bottom of a too-large glass. Lipstick crescents decorated its rim. A glance at the VCR showed the time as 1:12 AM or about two hours later than Em's internal clock would have guessed. Eleanor had had reason to be concerned.

"You know what they say about traveling these days," Em said with patently forced humor. "It doesn't matter whether you're going to heaven or hell, you're going to have to change planes on the way home. I missed my connecting flight. Headwinds."

Eleanor was not amused. "The Netherlands aren't a joke, Emma. You've got so much to learn."

"That's hardly my fault, is it? You're the one who couldn't hold on." Recriminations wouldn't help. Emma took a deep breath. "Look, I'd rather you didn't smoke in my home. I'm sure I'll learn whatever you need to teach me much better if my lungs aren't in rebellion."

Without comment, Eleanor stubbed her cigarette in a saucer she'd gleaned from Em's everyday dishes. The dishes were virtually indestructible: microwave, freezer, and dishwasher safe, and unbreakable to boot. A little charred tobacco wouldn't hurt them, but Emma cringed all the same.

"There were two calls before you returned. One from a woman, Nancy, who wanted to make plans for tomorrow afternoon. She said she'd drag you out of bed at eight if you didn't get back to her before midnight. The other was more serious, I think. Someone named Matt called to tell you that Bran had taken a turn for the worse and might not make it through the night. He left a number. I wrote it down, but it's on your tape, if you'd rather trust that."

Emma wasn't the only woman in the living room with empathy problems.

"You remember that Bran's the one with the curse?" Em asked.

"I recognized the name. Matt asked another question—had you done anything yet? I wondered what he meant. You haven't told him about the Netherlands?"

Em sighed as she navigated past Eleanor, en route to the phone. "He plays handball with Bran. We've talked. Just out of curiosity—could he become one of us, as it were? Can walking through time be taught or is it something you have to inherit from your mother?"

"It's a wyrd, Emma, mostly hereditary, though not always, and, yes, sometimes it crops up spontaneously. We're always on the lookout for newcomers in the Netherlands. The gift's there from the beginning, but the urge to explore usually hits during adolescence. That's why I expected to become aware of you years ago."

"Another example of puberty-linked magic?"

"You might say—or not. The wyrd simply *is* and if your friend Matt had it, most likely he'd have been found using it. Unlike you, he wouldn't have been named for his wyrd and wouldn't have denied it. It would have been part of him. More to the point, when you were noticed on Tuesday, you weren't with another newcomer."

Emma swallowed the information whole; there'd be a lot to ponder when the dust settled. Until then, Matt had dropped a new layer of urgency over everything. She reached for the phone. Eleanor had written a number with the university prefix and a hospital extension on the scratch pad beside the phone. Em had no trouble recognizing the handwriting or deciding that for the sake of short-term co-existence she'd simply dial the number rather than unreel the messages to confirm what Eleanor had written down.

Still, her mind raced in conflicting directions and a failure of concentration brought her index finger down on the redial button rather than one of the number-pad keys. Not much of an error, until she saw a ten-digit number pop up in the pre-dial window. The area code wasn't 212, the only New York code she knew, but Eleanor had said she lived north of the Big Apple. Eleanor had helped herself to Em's long-distance service the same way she'd helped herself to the liquor and the saucer.

Emma gave the number a good stare, trying to commit it to memory. It would disappear as soon as she tapped in the number on the scratch pad, although it should pop up again on her phone bill. Em could hardly blame Eleanor for check-ing in with—what was the name of the man she lived with?—the man she was married to on paper only? Harry. His name was Harry. He'd want to know that Eleanor had arrived safely. He'd want to know what had happened.

Was Harry the one who'd noticed her? Eleanor hadn't once claimed that honor. What was Harry's part in all this? Was he as unhappy with his part in a sham marriage as Eleanor was with hers?

There were too many things to think about. Emma had to narrow her focus. If she remembered the number, fine. If she spotted it on her next month's bill, also fine. Until then, she tapped the number that Eleanor had written. The connection wandered through several switches before it began ringing. After a dozen unanswered rings, Em hung up and tried a second time, with the same result. Well aware that Eleanor was watching her closely, Emma dialed the number a third time, leaving off the extension and tapping buttons until she reached a human being.

"Please connect me with the nurses' station in Section U," she said as professionally as any librarian could make her-self sound.

"There is no Section U," the obviously underinformed op-erator replied, beginning a strained negotiation that crept through two supervisors before someone transferred Emma to another extension that rang at least twenty times before someone who sounded more comfortable with mops than scalpels answered.

"There's no one here. They took him away this evening. Everything's closed up now."

In light of Matt's message, that had an ominous sound. Emma tried calling Matt at home without success then returned to the hospital switchboard, this time searching for Bran Mongomery. She had better luck than before. Within five minutes she was talking to a nurse in an ICU.

"If you're not family, I'm afraid I can only tell you that Brandon Mongomery is a patient and his condition is extremely critical. You couldn't see him if you came down here—not even through a window."

Especially not through a window, Em thought to herself. "Are any family members there now? Any friends?" she pressed. "One young man in particular—well built, a little on the short side, dark hair—starting to thin on top, glasses? He might be wearing khakis and a dark-green plaid . . ." She hesitated, thinking of more complimentary ways to describe Matt.

She needn't have worried.

"That one's here," the nurse assured her. "Got here before Mr. Mongomery got out of surgery and hasn't budged since. I can't call him in here to talk to you, but if you'll tell me your number, I'll pass the word that you've called."

"Fine," Emma agreed and gave the nurse her particulars before hanging up.

"Learn anything interesting?" Eleanor asked, though surely she had overheard everything.

"Not much—Bran's been moved from that funky isolation unit to an ICU, probably because he's had some sort of surgery. They'd only tell me that his condition was critical, but nothing more, because I'm not family."

"That's just a formality, Emma. They expect you to lie."

"I don't," she replied, which was the truth, even though she'd long since learned to lie when necessary. To change the subject, Em asked, "Who did you call while I was *non compos mentis?*"

"I didn't call anyone."

"Did another ghost come through then? Someone made a long-distance call, Eleanor. Who would it have been if it wasn't you?"

"I assure you, I don't know."

"I *saw* the number." Emma began to recite it.

Eleanor cracked between the fifth and sixth digits, which was a huge relief, since Em couldn't remember the whole thing.

"Harry," Eleanor confessed bitterly. "I called Harry. You were *non compos mentis* and I wasn't sure what to do. It was bad enough that I lost my hold on you as we transited from that moment when the curse rose back to the Netherlands. I looked for you as best I could. People don't just disappear, Emma, not even in the Netherlands, or between the past and the Netherlands. You could have been grabbed—but I should have felt something if you'd been. Someone should have felt something—that's why I called Harry. He'd have sensed something if anything had happened. He said there'd been no echoes, no absences. If you weren't where I'd left you, then you'd taken off on your own."

It was Emma's turn to feel wrongfully accused. "Not hardly. You said 'hold on' and I tried. I wasn't prepared for the way the wind beat us up—and for my money, I don't think you were either, Eleanor. You lost your grip and we got separated. It happens in the best of families. When mothers get careless, children get lost."

Eleanor stiffened, but otherwise ignored the bait. "I could have found you if you'd simply gotten lost after we were separated. But you weren't lost, Emma, not *after.* You took off with great confidence. I raced back here—you were out cold and I couldn't revive you, so I knew you'd gone someplace. Where else, I thought, and went straight back to the curse's root. Based on what you'd told me, there wasn't anywhere else that you knew. Believe what you want about me, Emma, but don't ask me to believe that you didn't take yourself somewhere after we separated.

"I was beside myself. I waited three hours and your body hadn't twitched. Of course I called Harry. If you'd fallen afoul of something dangerous, I needed to know . . . *they* needed to know. You may have bitten off more than you can chew in this Eudes-Bran misery, but you haven't glimpsed what a curse can do. The worst of them don't bother with the here-and-now—any here-and-now. The worst of them stalk one another, and us.

"And you'd gone someplace that I couldn't find. I called Harry, Emma—who did you call?"

"I didn't *call* anyone! I was head-over-heels falling through the middle of nowhere with my life flashing in front of me. I got lucky and managed to think my way back to the wasteland and that mirror-wall you'd shown me."

Eleanor seemed truly confused. "You didn't *meet* someone? You didn't call a name?"

Aramis. She had shouted that name—which wasn't a valid name—as she'd tumbled. He hadn't answered and a gut-feeling kept Em from honestly answering Eleanor's last question. "I tell you, I was alone from the moment we got separated until I woke up here."

Middle-aged daughter and decades-younger mother stood some five feet apart, measuring each other without subtlety. The mother-voice, so different from Eleanor Merrigan's voice, which had guided Emma throughout her life, advised her to tread cautiously. The immediate situation: laying an eleventh-century curse before it claimed another victim demanded her full attention. The rest—Eleanor Merrigan and all the mysteries she represented—would have to wait.

"I'll be more careful next time," Em promised and was saved from having to explain herself by a timely ring from the telephone. She lifted the receiver at once, without waiting for the answering machine to screen the call.

"Matt?"

"Yeah," he confirmed. "Where you been, Em? I tried to call you hours ago. We've all moved upstairs now. I gotta be a little bit careful what I say; I'm not the only guy here. If you—like—*did* something, or set something in motion, maybe you should reconsider."

The need for discretion and self-censorship was almost as great at the Maisonettes as it was at the hospital but Em couldn't explain that fully. She'd have to hope that Matt would read between the lines. He seemed to have the knack.

"I had company waiting when I got home—family—my mother, of all people! We went out for a little while; turned out I was gone longer than either one of us expected."

"Shit—your mother? I thought she was dead."

"Not hardly, cowboy. How's Bran? What I got from the nurse a few minutes ago didn't sound good."

"It's not good—*Your mother?* Is she for real, or like ol' Eudes coming back to haunt you?"

Actors had an easy time carrying on conversations where every line had two meanings. On the fly and well after midnight, the challenge was much greater. Emma scrambled for a clever, all-purpose response before mumbling—

"Don't worry about my mother, just tell me about Bran. The nurse said he was in extremely critical condition."

"The kim-chee hit the fan a couple hours after you left— that's why I thought it had something to do with you and all. When I couldn't reach you—Man, I thought it must be falling apart all over. That black stuff on Bran's neck—it started growing and moving real fast. You'd have thought it was a sci-fi movie the way people were running around there in Section U. From what I heard, Bran died a couple of times before they got him stabilized. They tried cutting away the crud and put him on a ventilator—"

Em interrupted to ask: "Have you heard what the crud is?"

"Bran's not the only patient anymore and the nurses up here are too busy with the inmates to fraternize with the visitors—but I've heard the word 'gangrene' mentioned a few times, and a lot of plain old 'crud.' The truth is, they don't have a clue what's eating him up—but I think they're taking it personally. It would have been easier to just let him die, but they're fighting overtime to keep him alive—at least until his mom gets here. Her plane lands at ten AM and—get this—the hospital's sending someone out to the airport to pick her up. It's *got* to be personal."

"Yeah," Em agreed idly.

Her greater attention was absorbed by her memory. The old woman—Edwys's mother—had attacked Eudes with a filthy medieval meathook. God knew, butchering animals wasn't a sanitary process even now and getting gouged with a weapon that had just slit a pig's guts was probably as sure a way to contract an infection as nasty as any humanity had ever devised, but putrefaction took time.

"Em? You still there, Em? You sure you didn't try something? It wouldn't be your fault, not if you tried something that didn't work."

Matt had a naive but unerring way of getting to the painful heart of the matter.

"We looked, but we didn't touch," Emma told her friend. "Not like the last time."

"There's got to be something, Em, some way to turn this around. You've got to try. If there's anything I can do—I'll face that swordsman, if that's what it takes."

"It's not the swordsman, Matt," Em whispered. She wasn't

good at this. Eleanor was scowling; she knew what they were talking about. "Have you seen or spoken to Jennifer? You know she's going to blame herself if Bran dies."

"Maybe not. I called her when I called you. She's got the same problem you've got right now. Her mother was listening to every word she said. She didn't make a lot of sense, but she's kind of backed off on her story about how it's all her fault 'cause she tried to poison Bran."

Em went "Um," in the way that meant agreement rather than disagreement or denial. She imagined Jennifer's parents could mount a strong "good cop-bad cop" assault and that Jennifer would be vulnerable to it. Especially since it was unlikely that Jennifer was responsible for Bran's condition.

Matt confirmed Em's suspicions by saying, "Her parents are giving her ten kinds of grief. She's still talking about how she'd do anything to make Bran better again, but her parents are talking doctors and lawyers—for her, not him. Now she's saying that Bran *thought* she put drain cleaner in his coffee."

"The Hoddens will take care of their own."

"Yeah, they won't let her do anything foolish."

"Are you still going to stay with Bran until his mother gets into town?"

"Yeah—there's not much I can do here, but it's one night out of my life, right? His mother should get here around noon. I'll decide what I do next after that. Maybe she'll be glad of the company—unless there's something you need me to do?"

"No—just call me if anything happens. Leave a message. Don't worry about what time it's gotten to be."

"You're going to try to untangle this, right?"

"*Try* is the operative word, though everything I've done has only proved to be a disaster for Bran. I'm thinking it would be better to let modern medicine fight this battle, but, well—we'll see what happens here."

Matt wished her luck with the wasteland and with her mother. There hadn't been much conviction in his voice. Maybe that was exhaustion speaking. Em had glanced at the VCR clock again. It read 1:50 and she knew from long experience that her judgment was lousy in the wee hours of the morning. She got Matt to repeat his promise to call the moment anything happened, then hung up the phone.

Eleanor was waiting for information. Emma sat down first. Thinking it was the teacup that more commonly sat there, she lifted Eleanor's glass and took a sip of Scotch. The shock left her gasping for air.

"Are you just going to sit there staring at me, or are you going to tell me what, if anything useful, that friend of yours had to say? You mentioned the name Jennifer and said she'd blame herself if Bran died. May I assume you've spotted a repeating pattern?"

Emma took another sip of Scotch, deliberately this time, and savored the warmth as it flowed down her throat. "Is there really anything we can do? Bran's got some sort of spreading rash—call it a fungus or maybe gangrene. It's gotten into his throat, maybe his lungs; he's on a ventilator. There's a good chance he's not going to last until morning. I'm afraid I got him into this crisis by blundering around with Edwys and Eudes. I don't think he'll survive another mistake."

"Then you'd best not make another mistake."

Em caught herself shaking her head again as the words, "First, do no harm," came out of her mouth. The stakes had become too high for comfort. "He's better off with doctors."

Eleanor flashed a skeptical frown. "Doctors aren't going to save that young man. We are—*you* are. As soon as you're ready, we'll link arms and go back there. No draughts this time; you'll like that—two doses in one night aren't worth the risk—not after I've seen you bond with Edwys."

The compliment fell on sterile ground. "Both times that I've *bonded* with Edwys, Bran's come another step closer to death. With friends like me, he doesn't need a curse for an enemy."

Since childhood Emma had defended herself with bleak, self-deprecating humor. The tactic had become so ingrained she was scarcely conscious of the words she'd spoken— until she noticed that Eleanor was rigid and staring at her.

"What?" she demanded. "What did I say? I'm just blowing off steam, Eleanor. You've made me responsible for Bran's life—I think I'm entitled to a little gallows humor. I'll tell you this—I'd feel a lot better right now if *you* were the one who's going to pull off this miracle. You're the expert, aren't you?"

Eleanor's stare became a quick frown. "I'm here to help you, Emma, not finish what you started. That's not the way it's done."

"You've got to be kidding," Em exploded. "This isn't a competition—or is it? Professionals can coach the amateurs so long as they stay off the field? Is that what you're telling me?"

"You take everything to extremes, Emma. Of course I'd intercede, if there was no other way. We have time—while that boy lives in the here-and-now, we have time. Oh, it would be nice to have more time. We could come up with some elegant solution—the finger-tap that moves mountains—if we had time. But a good kick will do as well as a finger-tap, if you know where to apply it, and we do."

"*We* don't. You might, but not me. Maybe I could get inside Eudes's head and get him to take another road home. Avoid Edwys's ambush entirely. If there's no one for Edwys to attack, there's no one for Eudes to kill, no body for Eudes to carry home, no reason for the old woman to go berserk, et cetera, et cetera."

"That *might* work," Eleanor conceded with the tone of a chemistry teacher confronting yet another doomed-to-failure experiment. "But that's just the sort of elegance we don't have time for—and you're assuming that Edwys hadn't tried before and wouldn't try again—"

"I'm assuming that if I can keep them from coming together in that courtyard, Hamlet won't happen. Edwys's mother and sister couldn't have butchered a pig every day—"

"Butterfly sneezes!" Eleanor interrupted. "Change the tiniest detail and everything comes out different: that's pure myth. Time is resilient. If Edwys was determined to murder his brother-in-law and managed to do it once, he'll do it again no matter how many times the butterfly sneezes. There's nothing accidental about Edwys and Eudes, nothing about Edwys's mother, either, from what I could see. The sister is the one who acted spontaneously; she's our target."

"That's too late! Edwys and his mother are dead before she makes her first move—and Eudes, too. Did you see that meathook the mother threw at him? At the very least it was dripping with pig guts and, considering what Bran's going through right now, I wouldn't be surprised if it hadn't been coated with some other kind of poison too. When she brought Bran to the hospital the other day, Jennifer was babbling about how she'd poisoned Bran. She hadn't—not in our here-and-now, but I'll bet her hands were dirty back in the eleventh century."

Eleanor beamed. "You're right. You're absolutely right. The sister *knew*—that's the piece I was missing. I kept thinking that she was as mystified as we were, but she wasn't. She knew what had happened and what would happen from the moment she saw her brother's dead body in her husband's arms. You've got the mind for this, Emma."

Never mind her long, dark hair or flawless skin, Eleanor was having a maternal-pride moment and Emma felt ill.

"If I were to stop her from killing Eudes, he'd still die—slowly and painfully. And I don't imagine she'd be in good shape once King William the Bastard's justice got done with her. Where's the improvement in that?"

The smile faded from Eleanor's face. "You're laying a curse, Emma; you're not trying to make anyone's life take a turn for the better—including Bran Mongomery's. If it wasn't that a curse gets stronger and more adaptable each time it claims its prey, we wouldn't care at all about Bran Mongomery. If we're successful tonight, the hospital might be talking miracles tomorrow morning, or they might be measuring him for a coffin; either way is acceptable to us, so long as the curse is gone."

"There's got to be a better way," Emma insisted. It was pure stubbornness on her part: everything Eleanor had said made sense, if getting rid of a curse were more important than rescuing any of its victims.

"A better way for whom, Emma? Better for four people who'd have died nine centuries ago no matter what we did or didn't do? To help them—if they can be helped—you're going to have to spend lots of time—lots of here-and-now time—untangling their lives and you'll sacrifice Bran Mongomery in the here-and-now. Is your conscience up to *that*? We're curse hunters, Emma, not menders of broken hearts."

Emma shook her head. There had to be a middle course.

"Don't give me that look, Merle Acalia Merrigan. Maybe you are smarter than me. Gods know you don't *think* like the rest of us—I didn't want you to. I wanted you to have the choices and chances I never did, but if you think you can wander the Netherlands doing what you want, when you want, then you're a fool. Oh, you're not the first to think of going it alone; there've been dozens—hundreds—of hunters who were seduced by the past. Curses got all of them. They

272 * **Lynn Abbey**

turned rogue and we hunted them down. There's nothing more dangerous than a rogue, Emma. It would break my heart to hear that you'd become one, but I'd lead the hunt—for your sake."

Emma heard Aramis describing himself as neither curse nor man. Was he a rogue? Certainly he'd looked the part. And acted it? The oldest stories in humanity's books were those of deceit and betrayal. It came to her then, like a door blown shut by the wind, that she wanted nothing more to do with curses or the wasteland or anything that either implied.

"You won't have to worry, Eleanor. From the moment I laid eyes on Jennifer in the library stacks, it's been one damned, unbelievable thing after another and I've felt like my life is someone else's playground. I'll finish this, then I want my old life back. I'll never complain about dull or boring again, I swear it."

Eleanor smiled. "You don't really believe that's possible, do you?"

"Maybe not," Em conceded, looking at the wall behind her mother's head rather than at her face. "But I'm going to try. I need to believe that if I go back to the eleventh century and do what you want me to do—what I want me to do, too—then I'll have earned the right to walk away. I'm not foolish enough to get seduced by anything you and your global corporation of curse-hunters—"

Eleanor let loose a sharp, bitter, and not entirely unjustified bark of laughter. "It's not foolishness that has me worried, Emma. We've both survived foolishness. I *am* here to help you. Yes, I was sent by people you haven't met and might not like, but I paid for my own ticket and cab fare. I never wanted you to wind up like me—that's why I left you here in Bower. I'll lie for you, Emma—if that's any consolation—but I won't let you go rogue . . . or go off with a rogue."

Tell her! the mother-voice screamed inside Emma's skull. *Tell her and be done with it.*

Em shook her head to clear the voice from her mind. "Don't let go this time and we'll talk again in the morning."

Eleanor held out her hands—the traditional gesture of trust and reconciliation, and also the method Eleanor said they'd use to return to the eleventh century.

"One thing at a time."

"One thing at a time," Em agreed and held out her hands as well.

She expected to find herself whirling off to the wasteland, but Eleanor moved between her arms to give her daughter a hug, then retreated.

"We won't get to tomorrow morning or anywhere else without a plan. Will you agree that deflecting the sister is our best strategy?"

Sixteen

Deflect the sister, Emma thought, as if her yesteryear namesake were nothing more than a billiard ball. Eleanor was just that cold sitting on the sofa, contemplating the ideal moment to abort the curse. Edwys and his family weren't people to Eleanor, they were hazards on the devil's own miniature golf course.

In a shameful way, Em envied Eleanor's detachment. Though she nodded at all the appropriate moments as Eleanor pondered whether to intervene before Emma-the-sister killed her husband or after, in her heart Emma longed for the magic bullet: the single small act that would make everything right both in the present day and the eleventh century.

It was a futile hope and Emma knew it, but it was still in her mind when Eleanor said they were ready to return to the wasteland. She considered suggesting that they grab a few hours' sleep—considered the idea and rejected it. The phone hadn't rung. They hadn't run out of time. And the Michigan dawn was still hours away.

Em and Eleanor sat face to face, knees against knees on sofa cushions spread across the living room carpet. The cushions were Eleanor's idea—concern for her daughter's comfort. Eleanor clasped Em's wrists, then brought them together, four hands touching.

"Let yourself drift," Eleanor advised. "The memory of the draught is fresh in your mind even if the draught itself is gone. Imagine movement—clouds in a gentle breeze or a soft rain carrying you away. Embrace the movement."

For Emma the working metaphor turned out to be neither clouds nor rain but balloons, a great bouquet of helium-filled balloons attached to her shoulders. Impatient and eager, they lifted Em out of her body. *Then* she imagined clouds: the wispy streamers flowing over a jet's wings when it took off through a light fog.

"I've done it!" Em said aloud when the clouds had thickened and she was aware of Eleanor's touch, but not dependent upon it.

"It's the wyrd," Eleanor countered. "You were born knowing a thousand ways to the Netherlands. When you're ready, reverse the images."

Despite the illogic, Emma landed her balloons on a dark, cracked-mud plain. She opened her inner eyes. There was Eleanor, luminous within a column of white light. There was the black-mirror barrier between the here-and-now—*her* here-and-now—and the future. They set out walking toward the eleventh century.

In the grand tradition of soldiers everywhere as they marched toward battle, Emma distracted herself with petty paradoxes.

"What would happen to our bodies if we got stranded here?"

"Whatever happens here, happens in the here-and-now," Eleanor replied. "It's all recorded: bumps, bruises, cuts, scrapes . . . death."

Considering that her neck was still tender when she brushed her hair, that wasn't a great surprise. "It's double jeopardy for flesh and blood then: what happens here, happens there, and what happens there, happens there, too."

"It's best—safest—to work in pairs. One to hunt, the

other to keep watch. There's an awareness—usually. If someone puts an ice cube in my hand, I feel it wherever I am. It's my signal to return. For what it's worth—I tried ice cubes with you after you disappeared. They didn't work."

Em bristled. "How could they? You hadn't mentioned signals."

"I didn't let go of you!" Eleanor snapped back. They shared an edgy temperament. "I didn't mention signals because I thought we'd be together the whole time. I didn't foresee that I'd be keeping watch! And the ice cubes *should* have woken you up. You'd have been disoriented and possibly frightened, but you'd be in the here-and-now—"

The night terrors. In the back of her mind, almost lost amid the excitement of the last week, Emma had gradually come to the belief that her terrors were the aftermath of earlier wasteland visits—now she was convinced.

Eleanor had continued talking through Em's moment of insight. "No, I think it's something more than that. The way you bonded with that boy and if you were out of your body for a whole day, the way you said you were . . . That's different. Your wyrd is different. Everybody's is, but yours seems more different than most. I wouldn't hunt without a partner, if I were you . . . and signals. You'll need to find a signal. You need something that works in a panic."

"What would happen if I had a heart attack back at the Maisonettes?" From the shock, perhaps, of ice cubes landing in her palms. She was older than Eleanor; her body was, anyway.

"You'd be as dead as your body as soon as you returned to it."

"And if I didn't return to it?"

"You have to return to your body. We live in the here-and-now."

"But if I knew I wasn't still living in the here-and-now,

could I stay here? Could I grab onto someone in the past and have vicarious immortality? Is that how rogues get started?"

The shimmering pillar that was Eleanor Merrigan in the wasteland flickered and dimmed profoundly. "Put that thought out of your mind, Merle Acalia Merrigan! Better to be dead than a rogue. We're safe enough if we keep moving—and absolutely safe when we return to our physical selves in the here-and-now. Curses aren't clever, Emma— they don't think or scheme—unless they capture one of us, someone with the gift for moving in and out of the Nether-lands. If you ever see someone here, and you weren't hold-ing their hand when you arrived, then get out! Don't take chances. Leave the rogues for the experts."

Rather late for that, if Aramis had been a rogue. "Are you an expert, Eleanor?"

Eleanor's presence brightened; they resumed their walk toward the horizon. "I'm all the expert you'll need tonight."

"And some other night? You said there are listeners. If a rogue crossed my path should I call your name real fast or call someone else?"

Another pause.

"I *thought* you wanted dull and boring for the rest of your life! Very well—we hunt rogues with artifacts and incanta-tions. You can call it magic, black magic. It has to be taught, so you need to have a teacher, someone who knows, some-one who's trusted, and you have to be trusted in return." Eleanor laughed bitterly. "I wasn't happy with the shape of my life in the Twenties and Thirties. I wanted dull and bor-ing too. When war broke out, I took advantage and slipped away. War isn't a curse, but it's fertile ground for breeding curses. Most of them are local—circumstances that don't lend themselves to repetition—but it only takes a few. We were frantic, trying to be two places at once—literally. It was easy to slip away—by the time anyone knew I was gone, it was too late to start looking for me. The hard part was going back. You can imagine that I wasn't welcomed with open arms."

Emma couldn't imagine that at all. "If it was so hard, why did you leave Dad and me in the first place?"

"That's a story for another time, Emma—when we're not walking through the Netherlands."

"I guess everyone has something they'd just as soon keep secret."

Eleanor let Em's remark pass. They picked up their pace until conversation would have been difficult to maintain. It seemed to Emma that they walked farther to find her eleventh-century namesake than they'd walked to find Edwys. Maybe it had something to do with Eleanor's opiate draughts or the lack of them. Em kept her curiosity to herself and divided her attention between the horizon, where she imagined the other Emma waiting for her, and the black ground in front of her. She'd had enough of falling into rabbit holes.

When the ground suddenly became like tide-washed sand at the ocean's edge, she stopped short.

"We're there."

"A little farther," Eleanor corrected.

"A little farther and I'm apt to fall into Edwys's mind again."

"You were *supposed* to be envisioning his sister."

"I'm not taking any chances. What's the official procedure for landing on my own feet in the eleventh century, rather than inside someone else's head?"

"No official procedure. The coming and going, that's subjective—we each do it differently—but until today I'd never heard of anyone falling into another mind. You'll find yourself the center of attention when we get to New York."

That was hardly reassuring.

Eleanor sensed Em's reluctance. "Would you rather take my hand again and let me lead? We have a physical presence in the Netherlands. Don't ask me how or why; we just do. We can touch each other."

Emma knew that much already. She accepted Eleanor's offer. There was no sensation of any kind as she reached into the light surrounding her mother, but Eleanor's hand was icy cold and dry when Em grasped it.

"Relax," Eleanor suggested, though she didn't take her own advice. "Practice your imagining."

As the bleak midnight landscape of the wasteland dissolved into the swirling clouds of another balloon-powered takeoff, Em wondered what was upsetting Eleanor. Was this business of "deflecting the sister" more perilous than she'd let on? Did she feel as awkward around the daughter she'd abandoned as that daughter felt around her?

They arrived in the butchering courtyard before Eudes and his Norman escort. Emma's namesake stood apart from the others, her apron already bloody and her arms folded. She was sniping with her mother who punctuated her equally biting replies with a foot-long meat cleaver.

"Sounds and looks familiar, don't you think?" Eleanor mused—the closest they'd come to irony in their brief acquaintance.

According to Matt's notes, King William's Conquest culminated a century of near constant conflict for the English throne. The native nobility was short on men and long on widows and daughters when William set out to consolidate his control over his new kingdom. He hadn't so much parceled out English lands and honors among his retainers as he'd turned them loose on the English noble women.

From a political and historical perspective the tactic had worked. Within a few generations, the nobility was English again. But viewed up close, Emma could see that the transition had been devastating for the women. Edwys's mother had seen her world destroyed and become a cultural dinosaur while the younger paid a high price for being part of the future.

And then there were the young Englishmen like Edwys—too young to have participated in defense or defeat, they found themselves brutally excluded from the society they'd been born to lead. No wonder, really, that Edwys had turned murderous, or that his name cropped up frequently in his kinswomen's bickering.

Emma strained her invisible ears to catch a few familiar words. A week, she thought, no more than a month and she'd have been able to understand the argument; she had a knack for languages. An hour, though, wasn't enough.

"You've got to try bonding with her sooner or later," Eleanor pointed out. "Why not right now? The better you know her from the inside—"

"How?" Em interrupted. "Those other times, I fell through the roof, as it were. How do I get inside her head deliberately?"

"It's all subjective. You'll have to find your own way—"

"Please, Eleanor, no more Zen and the Way of hunting curses!"

"But I find that getting in front of my chosen one, then wrapping my arms around him or her usually works. Try to get close enough to breathe her breath."

"She won't notice? I might not have any feeling, but I do have substance here."

"You won't know until you try, Emma—it's subjective. If my way doesn't work, you'll have to find something that does. You can. The wyrd is within you. Trust it. Believe in it."

Putting her arms around her namesake's waist was like swinging her arms through the grass when Emma had first arrived in the eleventh century: she could feel herself moving, nothing more. Em squeezed hard enough to hurt, and something gave way. If they'd been part of the same reality, they'd have become Siamese twins, but Emma was as far from her namesake's mind as before.

"This isn't working," she shouted to Eleanor who'd been behind her when she began her bonding attempt and could have wandered off to another century for all Em knew.

"Emma!"

The voice wasn't Eleanor's, but Em turned toward the sound, and so did Emma-the-sister. They were so close together by then that they could have been breathing the same air. Certainly they shared the same emotions: consternation, curiosity, and resignation.

Her mother had a right to be bitter, but that didn't make her easier to live with.

Either Em or her namesake could have had that thought. Synchronicity won the day. Em was swept up in her namesake's irritation. She floated in a mind that was, overall, much quieter than Edwys's had been, or even her own for that matter.

Emma-the-sister was quick-witted—the pattern of images through her mind's eye as she listened to her mother revealed a woman with an elegant understanding of cause and effect. But Emma-the-sister was slow-mooded. Her reactions were muted—even her perception of the world was muted: the sky was a softer shade of blue. The half-butchered pig's blood was red—dull, ordinary red, not the enthralling, horrific red that Em recalled.

Muted didn't mean timid. When Em wondered why they were butchering a pig—she didn't think medieval households ate meat except on special occasions—she was battered by a storm of irritation and images of a prized animal staggering wildly, dangerously, in a field until the household men rushed in to slay it with pitchforks and scythes. A sense of *wrong* throbbed in Emma-the-sister's conscience and, worse, a flow of words, most of them unfamiliar, but many that began or ended with a syllable that sounded very much like *curse*.

Much became clear to twentieth-century perceptions in those moments: the pig had been ill and to an eleventh-century mind, that sort of sudden, violent illness came from God, not an infection. Emma-the-sister had wanted the unfortunate creature dragged deep into the forest and left to rot; she certainly hadn't wanted it hung near the house where her children (there were three of them—two boys, one fair, one dark, neither of them older than seven; and the youngest, a little girl with hair so pale it was almost white) dwelt.

Butchering the animal and serving its meat to the cursed Normans was the old woman's idea: serve evil to evil. No wonder Jennifer had blathered on about poisoning Bran!

Em bought her meat in plastic-wrapped packages. She wasn't prepared for the vicarious sensations of making meat, particularly the sloppy, slippery meat that had to be torn out of a pig's belly. Neither, for that matter, was her namesake. Emma-the-sister was pregnant and exquisitely sensitive to unpleasant smells, textures, and just plain filth. Clenching her teeth, she took up the crescent-shaped tool with which she would shortly murder her husband and set about separating innards from red meat.

Em didn't want to cause an accident with idle or intrusive thoughts. Knowing the future as she did, and being determined to change it, Em was keenly aware of the absurdity of her desire to be inconsequential in her namesake's mind: the right accident now, before Eudes returned with Edwys's corpse, might be the magic bullet she dreamt of. She was shocked, then, when the thoughts swirling around her took on the very shapes she'd tried to deny.

Emma-the-sister, wife, mother, and daughter contemplated her own death in atonement for events she could neither prevent nor control. The trembling in her hand was not entirely due to nausea. A battle raged in Emma-the-sister's conscience: was suicide a greater sin than murder or the other way around?

A slide-show of portraits flashed at the center of Emma-the-sister's thoughts. Some of the faces were old, some young, some peaceful, others bloody or ravaged by disease. What the gallery had in common, Em understood, was that they were all English, all dead . . . and all people that Em's namesake had personally washed and buried. Even without the blood and brutality of William's conquest, the eleventh century was a time and place where everyone was on intimate terms with death and there were neither professional undertakers nor funeral homes to sanitize the process.

The battle in Emma-the-sister's conscience resolved. The forces of life at any cost and for as long as possible claimed the victory, but they won without triumph or hope as allies. Emma-the-sister was Emma-the-wife and the mind portrait of her husband cast a long shadow. Yet, Eudes himself was dimmed by a darker shadow.

The word "Grandmesnil" was Emma-the-sister's night terror. Grandmesnil was the lord, the man with his lips against the Norman king's ear and his foot on the neck of every Englishman and woman in the shire. Eudes was the wall between Grandmesnil and all that Emma-the-sister cherished. Em couldn't discern whether her namesake loved her husband in any twentieth-century sense, but beyond doubt she valued him and dreaded any threat to his safety.

She was an eleventh-century realist, then, making the best of life with the enemy she knew, rather than deluding herself with rebellious fervor. Emma-the-sister was young, too—though she didn't think of herself that way; that was Em's notion, along with the realization that she herself was probably older than the "old woman" who continued to berate her daughter as they worked side by side.

Emma-the-sister did love her brother—her *last* brother.

There'd been others; their portraits accounted for much of the pain in a sister's memory. And Emma-the-sister feared for him. Even in her thoughts, she strove to keep the two men, her brother and her husband, apart. A chance merging, triggered by one of her mother's remarks, set her heart racing. She lost her grip on the gut-cutter.

To Em's judgment, her namesake had no guilty knowledge of her brother's intentions—at least not the specific ambush unfolding in the nearby forest. But Emma-the-sister knew her little corner of the world wasn't large enough to hold both Edwys and Eudes. And that her brother didn't stand a chance against her husband.

Emma-the-sister said something to her mother—it was the first time Em had experienced the sensation of language forming in another mind. Framed with intent, the words were a little clearer than those she heard by eavesdropping, but not by much. Their gist seemed to be that Edwys was a reckless fool and his mother was a dangerous one for egging—the precise word had a meaning that hadn't changed in nine centuries—him on.

The old woman replied with harsh words and a stinging clout to her daughter's cheek. Emma-the-sister replied to that with a string of words that were almost certainly a curse no well-bred woman of the eleventh century should ever be heard uttering. They produced a standoff between the two women that hadn't ended when the man and woman Em remembered from her previous visit ran into the courtyard shouting and pointing.

Emma-the-sister turned. Through a gap between sheds and stalls she saw men leading their horses down the hillside path.

They're coming, Emma. Get ready. Can you deflect this one from her path?

Eleanor's voice, so clear and sharp that Em craned her neck, looking over her shoulder for the source. Of course,

Eleanor wasn't there and Em didn't actually have a neck or shoulder, but the implied movement got Emma-the-sister's attention. A hush came over the none too noisy mind as did a sense of waiting, hoping for something miraculous to happen.

Yes, Em said, knowing Eleanor would somehow hear her. *I'll find a way.*

Time, Eleanor would be pleased to hear, was pre-eminently subjective. Inside Emma-the-sister's head, it flew by while the Normans approached the courtyard and stopped dead the moment Eudes appeared with Edwys spilling out of his arms. Eleanor would also be happy to learn that her daughter quickly understood that all curses were born in futility. Emma-the-sister was not surprised to see her brother's corpse or to learn how he had died. Her mother's fury horrified her but it too came as no surprise. If anything, the Englishwoman's mood was one of deepening resignation: she had foreseen all this.

Em made her first attempt to change history when the old woman reached for the wood-shafted meat hook.

Stop her! Em shouted in her namesake's mind. *Take that thing from her and put an end to this before someone else gets hurt or killed!*

The mind around her perceived the urging. Em felt her namesake's attention shift inward. What was it Eleanor had said about the difficulty of changing expectations? Whatever her words had been, they didn't adequately describe the smothering negation that fell layer by layer, denial by denial, upon Em's heartfelt suggestion. A triathlon wouldn't have been more grueling. Defusing an unexploded bomb couldn't have been more stressful. In the moments while Em fought free, the meat hook spun and Eudes received the wound on his cheek.

The first time around Em had thought about infection and gangrene when she saw that wound. The second time, surrounded by the assumptions of another century, she perceived a simpler, more complete doom: the pig was cursed. Its meat and blood were cursed. And, struck by metal sleeked with that blood, Eudes became part of the pig's curse. He was as good as dead, doomed and damned before he picked up the weapon that had wounded him.

With those thoughts awhirl around her, Em was surprised that her namesake chose to intervene on her mother's behalf. Apparently the idea that blood was thicker than water was as old as the notion of egging someone into recklessness, and an apt description of the instinctive choice a daughter made between her husband and her mother. There was nothing Em could add to her namesake's pleas, nothing she could do to soften the blow from her husband's open hand.

Looking up from the ground, Em watched the old woman seal her fate with a futile second attack and endured the numbing shockwaves of a mother's death. When Eudes made his accusations—*Were you a part of this?* seemed to be the thrust of the Norman's anger—there was very little beyond grief and doom in Emma-the-sister's thoughts. She blamed herself; she blamed God; she blamed Eudes himself and dared him to put an end to their suffering. When he refused, her despair crystalized into rage.

The very absence of rationality fueled Em's hope that she would be able to "deflect the sister." In the absence of intellect, a single image might work a miracle, and Em knew exactly which one to use. She had considered using it when the crescent-shaped weapon first appeared in the Englishwoman's mind—but she hadn't been quick enough.

Em waited—anxiously—until Eudes slammed his sword back into the scabbard and turned his back on his wife. In the heartbeat before Emma-the-sister began her attack, Em let fly her own impression of three young children left without their mother.

They need you. No matter what else, they need you!

There was resistance: a dire chorus whispering "Grandmesnil" along with counter-images of hanged criminals, battered women, and a stark chamber that might have been in either a dungeon or a convent.

The distance between husband and wife expanded. They were already farther apart than they'd been the first time Em had witnessed this scene. History *was* changing but not enough, Em feared. She hurled another, more improvised, image into her namesake's turbulent thoughts: Chartres Cathedral as Claude Monet had painted it. Em would have preferred to assault her namesake with Westminster Abbey—Matt's notes said the late and good King Edward had consecrated it not long before his death in 1065—but she couldn't remember what it looked like.

Perhaps any impressive church bathed in light would have worked. The would-be murder weapon fell from Emma-the-sister's hand. The Englishwoman sank to the ground and, with Em as a silent partner, watched Eudes walk to the courtyard where he paused to talk with his limping comrade.

You've done it! Eleanor crowed. *Listen—the potential is gone!*

Reverse the motion.

Em imagined an embrace like the one that hadn't worked, then imagined herself letting go. Once again, the sensation was a little like floating behind a balloon, only this time there was no helium and her feet remained on the ground.

Eudes had finished his conversation with his second. He strode toward the manor house, very much a man in charge of his world. His wife remained crumpled in the mud, her face hidden in her hands, her back swaying to the rhythm of her sobs.

"We accomplished what we set out to do," Em said softly.

"Indeed you did," Eleanor agreed.

She'd made herself visible and was grinning broadly. Em

vowed to find out how her mother accomplished such a trick, but not this day.

"You said it would be hard work. I didn't guess how hard."

Two people who would otherwise have died this distant afternoon had survived; three people, if one counted the unborn child. Em could hope. In the end, her mother had been right: what mattered was that a curse which had ruined lives for centuries had been erased from time's record because it had never formed.

Quite an accomplishment . . . for an amateur, anyway. No wonder Em ached from her toes to her fingertips.

The limping Norman walked across the yard. His arms were plenty strong when he seized Emma-the-sister by her upper arm and yanked her to her feet. The words he spoke were nasty in tone; the shove he delivered to get her moving was unnecessarily hard; and he pushed her toward the humble cottages where the commoners dwelt.

The curse was gone, but there'd be no happy ending in the eleventh century. Eudes had a wound that would probably kill him and Emma-the-sister might well curse God before she died.

"I want to go home," Em said.

"You've earned it. I know you can manage yourself, but here—give me your hand again. I'll get you home. It's the least I can do after what you've been through."

With Eleanor holding her hand, the transition did seem to begin as a gentle rain which became a peaceful fog. Em closed her eyes and let her thoughts wander: she should come back to see exactly what she had accomplished, for good or ill. *Should* was the operative word, and Emma Merrigan had never been a slave to *should*. Even in Bower, she should find out how Bran was doing, but she didn't want to see him or Jennifer again. Her mind was burdened with memories not her own; it would be a while before she was comfortable with them.

Emma was reliving some of those memories and not paying attention when Eleanor let go of her wrist. She tried to maintain contact, but her reflexes were slow and her grip on Eleanor hadn't been firm to begin with. The soft fog instantly became a buffeting wind and Em was tumbling again. With every fiber of her being, she believed that it hadn't been an accident.

Seventeen

N*either anger nor* outrage would get Emma anywhere, but she had to burn through those emotions and despair as well before she could muster the conviction to get herself back to the wasteland. Her convictions had taken a beating from her mother's betrayal and she completed her timeless journey with a bone-jarring vertical drop out of nowhere. Em banged her knees and bit her tongue with the jolt; her pride absorbed the rest of the damage. She caught her breath.

The signs had been there. Eleanor Merrigan had posted them herself: *Yes, I was sent by people you haven't met and might not like, but I paid for my own ticket and cab fare.* And it was Em's own fault for letting that remark get by without a damn-the-torpedoes challenge. She'd just assumed that dealing with Bran's eleventh-century curse was everyone's top priority and the pressure would come later, when the nameless organization that appeared to run Eleanor's life would try to run Emma's as well.

Eleanor hadn't done anything to correct her daughter's assumption. Maybe she couldn't have. Eleanor might not be alone in her own mind. Possibly her dealings with Harry were closer to master and servant or slave than husband and wife. It was a far-fetched notion, but once a person started believing in curses and time travel, there really was no place to draw the line against unreason.

Yet, if dealing with Bran's curse wasn't the reason Eleanor had come to Bower, then what had been?

I'll lie for you, Eleanor had said, *but I won't let you go rogue . . . or go off with a rogue.*

Emma knocked her forehead against the wasteland's black dirt.

"How could I have been so stupid? She said that Tuesday was the day when I showed up on whatever she and her pals use for radar. Tuesday. Not Thursday when I found Jennifer. Not Friday when I found Eleanor's box. Not Monday night when Eudes showed up in my living room. But Tuesday, the day I can't remember. It wasn't Bran's curse that got their attention, it was the guy who pulled me out of the fire— Aramis."

Emma chuckled softly. The joke was on Eleanor and whomever had sent her. Aramis might be a rogue but his name wasn't Aramis; they shared no arcane or telepathic bond, and Emma couldn't have led them to him if she'd wanted to. Which she didn't. When it came to choosing up sides in the wasteland, Aramis had done a better job of ensuring Em's good will than Eleanor had, though Em had played enough social games to know a man who'd saved her life wasn't necessarily her friend.

Especially in the wasteland.

Things might exist in the wasteland, but they didn't live here. The air passed the more obvious EPA tests—or Em was getting by on the air her lungs had processed back in the Maisonettes—but for the first time in her admittedly limited wasteland experience, she was hungry and thirsty. The nearest refrigerator was on the other side of a black-glass wall.

Emma sat back on her heels, opened her "other eyes" wide, and looked around for the black mirror boundary between the wasteland and the here-and-now. It was there, glinting in what would have been the east, if Em were facing north, and farther away than it had been the last time. It looked different, too—less like a sheet of plate glass suspended in air, more like a slab of the Vietnam war memorial erupting from the ground. The wastelands were subjective, she reminded herself, and considering the way she'd dropped to the ground, she wasn't going to quibble over the shape of her escape route.

Emma got up, dusted herself off, and started walking. Neither flaming columns nor men with peacock hats sprang up to challenge her right to go home. The polished black surface was faintly warm and supple when she flattened her palm against it. Pond ripples radiated out from her spread-out fingers. She pushed, and her hands submerged—

"Madame Emma!"

She spun around. Distance was tricky in the wasteland— the voice had sounded close, but the man who'd called her name was too far away for her to see his face. Emma had no trouble recognizing Aramis by his hat and cloak. She had the time, if she'd chosen to take it, to push her way through the black glass to the Maisonettes. Em chose to stand her ground instead and hoped that she hadn't let reckless curiosity seduce her into making a terrible mistake.

Aramis waited until they were less than ten feet apart before saying, "Madame Emma, you continue to surprise me. You've learned to move quickly."

"I had help," Emma admitted, looking over her shoulder. She expected Eleanor to make an appearance—that was the reckless part of her curiosity. "My mother came looking for me in the here-and-now. She taught me the basics of coming and going. She's behind me now. I think she's really looking for you."

"Ah," Aramis said with a nod and a slow study of the twilight horizon. "You have seemed so alone in the past, but appearances are deceiving in au-delà, are they not?"

Em squirmed inwardly. It was easy to forget, when you were knee-deep in suspicion, that others might question your own motives and honesty. "Not mine," she assured him. "I'm still a beginner. I was sure I was alone until you popped up. I don't think I'd be able to spot Eleanor, either."

"Eleanor? This is your mother's name? I do not know an Eleanor from the end of time."

That statement made questions explode in Em's mind. She squelched all but one. "What *is* your name, anyway?"

"I was called Blaise Raponde."

Emma took note of the past tense as she sorted out the slighter difference between the sound of "blaze," as in bon-fire, and that of "Blaise," a not-terribly-common French name. He called her Madame Emma; she'd call him Blaise, unless he objected.

"Well, Blaise, what *did* bring you to this corner of the wastelands?"

Blaise pointed at the base of the black-mirror slab. "This is the place where I saw you last. I hoped you might return."

Interesting. She'd never have guessed she'd been here be-fore but, to her eyes, everything in the wasteland looked pretty much the same. Except for the rising slab, which she'd never seen before and Blaise didn't seem to see now. He was looking at the ground. It was the clearest demon-stration she'd seen of the subjective nature of the waste-land's reality.

"I've been through a couple times. My mother and I headed back to the eleventh century to stop a curse from happening. We did, I think—"

"Beyond doubt. I felt the wind as it was blown out. You have done well, you and your mother. But if a curse in the past was not your quest, then what were you looking for?"

Em shrugged. She was at a disadvantage whether she was talking to Blaise or Eleanor. They both knew the wasteland and curses better than she did. Their questions left her de-

fensive. Growing up in a football town, she knew that offense was the best defense.

"She told me about rogues, Blaise. About what happens
when someone like me doesn't make the curse disappear."

"You think that I'm a rogue."

"My mother does. I'm trying to reserve judgment. I have
no idea what she is, or the people she's working for."

"Perhaps we can ask her."

Blaise's voice had dropped suddenly in pitch and temperature. His attention was riveted to a point behind her left
shoulder, behind the black-mirror slab. She turned and saw a
narrow band of light slice vertically through the twilight. A
moment later she saw her mother.

"I said she was behind me."

Eleanor Merrigan shone painfully bright on the bleak
landscape and she came forward like a tank. She stopped
some forty or fifty feet away.

"Stand away from my daughter," Eleanor shouted. "Let
her go. You're caught now; it's over. Hurting her will only
hurt you worse, I swear it."

Blaise put another stride of distance between himself and
Emma, but he couldn't truly be said to have obeyed
Eleanor's command. Emma knotted her hands into fists but,
being keenly aware that she was an amateur playing a professional's game, kept her mouth shut . . . for now.

"Emma walk away from him. Go home, if you can. He's
a rogue, surely you can see that. What little of him remembers what he used to be knows that it's time for what he's become to be destroyed."

Wise though the suggestion might be, Em had no intention of leaving. Blaise couldn't be entirely human but
Eleanor was, at the very least, double-faced. It seemed to
Emma that her best hope of knowing which side the angels
lined up on in the wasteland lay in observing the confronta-
tion between her mother and Blaise.

"I am not a rogue, madame," Blaise said after Emma had made it clear that she wasn't moving.

Eleanor countered with, "Then lead the way to your body."

The peacock feathers emphasized the negative shake of Blaise's head. "It is true that I cannot do that. My body is long turned to ashes and dust. All the same, I am not a rogue. I knew how to make myself beneath notice before I became trapped here. It is a lesson you should practice, madame, and quickly. Or perhaps you meant to set the air aglow?" He removed his hat and bowed toward Eleanor. "Thanks to you, madame, the deaf can hear, the blind can see, and the three of us are quite exposed."

Blaise was extravagant with his gestures—in those garments, subtlety would have been useless—but he wasn't soft. There was an undercurrent of confidence—arrogance—surrounding him.

Eleanor was no slouch either in the arrogance department. "Unless you've summoned *your* allies, the only attention we're attracting is from mine. You're not beneath notice anymore. You haven't been since you meddled with my daughter. Your game is over. Emma, for your own good, if you won't go home, come stand beside me. If you're too close, I can't promise that you won't be hurt."

"What has Blaise done to you, Eleanor? He's saved my life twice in the past week. I think he's telling the truth: he's not a rogue. I'm willing to take that chance."

"Don't interfere, Emma. You know nothing about the Netherlands or rogues. You don't see it for what it is."

Everything was subjective in the wasteland. Em saw a man; her mother, apparently, saw a monster. She made a choice. "I trust what I see, Eleanor. Maybe you need to open your eyes a bit wider." She put herself between Blaise and Eleanor.

From behind, Blaise rested his hands on her shoulders. "I

am honored, Madame Emma," he said loud enough for Eleanor to hear. "But you must not endanger yourself on my account. I will make a stand here, but you need not. Run away home before it is too late."

Then the weight of his hands was gone and Emma heard his footsteps across the parched ground. That was hardly the reaction she'd expected, but when she turned her head, Blaise had that intense, stare-at-the-horizon look on his face again. She followed his line of sight. A half-dozen pillars of tornadic flame had popped up between them and the northern horizon. Distance measurements were tricky here, which meant size was trickier. Em would swear, though, that all of them were larger than any of the apparitions she'd seen before. She didn't need a Surgeon-General's warning to assume they were hazardous.

"Dear God," she murmured.

"I called them, Emma," Eleanor said without looking back. "I was sure you'd lead me to the rogue. It won't go down easily, but it will go down."

Blaise ignored the slight to his gender. "These are not your friends coming to savor a victory," he said in his deep, calm voice. "*Our* enemies have found us."

Eleanor dismissed the warning. "You won't catch me with that. That was old before even you were born."

The silvery light that surrounded Eleanor flared briefly. When it had faded there was a brass pipe about the size of a flute in her hands. Quivering Mylar ribbons dangled from the pipe which was topped with a large pink crystal. Emma was shocked that her mother actually carried a magic wand, doubly shocked that it was so kitschy. Blaise took the threats more seriously. His jaw clenched. His hand caressed his sword but did not draw it.

"One last time, Emma—move away. I don't want to hurt you."

"Then, for your daughter's sake, madame, turn around and put that stone to some good use. Time is not with us."

"Blaise is right," Em agreed. "We're not kidding. Turn around. If those are your friends, I don't ever want to see your enemies."

Eleanor shook her head with what appeared to be genuine sadness. "I found you too late to save you, Emma. I'm sorry."

She clasped the wand with both hands and raised it high above her head, then she closed her eyes. Her face contorted with supreme effort. Something that looked like laser light in fog arced between the crystal-tipped brass and Blaise's face. It seemed to Em, who could not see them both at the same time, that they each flinched.

Blaise drew his sword. He held it by the blade, with the pommel even with his eyes and the tip pointed toward the ground. The light strand from Eleanor's crystal took a magnetic curve and fastened on the sword's plain metal pommel. Eleanor cried out, possibly with pain, more likely with frustration—Em was willing to stake her life on the assumption that Blaise had thwarted her attack without launching one of his own. If he was a rogue, then he was an extremely patient and confident one.

He could afford to be, if the fiery columns were under his command, as Eleanor had claimed. Em counted ten of them now and they were picking up speed or size, perhaps both, as they got closer. On the great pool table of life, Em had left herself without an easy shot. Her shortest path to the black mirror passed between her mother at the far end of the light strand and Blaise at the nearer one. She'd have to duck low or circle behind him if she were going to make a run for the Maisonettes.

The columns were close enough now that Emma could see swirling eye holes and mouths within the flames. As she understood it, the columns were curses made manifest, and all identical to the one that had nearly claimed her. She'd have become a rogue herself, if Blaise hadn't intervened . . .

"Eleanor!" she shouted. "You're fighting the wrong—"

Without warning, a light strand, thicker and brighter than the one binding Eleanor and Blaise, hammered the ground a few feet to Eleanor's left. Morbidly fascinated, Em watched it put out sizzling, serpentine feelers. They stretched toward all three of them, but they touched Eleanor first.

Em thought she saw the luminous aura that surrounded them all in the wasteland glow blood red, but she couldn't be certain. When the serpents reached Eleanor, they set off an explosion that propelled Emma backward. She landed on her back, conscious but stunned. The shock had emptied her lungs and for several unpleasant moments she fought for every breath.

Crimson wind howled an arm's length above Em's face. A steady rain of grit from the wasteland's dry soil got in her nose and eyes. She could have been swallowed in an instant, but the curses were ignoring her. Emma rolled carefully onto her stomach and crawled until it seemed safe to stand.

By then, the curses had merged into one towering column of black-streaked flame. It covered her black-mirror escape route and had consumed both Eleanor and Blaise. Even if they'd set aside their differences at the last moment, Em couldn't imagine that Eleanor's wand and Blaise's sword together were any sort of match for the merged curses.

She looked around for a place to hide. The wasteland wasn't utterly flat—not when curses kicked up storms of wind and fire—but the closest thing she'd seen to a concealing landmark was the inaccessible black slab. Em considered a tactical retreat to the eleventh century and rejected the notion. Little as she wanted to watch the burning curses, she was afraid to get too far away from them lest she lose her way home altogether.

Emma retreated until her contradictory urges to run away

and to stay close declared a truce. She sat down on the dry crusty dirt. Was it only a week ago that she'd tied a clump in her nightshirt and thought it would solve all her mysteries?

For sheer novelty only the first week of her life could possibly equal this past one, and Emma's memory didn't reach that far. Bathed in grit and heat, she tried, without success, to make sense of what had become of her life. Her thoughts had wandered into sixth-grade Girl Scout camp—she'd been in charge of the bonfire on a rainy night—when the curse flames flickered. In the time it took for her to ask herself what was changing, the whirling pillars vanished and a dark silence descended over the wasteland. Em waited for the next assault on her sanity. Seconds became minutes and nothing leapt up to terrorize her.

When Emma stood up she saw the reassuring silhouette of the black-mirror slab and a smear of embers beside it. The innate human capacity for pattern recognition turned the smear into a corpse. Em tried not to anticipate which corpse the curses had left behind as she walked. About twenty feet out, she saw a sword near the embers. She ran the rest of the way. Blaise was recognizable within the ruddy glow. He hadn't burnt at all, but he didn't look good: his eyes were closed, his mouth was open, and the strands of dark hair draped across his cheeks weren't moving.

"Blaise? Blaise Raponde?"

Em had begun to lose hope when Blaise groaned and began the chore of sitting up. He'd fallen on his peacock hat. The stiff felt was crushed and the feathers were bent. In an ordinary place it would have been beyond repair, but Blaise restored both felt and feathers with a sweep of his hand.

"Thank God you survived!" The words were out of Em's mouth before she could censor them.

"Our Heavenly Father does not concern Himself with us here," Blaise replied and settled the hat atop his head. "I survive by luck and wits. This time, I survived by luck. And you, Madame Emma, how did you survive?"

"Pure dumb luck."

Blaise got his feet beneath him, then tried but failed to stand. Forgetting her doubts, Emma surged forward to offer assistance. He clasped her wrists and pulled. There was nothing ghostly or insubstantial about Blaise Raponde. He was as real as Emma herself and a good deal heavier. They both needed luck to keep their balance.

"I should have known better," Emma apologized. She meant that she should have planted her feet before she offered to help him up, but there was more that needed to be said. "I led her here. I'm sorry. I wasn't thinking and now— God knows what happened to Eleanor and you were nearly killed—"

"Don't trouble yourself over me," Blaise reassured Em. He gave her wrists a squeeze before releasing them. "There is no damage done to me that time won't mend—and here in au-delà, time is everywhere." He grinned; Em decided he'd made a joke and grinned back. "As for killing me, your concerns come much too late for that."

Em lost her grin. "I'm sorry."

"It is done and long ago. It is—" Blaise retrieved his sword and sheathed it. "It is my problem."

Blaise's English was accented, but it was Em's English, not whatever English the English had been speaking when that peacock hat was new. Emma would have liked to know how Blaise Raponde had learned idiomatic American English, but this wasn't the time for interruptions.

"Your mother believes I am a rogue. This is very understandable. I have hunted rogues myself—I was hunting one when I became stranded here. It is true: for all this time, I have had no allies, only enemies. I should not have survived; I should have been taken long ago. I would not believe me."

He'd used the present tense to speak of Eleanor. Em's French wasn't good enough for her to guess if that was a logical translation error. She asked, "Do you think Eleanor's still alive?"

Blaise stood in the place where Em's mother had been standing when the flames enveloped her. His aura had brightened but it was still more red than clear and he'd limped when he walked.

"We both warned her." Em made excuses for both of them. "We told Eleanor to turn around, but she was sure that she knew what was coming. Harry, I guess. She must have been expecting Harry."

"Your father?" He'd squatted and sifted the crumbling dirt with his fingers.

"No, her husband. I don't know him. I didn't know her until after I'd met you."

Blaise looked up from the dirt with a puzzled expression.

"Eleanor left me with my father when I was a baby—she tried to make it sound as if she'd done me a favor. I don't know what to believe, but she came looking for me because I'd bumped into you. There's a part of me that says she got what she deserved."

"No, Madame Emma." Blaise dusted off his hands as he stood. "I cannot speak for your mother, but she does not deserve what she has received. She thought I was a rogue. She knows what that means, as I know what it means, and as you, I think, do not. I do not blame your mother for what has happened here. It could easily have been you or me in her place. When you meet someone in au-delà, it is wisest not to trust."

Emma's mood soured. "I trusted you."

"I have been here for more than three hundred years, Madame Emma. In all that time I have met no one like myself. I would not have met you if you had not had the audacity to challenge a curse with your bare hands. That first time,

I was not there to rescue you, Madame Emma, I was there to extinguish a rogue before it caused damage."

Emma flinched and stifled another apology. Apologies were her default response to shame or embarrassment. After a hard swallow she asked, "Is Eleanor a rogue now? Will you hunt her down?"

"Do not lose hope, Madame Emma. Your mother is not a mouse. Unless I am very wrong, none of the curses that captured her has the strength to possess her so they will fight among themselves, possessing one another, until one of them has the strength. Before then, they will attract attention—they will have to battle other curses, even rogues, as they battle among themselves."

Em imagined some of the bloodier "nature in the wild" programs she'd watched—or, more often, decided not to watch—on television.

"Whether it's lions or hyenas, it's still a bad day for the zebra," she observed grimly.

"Usually," Blaise agreed with a shrug. "But while there is fighting, there is hope. A corpse is of no use to a curse. To become rogues, they need a whole man or woman."

The picture in Em's mind grew unpleasantly clear: "Eleanor's safe—in a manner of speaking—until one of them turns her into a rogue, then you'll kill her. Or, will you kill her before that?" Em had recalled the bruises on her neck. "*Can* you kill Eleanor before she becomes a rogue?"

"Can I? Yes. Will I? No. I am a gentleman, Madame Emma; I would never do such a thing. But this Harry, perhaps, will think otherwise, and no curses will stand in his way . . . or yours."

Emma understood what Blaise meant and was appalled. "I'm not going to murder my mother!"

Blaise's smile was sad and bitter. "If you don't, and I fail to free her or she fails to free herself, then what will you do? Will you play midwife to a rogue in your living room?"

"You can't be serious," Em muttered, but he was, and Harry would be, too.

"I propose that we work together to save your mother, Madame Emma. Return *au monde* and keep watch over your mother's body, while I pursue her here. She will seem to be in a deep and troubled sleep, but you will take care of her. And when she awakens, you will know it is time to return to au-delà to thank me."

Blaise had a dangerous smile, a rogue's smile, a smile that allowed Emma to think of nothing else as they embraced and afterward, when she pressed her palms against the black mirror.

The glassy surface had barely become supple when Blaise gave Em a between-the-shoulder-blades shove that sent her straight into the Maisonettes.

*   *   *

Deep and troubled sleep was a good description for what Emma saw when she raised her head and looked at her mother. Eleanor lay on her side with her eyes closed and her legs twitching. Before Em had risen to her knees, Eleanor opened her eyes.

Something held Eleanor's attention but it wasn't anything in the living room. Her breath became ragged and her skin had a shiny pallor; her pupils were dilated until scarcely any iris remained visible. Then Eleanor screamed.

Em shouted, "Eleanor!" and grabbed a wildly swinging fist before it connected with the sofa.

They wrestled briefly, very briefly. Eleanor whimpered once and went limp. Emma released her.

The scream lured Spin out of the basement. While Em glanced at the VCR—to her great relief, it read 6:13 AM and—in tiny, easily overlooked letters in the lower right corner—SAT, which meant that she'd lost just three hours rather than an entire day—the cat went nose to nose with Eleanor. He pulled back quickly, hissing and fluffing out his tail.

"I know," Emma assured him. "I know. I'm working on it."

A battle raged in Em's mind. On one side there was a panicked, emotional determination to wrap herself in secrets and privacy; hospitals, with their tests and questions, were beyond consideration. On the other side, reason said there'd be other screams that others would hear and, even if silence reigned, she didn't have the skills or resources to care for a violently comatose woman.

Reason won the battle, but not easily. Only a fool would call 911 with wasteland grime clinging to her face or before she disposed of Eleanor's suspect "cough medicine." And only a middle-aged fool would tell the med-techs, once they'd arrived, that the obviously young woman convulsing on the carpet was her seventy-year-old mother. Em scrambled to concoct plausible answers to inevitable questions on the way to the University Hospital emergency room.

She blamed the Internet with its abundant genealogical resources for sending a hitherto unsuspected niece to her doorstep Friday evening. When that deception passed muster, Em was free to answer most other questions with a truthful "We'd just met for the first time" or "She hadn't said anything about that," and the all-encompassing, "I don't know."

Eleanor's wallet had contained a better-than-average array of identification, including an insurance card, which promised to shield Emma from the financial consequences of a medical emergency, and a mint-condition business card for one Harry Graves in Red Oak, New York. There were two phone numbers on the card, one of which struck Em as the one she'd seen on her answering machine's recall screen.

Emma shared the waiting room at University Hospital with a quietly distraught mother and father, waiting, like her,

for someone to tell them something they didn't already
know. Emma wondered whether to call the numbers on the
business card. Blaise's warning that Harry might choose to
murder his wife rather than let her be possessed by a curse
echoed in Emma's thoughts. That was something Eudes
might have done, or maybe Blaise himself in his own time,
but Eleanor had referred to the secret society to which both
she and Harry belonged as a global corporation and no corporation would take that kind of risk.

Besides, Harry already knew where Eleanor was and why.
Quite possibly, he knew what had happened in the wasteland. He would come looking for his wife and offense was
the best defense. Emma made mental notes on what she
would and would not admit, dug out a credit card, and
headed for the pay phones. But after all her preparation, no
one picked up either phone. She was repeating a message for
the second number when a nurse came through the ER doors
and caught her eye.

"We're admitting your niece. She's stable now, but the
tests and x-rays don't show anything conclusive about her
symptoms. I'd like to ask you a few more questions."

Emma cringed inwardly and wondered how long opiates
lingered in the blood as she followed the nurse to an almost-
private corner in the waiting room. She wondered too if any
of the staff had been on duty when Bran Mongomery had
passed through the ER. The diagnoses were similar: critical,
life-threatening, with suspicions of drugs or poisons beneath
a thick layer of mystery.

At the end of the interrogation, the nurse gave Emma the
number of Eleanor's room on the head trauma floor and
started to recite the directions. Em waved her off.

"I know where it is. My dad was on that floor last February."

Em passed through the hospital cafeteria on the way.
She'd left her appetite in the wasteland but the aroma of cof-

fee, however bitter, was a magnet. With sixteen ounces of steaming caffeine between her hands, she detoured to a sun-lit window. As she waited for the brew to cool, it occurred to her that she wasn't ready to lose the mother who yesterday she hadn't known she had. Self-help books made much of the five stages of death; Em needed time for at least five stages of life with Eleanor.

She'd rarely felt so isolated. She hadn't been alone in February. John and Nancy had arrived at the Teagarden house before the med-techs had Dad loaded into the ambulance. They'd driven her to the hospital and she'd been with one or the other of them until after the funeral. This time the med-techs had bent the rules to give Em a ride in the front of the ambulance. She needed her car as well as her friends.

It was nine AM on a Saturday morning. Emma was sure John and Nancy would be home, but their phone rang until the answering machine cut in. She left a message with Eleanor's room number. Feeling sorry for herself, Em made her way to the elevators. The corridor on which the hospital segregated its head trauma patients was hushed, the rooms were private, the lights a little less bright, and everyone spoke in whispers. Em introduced herself at the nurse's station and got an all-clear to visit Eleanor Merrigan. She turned her head when she walked past the room where Dad had died and stopped short of entering her mother's.

A bandage covered Eleanor's eyes. Emma had expected that. The med-techs had complained that Eleanor's "blink reflex" wasn't working right and had bandaged them shut as a precaution. Downstairs in the ER, they'd shot Eleanor full of muscle relaxants to keep her from thrashing about. Em had expected to find her mother laid out like Sleeping Beauty or Snow White.

She couldn't have been more wrong.

Eleanor couldn't scream, but her mouth was open and a thin wail filled the room. She couldn't thrash, but that didn't stop her from keeping her arms and legs in constant, feeble motion. Already she'd slipped and pivoted around her left arm which was Velcroed to the bed frame and pierced by an IV line. Emma was in the process of getting her mother centered on the bed again when a nurse hustled her out of the room.

"You'll have to stay out here a few moments. I was afraid of this when your niece came up from Emergency, Emma. We're going to have to restrain her—"

Em said nothing, but her face betrayed her misgivings.

"It has to be done," the nurse said gently. "Eleanor will tear out her IV; fall, or worse, if we don't restrain her." She touched Emma's arm. "Your niece isn't *aware,* Emma. Even if she pulls or cries, she won't remember when she wakes up."

"I understand," Emma replied, though she had a bad feeling that somewhere in the wasteland Eleanor's suffering was about to increase.

"You'll be glad to hear that I just finished speaking to your niece's husband. He thought you might be here and wanted us to let you know that he'd gotten your messages and would be on his way as soon as he could confirm his plane tickets. He said he was very grateful for all you'd done for Eleanor and for him."

Em's gut went into free-fall. "Harry Graves called?"

"Yes. Poor man. It's so much harder when people get sick away from home. It must be a relief for you to know that he's on his way to take charge."

Relief wasn't one of the words that came to Emma's mind when she thought of meeting Eleanor's husband but she said, "A great relief," because it should have been—would have been in almost any other circumstances—and stammered excuses about taking a walk while the nurses took care of Eleanor.

The elevator doors opened as Em approached them and a

couple got out. She wanted them to be John and Nancy, but they were just two worried strangers. Emma fought a flash of long-buried anger toward Jeff and caught the elevator before it closed. If she couldn't take comfort from former husbands or old friends, she'd look somewhere else. The elevator let her out in the main lobby where the volunteers staffing the information desk gave her directions to Bran Mongomery's room.

Matt Barto was napping in the visitors' lounge in front of the elevator doors. Em called his name and his head came up wearing a smile. He was still wearing yesterday's clothes and needed a shave, but she must have looked worse.

His smile faded as he asked: "What's wrong, Em?"

Em wouldn't go down that road until she'd taken care of unfinished business. "How's Bran? Did his condition change after you and I talked last night?"

Matt's smile returned. "No one's using the word miracle, at least not out loud, but his fever cracked like an egg around four and the crud's in retreat. The big guy's not home free yet, but he's getting there. They're going to pull the ventilator before his momma gets here. She'll freak when she sees him, but nothing like she would have if she'd been here yesterday. From this end whatever you did was a raving success. So, why aren't we celebrating?"

Emma shook her head. "One thing at a time. Is Bran awake? Can I see him?"

Permission was granted and Matt led Em down a short corridor.

Bran Mongomery remained a frightening sight, worse than Eleanor. His muscles had melted away during the fever siege. Where he wasn't swollen up by the crud, Emma could count his bones. But there wasn't as much crud as there had been and in several places the dark sores appeared to have fallen away, leaving red-raw skin behind. IV lines ran to Bran's arms and monitor wires ran from his ribs to a chirping oscilloscope. His chest moved in rhythm with the twitch and hiss of the ventilator tube.

Bran's eyes were closed. Em hoped that meant he was asleep. She'd confronted her medical queasiness when Dad got sick, but, like Eleanor downstairs, he'd never had more than an IV line. The paraphernalia surrounding Bran was more than Emma could handle. Matt strode confidently into the room, but she stayed on the threshold with her hand clamped on the door frame.

"Hey, Bran—you've got company," Matt announced.

Bran's eyelids fluttered. He looked at Matt, then at her. There was no doubt in Em's mind that Bran knew who she was.

"You're looking better than the last time I saw you," she said, trying to sound more relaxed than she felt.

The ventilator made conversation impossible, but Bran communicated well enough with a weak smile and a wriggle of his fingers. Em let go of the door frame and braved his bedside. She slipped her hand around his.

"It's over, Bran."

He gave her a skeptical look.

"I swear it. You're going to get better—all better. The curse is gone; the demons are gone, as if they never were. You and Jennifer are free to start over."

The skepticism faded from Bran's stare. He closed his fingers around hers and squeezed. His eyes closed and his grip relaxed slowly. When, after a few moments, Em withdrew her hand, there was no reaction.

"I think he's asleep," she whispered. "I hope."

Matt agreed. "He's coming out of it now, but they've kept him pretty thoroughly 'zoned. You and your mom went back to do battle with Eudes?"

"With the sister—Edwys's sister, the one he used as an excuse to try to kill Eudes. I got inside her head and gave her a vision straight from God."

"Cool."

They retreated to the corridor.

"No, not cool. But she didn't die and Eudes didn't die, so the curse never got started. Everything that's happened this past week—we remember it and we'll keep on remembering it, but I think—if I understand what's going on—that it's been erased or, maybe, edited."

"Better than the last time when Bran went from having nightmares to having the crud. It still sounds pretty cool to me, so why aren't we celebrating? Why aren't *you* celebrating?"

"Finding Eudes in the eleventh century was only the beginning." Emma leaned against the nearest wall. "It's so much bigger than we guessed. Other curse hunters. History. A man named Harry Graves, who's Eleanor's husband. Her second husband. My stepfather." She stopped and let that revelation settle a moment. "It's so weird, I don't know where to start. My mother—it turns out she didn't come to help me take care of Bran's curse—or Bran's curse wasn't the only reason or even the main reason that she was standing outside my front door last night. I'd met someone in the wasteland—"

"You never mentioned that," Matt chided.

"I thought it was a dream—more of a fantasy—my imagination and loneliness working overtime. But somehow *that,* and not the stuff with Bran and Eudes and the eleventh century, were what got my mother's attention—well, probably not *her* attention. There's an organization of time-traveling curse hunters. A secret organization, as you can imagine. They think they're the good guys and they thought I was consorting with a bad guy—"

"Were you?"

"No—I don't think so. There was a scene, a bad scene, in what I call the wasteland. My mother tricked me and used me as bait to get to Blaise—the guy I'd met. It worked. He showed up and so did a bunch of curses a lot more potent than Bran's."

"You're here and Bran's getting better. The good guys must've won."

Emma shrugged. "My mother lost. The curses got her mind. She's in a coma on the fifth floor and the hospital's got itself another medical mystery."

"Is she covered with the creeping crud, like Bran?"

"No, at least not as of a few minutes ago. But she's in a bad way just the same. The doctors here can keep her alive, the way they kept Bran alive, but she's not going to have a miraculous recovery until someone rescues her."

"Someone, meaning you?"

"Not me," she insisted. They'd paced the corridor and were standing in front of the elevator. Emma pushed the "Up" button to return to the head trauma floor. "I got lucky, Matt—beginner's luck. I had no idea what I was doing and I nearly killed Bran with my blundering around. Eleanor's *surrounded* by curses and I've got a better idea of the dangers now. Rescuing her is a job for professionals, not an amateur."

"Merle Acalia Merrigan, since when have you been an amateur? Those curses keeping your mother prisoner, they all had to start somewhere. Right? We'll just have to track them down and erase them one at a time until she wakes up. Nothing to it."

Matt's optimism was ill-founded but contagious. "What's this 'we' nonsense?" she asked with a laugh.

"Research, Em. I told you, I could really get into this historical stuff."

The elevator dinged and opened, revealing John and Nancy. The timing was so perfect that they almost didn't recognize one another. That was an easily resolved problem and as for the rest, only time would tell.